Praise for *New York Times* bestselling author
E. Lynn Harris

"What got audiences hooked? Harris's unique spin on the ever-fascinating topics of identity, class, intimacy, and friendship."
—*Vibe*

"There is a universality about Harris's characters—so human, so earnest, so genuine, that crossover readers are embracing . . . stories told with warmth and humor from a perspective that is as refreshing as it is straightforward."
—*San Francisco Chronicle*

"An exceptional storyteller . . . [his] characters are both admirable and brave."
—*St. Louis Post-Dispatch*

Praise for *New York Times* bestselling author
Eric Jerome Dickey

"Wonderfully written . . . each character's voice [is] smooth, unique and genuine."
—*Washington Post Book World*

"Dickey was meant to write . . . [his] prose is poetic and sings with fluency."
—*Detroit Free Press*

"Vibrantly captures the voices of urban men and women, shattering stereotypes as [he] explores relationships between the sexes."
—*Dallas Morning News*

"A generous helping of humor and a distinctly male viewpoint."
—*Atlanta Journal Constitution*

Continued on next page . . .

GOT TO BE REAL

FOUR ORIGINAL LOVE STORIES

E. LYNN HARRIS
ERIC JEROME DICKEY
COLIN CHANNER
MARCUS MAJOR

NEW AMERICAN LIBRARY

Published by New American Library, a division of
Penguin Putnam Inc., 375 Hudson Street,
New York, New York 10014, U.S.A.
Penguin Books Ltd, 27 Wrights Lane,
London W8 5TZ, England
Penguin Books Australia Ltd, Ringwood,
Victoria, Australia
Penguin Books Canada Ltd, 10 Alcorn Avenue,
Toronto, Ontario, Canada M4V 3B2
Penguin Books (N.Z.) Ltd, 182–190 Wairau Road,
Auckland 10, New Zealand

Penguin Books Ltd, Registered Offices:
Harmondsworth, Middlesex, England

Published by New American Library, a division of Penguin Putnam Inc.

First Printing, December 2000
10 9 8 7 6 5 4 3 2

Copyright © New American Library, a division of Penguin Putnam Inc., 2000

"Café Piel" Copyright © 2000, Eric Jerome Dickey
"Kenya and Amir" © 2000, Marcus Major
"Money Can't Buy Love" © 2000, E. Lynn Harris
"I'm Still Waiting" © 2000, Colin Channer

Grateful acknowledgment is made for permission to reproduce the lyrics from "I'm Still Waiting" by Bob Marley. Copyright © 1968 Fifty-Six Hope Road Music Ltd./Odnil Music Ltd./Blue Mountain Music Ltd. (PRS). All rights controlled and administered by Ryko Music (ASCAP). All rights reserved. Lyrics used by permission.

(NAL) REGISTERED TRADEMARK—MARCA REGISTRADA

LIBRARY OF CONGRESS CATALOGING-IN-PUBLICATION DATA

Got to be real : four original love stories / E. Lynn Harris . . . [et al.].
    p.   cm.
      Contents: Café Piel / by Eric Jerome Dickey—Kenya and Amir / by Marcus Major—
Money can't buy me love / by E. Lynn Harris—I'm still waiting / by Colin Channer.
    ISBN 0-451-20223-6 (alk. paper)
    1. American fiction—Afro-American authors. 2. Afro-Americans—Fiction. 3. Love
stories, American. I. Harris, E. Lynn.

PS647.A35 G68 2000
813'.540803543'08996073—dc21
                                                                          00-045582

Printed in the United States of America
Set in Sabon
Designed by Leonard Telesca

Printed in the United States of America

PUBLISHER'S NOTE
These are works of fiction. Names, characters, places, and incidents either are the products of the author's imagination or are used fictitiously, and any resemblance to actual persons, living or dead, business establishments, events, or locales is entirely coincidental.

BOOKS ARE AVAILABLE AT QUANTITY DISCOUNTS WHEN USED TO PROMOTE PRODUCTS OR SERVICES. FOR INFORMATION PLEASE WRITE TO PREMIUM MARKETING DIVISION, PENGUIN PUTNAM INC., 375 HUDSON STREET, NEW YORK, NEW YORK 10014.

contents

Café Piel

Eric Jerome Dickey

chapter one

When the elevator dinged and opened, over twenty mad-as-hell people were congregated outside of John's office. Camped out like they were trying to get tickets to a Jerry Garcia concert. Not one happy face.

An eviction notice from the L.A. county sheriff was stapled on John's mahogany door. The door was padlocked. By the date on the notice, all of that was at least a week old.

A middle-aged Asian, dressed in a pinstriped suit and suspenders the color of the American flag, was the loudest. Face flaming red. Spit leaping from his mouth as he screamed in his native tongue, his hands flying in kung-fu motions. Everybody stayed out of his way and let him Tae Bo his way up and down the brown carpet.

I asked the Mexican I had stopped next to, "What's his trip?"

"He lost a hundred thousand in restaurant equipment. From what I understand, John leased his equipment before he vanished."

"One hundred thousand?"

"One hundred thousand in top-of-the-line restaurant equipment. Enough to have him looking at bankruptcy."

"Makes my loss sound like chump change."

"Same here. But it doesn't mean I need my money any less."

"No sign of John?"

"Are you kidding?"

He said he heard John had packed up and moved everything. He was down today because of the check John had given him. A check drawn on the same account mine was.

I said, "Your check bounced too."

"No. Bank said this account was closed last year. I was hoping John's accountant accidentally wrote me a check on a wrong account, but"—he made an irritated motion at the eviction notice on the door—"I don't know. With this many people, this is fraud. I needed this two hundred dollars. I've got to get my kid a uniform for school and supplies and stuff."

"This is messed up."

"My name is Manuel Torres."

"Robert Davis. Call me Bobby."

A woman and a child were standing next to him. His wife and ten-year-old daughter. His wife was hardly five feet tall, long black hair that touched her waistline. His child was slim, had Bambi eyes, dark hair, and despite all the ruckus, she was polite with all smiles. He and his wife held hands in a way that spoke of love. Real love. Something I've dreamed about, but never had.

He suggested, "We should start a list so if we can get some sort of class-action thing going, all parties involved can be informed."

"Good idea."

Manuel Torres turned to the crowd, put two fingers into his mouth and whistled over their riot-level chatter. Everybody congregated at his feet. Everyone except for the Asian, who stood in front of John's door and scowled like he wanted to kick it down.

Manuel suggested that we investigate legal options and file against Jonathan to try and recoup some of our loses.

Avenues that would cost new cash to chase owed cash.

One of the women in the hallway blew out air that sounded like weeks, if not months, of frustration before she snapped, "There's no telling how many people he ripped off. That Asian man lost one hundred thousand. I lost three grand."

Another said, "It hurts like hell, but anything legal will take well over a year to settle. I've got a cleaning service to run, and I need every last dime of the capital I have. Most of you are probably in the same situation. We should just take this as a lesson learned and move on."

Two more left without apologies.

I didn't feel comfortable with nonblack people attacking a brother. Not one of them would spend the night in our community, let alone spend a dollar where a black man roosted behind a cash register. But this wasn't about being black. This was about business. All about the green.

Something must've happened, like John had gotten ripped off at a higher level, and we were feeling the trickle-down effect of his hard time. If the sheriff had ridiculed me and tacked an eviction notice on my door, I don't think I'd be in the mood to rap with people over a few dollars. I'd be somewhere attacking my liver with a fifth of Bacardi 151.

Manuel said, "Everyone should contact this number if you hear anything. If you help one of us, you help all of us."

A couple of brothers got off the elevator. Both were draped in gold designer clothes from head to toe, each had thick upper bodies and weak legs. They looked like South Central buffalo. They swaggered by without a word and stood in front of the door.

They rumbled like an urban glee club, "Ain't this a bitch?"

We told them what we were doing with the mailing list.

The smaller of the two sneered. "What y'all plan on doing, sending out Christmas cards?"

Manuel explained to them what he hoped to accomplished.

One of the buffalo had a hard expression that said he thought all of us were idiots for thinking about dealing with John on that level, but the other one nodded his head and sighed like he had come to the conclusion that he had nothing to lose, signed the sheet of paper. Then both of those buffalo snorted, about-faced and left with slow and angry strides.

I spent the rest of the morning in the sunshine and dry heat of Pasadena, on the streets of Old Town. Walking through the smog that spread over Colorado Boulevard, I held the classified ads in hand like a man in search of a dream deferred. The place I wanted to lease and turn into a photography studio, the opportunity that had been vacant for a few months in the heart of

Old Town, was still there. Waiting. But like any woman worth having, she wouldn't wait for long before somebody passed by and noticed her beauty, saw her true value. She would wait until she was seduced by some brother with a few more dollars in his pocket and better credit than I had on my TRW.

A couple of nice-looking sisters—both caramel-coated and looking fine and wealthy in pastel-colored business suits, shades with yellow lenses, and corporate temperaments—sailed across the street at the diagonal crosswalk. Came toward me like I was luring them in. I struggled for a little eye contact, then spoke and gave them compliments like they were the finest of the fine.

They glanced at me, saw I was in Levi's, sandals, and a white T-shirt from the Minnie Ripperton 10-K, but they didn't stop their conversation or slow their stride. However, two or three white women on their heels gave me a peppy "Hi."

I said, "Hi."

"I really like your hair. Awesome, dude."

I ran a hand over my reddish-brown dreadlocks, my mane that hung below my shoulders and smiled. "Thanks."

The snow bunnies even glanced back and showed those pearly whites. The one in the sienna miniskirt and white see-through top actually had a nice butt. Enough cleavage to show off her bought and paid for breasts. When she stopped in front of a store, she openly stared back at me like she was contemplating some flirtation. Had a gleam in her eyes like she was wishing on a star. Pasadena was liberal, but my mind wasn't in that mode.

A few feet down, the women of African ancestry had stopped and chatted with some white boys. The Nubians were standing on the curb, kissing them on the cheeks. Blushing and smiling and touching them on the sleeves of their Brooks Brothers suits.

I couldn't get a sister to give me a conversational crumb let alone a whole colloquial cracker.

Time to move on.

I stopped at a pay phone and called the office that was handling the lease. I had called them at least ten times over the last few months. Had called so much they knew my voice.

I said, "What are the terms?"

"Still the same."

"Two-year contract."

"Yes, it is. Two-year contract with one year up-front."

"Is that negotiable?"

"Everything in life is negotiable."

I was facing Z Galleries and the space for lease. I checked out the number of people who were shopping Colorado Boulevard during off hours. The nonstop consumers were better than the regulars at most malls. Weekend nights up here had a party atmosphere, sidewalks crammed with street performers, boulevard with bumper-to-bumper nonstop traffic on the mile-long strip.

I said, "That's what I need to hear. I've noticed the space has been empty for a while."

"Yes, it has. I thought you were coming in."

"Having a cash-flow problem."

"At least yours is flowing."

"Could you do a month-to-month?"

"Depends on the credit."

"Now, how much would actually be required to secure a lease?"

"What would you be using for collateral?"

"Would a used Nova be considered collateral?"

She laughed hard. "Used Nova? Isn't that redundant?"

I ran my hands over my dreads, chewed my lip.

She asked, "Will someone be co-signing the lease?"

"No. Not if I can help it."

"Think about it. Whew. Used Nova. I'm dying over here. You must be a comedian?"

She was still cackling about my Nova. Her laughter calmed down, sounded like she drank some water, and she went over the actual dollar amount they would need a month. A dollar amount that didn't include utilities, phone, liability insurance, and a few other things. Like food. It sounded hard. With the amount of money I didn't have in my pocket or in my bank account, I was living one block from impossible. But I knew I could do it.

She said, "You want to stop by and fill out a lease?"

My hand bounced against my pocket. Not even a jingle.

Too bad dreams didn't have sounds, didn't make noises that others could hear, nothing they could see or feel or taste. Nobody can taste the dream but the dreamer. Nobody could smell what I wanted for me but me.

I said, "Not today. Thanks anyway."

"Well, why don't you give me your name and number, and if anything changes, if the proprietor revises his stipulations and makes them more auspicious, I'll give you a call?"

I said a bland, "Sure. If it's disconnected, call back in a day or two."

She laughed again. "You need to be onstage."

I hung up.

I stopped by the bulletproof post office on Crenshaw and Thirty-ninth, and sent a certified bill to the only address I had for John. Then I used my calling card to phone every number I could think of, including his sister back east. Nobody knew where he was. At least nobody was saying. His family didn't care where he was. Sounded like they hoped he vanished for good, then hung up on me.

I made it back home late afternoon. Walked into my castle that had a mattress on the bedroom floor next to plastic milk crates with my clothes folded inside. Walls were plastered with pictures, black-and-white scenes of Los Angeles, Vegas, and Arizona, photos from the riots, head shots I took for struggling actors who never paid me for the work.

A roach was in a corner. Staring at me.

My answering machine was flashing like it was mad at me too. It had one message that had used up a lot of tape. A message was from Jonathan Curry. He left me a number in the 619 area code to call him back. That southern California area code spread out south from below the Republicans in Orange County, all the way to the Tijuana border.

"Yo! Bob-bee! Heh, heh. Look'a here, sorry about the mix-up. I just got word through the grapevine that things got pretty wild up there in Los Angeles. Good thing I was gone, right?

Heh, heh. I tried to contact you so I could straighten you out, but I guess you were down at the office too. Look, I'm moving everything, and I want you to finish up the work for me. I've got a no-lose thing working. Same thing, different hotels and I don't have to deal with labor unions or—"

And it went on and on for two minutes.

I called the number. A female with a strong Latino accent and a no-nonsense business voice answered on the second ring. It was loud, lots of street noises. Too clear to be a cellular phone, so she had to be squatting at a phone booth.

I said, "John around there?"

"Who is asking?"

"Bobby. I'm looking for Jonathan Curry."

"You are who?"

"I'm the photographer. I did some work for him. He wrote me a check, and it bounced. I need the money so I can—"

"He is gone."

"Is he coming back?"

"No. He told me to give you a message."

I grunted. Ran my hand through my hair. I said, "Go ahead."

She told me where John was going to be working. When he needed me to get there. Where I would be staying.

I said, "That's a long way to go on a secondhand promise."

"Secondhand promise . . . I no understand."

"Your words are hearsay."

She paused, then sounded flustered. "I no understand."

"A long way. It's a long way from here to there."

"Yes, it is. That's why you must fly. He will send you tickets to fly. He will send a note and tell you where to come to do your work."

The best I could figure was that he'd fled with all the equipment and machinery he had "borrowed" and landed in a place with an attitude the opposite of the TV show *Cheers*—he went where nobody knew his face and nobody knew his name. It basically boiled down to me lugging my camera equipment to a designated spot and waiting for him to show up. Hoping he'd show up.

I said, "What about the money he already owes me?"

She said, "He say he pay you when you get there."

"Look, his check was no good. That made my checks bounce. I have people here I owe, and I need to pay now."

"He say he pay you for what he owe you and pay you for your travel expenses when you get here."

"So is the ticket he's sending one way or round-trip? Last thing I need is to get strand—"

"All I know is what I have already told you. He will send you the ticket you need to fly. It will be at your home in the morning. He will tell you where you need to go."

"What is your name?"

"Who I am is not important."

Whoever she was, she must've had cataracts in her ears, because she sure couldn't see what I was saying.

"Whoever you are, give John a message for me."

She replied an ambivalent, "Okay."

"Tell him I said fuck off."

First she paused, like she was caught off guard; then in a harsh tone, she snapped a few things in Spanish before she switched back to English and said, "What you say is not nice."

More rugged words came in Spanish. I tried to say something, but she hung up. Every damn body was hanging up on me.

Now I was pissed off more than I'd ever been pissed off. I picked up the phone and dialed Manuel Torres.

He said, "Bobby, what's going on?"

I paused. Looked at the number I had for John. A quick call to 4-1-1 with the area code and prefix could tell what area John was in. Might even be able to call the phone booth back and ask whoever answered exactly where they were. Thought for second.

I rubbed my temple, said, "I called to say thanks for what you did today."

"Are you okay?"

'Just a little stressed."

"We all are."

"Thanks for . . . uh . . . for . . . looking out for everybody."

"Keep the faith, Bobby. This will pass."

I hung up. Hung up feeling bad. Like a fool to John's dealing. Like a coconspirator to Manuel Torres. How could I be a co-conspirator if I didn't know what I was a coconspirator to?

All I knew was what was real: that my rent would be due soon. I had borrowed all I could afford to borrow. I looked up at my own wall. Saw that one lonely roach. Thought about me. My own restlessness and anxiety. My needs. My wants. My future. So many thoughts.

Right now I had less money than a high school dropout. I was in a grind. I know that this time next year it wouldn't matter. It would be chalked up to experience. For better or worse, my life would have changed. That would be next year. But right now my situation was all that mattered.

chapter two

Somebody banged on my hotel room door. Harsh, short strikes that made me jump and flounder with my camera. I fumbled with the Minolta and caught it before it dropped. It was damn near nine A.M. and hotter than July. I'd been waiting since seven for John to show up. Anticipation had me on edge. I'd flown south to San José del Cabo on a promise. On a dream. All but thirty dollars of the money I'd borrowed from my cousin Debra and my friend Shelby was gone.

I stood straight and said, "Yo, John. It's open."

The Spanish-style door creaked open and brought in a blast of the one-hundred-degree dry heat. Serious, stinging heat like I'd never felt in any part of Los Angeles. That heat made the cigarette odor that permeated every damn thing in the room worse. The whole damn country was crammed with chain-smokers. The hotel people laughed when I asked for a no-smoking room.

It wasn't Jonathan Curry who stepped inside. It was a stern-faced, petite female dressed in a sleeveless money-green blouse and short golden slacks. Roman-style sandals showed off her manicured and golden painted toenails. Her dark brown face didn't have any expression. She was overdressed for this kind of heat. My jeans and T-shirt felt like too much clothing. Naked would be too much material for the heat down here by the equator.

I thought she was from the receptionist desk, but she wasn't in a cheesy blue-and-white uniform. A small green duffel bag with the emblem for the L.A. Kings soccer team hung on her right shoulder. Her legs were thick, calves damn near the size of her thighs. A beat-up novel, *Like Water for Chocolate,* was in her hand, along with a Spanish-English dictionary. Both books were worn-out beyond belief. The novel had a bookmark three-quarters of the way through.

She stood and stared at me. Glanced at a piece of paper in her hand. Then looked at me again. I couldn't remember any Spanish worth knowing, so I hoped she spoke a little English. Since I'd gotten off the airplane at the desolate field and walked into the sardine-packed warehouse they called an airport, I hadn't heard a word of English. Hadn't seen a single sign in English. As far as I knew, my ancestors' coerced language had become obsolete.

I said, "Hola."

She eyed my hair before she returned a dry, "Hello."

"Como está?"

"I am doing all right. You are the friend of John, no?"

"Sí."

Her face was brown, but not darker than mine. Her hair was dyed reddish-brown. Her mane was straight, but not as straight as most of the native women I'd seen.

From the first rude syllable, I recognized her voice and accented English. The tone. The hostility. It was the same woman who answered the pay phone when I dialed the number in the 619 area code in search of John and my lost funds.

She folded her arms, looked away. Since I was the foreigner and was struggling with the language, the shoe of racism was on the other foot. It made me shift side to side.

I said, "Cómo te llama?"

"My name is Alejandria Sanchez."

"Al-ex-ann-dree-ah?"

"No." She made impatient eyes. "Alley-han-dree-hah Sanchez."

Calmly I repeated, "Alejandria Sanchez."

"Yes," she replied. She glanced at a piece of paper in her hand. "You may call me Alejandria."

"Thanks for the privilege."

"John sent me for you. What is your name? I do not want to say it wrong and offend you."

"Robert Davis. Everybody calls me Bobby."

"What should I call you?"

"Bobby."

"B-o-b-b-y." She read the paper in her hand again. "What did you say? Bob-bee?"

"Yeah. Bobby."

"I talked to you before."

"When I called San Diego. At the phone booth."

She nodded. "You were the rude man. You say evil things."

"If you say so. Mucho angry when a grande check bounces."

"In case you did not notice"—she crunched up the paper—"I speak English. Better than your Spanish. Much better."

I said, "I concede. My Spanish is not so good."

"It is awful." Her lips were tight; then they curved down. "Gringo's disrespect us by coming here and slaughtering my country's language."

"Well, I just got here. I can't take the blame for that."

"Do not patronize me."

"Eh, sorry." She had said patronize syllable by syllable, pay-tron-eyes. I said, "I was just being—"

"It is hard on my ears. Speak your English. I understand."

I chilled, held my attitude in check. Everyone in Los Angeles and Pasadena had dissed me left and right, and now this south of the border bullshit. This was going to be a long-ass day.

I said, "Thought John was coming to get me two hours ago."

"He is a busy man."

"He is down here, right?"

"He is back and forth between hotels in San José del Cabo and Cabo San Lucas. He is a busy man. I come to take you on tour so you can start photography on the brochure to represent his other hotels for American and Canadian tourists."

She sounded stiff, like she had memorized what to say.

I said, "Somebody else mentioned Canadians being here."

"Canadians have winter homes in Cabo. Others visit as well. He wants something to show the beauty of the cities and generate tourism directed toward him and his growing franchise."

'What am I supposed to photograph for the brochure?"

"I will show you. He tell me where to take you. The final decision will be up to you. You have the freedom to choose."

"Thanks for the freedom." I paused. "Did he send my money?"

"No."

"What?"

"I have the film and other things John said you requested here in my bag."

"No money?"

"Only film. No money."

I grunted, sighed, sucked my bottom lip.

She said, "You want me to give it now or later?"

I rubbed my temples. 'What was that?"

"Do you want the film now or later?"

"Later. Just hold on to it."

She said an emotionless "Welcome to Mexico, Bobby."

I said a grim "Thank you."

She ran her hand over her hair, then mumbled an irritated "De nada. I mean, thank you. No, I mean, you are welcome."

"I'm sure."

She extended her limp hand. Gave a brief handshake.

I said, "You work for John?"

"Sometimes. Yes. I am his special friend."

"What does 'special' mean?"

"Do you not understand English?"

"Yes, I do."

"Then, you understand what special friend means."

I motioned her toward a hard chair. I said, "Have a seat."

"No, thank you. I will wait where I stand."

Alejandria spied around the room in the same spot she had been waiting since she came inside. She kept her distance and left the door mostly open, the way maids did. She tunneled her fingers through her hair, sighed and stared down at her feet.

A moment later Alejandria turned her back to me, flipped

through her dictionary, went back and forth through the pages, then exhaled and closed it hard when she saw me watching.

She cleared her throat. "This your first time in Mexico?"

"First time going through all the shit they put you through at customs. It was a madhouse down there. About one hundred people. I could've used a translator to help speed things up. Why didn't you show up at the airport?"

She wasn't paying attention. Her nonchalance irked me.

Alejandria had on a body lotion. Her thick legs had a subtle shine. The women I'd seen here at the horseshoe-shaped Tropicana hotel were pretty. They had an ethnic difference that gave them an exotic appeal, but Alejandria stood out. She was the only one who looked mixed. Stood out the way a mulatto did in a flock of purebred Africans. She had to be part black, but I didn't know what part. I didn't care to ask. Her stoic professional demeanor made her read unapproachable. Straight to the point. Stone-faced. A south-of-the-border bitch. I didn't know they had a bitch factory this far south.

Her hairstyle was the first cosmopolitan blunt cut I'd seen since I arrived. I'd been here a few hours, and hadn't ventured from the hotel. I'd stepped and peeped at the Baja Properties Real Estate and inside Sandrick's, a hamburger joint, but that was about it. Three men dressed in Russian military fatigues carried loaded rifles and were on the corner across the street by the Iguana restaurant. They looked at me when I stepped out of the archway onto the cobblestone, watched me while I walked the heat and the dirt road and took a few snapshots, made me feel like Rodney King on parole, so I decided it was best for me to come back and chill inside until I was called to come out.

I went to the closet to grab some equipment. Alejandria closed her dictionary, then stared at me with no emotion. I saw her watching me in the mirror. I turned and faced her. Our eyes met. She frowned.

I asked, "Is there a problem?"

"No."

She turned away. Opened her dictionary again.

Made me feel she was more irritated than a few seconds ago.

Maybe because of the ripped Levi's I was wearing. My lime T-shirt had red letters: "THE HARDER YOU WORK, THE HARDER IT IS TO LOSE." What I had on was just as good as the locals. Actually better.

Outside the two-level, beige stucco hotel, beyond the glitter of the rectangular pool and the jungle of palm trees, the whole city was beat-down and straight-up, impoverished. Filled with bungalows and ragged roads and stray dogs and chickens clucking in the middle of the streets. Made East Los Angeles look like Beverly Hills lite. Made houses in Compton look like castles.

I said, "Want me to hurry up?"

"It is up to you. I am just the driver."

"Am I dressed okay?"

"I am just the driver."

She folded her arms, turned and stared out of my open window. Put her attention in the direction of the white people lounging poolside, underneath the palm trees and archway that led to the main street and other businesses. A few feet from that, smiling Mexican women in shiny green tops and short skirts catered drinks and meals at the outdoor part of the restaurant.

Alejandria left with a kick-ass pace. I followed her to the backside of the hotel. Her VW was sea blue with red doors and hood, golden Baja California plates. Down here, I hadn't seen but a couple of decent cars made since the eighties. This place had to be where Pintos came to die.

I lagged behind her because I had slowed down to take a picture of a pregnant woman smoking a cigarette. Different culture, different habits. I took some shots of dusty little girls wearing plaid skirts and boys in school uniforms running in the streets, then a man riding a horse. Alejandria was still keeping an eye on me.

I ignored her.

When I finished I put my equipment in her backseat. Laid it on top of her books and magazines. Worn paperbacks fiction novels, used nonfiction textbooks, some in Spanish, most of them in English.

We zoomed down a narrow street that sloped upward and

had barrio stores which sold American movies dubbed in Spanish, travel agencies, mostly shops that sold trinkets and blankets like the ones in border town Tijuana. All the signs were in Spanish, all the prices in pesos, so I couldn't tell what kind of stores they were or what anything cost. But they all looked five-and-dime.

We headed toward the Mexican police. These had on blue pants and white shirts. They didn't carry rifles, but their attitudes seemed loaded and they were stopping cars at random. Mostly cars with white tourists. White people were getting pulled over for no reason. That got a smile out of me. But that smile vaporized when they gave Alejandria an evil stare, me a difficult glare, then waved us over. They questioned her and let us go.

I said, "What was that all about?"

"They wanted to know who you were."

"And?"

"I tell them you are a friend of John."

"They know John?"

Alejandria frowned. "His sister works for John."

"What if I wasn't a friend of John?"

She rubbed two fingers together. "Then they would find a reason for you to give them money."

I took more pictures while we rode. Took shots of other tourists who were taking advantage of the fact that they could drink and drive.

Then we were away from town. It was quiet. No music. She never glanced my way. I figured she didn't feel like talking, wouldn't give up a conversational crumb, might be having one of those women mood swings with a Mexican twist.

She said, "Will you tell me something I do not know?"

"What?"

"The word you used. Concede. What does it mean?"

"It means to give up."

She said, "Give up."

"Yeah."

She asked me to spell it for her. I did.

She said, "Oh. I thought it start with letter *K*. That is why I could not find it in my dictionary."

I said, "Nope. Starts with a *C*."

"Gracias. I'm sorry."

"For what?"

"Being rude. I meant to say thank you."

"You're welcome."

"Concede. Give up. Small word with big meaning."

She quieted. The view of the ocean was breathtaking. The silence, nerve-racking.

She turned to me and asked, "What is Los Angeles like?"

"You haven't been to L.A.?"

"For a few days. To help John pack up his things. Then San Diego. To help John pack more things. That was when John had, eh, trouble with his business and had to return here."

"You didn't get to see Griffith Park or Universal Studios?"

"Nada. I'm sorry. I mean nothing. I only worked."

I said, "Los Angeles is . . ."

She laughed. Not much, but a genuine giggle. I thought she was going to jerk her VW off the road when she dropped her head into the steering wheel.

I said, "What's funny?"

"You sound like you choke. The word is Angeles."

I tried again: "Angeles?"

"No, Angeles."

"Eh, Angeles?"

"Sí. I mean yes. Much better. Okay for now."

Her engine roared and she shifted gears without a thought, sort of like a drag racer at the Long Beach Grand Prix. She had left the top down; the sun was beating me into dehydration and a mild sweat. I would've complained, but I liked the way her hair flew in the winds. If some of her mane swung and covered her face, she flipped her head and it moved out of her eyes, moved like it had been trained. A few strands stuck to her dark red lipstick. When she smiled, I saw she had a slight overbite. Very slight. Not enough to call an orthodontist about.

I said, "John never tells you about Los Angeles?"

"No. He does not tell me much of anything."

"What do you guys do for fun?"

"Work. No fun."

"How long have you known John?"

"Too long."

She went down a stretch of highway and passed by a few sets of stucco condominiums being constructed, others already in place. That sect looked very American, extremely European.

San José del Cabo had concrete roads, but when we left town we left pavement and asphalt behind. The view of the ocean was awesome, but the unpaved roads between cities were rough and bumpy. Most had more potholes and dips than Pico Boulevard and Wilshire combined. And twenty minutes of getting tossed around on a rough road was a long time. A few more minutes and I'd be out searching for a tube of Preparation H. She didn't slow down or downshift in the blind curves. That had me gripping whatever I could whenever she made a sudden turn.

We zoomed along the coast, stopped long enough for me to take photos of a group of fishermen at a splintered wooden table set up near the shores. They were shirtless and dissecting the catch of the day. Then she stopped by Supermercado Plaza and got a six-pack of sodas, and cruised on into Cabo. Back in a city again. Back on roads. Stucco business, vendors on the streets selling blankets and trinkets and knickknacks to well-tanned tourists. All the signs were in Spanish. It was like East Los Angeles, without the graffiti and attitude. In Los Angeles I would've been watching my back and looking for an escape route.

Not a black person in sight. I was beginning to think I was the only one left in the galaxy. I'd never felt so far away from home in my life. Damn shame that when I saw too many black people I felt uneasy, and when I didn't see any I felt lonesome, like there was a conspiracy I didn't know about.

Alejandria zipped through town, up a cobblestone hill at warp drive, and came to a stop at a high point in a secluded area filled with big extravagant mansions. She killed the motor before the car stopped rolling. I could see the ocean, the town, the houses, and businesses carved into the city, and the mountains in panoramic view. One of the most beautiful things I'd ever seen.

Click. Whirr. Click. Whirr. Click. Whirr.

It was overcast, but the skies were the clearest blue. It was nice not to see a grayish hint tinting the heavens and no carbon monoxide flooding the air. No rush-hour traffic.

She strayed over to the cliff's edge, then pointed down at a big white house under us with several people outside by the pool lounging, tanning, swimming.

She said, "John wants this one to be in the photograph."

"Why that one?"

"That is"—she hesitated and struggled—"Silver-Star Stale-Leon. That is his house."

"Who?"

"The person in the movie. He kills everybody by himself."

I thought for a moment. "Sylvester Stallone?"

"Yes. I have a hard time with some American names."

"Me too." I laughed. "Like Shan-knee-qwa, Sha-nay-nay, Sha-qwon-dah. Stuff like that."

She didn't laugh.

I attached my telephoto lens and aimed at the big white house with the mushroom-shaped domes at opposing ends of the rectangular roof. I thought I saw Sly in a tight black shirt and shorts strolling by the pool.

Click. Whirr. Click. Whirr. Click. Whirr.

"What do you know about this area?" she asked. "Did you take the time to learn anything about Cabos before you came to take your pictures?"

"Eh, no."

"So you take my country for granted, no?"

"I'm only doing photos. Not an archaeological dig."

"Then, I will tell you some things. No?"

"That would be nice."

Alejandria walked out and stood on the edge of the cliff and pointed out to the sea. She stood so close to the edge it scared me. But she looked comfortable being on the edge.

She said, "That is El Arco, the Arch. On the left of the Arch is the Sea of Cortez, the other side is the Pacific Ocean. Los Cabos is known as the Capes, the southern tip of Baja California Peninsula, where the desert meets the sea. This is a fishing city. We fish for marlin, tuna, trout, shark, dolphin."

"So, Flipper is the catch of the day."

"Who?"

"It was a joke. *Flipper* is a television show."

"Let me know next time you tell a joke, so I can laugh."

"No problem."

Click. Whirr. Click. Whirr. Click. Whirr.

I asked, "Where're you from?"

"I no understand."

"Were you born in Cabo?"

"No." She paused. "Mexico City."

"'Mexico City."

"MEH-hee-ko. Mexico."

"MEH-hee-ko. Mexico."

"Yes."

"I'll work on the pronunciation."

"Please do." She turned and strolled down the edge like she was tightrope walking without a safety net. "Where did you learn to speak Spanish? It sounds so funny."

"College. I had a couple of semesters."

"College." A numb look came over her face. "Oh. You go to college, Bobby?"

"Went. Graduated from USC. And I have less money than a high school dropout."

"You graduated? How long did you take to graduate?"

"Four and a half years."

"Oh." The tone in her voice dropped, deepened. "I see."

"How far away is Mexico City?"

"Lejos. I mean"—she thought—"eh, far. A long way."

"How far?"

"Too far."

Alejandria walked down the edge and stopped long enough to point out a few places between the sea and the ocean. When she moved, it was slow and easy, the roundness of her backside doing a subtle shuffle side to side.

"Alejandria?"

She turned around. "What?"

Click. Whirr. Click. Whirr. Click. Whirr.

"Stop, please stop! I no like my picture. I do not photograph good."

Click. Whirr. Click. Whirr. Click. Whirr.

"*Deje de hacer eso!* Stop it! No photo!" She blushed and covered her face, then turned her back to me. She peeped at me. Turned around. Threw her head in a circle. Moved her reddish-brown hair from her face. Planted a hand on her hip. The other on the back of her neck.

Click. Whirr.

She struck a series of sexy poses. "Okay, Hombre Negro. You can waste your film if you like."

Click. Whirr. Click. Whirr. Click. Whirr.

Two rolls of film later, we sat on the rocks and talked. When I asked, she told me a little about her family. Very little. She had a high wall and was closed about who or what she was. Her father was black and Panamanian, her mother from Mexico. That was all she said.

I told her a lot about me. I was hungry for conversation in English. I talked about growing up with Debra and my cousins.

She said, "We have a lot in common."

"Really?"

"We were born poor, still poor, neither of us have been to a lot of the places in the world, and today, we work for John."

I said, "Victims of economic circumstance."

"That means poor too, no?"

"Yeah. But I'm gonna open my own business one day."

"Good. I believe you gonna."

I smiled, chuckled. "Nobody else does."

"I see passion when you put camera in front of your face."

"It's my love. Everybody should love what they do."

"Why do you choose that job? The photography."

"I want to do something that has personal meaning and can

be passed on from generation to generation. Capturing time, saving history through personal moments. So a child can know what his or her parent looked like when the parent was young."

"You photograph your mother, no?"

I told her that my mom was married at sixteen, had me at nineteen, died from asthma at twenty-two. Outside of the obituary, I hadn't seen a single picture of her. I'm older than my mother lived to be. I've had more days and nights. More sunrises. More sunsets.

It was a strange feeling when you outlived a parent's youth. I don't really have proof, that connection, that my mother ever existed. My only proof is me. My dad wasn't big on taking photos. I have three photos of him. Two of those were taken after Mom died—one at the funeral and the other the day my old man left me with Debra's family. Two good-byes.

I wanted to become a photographer the first time I flipped through my aunt's photo album and saw snapshots going back fifty years, back to when Grandma Ida was young, not a wrinkle anywhere, holding a cigarette on the tip of her fingers, a bottle of Vodka in the other, lounging on the sofa, looking as frisky as she could for the camera. A diva in her prime.

Alejandria listened to me babble. Added nothing to the conversation. Her eyes were toward the ocean and the gulf.

She said, "I understand."

"Do you?"

"Yes, I do."

"So I'm down here, hoping John comes through for me this time. But even if he don't, it won't be the end of the road. I'll still get my own business and get me a better place."

"Do you trust him?"

"Not really."

"How can you work for him, then?"

"I'm asking myself that. I should've cashed in the tickets he sent and used the money for bills and food."

"I believe you. I believe you will get your business."

"Thanks."

"Does your family help you?"

I shook my head. "In some ways. I guess."

Down the mountainside, a huge clock was high on a building in the middle of Cabos. The minute and hour hands were straight up. Somewhere down there, a church bell tolled twelve times.

I said, "Do you trust John?"

She shrugged, shook her head, then another shrug.

"Then, why are you working for him?"

She was quiet for a moment. Alejandria was staring at her nails when she asked, "Are you hungry, Bobby?"

"Did John give you money to feed me?"

She whispered, "Yes. That is what I am to do."

"Then, I'm starving."

"We shall go eat, then."

"Okay."

I finished two more rolls of film, and we made it down the hill by two P.M. It was early, but people were in shorts, tank tops, and sandals, drinking, dancing, and sweating like it was the middle of the night in Las Vegas. Old white men were hanging on to Latino girls young enough to be their granddaughters.

The workers wore shiny purple pants and shiny gold shirts. Every place we went looked like we'd stepped inside of El Torito, every worker like they'd been beamed up from the seventies. There wasn't a sound in the air that reminded me of the states. No news on the tube about Los Angeles. Even the birds chirped with an accent. The music in the restaurant was outdated, too old to be old school, but the way everybody reacted when the Pointer Sister's "Neutron Dance" came on, you'd think it was new.

Then they turned on the macarena song. Everybody got up and headed for the floor. We had just finished a chicken enchilada platter. I asked Alejandria to come to the floor and dance.

She said, "No. That would not be, eh—this is business so it would not be, eh, would not be, eh—"

"Appropriate."

"I do not know that word."

"It means—hell, I know but I don't know."

"Then, why do you use it?"

"That's what we do in America. We use words when we don't know what they mean."

"Why?"

"Let's dance while I think about it."

She sighed, but she didn't move away when I reached for her hand. It took minimal coaxing. And she danced her ass off. I thought she wouldn't know the song, but she did the stupid hand movements without missing a beat, started smiling and got into it, dipped and rolled her hips with each move.

I said, "How old are you?"

"I am very old." She fidgeted. "Twenty-five."

"You're not old." But she looked a little older. The kind of age a person had when life had dealt them wisdom in the form of hard times. I said, "You're very pretty. And you're a young woman. Very attractive woman."

"Thank you." She blushed. "Thank you very much. Your words are kind."

"It was nothing but the truth."

"What is you age, Bobby?"

"Twenty-nine."

"John is older than you."

"Twelve years."

"Sí, twelve years."

I said, "Sí. He was the oldest freshman I knew in college. Most people thought he was a professor. Professors included."

She smiled. "Was that a joke?"

"Afraid not."

A slow record came on and I took her hand, stopped her from swaying back to our table. While we rocked to one of her native ballads, she rested her head on my shoulder, hummed along. Put a hand around my waist and drew me closer.

I said, "You like that song?"

"Sí. It is Selena."

She wore a sweet perfume that had mixed with sweat. During the second slow song, I felt an erection coming on strong. She was close enough to rub against it. She stopped dancing, pulled her head back and gazed into my eyes, grinned briefly at her thoughts, then cradled her head back into my chest. The tip of her fingers stroked by back. She did that over and over.

Alejandria said, "You are a kind man."

My fingers stroked circles in her back.

"You're a kind woman."

She hummed along, but stopped in the middle of her hypnotic tune. Her voice was low when she asked, "You have a lot of girlfriends back home, no?"

I shook my head. "I'm too busy working on myself to get a girlfriend."

"Too busy?"

"Yeah. And American women are expensive. They want a man with much pesos. Most women, especially the ones in Los Angeles, are pretentious and materialistic. They wear fake nails and fake hair and want a real man with real money."

She laughed a little.

After the record ended we left the laughter and smiles on the dance floor, went to the table and gathered our things—her purse, my equipment—then we left. We didn't talk as we headed back into the dry heat. Didn't look at each other. My erection wasn't gone. I wasn't wearing underwear. Hardly ever did partake of the Fruit of the Looms. It wouldn't take but a peek to see my bulge, so I held my camera in front of me when I walked. But I wished I could hold Alejandria right there.

Then we were back on the road, in her VW with the windows down so the hot air could blow over our sweating bodies, zipping over cobblestone roads. My hard-on was almost gone, but the sensation was still alive. Tingling and lingering. With another man's woman, I'd gyrated some semen into my dungarees.

I said, "Let's stop by John's on the way back, okay?"

"No, I do not think so."

"Pretty please?"

She exhaled, then sighed out a heavy "Sí."

My nerves were making me shift around, pretend I was more interested in the country than I would ever be. The truth was I didn't want to see John. But I wanted what he owed me, needed what he promised to pay. My money was almost as important as air, but other things had happened. I needed to see them together so I could extinguish this fantasy stirring in my mind. I felt a chemistry. Because she was a woman. And I am a man. And chemistry recognized no boundaries. Friend or cultural, the right kind of chemistry and the wrong kind of moment would make a man weaken enough to sex his brother's wife.

My veins were chilled with carnal danger, so something definitely needed to be diluted. The smell of her perfume, the aroma of her sweat, how she felt next to me. My erection that wanted to throb back with every beat of my heart. I'd lost count of the months that had passed since I had had a woman. Not sex. Not a rental. But had a woman in my life for more than a few hours at a time. Either they never stayed or they never came back. Half of my regular-sized bed was always empty.

Alejandria parked her car in front of a one-level mauve building. Square and surrounded by a safari of palm trees and other greenery. The same style as the rest of the area. She parked, sat, and stared at nothing.

I said, "This is his place?"

She nodded without blinking.

"What's wrong?"

She said a brusque "Nada."

She reached into the backseat and grabbed her novel.

Alejandria said, "You want to see your friend, no?"

"Yeah."

"Then, go see your friend."

When I went inside, a young waitress in white shorts and a red-flowered top smiled and spoke to me in English. Alejandria came inside a few seconds later. That was when the waitress killed her smile and stormed away. Alejandria ran her hand through her hair and breezed past me. Her other hand was slapping her book against her thigh. I matched her pace and followed her rage.

I said, "Was she pissed off at you?"

"Pissed off?" She was growling. "I no understand, pissed off."

"Mad, ah, angry."

"Yes, angry." She said some rough things in Spanish. "Always pissed off."

John was standing in the middle of the room, scratching the exposed portion of his hairy stomach. Dark brown flesh drooped over his belt, spilled onto his Bermuda shorts. John had thin legs, a big top; his hairline was receding on his pear-shaped head. John claimed he was part Ethiopian, two generations removed. But none of the Ethiopians I knew would claim him.

John was supervising the installation of a stage in the bar area. Alejandria had told me John wanted to add live music, American bands, to his agenda.

I said, "What's up?"

"What up, homeboy?" John screamed and crossed his arms like he was a rapper from the early eighties. Mexican workers stared at him. I hated that shit. Hated it when he mocked our culture outside of our culture. John had zero rhythm. Alejandria wasn't amused. She dismissed us with a slight wave of her hand, strolled to the other side of the room, sat at a wooden corner table, opened her book, crossed her legs, got comfortable. John glowered, licked his lips, jingled his hand in his pocket, then winked at me.

John said, "Watch this."

I said, "What's up?"

He called to her. "Alejandria."

She didn't raise her head. But her leg quit bouncing.

He said, "Go get me and him something to drink, will ya?"

She pushed the chair back under the table, allowed the wooden leg to screech across the concrete floor. The noise dragged on. When her head rose, her eyes had darkened. She looked wicked. Her cold demeanor had returned. She grabbed her purse, her book, and came toward us. Very slowly. Took her time. Never took her eyes away from John. Never blinked. Her book slammed against her leg again and again.

Her voice was at a whisper when she said a stiff "Qué?"

"Two margaritas." John commanded without so much as a glance in her direction. "And speak in English, please."

Alejandria nodded once. "Again, I apologize for being rude."

The phone in a side office rang, and John ran off to catch it. He screamed, "I'm coming, dammit."

Alejandria avoided me. She lowered her head and went toward the bar. I said her name as soft as I could: "Alejandria."

Her eyes arrived at mine with enough force to push mine back into my head. Her face was unfriendly when she snapped, "What?"

I stepped closer to her and touched her hand. I smiled. "May I have a Coke, no ice? Pretty, pretty please? I still think you're pretty."

Her face didn't change, but her eyes brightened. Now her walk changed from a harsh strut into an easy sashay.

I said, "Thanks."

She raised her hand in the air. Wiggled her fingers. Her bracelets danced a jingly song when she did that.

Something sparkled in the mirror at the end of the room facing us. It was the waitress I'd met at the front door. She was peeping around the corner. Watching Alejandria with pursed lips and tight eyes. Her hand with the silver ring held the opening to the doorway. She pushed away and moved in the opposite direction when we made eye contact. She was gone, but I heard her feet moving. Sandals flapped a violent offbeat cha-cha-cha across the concrete floor. A moment later a bell tinkled. The front door slammed hard enough for me to feel the vibrations.

When John came back into the room, he showed me around the place. The kitchen had equipment that was top of the line, state of the art. About one hundred thousand dollars' worth of machinery. The hotel was adjacent. Three hundred rooms filled to capacity.

I said, "Is that the stuff the Asian sold you?"

John patted my back and laughed. "You mean the crazy Korean? I heard he was running up and down the hallway chopping up shit."

"I heard he lost a poor man's fortune dealing with you."

"His insurance will cover it."

"Somebody said he didn't have any insurance."

"Duh. That was a fool's move."

"Heard he might go under."

"Shit happens. He'll pull through. Hell I used to be homeless—"

"I know."

"—but did what I had to do to stop living inside a broke-down Chevy to being the man at the top of the hill."

"What about your credit?"

"I'm not going back stateside for another seven years anyway. I'm going to be the BMOC down here in less than a year."

John gave me a ride back to my room in his brand-new imported Benz. A C280. Alejandria was already gone. She had left without a good-bye. So I had to wait around until almost eleven P.M. for John to wrap up his business.

We drove through a town of neon lights, people staggering from club to club and bar to bar. One drunk tourist urinated on the sidewalk and got snatched up by the police before he could zip his pants back up. Tipsy women were being grabbed at by strange men with sticky fingers. Pretty faces in seductive outfits were being followed and teased. Something about leaving home made a woman feel the need to dress like a whore.

John said, "Up in Tijuana, they have twenty-three million tourists a year, and they spend at least thirty dollars each."

"That's a grip."

"And I plan to get that kinda business down here."

"Go for it."

"Why don't you move down?"

"And do what?"

"The hotel and restaurant business."

"Not my bag. Unless you wanna lease me a place."

"Photography?"

"Yeah. A studio."

"Down here?"

"Up in Pasadena."

"I'm through with the U.S. of fucking A. Why don't you do it here? Tourist season could bring you a grip."

"What would I do in the off season?"

"Fish. Snorkle. I dunno."

"I can starve in L.A."

"You'd think of something."

John babbled nonstop, first about his latest ex-wife, who was down visiting last week; about his nine kids, who he wouldn't have to keep sending child support; then about the three waitresses at the club he was screwing: Dehlma, Sylvia, Alejandria.

Sylvia was the girl who had stormed out when Alejandria came in. He said he screwed her this morning in his office.

"Sex in the A.M. is better than coffee." John opened a beer and said, "Want me to get you a couple of babes? I know some hot firecrackers that'll straighten you out. Whatever you want, they'll do. They'll do some shit you never—"

"No, thank you."

"What's wrong? You're too quiet."

"Tired. Long day. Jet lag."

"Let's grab some honeys, go to the beach and get massaged."

"Nah. I need to unpack, write some postcards, call Debra."

"How is her fine ass doing?"

"She's all right."

"Lord knows I wanted to pop them panties for GP."

"Don't talk about my cousin like that."

"Ouch. Why are you so damn sensitive about her? She's just your damn cousin."

"Right. She's my damn cousin. And your reputation precedes you. Let's keep this business until the business is over."

"Forget that. Let me take you to a few places and show you my real reputation."

"Maybe later this week after I've done some more work."

"All work and no play?"

"Business first. You want quality work, right?"

"Okay. I'll pick you up at eight in the morn for breakfast."

"Sounds good. I assume you'll be on time."

"You know what they say about people who assume."

"Like I assumed your check was good. Where's my money?"

"I don't have it on me. You'll get it."

John dropped me off curbside. Left with his music blasting Gladys Knight and the Pips. I walked down by the church, peeped inside a store and bought a pack of Chicklets.

Then I went back to my empty hotel room.

Alejandria flowed through my mind while I unpacked. I wondered where she lived. How far away. If she inhabited one of the overcrowded stucco shacks like I'd seen a block away. Wondered where she lived, how she lived. Wondered what she did when she wasn't letting John tell her what to do.

I looked in the mirror at my dreads, stared at myself for a while, eyed my ripped jeans and wrinkled T-shirt. Smelled underneath my armpits. Damn I needed to take better care of myself.

While I took a cool shower, I wondered what she thought about me. Didn't matter. She wasn't American, and no matter what her lineage, based on culture, she could hardly be called black, and probably had a thing for the white men who stopped through to spend nickels and dimes. Or for long-term shysters like John. Brothers who could offer her more than crumbs of conversation. Because no matter what country I was in, talking didn't pay the bills. Good intentions couldn't be cashed at the bank.

All I remembered about the day was the view from the top of the hill and the details of Alejandria—what she had on, what she looked like, what she smelled like, how her hips moved when she walked, how her lips moved when she talked, how she had thrown pounds of sensuality into the macarena, what her body felt like against mine during the slow dance, the emptiness I felt when she pulled away from being that close to me.

I picked up the phone to call Debra. It was time to make that call to let her know I had landed safely. I charged the call to the room. John would have to pay for that call. She wasn't home—either that or she just wasn't picking up when she heard my voice on the machine.

Everything on television was in Spanish. Not an English station on the radio. I was isolated. But I was used to isolation. Used to being a loner. One who didn't quite fit in because I didn't follow the standard program. Hair too long, hair too different, clothes not the style of the week.

Boredom took over and I opened my window and gazed at the people lounging by the pool, swimming under the pale moonlight.

I mocked her accent and attitude and said, "Alejandria."

chapter three

I woke up before six the next morning. It was warm all night; this part of the world didn't cool down with the sun's falling, didn't get a chill like the summer nights of Los Angeles. I had the air on for a while, but too much air-conditioning stopped me up. The last thing I wanted was a summer cold. I got up before the real heat came back to town, did some stretching, put in three hundred sit-ups, took a brief jog past the restaurants, sidewalk vendors selling silver bracelets, hoofed it two miles toward the Pacific Ocean, then turned around and came back.

While I showered, the television in the room next door blasted country music, screaming about an Achy Breaky Heart. I needed to buy some repellant because I fell asleep on top of the thin covers and had six mosquito bites on my leg. My back was stiff. The bed wasn't shit but a cheap mattress on top of a concrete slab. The floor was concrete, the walls were concrete. I didn't put on any body lotion because I didn't want to attract any more miniature bloodsuckers.

Just as I pulled my jeans up over my butt, there was a knock at the door. My travel clock had 8:50. That meant it was 7:50 here. John was early. For him to be on time was unusual. He always made people wait. The clock important to him was his clock. And he never put batteries in it.

I said, "It's open, John."

Alejandria walked in. Moved in her slow-and-easy style that made her backside sway with hypnotism. She grinned and said, "Good morning, Bobby. How are you today?"

"Morning, Café Piel."

She mocked me, "Café?"

I said, "Café means brown, right? Piel means skin, right? I was saying that you have pretty brown skin, right?"

She playfully rolled her eyes and laughed. "Café means coffee. Morena means brown. I told you about your bad, terrible Spanish."

Terrible had sounded like terry-bull.

I chuckled. "It sucks."

"Yes, it sucks."

"Sorry."

"Café Piel sounds nice when you say. I will be your Café Piel."

I reached out to shake her hand, but she pushed my hand aside and hugged me. Tight and long. Rubbed circles in my back.

I said, "How're you today?"

"I am fine."

"You looked upset the last time I saw you."

"Yes. I was pissed off. Very, very pissed off."

She released me and walked deeper into the room, swished her yellow-and-blue sundress side to side.

She said a sincere "Thank you for bring nice yesterday."

"No, thank you. For what you gave me."

"For what I gave?"

"The slow dance. It was nice."

"You're a good dancer. Excitable is the word I think."

"Yes. Excitable is the word of the day."

She blushed for a second, jumped up on top of the dresser, crossed her legs and pulled her naked feet up under her dress.

I said, "Where's John?"

"John is a busy man."

"You're taking me to the busy man?"

"John told me to tell you he couldn't make it. He will try to get free later today, maybe early tomorrow and take you more places. You'll have to put up with me for now."

"Too bad."

We looked at each other for a moment; then we both laughed.

She jumped off the dresser, did a ballet move, fell on top of the hard bed, bounced back up. She said, "Let's go."

"Let me grab my shirt."

"Andele!"

When I picked up my camera, she said, "No, leave it."

I nodded.

First we had a quick breakfast in Cabos before we headed to Bahia San Lucas; then we stopped for lunch at Playa del Amor, Lover's beach. White sands, clear blue waters. Enough euphoria to make me not want to go back to my one-bedroom, one-roach apartment in Hyde Park. The sun reflected off the calm ocean. A slight breeze came down on us from the Tropic of Cancer. Water splashed on my rolled-up jeans while I chased Alejandria along the shores. She was agile as a gazelle and dashed into a cove. She could run fast as hell. Her arms pumped like she was Flo Jo going for the gold. When she got tired and a little winded, I caught her in a gentle hug. She broke away, laughing. I chased her finesse a few hundred yards. It was damn hard to play catch me in the sand. Today she was acting youthful, uninhibited. Free. Looked about twenty with her hair damp and makeup off. The second time I caught her I held her tighter. She kicked her legs in the air and cackled. We tussled and fell down hard. She was on top. Her face changed back to stoic.

I said, "You okay?"

She stared at me for a moment, lost her humor, then leaned over and pressed her lips against mine.

She said, "Sí?"

I said, "Sí."

Her mouth eased open, and I put my tongue inside her mouth. Chased hers. Felt my heart beat hard and strong. She kissed me with her eyes open. Stopped and stared. Then ran away again.

We drove back to San José del Cabo and stopped by the Stouffer Presidente Hotel. It was huge, three stories and spread over a few acres. The place was no joke.

I said, "This one of John's hotels?"

"It is his competitor. The one John wants to be better than."

She didn't park on the grounds. She left the car a block away

on the same street that led back to the Tropicana Hotel. I knew
the street because I had jogged down here and turned around
this morning. Alejandria led me around the hotel, cut through
the palm trees and shrubby, hiked to the outside beach and sat
out by the ocean on a railing. We watched the sun sparkle on
the warm waters. A waiter came out to where the land met the
ocean, and we ordered. She spent a few more of John's dollars.
We sat around sipping on blended beverages. Alejandria lit up a
cigarette. I frowned a little. She saw.

She asked, "You smoke?"

"No. A lot of people here smoke."

She handed me the cigarette. "Here."

"I don't smoke."

"Never?"

"Nope."

"Help me finish these, and I will quit smoking forever. The doctors said that is how mi madre got her cancer. From smoking."

I puffed, but did the presidential thing and didn't inhale.
Choked. I never would've done that at home. Would've walked
away from a woman with a cancer stick between her fingers.

She stepped down and strayed across the white sand out into
the clear ocean. Her dress ballooned under her. She cupped her
hands, grabbed water, and dropped it across her hair and back
and yielded a look of pleasure. Flipped her head to sling the wet
mane out of her face. She wasn't vain, wasn't concerned about
her hair, not like most women I knew. She had another kind of
freedom. She faced me, her eyes calling my name. I jumped off
the wall, threw her cigarettes in the trash and went into the
water. When I got close she started a water fight. She was very
competitive. Wouldn't stop until she was sure she had won.

She said, "Do you concede, Bobby?"

"Nope. Do you?"

"I never concede."

I tried not to concentrate on her wet bosom, how the water
made her top almost see-through and her breasts see-all, but her
large, dark nipples, their standing-at-attention reaction let me
know she was a little cold.

I said, "Ready to go in?"

"No. John wants me to keep you busy. Keep you company."

"So I won't be bored?"

"No, you are an excuse."

"An excuse?"

"He wanted to get rid of me so he can see his other women."

"What makes you think he has others?"

"I have eyes and see the truth in their eyes. I have ears and hear what they do not say."

"I see."

"He says he trusts me with you because you are what he calls a nigger. That is a bad word. Not nice to call a person that."

"It is."

"He does not respect you."

"I guess not."

"He respects no one. He has hurt a lot of people."

"How does that make you feel? Knowing that your special friend hurt a lot of people."

"I do not know. It troubles me. I think about it a lot."

"So he called me a nigger."

"That word was on the murder trial for the football player from America. John laughed and said that word was why he did not go to jail. Is that true?"

"Maybe, maybe not. Anybody ever call you a nigger?"

"Yes. When I was on the freeway in San Diego."

"What did you do?"

"John said I wasn't going fast enough."

"How slow were you going?"

"The speed limit."

"That'll do it."

"They are so impatient and rude. Why do they shoot at each other on the freeway?"

"Because they can." I wrung some of the water out of my hair. I said, "What did you do when they called you a nigger?"

"I did not answer. That is not my name. If I become angry, then I surrender my power; I lessen myself. Do you agree?"

"Next time I won't turn around either."

"I told John I dislike you and you act like a *pendejo*."

"*Pendejo?*"

She paused. "Asshole."

"Really?"

"Sí."

"Sounds like this is going to be hard work. You and an ass-hole-nigger in Mexico."

"Very. I am working very hard."

She took my hand and helped me out of the way of the in-coming surf, and never let go. We went to the edge and watched the boats in the distance, fishermen hard at work.

Alejandria said, "Poor Flipper. But we have to eat."

We laughed.

After we'd spent an hour walking and talking and air drying, my bladder started yelling at me. Screaming to be emptied.

I said, "I need to go to a bathroom."

"There is one inside the hotel. In the lobby."

"Okay. Is it okay to go in there?"

"John would be mad. But he does not come down here. He does not want anyone who works for him here. That is why I come down here to be by myself. Because others will not come."

"John is your boyfriend."

She nodded, bit her lip, whispered, "Yes."

"You love him."

"Sometimes. But not the way a woman should love a man."

"How long have you been with him?"

"Too long."

She led me back toward the lobby of the Presidente. I par-doned myself and went across the squared concrete tiles to the Cabrillo Banos to relieve myself. Alejandria stayed by the counter, closer to the end facing the front. Almost as if she was positioning herself so she could see who came in.

When I came back, Alejandria was sitting in a leather wing-back chair across the lobby next to the reservation desk, legs crossed, right leg on top, bouncing up and down. She smiled, walked to me, extended her closed fist to give me something. I opened my hand to receive it. It jingled when it left her hand and landed in mine.

A key. With the numbers 214 engraved in the metal.

Her lips hardly moved when she whispered, "Sí?"

My lips hardly moved when I nodded, then said, "Sí."

chapter four

Café Piel spoke broken English, but was amorous in perfect Spanish. Passionate and ravenous.

After we finished the second time, she cradled her head on my chest and eased into a relaxed sleep. A siesta. The lines of stress that were riding her face had been erased. At least for now. She was peaceful. And for the first time in a while, all of the bullshit that had been troubling me didn't seem worth the power I'd been giving it.

I peeped out of the window facing the Gulf. The sun was resting on the top of the waters in between the rocks of the Arch. Reddish orange had shaded the sky. The hue of sunset. Colors of the ending of the day.

I gazed down at Alejandria's brown skin, then at my darker brown skin, put my flesh next to her flesh. Studied her hair. My hair. Her eyes. Mine. Imagined what the combination would make. She twitched. I pulled her damp hair from her face and rubbed circles on her nose. Her lips.

I wondered how an asshole like John could end up with an angel like Alejandria and I spent most of my nights touching myself while I stared at *Ebony Man*'s calender girl of the month. How he could he end up with a supportive woman like this, and on most days I couldn't depend on my shadow to have my back?

I got pissed off because this was just a fantasy. Well, it had happened, so it wasn't a fantasy anymore. It was more than a release for me. In a few hours she'd be back with John. Doing the same for him that she had done for me. Back with him, living in a loveless exchange. Master. Slave. I'd be back to being who I was before these snatched moments. Cruising clubs in search of the next disappointment, hunting for a new heartbreak.

Soon I'd be going back to Los Angeles. I'd be gone and it would be like this never happened. I'd be back to being myself. Back to being by myself. All of this would be fading in my mind. Alejandria would be gone. My heart would move on to other things.

But I couldn't abandon the woman who wanted nothing from me, smiled at my ambition, and had bedded me from her heart. Even in her own misery, she had a control I wish I had in my own struggle.

The room was getting dark. I closed my eyes and tried to catch up with Alejandria in her sleep. I wanted to intrude and become a part of her dreams, and in her dreams have her make love to me until we woke up, refreshed, and ready to do it again. I wanted to steal as many moments as I could.

My eyes got heavy. I drifted off. Dreamed about her running in an open field, turning cartwheels and singing the slow song, the Selena tune we danced to. She disappeared behind a magnolia tree. And when I ran there, she was gone.

I felt someone pushing my shoulder.

Again and again.

I woke up to a dark room and a star-filled sky.

Alejandria had her chin resting in my shoulder. Her hair in her face. She licked her lips and kissed me.

"Hello, Bobby."

"Hello, Alejandria."

She eased her hand under the sheets. Her soft palms rubbed across my chest before her touching flowed south. She kissed my chest while her hand touched me and made me grow. Her eyes held passion. I kissed her breasts, licked them, sucked them, made her back arch. Her words were long moans.

She said, "Not so hard."

I eased up a bit.

Her body shuddered. "Yes, Bobby."

She said some sensuous words in Spanish. Words and phrases and moans that excited me, made my desire for her mushroom.

I said, "What does that mean?"

"That feels so nice." She ran her tongue over her lips, smiled. "So, so, very nice."

Her moans deepened. My appetite became more intense.

She spread her legs, welcomed me. She whispered, "You can?"

"Yeah."

"Good."

I kissed her. Tried to find my way in, but I kept missing.

She reached down and took me. "I'll help you, sí?"

"Okay."

"Slower this time."

"Okay."

"Much slower. Follow me. Do not hurry. We have time."

"Okay."

She returned my kisses. Showed me the way to her pleasure.

chapter five

An hour later we slipped into our damp clothes, left the key on the dresser, and tipped out the back exit. She wanted to take the long route again, avoid the lobby and slip through the pool area to the side streets.

Everything was awkward. The way she strolled without touching or holding my hand. The lack of words. The hard expression on her face. I wondered if she'd be fucking John by midnight.

I said, "Well, your car's still here."

"Sí."

We hopped in and she started her engine without a word.

I said, "How long have you been working for John?"

She didn't answer. She closed her eyes for a couple of seconds, then opened them again. Thin lines come back into her face, and her lips scrunched tighter than a boxer's fist.

I realized what we had just done. What I had just asked.

"I'm sorry. I didn't mean it like that."

"I see. I understand. What do you mean, then?"

"I meant, I was wondering how long you had been knowing him. Why you, eh, tolerate him. His attitude. Understand?"

"Sí, I understand." She whispered that. "I understand."

"You said you love him."

"Some. Not enough to be concerned with."

"Okay, some. But do you like him?"

She paused. "No. Why are you concerned with how I feel for John? Why are you concerned after we were intimate, if you were not concerned before?"

"Why are you with somebody you don't like?"

"John used to be very good to me, very attentive. But men are like that at first. He still is good to me in his own way. Mi madre is ill with cancer, mi padre is dead. I have a sister younger than me. And two brothers older. I had three but he and my husband were killed."

"How were they killed?"

"The earthquake. Home in Mexico City. Belushi, my husband, and my big brother Oscar were sleeping in the living room. I was still at work at the restaurant. I was hurt, but not bad."

"I'm sorry."

"It is no need to be sorry. They are in heaven now. We are the ones in hell. No need to be sorry for them. No need to be sorry for me."

"Why haven't you met someone special or married again?"

"In my life I have met two people special, who are good to me, who I liked. Belushi and you." She smiled. "I like you. You are different."

"Why don't you leave John?"

"And what would I do?"

"What would you like to do?"

"You promise not to laugh?"

"I'd never laugh at someone's dreams. Can't afford to."

"I would love to go to college. To get an education, to be smart like you."

"I'm not that smart."

"I see the thing you do with cameras. The passion. John has shown me other pictures you took. You have a gift. Do not take what you have for, eh"—she paused—"I do not know the American word for—"

I said, "Granted?"

"Yes. Granted. Understand what belongs to you." She nodded her head. "I want to have something nobody can take from me. So for now I buy books, and I teach myself things I need to know."

"Then, leave here."

"When it is time, I will leave."

"How'll you know when it's time?"

She hesitated. "Where would I go?"

"Come to America with me."

"John promised me the same thing."

"What happened? I mean, you were there, right?"

"He took me to San Diego. He tell me that he will let me go to the city college. That was what I wanted. To learn."

"But he got in trouble."

"We had to leave." She nodded. "And I could not go to school. I could not stay without him."

"Why not?"

"Where would I stay?"

I said, "If you wanted, I live alone, I'm never home, and you could stay with me until you decided what you wanted to do. You could get a part-time job and, hell, damn near every city has a city college you can go to."

"Shhh." She sounded angered. "Be careful what you say."

"I say something wrong?"

"All the gringo come here and make promises they do not plan to fulfill. They come in your winter season, make babies with young girls and go home to their country's spring and never come back. That is what mi padre did. My father did that."

"I thought you said he died."

"He is dead to me. As I am dead to him. I say that so others will not think bad of me, bad of mi madre. No one questions the dead. Everything else, about my husband, my brother, everything else is the truth."

"Where is your daddy from?"

"New York." She chuckled. "He was here for business. Like you."

A moment passed.

She said, "We did not use a condom."

I nodded. "I know. I was there."

"We should have used a condom."

"I know."

"We were not wise."

"I know."

Another moment passed.

Alejandria said, "Do one thing for me."

"What?"

"Do not make promises. Do not make lies."

"I promise not to make any promises."

"Was that a joke?"

"I was trying to be funny, yeah."

"It was not funny. No promises. No lies. Comprende?"

I replied, "Sí. I understand."

Nothing was said for a few tense minutes.

I said, "John's not good for you."

"John is not so bad. I have seen worse. I have met those who are not as good. At the restaurant John pays well, six dollars for one hour of work, better than all of the restaurants in Cabos and San José. So for some he is a hero. Most will do almost anything to get a job with him."

"Can't you work another job?"

"John pays me more than the others. I get almost ten dollars. Eighty dollars a day. We do not have all the jobs you have in your country. I do not want to work in a restaurant and cook and be a waitress all my life. But I need the money to send home to my family, mi madre. Madre can't work. Like I said, cancer. My family needs the money. I think of others first."

"What about what you want?"

She shook her head. "That would be selfish."

I said, "What about love?"

"Love is not necessary for survival."

"Maybe not, but it makes life worth living."

"Love not necessary for survival. I think of others first."

"Who thinks of you first?"

"No one."

Another talkless hour passed. We rode around town and stopped for dinner at the Iguana, then went back to my hotel. When we got to my room, the television was playing loud on a Spanish channel.

I turned the noise down and said, "Maid must've left the idiot box on."

Alejandria came just inside the door and gave me less than a shallow hug. A leaning, one-arm hug at that. I tried to hold her and kiss her lips, but she shifted and I barely tasted the side of her face. Ended up French kissing nothing but air.

She lent me a hypocritical smile and flipped her hair. I started to speak, but she shut me up me with the raise of her hand. Then with small, difficult words, she stepped away, expanded her false smile and said, "Today I took you to the beach and drove you around the city. We had breakfast here, and dinner at the Iguana. Nothing else happened. Nada, understand?"

Her delivery was straight. Emotionless.

I shook my head. "Not really. What's wrong? Did I offend—"

"Sí, but no?" She forfeited the remainder of her smile and dropped her head. Again she made a sound of frustration and tunneled her hand through her damp hair. Without warning, she spun around and rushed out the door without another word.

I called her name. Tried not to sound like I was pleading, just to sound like I cared. She crossed over by the pool. The few people lounging stared at me, peeped at her, went back to working on their tans.

Alejandria didn't slow her pace. She sped up, whisked by the white wrought-iron tables and chairs that were on the sidewalk part of the tavern, and vanished through the arch of hotel leading into the restaurant area.

chapter six

"Alejandria said you called me a nigger."

"Black, white, purple, I call everybody a nigger. It's an adjective of affection and endearment. Don't take it personal."

"John?"

"Yeah."

"Kiss my ass."

"You gay?"

"Hell, no."

"Then, why are you inviting me to your booty?"

"John?"

"What?"

"Kiss my ass."

John had been driving me around for the last two days. Being in his presence was a true test of what was left of my character, which I felt was weakening with each passing moment.

"I don't appreciate what you said."

John said, "Black men on the streets of L.A. call each other nigger all the time. Scream it across Crenshaw Boulevard. Shout it over the balcony at the Hawthorne Mall."

"Hawthorne Mall closed down."

" 'Cause too many niggers were down there. Tell me I'm lying?"

"Not the point," I said. "And every now and then, a brother gets his head cracked wide open for saying it."

John laughed. "Sounds like you're retaining water. You come to Mexico for money, or to start some righteous shit?"

I didn't answer. I raised my orange juice to my lips and enjoyed the view. John was right. What I had come here for was to get the money. And make a few dollars more. Getting a chance to freak his woman was an under-the-table bonus. I needed to put things in perspective, had to shake the agitation and aggravation she had left behind. Alejandria was right. Nothing had happened between us. Room 214 had never happened. Even when it was happening, it wasn't happening. Nothing was going on.

John drove and belched a couple of six-packs while he took me from sight to sight. Bumpy roads were smooth in his Benz. The windows were down and a Tracy Chapman CD was on his sound system. I hated Tracy Chapman's depressing music. Every sad lyric made me want to run out into the ocean screaming. I didn't give a damn about a fast car. But I was glad to hear something in English. Something with a familiar beat. Right now Tracy had the most beautiful voice in the world.

John said, "Beautiful country."

"Yep."

"Inhale."

"What?"

"Take a deep breath."

I did.

He said, "Smell that?"

"I didn't smell anything."

"Exactly. Can't do that up in Los Angeles without choking on smog. And the water at the beaches up there, yikes, that crap is too cold and you can't even see your feet in the shallow part."

"True."

"You should step into this ocean, walk down in the warm waters of the Gulf, and get your feet wet up to your neck."

"Maybe I'll find a senorita and dance around on the beach."

"Now you're talking. Dance naked. Get some fucking in while you're down here. You still like women, don't 'cha?"

"Black women."

"Close your eyes. It'll feel the same."

"I just might do that."

Click. Whirr. Click. Whirr. Click. Whirr.

We stopped at his three-hundred-room hotel, where he arranged for a lot of native beauties in flossing bikinis to be available for photography at poolside. There were a couple of girls I hadn't seen before. All of them worked for John. They were cutting eyes at each other and avoiding getting too close or even being in the same photograph. I played naive and made Dehlma and Sylvia pose together. Made them hug and cheese like long-lost sisters. Somebody said Dehlma was around eighteen, Sylvia was around nineteen. John blew kisses to one as he squeezed the other's rump.

Click. Whirr. Click. Whirr. Click. Whirr.

I said, "You've got a lot going on down here."

"Yeah."

"So you had planned this before you left L.A."

"Damn right. The U.S. of fucking A. was an end to a means."

"Ripping people off was premeditated."

He laughed. "I plead the fifth, then drink it in celebration of business well-done. They'll get over it."

"A lot of people have a bounty out on you."

"That legal bullshit up there don't mean shit down here. I'll be Chapter 7, and my accounts are out of reach. You been in contact with all of those other people who were hunting me down?"

"Nope."

"And make sure you don't."

"Why?"

"I'm on the run and don't need to be found for a while."

"You paying me by cash right?"

"You still mad?"

"You screwed me over. What d'you think?"

"No, I didn't. Yours was an accident."

"Why was mine different?"

"If I knew I'd tell you."

"I forgot to tell you, a couple of rough brothers came by your office hunting for you too. Mean-looking brothers."

John lost his humor that time. His sarcasm and cynicism fled as his voice turned dark, and I would swear that he was terrified when he asked, "What they look like?"

"Over six feet tall, prison builds, gold teeth, frowns."

"They have tattoos on their necks?"

"Think so."

"Damn." His breathing changed, hands opened and closed. "Those are the last motherfuckers I want to see."

"What's up?"

He ran his hand over his head. "I got this chick pregnant back in ninety-four. And I got a little behind on the child support."

"When was the last time you made a payment."

"Back in ninety-four."

"Which chick was this?"

"Waitress who worked at Dulan's. Cutie with the Jamaican booty. Kinda like Shelby's ass, just not as tight. Actually it wasn't tight at all. Sisters sho' be letting themselves go."

"She worked at the restaurant on Crenshaw?"

"Ain't but one."

"Looked like they were ready to get a rope and find a tree."

"They'll never find me."

"And since I've found you, I need my money."

"Quit whining about a dollar or two."

"Quit gaming me."

"How much I owe?"

Click. Whirr. Click. Whirr. Click. Whirr.

"Your check bounced. I have to pay returned check fees, pay for phone calls—"

"What phone calls?"

"I made phones calls to New York six times to try and get in contact with you through your stepsister, and she left me on hold for over fifteen minutes."

"Nobody told you to hold on that long."

"Your bounced checked made three of my checks bounce."

Click. Whirr. Click. Whirr. Click. Whirr.

"All right, I'll pay you before you leave."

"Before tonight. I want to sleep with my money."

"You're about to lose your job."

"Like I said, you're paying me by cash, right?"

"All right. You're worse than the Koreans at the swap meet."

"U.S. dollars. Not pesos."

"All right, whatever." He popped open another beer.

"I'm serious, John. No bull, okay? I had to borrow half of my rent money from Shelby and I have to pay her as soon as I get back to L.A."

"That's another one I'd like to get doggy style. I'd love to sniff her drawers."

"John. Don't disrespect Shelby in my face."

"Then, turn your back. Women down here don't have an ass like that. Most of 'em don't have an ass at all. I'm longing for a real booty. Can't close my eyes and make that feel the same."

"My money, John. Stay focused. What's up with my grip?"

"Give me some credit. Didn't I pay for the fucking plane ticket?"

Click. Whirr. Click. Whirr. Click. Whirr.

"Two hundred eighty-eight. Big fucking deal."

"And that was too much. I need to get a new travel agent."

"I want my money plus six dollars for the shuttle to the hotel plus eight dollars in tips."

"Eight dollars in tips? Why you give so much?"

"It's called respect. You've heard of that right?"

"In my book it's called stupidity. You could've gave 'em two quarters and a jujube and they would've been happy. What you think I am, a damn Rockefeller?"

"I want all of what you owe me, plus I want half for this shoot now, before dinner, the rest when I finish."

"Who keeps the negatives?"

"I do."

"No, I do."

"Nope. You need more copies, you come through me."

"How much to buy you out?"

"An extra four hundred."

"No speaky dee English, misstahr."

"I'm not joking, John."

"We'll have to go by the house."

"No problem."

"And I ain't giving you eight dollars for no damn tips."

Click. Whirr. Click. Whirr. Click. Whirr.

John dropped his beer can where he stood. Before it bounced twice, two of the helpers dashed over, bumping each other like soccer players combating for a loose ball.

John chuckled and popped open another can. "Hungry?"

"Hungry for my money. I'm serious. Don't screw me."

chapter seven

We stopped by John's house in Cabos. A two-story five-bedroom spread up a cobblestoned hill. The Pacific and part of the Gulf faced his floor-to-ceiling windows. Looked like I could toss a rock from the hillside, and it would drop and hit the ocean. He had this big-ass house with central air, and had me in a hotel room tossing and turning on a concrete slab, fighting off mosquitoes.

When he opened the door, the smell of well-seasoned meat filled my nose. That made my stomach rumble and growl. Pots were banging a not-too-pleasant song. Some of John's help was stirring in the kitchen. John went in before me. I pulled the door up behind me a little too hard. It banged closed.

John cringed. "Take it easy with that, will ya?"

A cabinet slammed.

John shouted, "Take it easy with that, will ya?"

"John, are you ready to eat lunch?" Alejandria said as she stepped out of the kitchen. She had on one of John's restaurant shirts. Bare feet. Hair was pulled back from her face and tied. She had on a shallow, open-cleavage shirt, open enough to show off her rust-colored French-cut panties. No bra. Dark nipples on parade. She saw me and looked at John. Kept her eyes away from me. Pulled the shirt and covered what she could.

She asked, "Should I prepare lunch for you and your friend?"

I said, "How have you been, Alejandria?"

"I am fine, Mr. Davis. How are you?"

"I was beginning to think John was holding you hostage."

She turned back to John. Alejandria said, "I should prepare lunch for your friend as well, no?"

"Eh, excuse me, Alejandria." I looked at John. "Does she have to clear everything through you?"

John laughed. "No. Ask him, babe."

Alejandria gazed at me. Eye to eye. Then she made herself busy buttoning up her shirt.

She said, "Would you care to join us, Mr. Davis?"

"Is it okay with you, Senorita Alejandria Sanchez? I wouldn't want to intrude."

"No, you would not intrude, Mr. Davis. This your friend's home, Mr. Davis."

I said, "Bobby."

"Qué?" Her hand flew up and covered her mouth. She looked at John, then back at me. She said, "I am sorry for being rude. I mean, what?"

"My name's Bobby. Mr. Davis is my daddy's name."

"I was sorry. I thought . . ." She kept readjusting the shirt like she was trying to hide herself. "Bobby is not your name?"

"It was a joke, Alejandria. I was kidding. Next time I'll tell you it's a joke first so you'll know to laugh."

Her skin reddened on her cheeks. Alejandria had a panic in her eyes that asked if I had broken down and exposed her secret. If I had told secret. A second later her eyes calmed.

John patted me on my back. Patted me hard and got his hand tangled in my dreads. He freed his hand and said, "I'll be right back. I gotta go see a man about a horse."

Alejandria hurried toward the kitchen. She said, "I have to finish. Five more minutes and it will be done."

When I glanced down the hall, John was walking toward the back of the house. I assumed he was going to use the bathroom in his bedroom. I took easy steps and followed Alejandria's fast pace into the kitchen.

Alejandria continued chopping onions and tomatoes for the tacos, ignoring me. I took her hand. At first she tightened her grip on the knife. Then she loosened it. She didn't pull away, but she let out a weak "No."

Even though it was the same word, the "no" sounded more Spanish than English. It mad me wonder how many men she had told no. Made me want to know how many had listened.

I said, "I'm not going to hurt you."

"Go with your friend. Go, Robert Davis. Go."

I held her hand for a moment and said, "Look at me."

I put my hand on her round chin and helped. Tears had formed in her eyes. I kissed her forehead and said, "It's okay. Everything's cool. He don't know."

She moved my hand and resumed her cutting. "Go. Get away from me. Do not ever touch me in that way again."

"Alejandria—"

"Bobby, please. Respect what I say."

I left the kitchen and went into the living area in time to hear John coming back up the hall. He was zipping up his pants and calling out, "Bobby, come here, will ya?"

I followed John into his bedroom. The way the sheets and covers were convulsed on the bed, something violent had happened. And the stale odor in the air told me it had been very recently. Across the room was a chair with a brown-and-yellow paisley sundress and a bra draped across its back. Neatly folded. Like she had undressed at his command. Like it was nothing but business. At the foot of the bed was an empty wine bottle with one glass. No lipstick was on the rim. Like she hadn't been invited into all of the pleasures. I backed up and stayed close to the door. Reneged full entry into Alejandria's discretion.

John took down a large picture of himself standing in front of USC and revealed a wall safe. He licked his fingers, rubbed his hands and turned the dial right, left, right, then turned a handle. It clicked open. He reached in and took out a stack of American money still in the bank wrapper.

John threw me the bundle. He smirked and said, "Here you go. That should cover it all."

The bills hit the opening to the door and bounced into the hallway. I picked the bundle up and flipped through the money. Almost three thousand. My heart thumped. Hard. Some of my old headache went away. It was replaced by a new headache. A headache brought on the vision of all the people who had been out in the hall of John's old job crying over money that had been stolen. Money that I was holding. But I had money. I had touched it, so it was mine. Enough to set my dreams in motion. If I could get my cousin Debra to co-sign, and if I negotiated the right way, my lease could be obtained by this time next week.

John said, "About time I saw you smile."

Felt like somebody had lifted an anvil off of my shoulders. My hands sweated as I flipped through the bills. I held a few up to the light. Checked the serial numbers to make sure they were all different and not consecutive. Tested the ink to make sure it was dry. Made sure the right president's face was on the money.

I said, "This is enough for the entire job."

He winked. "No bad checks this time, huh?"

I put the money in my waist, pulled my T-shirt over the wad.

Alejandria came up behind me just as John started to babble about where he bought his Italian bedroom furniture from. More like got it on credit from a Beverly Hills store and fled without paying.

Alejandria peeped in at her clothing, glanced at me.

She said, "Excuse me, Mr. Davis."

She tried to ease by me. I turned and bumped into her, then accidentally on purpose pressed into her front. Touched her the way we touched when we had slow danced to the Selena song. When we had danced between the sheets at the hotel. She tried to push me away. I stumbled into her, forced her to catch me, made her acknowledge me. Our faces bumped at the lips.

I said, "Sorry."

She pushed me hard. Stared and gave me the stone face from the bitch factory churning deep inside her. She grabbed her belongings and shoved past me. John was struggling to put the picture back over the wall safe. This time she bumped hard into me. Shoved me with her body.

Her eyes cut into my face. She growled, "Sorry."

There was a knock at the front door. John screamed, "Answer that, will ya, Alejandria? Hurry it up."

By then Alejandria was halfway down the hall, fighting with

herself, yanking on her sundress, struggling with her bra. She finished dressing and threw John's shirt over her shoulder.

John was still babbling. Narcissistic rambling.

He said, "Ain't that right?"

I said, "Ain't what right?"

Before he could repeat himself, there was a lot of shouting coming from the front room. Loud overlapping curses.

John broke out, running up the hall. "Oh, shit."

I followed.

Alejandria and one of the girls I had just finished photographing were in the living room screaming at each other. The other girl was Spanish, but more Native American looking. She was in a thong bikini and flat shoes. A strong tan and shades on her eyes. They were about a half second from a fight.

Alejandria snapped, "Cabron!"

"Hijo de la chingada!" the girl in the bikini screamed and swore at Alejandria. "Chinga tu borracho madre!"

Before the girl made a step, Alejandria reached up the two steps, grabbed her by the hair, and snatched her off the foyer landing down onto the concrete floor. The girl's shades flew across the room, and she landed on her shoulder. Her head made a hollow sound when it thudded and bounced on the floor.

She moaned, "OoooOoooOooo."

Alejandria grabbed a handful of the girl's black hair and closed-hand hit her over and over with her left hand. The girl swung wild and slapped Alejandria. Hit Alejandria hard enough to echo. Alejandria didn't back off, charged at her growling. Rabid and clawing. Alejandria bit the girl's arm until the girl wailed and cried. All of that happened before we could get to them. And when we got to them, we couldn't get them apart. Alejandria scratched the girl across the face like a lioness striking injured prey.

Alejandria screamed in a mixture of Spanish and English to never, ever disrespect her mother.

The girl flipped around and screeched out like a wounded animal, one loud long continuous shrill that gave my skin goose bumps. John threw Alejandria toward me. Slung her up in the air in my direction. In the air, she was still fighting. Alejandria landed, found her footing, got ready to charge back at the girl, but slipped on the carpet. One of her legs flew up into the air. She spun and fell backward, head first, but I caught her before she crashed on top of a glass table with an iron base. Alejandria found her footing again, tried to move back toward John or the girl—maybe John and the girl. I didn't know who she was after, but I didn't let go of her left arm. She yanked and tugged, tried to scratch my hand, but I didn't let go.

John said, "Cut this shit out before you break some of my furniture! You know how much this stuff costs, dammit?"

The injured girl whined something in Spanish. Something fast and desperate that sounded like a ten-second word.

John screamed, "English, dammit! English!"

"What is she doing over here?" the girl cried out.

"None of your fucking business. Alejandria, get her a towel and some ice."

Alejandria didn't move, but reached over to grab a brass lamp on the table. She gripped it and brought it up over her head, high over her head. I caught her hand and she looked at me.

She said, "Let me go!"

I said, "Don't."

She loosened the lamp and jerked away from me. She turned to John and screamed in Spanish.

John said, "English, dammit! English!"

"Fuck you, fat, lazy bastard! You get your ugly stupid bitch a towel yourself, mudderfucking fat asshole!"

"Alejandria, that's more like it." John chuckled. "Your English is improving. Now, go get a towel, please."

The girl rolled side to side and cried, "OoooOoooOooo."

John turned to the girl on the floor. He said, "Angeles, you all right? Don't get blood on the carpet. That's from the States and hard to find. You might not be able to work tonight."

"She scratch my face. My heard hurts. Sí, pero no."

"Alejandria, you might have to work her shift tonight."

Alejandria tensed. I moved between her and John. I put my hand on her shoulder and said, "Are you okay?"

Alejandria jerked away from me and stormed through the kitchen and out a side door. The garage door whirred open. A VW engine roared. Then a wicked screech out of John's driveway. It sounded like her Volkswagen banged and scraped the top of the garage door before the door was all the way up.

John shouted, "Take it easy before you tear my house down!"

The sound of gears shifting faded with distance. Faded at breakneck speed.

John whistled while he walked into the bathroom. He came back about ten minutes later with a dry towel. He handed it to the girl and told her, "Straighten up my furniture and the rug. Then go into the kitchen and get some ice, babe. Take care of that, will ya? Try not to bleed on the furniture."

Minutes later, with her head wrapped, Angeles smiled and prepared the tacos. Laid them out like she was serving a king.

John grabbed a taco and headed to the bedroom. She followed. Held her head and smiled all the way down the hall.

That lasted about fifteen minutes. I heard the last five minutes of her moaning and Spanish screams coming up the hall. Heard them loud and clear because John didn't close the door.

John came out of the bedroom first. Wobbling like he was punch drunk. Half a taco in his hand. He walked into the living room and asked me, "You want some before she goes to work?"

I shook my head.

"She won't mind."

I shook my head.

He waved me off. "Damn, this taco is good. I'm going another round. Make yourself at home. Sure you don't wanna?"

I shook my head.

chapter eight

Fifteen minutes later Angeles came out half naked with her head bandaged. She sang her way toward the hall shower. When she finished, she came into the living room for minute. She was holding her head and grimacing in between smiles. John wouldn't allow her to use the one in his back room of sin. John put his pants back on, grabbed a couple of brews and left me there with her. Said he had to run down to the hotel to meet with a vendor and check out a band.

I said, "How am I getting back to the Tropicana?"

"She'll take you."

"She's injured."

"No, she's not. You injured, Angeles?"

She shook her head, groaned, and limped across the room.

Within ten minutes Angeles had dressed herself in the same sundress Alejandria wore the day we went to Lover's beach. Wore the same perfume, but it didn't smell as sweet. Angeles drove a VW. The same year as Alejandria's. Only this one was yellow with orange doors. John must've had a two-for-one coupon.

We were about fifteen minutes from my hotel, on the bumpy and winding road I had ridden on my first day with Alejandria. The same road John and I were on this morning.

Angeles said, "You John's good friend, yes?"

"No," I replied, then stared off into the night filled with a thousand stars as I mumbled, "I was just a nigger who was selling out for him."

"No understand. Eh, hablo Español?"

"No Spanish. I understand better than I speak it."

"Sí."

"How old are you?"

"Diecisiete."

I paused and did a mental count in Spanish. "Sixteen?"

She looked confused. Nervous. I knew she didn't understand the word sixteen. She shrugged, smiled, and said "Sí."

After jailbait dropped me off, I sat in the lobby and watched repetitive videos on the screen. Over the hour I downed three margaritas. When I finished I left a five-dollar tip. I stopped by the pool and looked at the employees. They were on break. Smoking Marlboros and sipping on bottled Coca-Colas.

The one with the silver tooth smiled and said, "Hola."

I said, "How're you today?"

"Bueno, y tú?"

"I'm doing fine too."

I glanced around at the country, listened to the language. For a moment I wondered who or what I would be if my ancestors hadn't been taken from Africa. But I let that rest. I needed to keep focused on reality and let the fantasy go. Who I am is who I am. Being in Africa wouldn't make my life any better. Just like being in Mexico didn't make theirs any better. It wasn't like every brother over in the motherland was getting forty acres and a mule and being treated like a king.

I mumbled, "Seventeen. Diecisiete means seventeen."

In my mind that simple translation was a major victory. Helped me understand how Alejandria had felt when she struggled to get words and phrases right.

I looked on the other side of the restaurant and the pool lined with palm trees, saw the light in my room was on. That didn't bother me because I usually left the lights and television on when I was in a hotel. But my front windows were open. The television, on a Spanish channel. The maids wouldn't have left the windows wide open. I thought about my equipment. That made me hurry.

When I rushed and bumbled in the door, Alejandria was lying

across the bed closest to the bathroom. Asleep in jean shorts and a L.A. Kings T-shirt. Her duffel bag was near the foot of the bed. She jumped up when the door shut. I took the money from underneath my shirt, the money I'd gotten from John. Tossed it on the dresser next to a few books. Her books.

Nothing was said for a few moments.

I said, "Good evening, Senorita Alejandria Sanchez."

"I do not like the way you sound."

"Why are you here?"

"I came to apologize. I hurt you today."

"How did you get in?"

"I told the man at the desk I was your special friend."

"He let you in just like that?"

"He saw us together. And I gave him money."

"How much."

"Two American dollars."

I looked at the camera equipment.

She said, "Are you angry with me? Pissed off?"

"Why would I be pissed off?"

"The way I behaved. The things I have done."

I shrugged. "I'm visiting. This is your lifestyle. Survival, re-member?"

She sucked her lip and nodded. "Sí."

"Are you okay?"

She nodded, short and sweet.

I saw her arm was scratched. Face bruised a little. Eyes swollen. Her voice was sad. Very heavy. Very sad.

I said, "Did that girl hurt you?"

"Her words hurt me."

Another moment passed.

She said, "I will leave Cabos. For good."

"Why?"

"Because it is time. Time to concede."

"Where you going?"

"Mexico City. To be with my mother. She is not doing well. Heaven is calling her name. My family needs me."

"What did John say?"

"I do not tell him. He will not miss me. That girl you saw today, the one who fight for John."

"Yeah?"

"That was me a while ago. Fighting for John."

Another moment passed. "When are you going?"

"Tomorrow or the next day."

"Why so soon?"

"I have to do it now or never. I wanted to tell you."

"Why?"

"Remember when you asked me what I wanted? My dreams?"

"Sí."

"You make me like me. I want to follow my dreams. I want to be happy, like you."

"What makes you think I'm happy?"

She shrugged. "Maybe because I feel happy when I am around you. When you smile at me, I smile and my heart goes very fast."

"Mine too."

"I am glad." She hand combed her hair. "May I touch you?"

"Yeah."

I held her for a few minutes, we hugged and rocked, and then she pulled me over to the bed. We sat and talked with the news giving us background noise. I gave her one of my business cards. She wanted my address so she could write me.

"Maybe one day, I will come to back to America. Get to see Los Angeles."

"It's overrated."

"I would still like to see it."

"If you do, you'll always have a place to stay."

"Be careful what you say."

I kissed her. When I stopped, she kissed me. When she stopped, I kissed her. She turned the television off. Clicked the radio on. She lay on top of me and restarted the kisses.

chapter nine

Alejandria drove me to the airport early the next morning. Since I wasn't scheduled to leave for another week, I had to pay to change my ticket. Last night I was going to have a few words with John, but I didn't see the point. My words could never convince a leopard to give up its spots. But I did run up the phone bill at the hotel room before I left. After I had called Los Angeles and talked to my cousin Debra, made sure I had a ride home from LAX once I made it back, I made a few more phone calls.

I guess you could say I took a page from John's book on how to scam and mistreat people, and decided to flee with the fee he had paid for work I wasn't going to do. My conscious was clear because I was leaving on my own freewill.

In the dryness of the morning, I packed and headed toward the barren field that welcomed foreigners to this land and waited right outside the sardine-packed warehouse. A place that was congested and looked as aggravated as I had felt a few days ago. Waited right outside the din and bustle of the airport's customs area. Alejandria was standing next to me, rocking side to side, her palms sweaty, dampening my flesh as she held my hand.

A plane coming in from the north landed.

We waited awhile. Not long. Only a few minutes. Long enough for people who had just flown in from Los Angeles to get off their rented chariot and make their way through customs, which, for a few, didn't take long because they had no luggage.

The Korean man who lost one hundred thousand dollars in equipment, a man on the verge of bankruptcy, appeared first. I recognized his suspenders, the ones that echoed the colors of the American flag, a symbol of the American dream, more than I remembered his face.

Right behind him were two black men with well-developed upper bodies. Men that no one could ever forget. Dressed in gold hip-hop attire from head to toe, thick upper bodies and thin legs. The men I had once thought of as South Central buffalo. Righteous men who, by any means necessary, were looking out for the well-being of their sister and their sister's child.

Four others were in that group. People I'd seen in the hallway at John's old office in downtown Los Angeles, all standing in front of a padlocked door decorated with an eviction notice. Hardworking people who had been ripped off.

Last night I had called Manuel Torres. I talked to him awhile and got him to give me the phone numbers from a few people off the list he had. The ones who had lost the most. I'd made late-night phone calls and told them all about an early-morning flight. I didn't want Manuel Torres involved. He was a nice guy. Family man with too much to lose over two hundred dollars. I liked him and wouldn't want him to jeopardize what he had. I've give Manuel two hundred dollars of my money when I made it back home. Money to cover his little girl's uniform and school supplies.

My last call was to John He told me what time he'd pick me up today. He was busy and pissed off because he couldn't find Alejandria to run his errands. Too bad. That was too bad.

Alejandria and I lingered outside the terminal, on the other side of the doors, where customs was giving the travelers a hard time. The crowd coming toward me was looking anxious. Anxious enough to make me feel some fear for John. Anxious enough for me to wonder if this was the right thing to do.

In this world, with my hair and complexion, I was an easy one to spot. One of the brothers stepped forward and in a heavy voice said, "Asaalam Alakium."

I shook his hand. His grip almost powdered my bones.

The other one said, "Hotter than a bitch in heat down here."

I said, "Yeah. Get's hotter."

"Today's gonna be the hottest day Mexico has ever seen."

I didn't ask what he meant by that.

First I told them the name of the hotel I had left early this morning, the horseshoe-shaped Tropicana, told them I had left without checking out. Then I let them know that the taxis out front would take them there for a few dollars. I dropped the key to the room in his massive hand.

I said, "John will be there around noon. CP time."

He slid the key inside his shirt pocket. "And we'll be inside the room waiting. We ain't in no hurry."

Alejandria finally said something, spoke with a nervousness, a softness that held her own cultural cadence. "John . . . he has a . . . the box in the wall . . . it's called a . . ."

I added, "Safe. He has a safe in his master bedroom."

"Yes, a safe. He has a safe at his home. A safe with American money. You would like to know the combination, no?"

The brothers actually smiled.

I knew what she was doing. She was making sure she couldn't go back. No way to undo her part in what was about to happen.

And the people who got off the plane all assumed I was a righteous man, doing this for them. I was doing it for selfish reasons. For Alejandria. I wanted to make sure there was no way she could go back to the life she was fleeing.

When all was said and done, the crowd from America all walked away, moved by all the stone-faced armed guards, and went out into the sunshine rising high over the southern tip of Mexico. The Korean lead the way, occasionally chopping air, either practicing breaking boards, or breaking a neck.

Then it was close to time for the next flight to Los Angeles.

My flight.

Alejandria was at my side. Wiping her eyes every other second. That stoic woman I met had melted and become human.

It was hard to say good-bye when you felt it would be the last time you saw somebody. Finality could be overwhelming. For me, I think I felt remorseful because it was the death of a relationship that never happened. I had so few worth remembering.

Alejandria kept wiping her eyes and held my hand.

She said, "You are a good person."

"I care for you too."

I counted out fifteen hundred dollars, handed it to her.

She stepped away. "No."

"Yes. Take this. This'll help some."

"No. I can work at a restaurant or something. I can cook at a restaurant or be a waitress again."

"Take this."

"It would not be right."

"Today, I think of others first. Take the money, please?"

We pushed the money back and forth. She finally took it and gave me a big hug and many kisses on my face.

"I love you, my friend," she said. She pulled away and looked at me. "I was wrong, Bobby. Love is necessary for survival. I wish I could survive with you."

"I feel the same."

She grinned. "Maybe one day, huh?"

I nodded.

"Good."

"Yes. It is good."

She walked in with me. Then I followed her to the ticket counter. She bought a one-way to Mexico City.

I asked, "What are you doing?"

"I am leaving."

Her flight was scheduled to leave minutes before mine. Then she asked me to walk back to her car. A small suitcase was in the backseat. It had been there since yesterday.

She said, "I was going to drive home, but now I will not."

Alejandria took as many books as she could carry and put them in the duffel bag she had had the moment I met her. She held on to her dictionary and *Like Water for Chocolate.*

I said, "What about the rest?"

She said, "What can't be carried should be left behind."

She left the keys in the ignition.

I said, "You sure you want to leave like this?"

"I have the clothes I need. Clothes are clothes. Clothes are things. The car belongs to John. I only need my books. What I learn will last longer than what I own. I read that owning is an illusion. I will not fool myself with other things."

I smiled. Wished I could touch her and become more like her. She didn't have a cent to her name, but she had more than most.

She squeezed my hand, like she was trying to keep part of me. She said, "I will see you again, no?"

"I hope so."

"Promise me."

"You said no promises."

"I changed my mind."

"Just like a woman."

She laughed. "That was a joke, no?"

"Yes, it was a joke."

"Promise me, Bobby. Promise me, promise me."

"I promise."

"I promise you back."

"I'll write you."

"I will write you back."

"I'll send you a copy of the pictures we took."

"Then, I will write you today. Send a photo of you so I can show mi madre. I will tell her all about you. She will be happy to know that you make me happy."

"Okay."

She held the money to her heart. "This will be a loan."

"Sure."

"And I will find you and put it back in your hands."

Yes, she was a woman worth waiting for. I had passed along, seen her beauty, recognized her true value, and now, in my heart, she was mine.

I said, "I'll keep a light burning in the window."

"What does that mean?"

"Means I'll wait for you."

"I will burn a light in my window for you too."

I hugged her again. Felt her flesh. Smelled her perfume. Tasted her tongue. Heard her laugh. Saw everything from her golden toenails in her Roman sandals up to her schoolgirl smile. Until I saw her again, when darkness comes and I fly away into my dreams, as I lived inside that euphoria, those were the things I wanted to take into my midnight meditations with me.

They called for her plane's final boarding. She let go of my hand. Took almost a minute for her to do that.

Then she said, "This is for you. This is part of me. I will get it from you when I see you again."

She handed me *Like Water for Chocolate*.

I gave her one of my cameras. A Nikon that was one of my favorites. Told her to take plenty of pictures and I would get the camera when I saw her again.

Neither one of us wanted to say good-bye. I'd never before lived a moment this hard. Never in my life had I felt so overwhelmed.

I put my hand on her chin and said, "Keep your head up."

She wiped a stubborn tear from my face, put her hand on my chin and told me to do the same.

She bumped through the crowd at customs. Along the way she stopped long enough to raise the camera to her face and aim the lense my way.

Click. Whirr. Click. Whirr. Click. Whirr.

Finally she boarded her plane. Looked back the entire way. Her looking back meant a lot. Her face was set, reflected in the dry heat of the morning sun. She sucked her bottom lip inside her mouth and waved nonstop.

I waved until her plane door closed. Then I waved while it backed out of the gate. It taxied down the runway. Took to the sky. Then it was out of sight. So I stopped waving. Stopped waving and held on to *Like Water for Chocolate* like the book was my favorite girl.

Alejandria Sanchez was gone. The taste of her still on my

tongue. The smell of her still in my nose. The rhythm of her forever in my chest, giving my heart a new beat.

It was time for me to get in line and struggle through customs. Time to get on my plane. Time for Los Angeles.

Kenya and Amir

MARCUS MAJOR

July 8, 1995

Amir rolled over and looked at the clock on the nightstand: 11:56.

His gaze traveled to a porcelain vase on the same nightstand. It was full of once proud peach roses, now slumped over, barely clinging to life.

Amir sighed and looked at the ceiling. Three weeks ago your ass was on top of the world, playa. You were a contender. Naw, fuck that, you were the *champ*. And life was good, king. Yeah, king is better. After all, you had the *most* regal queen on your arm. When the two of you walked in a room, with your varying but equally striking hues of shiny chocolate, people paid homage. Y'all were out of place, they were often told. They looked like a royal couple of ancient Nubia. A majestic pair. Like they should be somewhere holding court and subjugating those who disobey rather than slumming at some function with the great unwashed.

And now, Amir thought, the only thing that was unwashed around here is your ass. And you lack the motivation to get out of bed. Not even able to summon up the courage to go to work today.

For the past few weeks, no one other than his mother could detect anything was bothering him. Amir prided himself on that. The world shouldn't be able to detect desolation in a man's face, especially if it was over a woman. A man shouldn't let everybody know his business by walking around all gloomy and stupid. Not if he was a *real* man. But Amir knew even he might have had difficulty today with keeping up the facade, which was why he had decided to take the day off.

Because today was the one-year anniversary of their first meeting. Amir wasn't sure if Kenya remembered, but he sure as hell did. And man, did he have plans for them to celebrate.

But it was all for shit now.

How did you get to this point, dog?

Damn. Had it been one year already? He could honestly say it was the best year of his life.

Nature's call was the only thing that could pull him out of bed. Amir walked into the bathroom.

The memories were far too vivid for it to already have been a year. The passage of the seasons had not clouded his recollections in the least. He could still remember the first time he felt the sweetness of Kenya's tongue. The cleverness of her hands. The warmth of her breath on his neck as they slept, her arm protectively draped over his body, as if she had to stake her claim even when she was unconscious.

When autumn arrived with all its many changes, Kenya's adoration had remained a constant in his life. When winter kicked up its angry heels, a kiss from Kenya would temper the coldest night. Spring brought rebirth and a rekindling of Kenya's affection. Amir considered himself a creative lover, but Kenya took it to another level. Amir swore that she must have devoted her every waking hour to thinking of ways to make him happy.

An excellent lover, and not just in the typical sense of the word, either. See, Kenya appreciated any and all things pertaining to life, everything God-made right down to the skin she was in. She surely had to be the purest soul that he had ever encountered.

And above all, Kenya loved her Amir.

Which is probably where she thinks she went wrong. Amir figured she was probably beating herself up for letting herself get caught out there, which troubled him even more. Amir hated the thought of Kenya being pained over anything, but to think he was the cause of her anguish was damn near intolerable.

Amir looked in the bathroom mirror. As was often the case lately, he didn't like what he saw.

Damn, it had been a whole year. It seemed like only yesterday that he first walked in that restaurant and saw Kenya sitting there nervously, facing the door so she could see who her friend had set her up with.

Amir turned the faucet on and let the cold water run through his fingers. Then he wet a washcloth and held it against his face to soothe his eyes. He wiped the remnants of sleep out of them and looked back in the mirror.

Amir never accepted blind dates. Never had any reason to. He'd always had more than enough willing pussy at his disposal. He had only agreed to meet Kenya as a favor to one of his customers, who kept insisting that she had a friend who was perfect for him. He left the bathroom and headed to his kitchen.

And she hadn't been wrong, either, Amir thought as he poured himself a glass of orange juice. He and Kenya had clicked from the moment he joined her at that table. Kenya.

And you weren't wrong either, babe. You weren't wrong to love me. I know that and you will know that, too, if you would only let me prove it to you.

But that wasn't going to happen. Amir set down his glass and leaned on the counter. Kenya had told him in crystal-clear terms that it was over. No yelling or tears, either, at least not after the original cursing out. The next day she had called him over, sat him down, and coolly laid out what she found acceptable and not acceptable in a man and how he had fallen short. Amir shuddered as he thought of her frost that evening when she told him that he was finished being a part of her life. As far as Amir and Kenya was concerned, there was no present or future—only past, she had said.

I may have disappointed you, Kenya, and you have been wronged, but you weren't *wrong* to love me. Believe that.

July 9, 1994

"Now see, Kenya, I believe that's where you're wrong." Amir dipped a piece of bread into a saucer full of olive oil. "Men definitely have it harder than women when it comes to finding a mate."

Kenya had to put her fork down on that one. "You're gonna have to explain your reasoning to me," she said. "I just read somewhere that there are one hundred sisters for every eighty-five black men between the ages of twenty-five and forty-four."

Amir swallowed and gave her an incredulous look. "That's a pretty expansive pool. Forty-four? What, are you looking for an old man?"

"No, but I'm only twenty-three. Take Karen, for instance. She's thirty-one and looking to get married and have another child. Let's just say that she's a little more flexible than she was five or six years ago."

Karen was the woman who had set them up. She was a fellow congregrant at Kenya's church. She knew Amir from his barbershop, where he often cut Karen's son, Jeremy's hair.

"She still has plenty of time," Amir said.

"Um-hm. So tell me again why we have it easier than brothers. The numbers don't lie."

"No, they don't, but they don't tell the whole story, either."

"You're right." Kenya said. "I don't know what they mean by 'available.' Are they including bisexual men? Criminals? Drug addicts? And what about those brothers with a penchant for white meat?"

Before Amir could respond, their young blond waitress came out onto the veranda, where they were sitting. Carrying a platter of food, she set Amir's plate of chicken and linguini in front of him and handed Kenya her vegetable lasagna.

"Can I get you anything else, Amir?" She smiled at him as she cleared their salad plates. "A refill or anything?"

Amir looked at Kenya, who shook her head slightly, then back at the waitress. "No, thank you, Susan. We're fine."

As she walked away, Kenya hoped that Amir's penchant for white meat didn't go beyond that chicken breast on his plate.

"She certainly seems friendly," Kenya said.

Amir didn't answer right off, as he was saying a quick grace over his food. When he was finished, he sprinkled some Parmesan cheese on his linguini. "Yeah, she is."

"I noticed you know her by name," Kenya said.

Amir looked up. "She was wearing a name tag."

"But you aren't. I noticed she knew you by name, too," she added humorously but with intent.

"She did say Amir, didn't she?" he said with mock agitation. "She's getting a little too familiar."

Kenya chewed a forkful of lasagna and studied Amir's face. He noticed her skepticism.

"I'm a regular here, Kenya. The food in this place is excellent. My greedy little brother found this place—he and I come here all the time. I know all the waitresses here."

Kenya broke eye contact and concentrated on her lasagna. "Oh, I figured it was something like that."

Amir had a sly grin on his face. He tried to hide it by taking a sip of iced tea, but Kenya caught it before he could.

"Now, tell me, why do you think that men have it harder than we do when all the data points to the opposite?"

"Don't misunderstand me. I'm talking about just in finding a mate," Amir said. "I don't mean in the workplace, or in life in general. Of course, sistahs have it harder with that. Dealing with the double whammy of sexism and racism."

"But with finding that special someone, you believe we have it easier?" Kenya put down her fork, slid her plate back, and rested her chin on her folded hands.

Amir looked at her rapt posture. "I see you're giving me your undivided attention. Like you expect to hear something important."

"Or maybe I expect to hear some bullshit, and don't want any food in my mouth when I do."

Amir rolled his tongue around his mouth and leaned back in his chair, suppressing a smile. So, we have an honest one here, he thought.

"All right," he said. "Now, what I'm about to drop on you,

are you sure you can handle it? It's too distressing for many women to deal with. It might upset your applecart."

"Wait, let me prepare myself." Kenya closed her eyes and took a deep breath. "Okay," she said when she opened them again. "Proceed."

"I submit that men have it harder than women when it comes to finding somebody, because despite what that data would suggest," Amir said, "we have more competition than you do, more factors to overcome." He paused to take another sip of his iced tea.

"That must be an example of the new math that they are teaching now." Kenya said. "Where I'm from, one hundred is more than eighty-five."

"Kenya, let's say there is a limited pool of quality brothers out there. Who is your competition as far as landing one?" Amir asked.

"Other women."

"Of course. Anyone else?"

"Well, the only other people are men," Kenya replied, "which brings me back to my original point of bisexuality."

"Assuming all the brothers in your pool are strictly heterosexual . . ."

"Well," Kenya said, noticing the waitress serving a nearby couple, "there's white women."

". . . and haven't come down with a jungle fever. Is there anyone else, besides sistahs, that you have to compete with?"

"No."

"Well, then," Amir said triumphantly, "my point is made right there." He twirled a forkful of linguini and put in his mouth.

Kenya stared at him like he was touched.

"How do you figure that?" she asked.

Amir swallowed before responding. "Kenya, as a woman, all you have to compete with to land a quality brother is other women. Men have to compete with other men"—Amir put his fork down and adopted his most professorial posture—"and *women* when searching for our soul mate. Understand?"

"No," Kenya said. "I thought you were excluding bisexual people from our available pool."

"We are," Amir insisted. "Kenya, let's use the figures you gave earlier. Let's say there was a huge room, and inside there are a hundred quality single sisters and eighty-five quality single brothers. On the surface, it would seem that the men have the natural advantage of having a surplus of fifteen woman. Right?"

"That would be correct, sir. I'm with you so far."

For some reason, Amir chose that moment to give her what had to be the most dazzlingly perfect smile she had ever seen. Kenya swore that there must be some hidden mechanism that attached its arrival to her legs, because they reflexively parted under the table when he flashed it. She quickly stopped herself from staring, hoping that he hadn't caught the lust in her eyes.

Amir paused to twirl some more pasta methodically around his fork. Kenya wondered if it was a metaphor for his finger and her.

"Peep this, Kenya," he said. "Out of that eighty-five brothers, it would stand to reason that some would be more attractive to the women in the room for any number of reasons. Be it because he is better-looking, has no previous kids already, too tall, too short . . ."

"How about being employed?" Kenya added.

"A job, and so on. Agree?" Amir popped a piece of bread into his mouth.

Kenya nodded and watched him lick the excess olive oil off his too-damn-chewable-for-a-man-to-have bottom lip. She forced herself to look down at her plate and took a bite of her lasagna. Amir continued.

"So, let's take the middle-of-the-pack brother. Number forty-three out of the eighty-five. He watches the top forty-two men and women pair off—"

"Which still leaves him with fifty-eight women to choose from," Kenya said.

"Ah, but that's where I beg to differ. He might have twenty-five, thirty tops."

"Huh?"

"Because while it's wholly acceptable for a woman to pair off with a man making more money than she does, the reverse is not true," Amir stated unequivocally. "At least, twenty of those remaining women are gonna have better-paying jobs than him and are, therefore, off-limits."

"That's not necessarily true," Kenya protested.

"But, thirty seconds ago, you brought up economics as the quality that makes a man desirable. You didn't say good character, morality, being religious, creativity, and whatnot. First thing out of Ms. Kenya's mouth was *being employed*," Amir reminded her, mimicking her voice.

She accepted his needle willingly, unable to contain her laugh.

"I simply said he had to be working. I didn't say he had to be making more money than me."

Amir paused in midchew and took a sip of his iced tea, giving her a disbelieving look.

"What?" she asked.

"Kenya, don't be cracking jokes while I'm trying to eat."

"I'm serious," Kenya insisted. "It's y'all's ego that has a problem with a woman making more paper than you."

"And I wonder why?" Amir responded. "Don't dismiss the intimidation factor a man feels when he tries to step to a woman making more loot than him. He can come away from that encounter feeling quite small."

"Come on, Amir. I understand you're trying to make a point, but aren't you being a bit extreme?"

"Am I?" Amir reached for another piece of bread, this time deciding to butter it. "Unless I missed something, has there been a sudden glut of female attorneys running off to marry sanitation workers? But does society bat an eyelash when a male lawyer marries a waitress? Or a doctor marries a nanny? Aren't those equivalent to a man's blue-collar jobs?"

While Kenya was mulling that one over, Amir continued.

"I think a lot of professional women want a man that's on their level. A man that 'leaves for work clean and comes home from work clean.' If that's the case, that rules out construction workers, sanitation workers, mechanics, plumbers, carpenters, and almost every other kind of blue-collar job I can think of. Brothers know that. That's a hell of a thing to contend with."

"Yeah, I see your point," Kenya acceded. "Women can aim high in marriage and think nothing of it. A man aiming high is frowned upon. He has more pressure to deal with as far as the expectation of being the primary breadwinner to prove his worth. Even if he's with a woman that loves him regardless of what he does for a living, other people look down on him. You're right."

Amir's mouth opened in amazement.

"You know, we're outside," Kenya said. "You're gonna swallow a fly."

"It's just that I'm surprised you agreed with me so easily."

"Why? Do all your other dates put up more of an argument?" Kenya smiled knowingly. "Is this your litmus test to find out where a woman's head is at?"

Amir suddenly felt the need for a refill and began to search for the waitress, making sure he looked everywhere except at Kenya. So she was pretty sure she had hit the mark.

She smiled. "Don't get me wrong. I still think men have the natural enviable position, as a whole."

"Agreed," Amir said.

"Not feeling the pressure to make as much money as our spouse is one of the few positions where we have an advantage."

"Positions?" Amir asked.

"Yeah, plural."

"Like, when else do you?"

"Why?"

"Please, I'm curious." Amir pushed his plate back and rested his elbows on the table, like Kenya had done earlier.

She put her fork down, sat back, and crossed her legs. "Well, another one I can think of offhand is with children. From the moment a woman gets pregnant, she holds all the cards. Everything a man does is reactive to whatever she does. She can decide to keep it, abort it, or carry it to term and give it up for adoption. Each choice she makes will impact the man in one or another. But it's totally her choice."

"Yeah," Amir agreed. "Most women I know will say, *Well, he should have thought—*"

"*. . . about that before he lay down.*" Kenya and Amir spoke in unison, which made them both laugh.

"I don't like that mentality," Kenya said. "Only the most foolish woman would want to trap a man by using a child. Personally, I don't want anyone that doesn't want to be wanted."

Susan came over with a pitcher of tea. While she watched their tea glasses being refilled, Kenya felt Amir's eyes poring all over her body. Making their way along the contours of her face, pausing at the ripeness of her lips, before continuing down the elegant slope of her neck and along her almost bare shoulders.

Susan finished and walked away.

"You have very nice skin, Kenya."

"Thank you." She opened up a packet of Equal and poured it into her glass.

"You know, you're a very unique woman."

"Don't be silly. A lot of sistahs have nice skin."

"I *know* that—"

"I'm *sure* you do," Kenya teased.

Amir smirked. "I was referring to your outlook, your openness."

"Amir, whether we know each other for a hundred years or this will be our one and only meeting, one thing you won't be able to say is I'm not real. With me"—Kenya extended her arms grandly, like Tina Turner accepting a curtain call—"what you see is what you get."

Amir brought his eyes up to meet hers, taking the scenic route along her breasts.

"Oh, I hope so."

Kenya brought her arms back in, but she wasn't angry at his leering. She had left herself open for it. Besides, he was just being a man, after all.

She turned her attention to the dessert tray nearby. "That cherry cheesecake looks good."

"Then, have a slice."

"I can't. I'm watching my figure."

"Why don't you let me do that for you?"

Thinking it was one thing. Verbalizing it was a whole different matter. Kenya decided to check his ass right there.

"Ah, I see you're very unique as well," she said.

"How do you mean?"

"I figure you must be purposely providing such a blatant example of that sexism that you say we sistahs have to contend with. Because someone as *progressive* as you, if you really wanted to compliment a lady, would have focused on her creativity, her good character, and morality . . ."

Amir half blushed, half cringed. Busted.

"You got that one, Kenya. You're right."

"Um-hm," she replied. But she wasn't mad. He had won points with her, for she always liked when a man accepted his comeuppance gracefully.

"By the way, does what you were saying earlier apply to you?"

"What was that?"

"About brothers being scared to step to a woman who makes more money than them."

Amir gave her a comic double take worthy of Don Knotts. "I was talking about *other* cats, Kenya. God, in His infinite wisdom, hasn't seen fit yet to craft the woman too good for Amir Moore."

Kenya and Amir walked up Chestnut Street toward his Jeep, leaving Kenya's car in a nearby parking garage. They had decided he would do the driving for the remainder of the date.

Kenya squinted as they walked in the sunlight. They had been sitting under an umbrella at the restaurant and she hadn't noticed how bright it was. She reached into her purse for her sunglasses.

Kenya looked over at him uncertainly. "Are you sure you don't mind going there?"

"Oh, no. It's fine." Amir sighed loudly for effect.

Kenya smiled. "Well, you *did* ask me if there was anything in particular I'd like to do."

"I know, I know," Amir agreed as they reached his Cherokee. He unlocked Kenya's door and helped her in before walking around and getting in himself. "And I'm a man of my word." He took off the steering wheel lock and laid it across the backseat. "So, it's off to the flower show, we go," he muttered.

"If you give it a chance, Amir, you just might enjoy it."

"The land of petunias and daisies? I don't know, Kenya. Excuse me."

Kenya flinched slightly as Amir reached in between her knees and opened his glove compartment. After fiddling around in there for a couple of seconds, he pulled out a pair of sunglasses, closed the door, and started the engine.

Kenya was disappointed. Now hidden from her view was the loveliest pair of eyes she had ever seen on a man. She hadn't complimented him because she figured every other woman he met probably did. What Kenya liked wasn't so much their unique shade of chestnut, though she had to admit it was quite dazzling. What had really captured her was the way they sparkled. The life behind them.

At least she could still see his bushy eyebrows. Her thumbs had been longing to smooth them since he had first sat down at the table.

Kenya picked up the edge of her peach-and-purple Anne Klein summer dress to shake out the wrinkles, letting the hem fall just above her knee.

"Did you ever run track, Kenya?" Amir saw an opening and pulled out into traffic.

"Yes, I did. How did you know?"

"As a former track stud myself, I can tell by looking at your legs."

So he had noticed.

"Yeah," she said as she reached in her purse to take out a Certs. "My first couple of years of high school, I was a star. My coach thought I was bound for Olympic glory."

"Yeah?" Amir glanced at her. "So what happened?"

Kenya sucked on her mint. "The number-one scourge to as-piring female track stars." She placed her hands on her waist. "One summer my hips arrived and spoiled the party."

Amir stopped at a red light and gave her body a quick but thorough once-over, starting at her open-toe mule sandals and ending with her shoulder straps.

"That's just God's way of reminding women of their duty to go forth and multiply," he said.

"Oh, is that what it is?" Kenya laughed.

"Yep. Trust me, I know these things." The light turned green.

"Well, you may be right," she said. "I'm gonna need these childbearing hips to carry my twins."

"How do you know you're gonna have twins?" Amir asked.

"They run in my family. My grandmother was a twin. I have twin uncles and twin cousins, too."

Amir was quiet for a couple of seconds. Kenya noticed his pensive look.

"A penny for your thoughts," she said.

"I was just thinking how nice it would be to have twin sons. Wreaking havoc on the gridiron. Dunking on suckers on the basketball court. Smacking home runs on the diamond. The mere mention of their names would strike terror in the hearts of people. People would be like, 'The Moores are coming, the Moores are coming.' " Amir beamed. "My boys would do more damage than those other Moors did in Spain."

"Before you put your yet-to-be-born sons into the halls of fame of three different sports, how do you know you wouldn't have girls?" Kenya asked.

Amir scoffed. "Moore men have sons." He stopped at an-other red light. Kenya looked into the window of a shoe store at a cute pair of boots. She could feel Amir's eyes roving over her body again. She turned to face him. He didn't turn away but looked her in the eyes instead.

"What?" she asked. The light turned green.

"I was just thinking, you still look fast to me."

"I am, let me assure you."

Amir merged onto the Schuykill Expressway and shifted into a higher gear.

"I can take you."

Kenya looked over at him and noticed he was wearing a mischievous grin. "I doubt that very seriously."

"No, I'm pretty confident I can," Amir replied.

"Well, we'll just have to give it a run then someday, won't we?"

"We shall."

They didn't talk for a couple of beats. Both thought about turning on the radio, but each was more interested in conversing than in listening to music.

"In the meantime, can you tell me where we are going?" Kenya asked, breaking the silence.

Amir turned to her. "To the Civic Center, for the flower show—that's what you want, right?"

"Yes, it is." Kenya folded her hands on her lap and dropped her chin demurely. "I'm just wondering how you knew where the flower show was being held."

"What do you mean? At the restaurant you told me . . ."

Amir's voice trailed off at the sight of Kenya emphatically shaking her head no. She was suppressing a laugh, and not doing a very good job of it.

Busted yet again.

His sheepish look provided all the push that she needed. The dam had burst and her laughter came spilling out.

"Okay, listen. I may have been to one or two of these flower shindigs in my life," Amir admitted, "but I'd appreciate it if you'd keep that between you and me."

"Hey." Kenya had almost exhausted all her giggling. She motioned like she was buttoning her lips. "It stays with me. Though I don't understand the reason for all the secrecy."

"Are you serious? If the fellas found out about me going to flower shows, I'd be ruined." Amir gave a fake shudder. "I could hear it now. Tulip boy. Daisy man. Rose Petal—"

"Mr. Marigold?" Kenya offered.

"Exactly. You *know* I can't have that!"

Kenya chuckled again. This time it quickly subsided, however.

"So, you've been to a couple of these before, huh?" she asked.

"Yeah."

Kenya hesitated and looked out her window. She knew she was being too forward but decided to press on anyway.

"So, with some other female, I can presume."

"That would be correct."

"Well, you must be a nice person to let women drag you off to a flower show so easily."

"Believe me, Kanya, I'm not accustomed to getting dragged off anywhere I don't want to go. And with women, it's usually me that takes the wheel."

I can believe that, Kenya thought. Fine as your chocolate ass is.

"I only let a woman get her way if I really like her."

"Did you plan on going to the flower show today?" Kenya asked.

"No." Amir glanced at her. "But I like you already." She was still looking out the window, and he thought he saw a trace of a smile.

Kenya caught herself blushing, for which she felt silly. No, she felt moronic. She had almost bought that bullshit.

"So," she said, turning back to face him, "the other women you went here with—"

"Other *woman*," Amir corrected. "There was just one."

"This other woman took you to two flower shows? I guess you must've *really* liked her."

"Correction, Kenya. I took her because I loved her. Still do."

Like your smooth, sweet-talking ass knows the first thing about love. And if you still love her, then you need to be with her, Kenya thought. But he probably cheated on her and got caught out there, and she got tired of his bullshit. He looked like the creeping kind.

"What happened?" she asked.

"Nothing, she is still in the picture," he replied casually.

Oh, so you are a brazen *motherfucker*. I peep your game now.

If you tell me that you have a girlfriend at the beginning, I can't throw it in your face later. Can't say I was lied to or led on. So now either I'm gonna roll with the situation and be your woman on the side, or I'm gonna be the dummy that expends energy, heartache, and pussy trying to take you from your lady. Uh-uhn, you got the wrong one, baby. I don't care how fine you are.

"Then, why aren't you with her?" Kenya asked, trying to voice indifference.

"Because my grandmother couldn't make it this year," Amir replied coolly. He looked at Kenya out of the corner of his eye.

She all of a sudden became extremely interested in the view outside her window again.

Score one for Amir.

Kenya was getting ready for bed when the phone rang. She glanced at the clock—it was a quarter past midnight. Who would be calling her this late?

"Hello?"

"Hello, Kenya. Am I calling you too late?"

She smiled and lay across her bed. They had just said their good-byes an hour ago. "Yes, but I'll forgive you this time."

"I won't keep you long. I just wanna tell you what a good time I had today, and to thank you for making it so."

Was this guy for real?

"Even though I took you to look at a bunch of plants?" Kenya asked.

Amir's laugh sounded even sexier over the phone.

"Actually, Kenya, my grandmother has instilled in me a love of flowers, so I enjoyed it."

She could tell. While they were walking among the different exhibits, Amir had looked entranced at certain points. "That's good. I like a man that can appreciate beauty."

"I was surrounded by it today."

"Yeah, the place looked like something out of a fairy tale, didn't it?" she asked.

"I wasn't talking about the flowers, Kenya," Amir said quietly.

She was so grateful that this conversation was taking place on the phone and not in person, where Amir would be able to see her girly blush. Unable to think of something clever to say, she just lay there with the phone resting on the pillow next to her ear.

"I also enjoyed the movie you chose," Amir added. "What was the name of it again?"

"*I Like It Like That*," Kenya told him. "You know, it was written and directed by a black woman."

"Yeah?"

"Yep. First time ever for a major movie studio."

"It's a damn shame that in 1994 we're still talking about 'first-time' anything for African Americans," Amir said. "We should have been done with trailblazing at least a generation ago."

"You know it," Kenya agreed. "Though remember I said black *woman*. Black men have done it before."

"I know. Sexism and racism—the double whammy." Amir fell silent as he replayed some of the more enjoyable scenes from the movie in his mind. "That sistah got skills. I'm impressed."

"I'd imagine her ability might be intimidating for a brotha. Even you might be too scared to step to a woman like that, huh?" she teased.

Amir scoffed. "Kenya, please. I've already told you that that woman doesn't exist."

They shared a chuckle.

"Besides, I'm not looking to 'step to' anyone right about now," he said.

"No?"

"Nope."

"So. You don't want that somebody special?" Kenya asked.

"Of course I do." Amir insisted.

"Now, I'm lost."

"Kenya, I'm not looking for that 'somebody special' because I might already have a person like that. Why would I need another? Though I will admit to being a selfish person, I'm not greedy."

"You're not talking about your grandmother again, are you?"

Amir paused before answering. "No, I'm not."

"Oh," Kenya said quietly. So, he did already have a woman in his life. At least he was telling her now and giving her the option of what she wanted to do. That was fair. All she had invested so far was a good-night kiss on that smooth cheek of his.

One thing for sure, the attraction between them was too strong for him to just be interested in friendship. Not with the way his eyes had been all over her ass, hips, and legs whenever he thought she wasn't looking.

"Look, Amir. I'm not gonna be able to make it next weekend. I don't want to monopolize you two Saturdays in a row. Maybe you should be with your special lady."

"But I'm gonna be."

Kenya was lost again. Slowly it dawned on her what it was he was getting at. She could practically see the sly grin on his face.

"Oh, so I'm 'special' already, am I?"

"*You're so spe-cial. If you only, only just be-lieeeve,*" Amir sang.

"I remember that song," Kenya said enthusiastically. That was an all-time favorite song of hers, and she liked hearing Amir's rich baritone voice singing it. "That used to get everybody on the floor back in the day!"

"True," Amir agreed.

Kenya continued her stroll down memory lane. "I remember that group was from Newark." She racked her brain, "Ohh, what was the their name?"

"Blaze."

"Yeah, that's it. Blaze! What happened to those brothers?"

"I don't know. Maybe they're stranded on the same island as Colonel Abrams and Adeva."

Kenya laughed. "Speaking of blaze. I hope the sun shows us a little more mercy next week than it did today."

"So we're still on for next Saturday?" Amir asked.

Were they? Kenya could hardly wait to see him again. "Yes."

"And you'll set aside the whole day for me again, like today?"

"Yes," she repeated, softer this time.

"This time I choose what we do?"

"Yes, Amir," Kenya whispered.

"Great," Amir said. "I'm looking forward to seeing you again."

"Because I'm just so damn *special*, right?"

"Exactly." Amir answered, conveniently ignoring the sarcasm.

"How many women have you told they are special, Amir?" she asked.

"Why?"

"Just curious."

"How many have I told? Too many to count. Now ask me how many times I meant it."

"How many?"

"You'd be the first, Kenya Wallace."

Though she was growing sleepy, that comment caused her to laugh. This guy was so full of shit.

"See, women are always talking about how they want a man to reach out to them and verbalize our feelings. When we do, we get ridiculed."

"Yeah, but we're talking about men we've known for longer than twelve hours!"

"Well, y'all should be more specific, then. Let a brother know the guidelines."

After they finished their laugh, they decided to get off the phone, each thinking that the other one was probably ready to go.

"Good night, Kenya. If I see you again before Saturday, it'll be in my dreams."

"Good night, Tulip boy."

Kenya clicked off the phone, rolled over, and stretched out. Amir certainly had personality to spare. He was a smooth talker—that was for sure. When she combined that with his looks, well, hell, he could almost be considered lethal. Kenya reached toward her nightstand and turned off her lamp.

In the darkness, she had one final thought before she slipped off to sleep.

She'd better keep her guard up.

July 10, 1994

Kenya and her friends Tonya and Racquel were walking along the many tables set up at the Willingboro indoor/outdoor flea market. It was a pleasant Sunday afternoon, not nearly as humid as the day before. The three of them were sharply dressed in their Sunday finery from attending church earlier and were drawing stares from the men in attendance. Whenever they stopped at a table to peruse the different books, cards, music, or Kente cloths, the vendor, if it was a man, would give them his undivided attention. Kenya knew it was mainly because of Racquel. Though she and Tonya were by no means ugly, men drooled over Racquel. She had skin the color of café au lait and had a tight little body that jiggled in all the right places, which she didn't mind showing off. And what God didn't give her naturally, she had no qualms about enhancing artificially. She spent more time, energy and money on her appearance than anyone Kenya had ever known.

Racquel stopped at one of the tables full of books, causing the other two to stop. It wasn't much different from any of the other tables, except it was watched by a very handsome man with dreadlocks.

"How much for this soul food cookbook?" Racquel asked the vendor as she opened a huge, heavy book.

"Sister, just 'cause you're making my day by being so pretty," the vendor looked around furtively, then whispered, "half price for you."

Racquel flashed him a quick smile to acknowledge his compliment. "Are there a lot of good recipes in here?"

"All types of dishes, real food, the kind like your grandmother would make." The vendor leaned forward, resting his palms on the table, all the better to sneak a peek at Racquel's cleavage.

"Are you a good cook?" he asked.

Tonya and Kenya looked at each other, thinking the same thing. If it wasn't for men taking her out to eat, Racquel would starve to death.

"I can do a little something," she answered, looking at him over her shades.

Kenya and Tonya decided to leave Rachel to her flirtation. By the time she was done, she would have that book for free and the vendor would have her phone number, if she had deemed him financially viable.

The two of them walked farther down the aisle to the table where they always bought their oils, candles, and incense. After exchanging greetings with Sister Delores, the elderly woman who sold the items, Kenya and Tonya started to sample the different fragrances. Kenya liked the opium and musk scents best.

"What are you getting?" Racquel joined them, standing in between the two.

"I need some oils," Kenya said.

Tonya noticed that Racquel was holding the cookbook. "Since when did you gain an interest in anything culinary?"

"Hey, I like to eat," she said holding up the book to look at the cover. "Besides, Hakim insisted on giving it to me."

"Oh, did he, now?" Tonya asked, turning back to the table. "And what did you give him? Besides false hope."

Kenya chuckled.

"Nothing, girl," Racquel said. "He gave me his number. Told me he wants to cook for me."

"Are you gonna call him?" Kenya asked.

"Maybe. He's cute and I do like to eat. Besides, it'll give me a chance to see how he's living." Racquel looked back at Hakim, who was still leering at her, and gave him a wink. "I see ya, boy," she whispered.

Kenya shook her head. Fresh out of church, and Racquel was already in manhunting mode.

"You're a trip, girl," Tonya said.

The cookbook bounced off Kenya's leg and landed with a thud on the toe of her pump.

"Ouch!" Kenya yelled.

"Be careful, Rocky," Tonya said, looking at the cookbook on the ground. "I know cooking ain't your thing, but damn!"

Kenya handed the items she wanted to Sister Delores. As she

waited for change, she slid her foot out of her shoe and flexed
her toes, making sure they were all still there. She noticed Racquel was making no effort to pick up the book. Tonya had
grown still, too.

She put her shoe back on and glanced over her shoulder at
them. They looked like they had seen a ghost.

"What?" Kenya asked.

"Would you look at this Mandingo motherfucker coming
toward *me*?" Racquel mouthed, awe plain in her voice.

Kenya turned around to see what they were gawking at.

Majestically making his way down the aisle was Amir. He
was wearing matching white linen drawstring pants and vest,
with no shirt underneath. The contrast of the gleaming white
and his chocolate skin was striking. As he negotiated his broad
shoulders down the walkway, the sea of people parted for him
like he was Moses.

Kenya noticed the men's looks of envy and of women's out-
right hunger as he passed. She had to agree. He did look good
enough to eat. As he got closer, he whipped off his shades and
smiled.

There. Now it was perfection.

Racquel turned away, quickly wet her lips and prepared to
put on her best take-me-I'm-helpless-but-I'm-tasty act. She put
her pouty smile on and timed her turning back around to coin-
cide with Amir's arrival.

The smile turned into a full-fledged pout when Amir brushed
past her and kissed Kenya on the cheek.

"It's either Saturday already, or I *must* be dreaming," he whispered in her ear.

He smelled delicious. "Hey," she said returning his warmth,
"what are you doing here?"

"I come to the mart occasionally to buy some artwork."

"Oh, you mean like pictures of flowers, tulips, and daisies?"
Kenya asked innocently.

Amir rolled his tongue inside his cheek and gave her a "you
got that one" smirk.

"No, not today. Actually, I prefer African art. As a matter of fact, I'm looking for something in particular. Maybe you can help me. This morning, as I was looking at the different prints, pieces, and figurines around my place, I felt that something was missing. What I need is a regal Nubian princess with heart-shaped lips, high cheekbones, and shimmering mahogany skin. You know, the kind of sister whose elegance and allure jumps out at you every time you lay eyes on her. Whose natural charm is such that it would inspire me to conquer the world if it would please her, and lay waste to that which would do her harm." Amir put his sunglasses into his vest pocket. "Yep, that's what I'm missing. So, have you seen anything like that around here?"

Kenya turned back to Sister Delores's table to hide her embarrassment. Damn, this guy was forward. She picked up a metal candleholder that had caught her eye earlier and looked it over.

Racquel cleared her throat. Kenya turned back around.

"No, I haven't seen anything like that, Amir," Kenya said demurely, putting the candleholder down.

"You must not be looking too closely," Amir asserted.

Racquel coughed louder.

Kenya relented and made the introductions. "Amir, this is Racquel. Racquel, Amir."

Racquel stuck out her hand, and her breasts, at Amir.

"Hi, Amir," she said, coquettishly.

"Nice to meet you, Racquel." Amir shook her hand gently. He then turned his focus back to Kenya, much to Racquel's dismay.

"And this is Tonya."

"Hello, Tonya."

Tonya, who had been eyeing him warily, stepped forward to take his hand.

"Hello, Amir, but I believe we've met before."

Amir released her hand and studied her. He prided himself on his ability to remember faces, but hers wasn't ringing a bell. "I don't believe I've had the pleasure, Tonya."

"Well, we haven't been formally introduced. You're from Lawndale, right? Same town as my fiancé, Brandon—Brandon Thompson."

"Oh." Amir nodded. Now he remembered. He and Brandon weren't close, but they often played ball on Wednesday nights at the recreation center. "Okay, you sometimes watch Brandon down at the rec."

"Yep, that's me."

Amir turned his attention back to Kenya. "What did you buy?" he asked her.

"Some oils."

"Which scents?"

"Opium and musk."

At that point Amir noticed the book on the ground.

"Did one of you drop this?" While he bent down to pick up the cookbook, Racquel looked at Kenya. Kenya could tell she was brimming with questions.

"It's mine," Racquel said as Amir stood back up. She stepped toward him to accept the book, far closer than was needed.

"Thank you," she said, shamelessly batting her lashes up at him.

"You're welcome." He handed the book to her.

Racquel took the opportunity to squeeze his bicep with her free hand. "Wow. You must work out."

"I try to take care of myself."

Racquel, who didn't feel like holding the heavy book, set it on the table. All the while she kept her hand on Amir's arm.

Racquel's flirting was beginning to irk Kenya. "We're still on for Saturday?" Though the question was for Amir, she looked at Racquel when she asked it.

Racquel's mouth fell into a perfect oval. She put a halt to her fondling. Tonya noticed her reaction and stifled a laugh.

"You better believe it. I've got big plans for you, Kenya." Amir smiled. "Something *special*."

Kenya grinned, her enjoyment at his comment greatly enhanced because it excluded Racquel.

Racquel glanced at her watch. "Ladies, I think we should be going, if we're gonna see Taz before she leaves."

Kenya and Tonya looked at her. Since when was her perpetually late ass concerned about being punctual?

"We got time," Tonya said.

"Not really," Racquel insisted. "Didn't you tell Taz we'd be there by three?"

Even though Racquel was being a pain, Kenya knew she was right and acquiesced.

"Amir, I do have to go. I promised my sister I'd stop by and say good-bye before she left for Morristown."

"Your sister's name is Taz?" Amir asked.

"Short for Tanzania."

"She's also named after an African country, huh? Let me guess. Your parents were actively involved in the Black Nationalism movement back in the day."

"Power to the people, baby," Kenya replied.

"You'll have to introduce me to your brother, Zimbabwe," Amir said.

"Sure," Kenya answered smoothly, "but the family calls him Bob, for short."

They both laughed. Neither of them was in a hurry to leave. A feeling that wasn't shared by Racquel, who was shifting her weight from foot to foot impatiently.

"Well, don't let me hold you up," Amir said. "Family is very important."

"Okay. Give me a call sometime this week."

"All right." Amir turned toward Tonya while Kenya was gathering her things. "It was nice meeting you—formally."

"Likewise," Tonya agreed.

"And nice meeting you, Racquel."

Racquel, purposely brushed her nipples along his arm as she reached back for her cookbook. "Likewise." She looked up at him to gauge his reaction and was disappointed when there was none. She pouted again.

"Let's go," she said, irritated.

"Bye, Amir," Kenya said sweetly. "Good luck art hunting. I hope you find what you're looking for."

I already have, Amir thought. "Thank you."

Racquel spun on a heel. "Yes, Amir. I *do* hope you find what you're looking for," she said, her voice laden with acerbity.

Oh, fuck you, too, skank, he wanted to say.

"I hope you do, too, Racquel," Amir answered dryly. "And good luck hunting."

"What did he mean by that?" Tonya asked as they headed for the parking lot.

Racquel shrugged her shoulders. "Maybe he means cookbooks." She shifted the massive tome she was carrying from one arm to the other. "Anyway, how should I know? He's Kenya's friend."

"What's that supposed to mean?" Tonya asked.

"Nothing. It's just that he strikes me as a dog."

Kenya's patience with Racquel was wearing thin. "Oh, really? And you feel qualified to offer an opinion after knowing him for all of five minutes?"

Racquel looked at her icily. "And you feel qualified to defend him already, huh? How long have *you* known him?"

Kenya rolled her eyes and slightly quickened her stride. Though Racquel was sometimes fun to be around, she could also wear on her nerves. She was more Tonya's friend than hers, anyway.

"Rocky, why are you being such a bitch?" Tonya asked.

Racquel shrugged her shoulders. "I'm entitled to my opinion."

"You're also entitled to keep it to yourself," Tonya said. She looked over at Kenya. "Though, if you would like, I could ask Brandon about him."

Kenya looked at her.

"It's just that I've noticed a lot of women going to those rec league games. That one"—she nodded her head back in the direction of the flea market—"always seems to have his own cheering section."

Racquel glanced at Kenya and smirked. She wondered how Ms. High-and-Mighty felt about that little tidbit.

Kenya pondered Tonya's offer. It seemed wise to know what she was getting into. She nodded at Tonya to give her the go-ahead to do so.

Racquel, who had all of a sudden become cheery, put her hand on Kenya's arm. "I apologize, Kenya . . ."

Kenya noticed her voice didn't have the slightest bit of remorse.

". . . it's just a first impression. How did you meet him anyway?"

"Karen introduced us."

"Karen?" Racquel stopped dead in her tracks. "From church?"

"Yep." Kenya reached her Tercel and unlocked the door. Tonya got in the front seat. Racquel trudged to the passenger side slowly, lost in thought. Kenya knew what she was thinking. Why Kenya and not her?

"Y'all don't remember her telling us about him a couple of weeks back?" Kenya asked as they slid in.

Racquel shook her head.

"I probably wasn't paying attention," Tonya said. "You know other men don't interest me anymore." She held up her ring and admired it.

Kenya started the car. She turned on the radio to WPRS. Jackie Moore's "This Time, Baby" flooded the car. Kenya put the car in reverse and started to back out, looking at Racquel in the backseat.

"I don't know why you don't remember. You were sitting right next to me. In fact, you were the one who asked Karen what he did for a living."

Racquel stared at her dumbfounded.

"She told us he was a barber who cut Jeremy's hair—" Kenya stopped and shifted the car into drive. "Now, that I think about it, that's when your interest dropped off. When you found out he was only a barber." She turned and accelerated.

Tonya giggled.

Your prissy ass is gonna pay for that, Racquel thought. She looked out the window, refusing to let Kenya or Tonya see her irritation.

July 12, 1994

Kenya walked into her apartment and picked up her ringing phone. "Hello?"

"It's me, girl."

"What's up, Tonya?" Kenya asked as she kicked off her shoes.

"You just getting in from work?"

"Yeah, I had a few errands to run." Kenya started going through her mail. "What's up?"

"I asked Brandon about your friend."

Kenya sat down on the sofa. "And?"

"Well," she hesitated, "from what he tells me, your buddy Amir is quite the womanizer—has slain more sisters than a little bit."

Kenya's face tightened. "Yeah?"

"Yeah. He started reciting just the names of women that he knew about. I made him stop at around twenty."

"Damn." Kenya said.

"Ya know."

They were both quiet for a couple of seconds.

"I guess it would be too much to expect a guy that good-looking not to be a dog," Tonya said.

"Yeah. So Brandon is sure, huh?" Kenya asked.

"Afraid so. It didn't take a lot to get it out of him, either. He was surprisingly forthcoming."

Not so surprising, Kenya thought. Brandon was probably envious of Amir—more than a little bit.

"Well, Kenya, now you know."

"Yep."

"So what are you gonna do?"

"I'm about to make me something to eat." Kenya walked into her kitchen.

"You know what I mean."

"Well, I have a date with him Saturday. I intend to keep it."

"O-kay. As long as you know what you're walking into."

Kenya took a pack of noodles out of the cabinet and set it on the counter. "What a man does with other women before he meets me is none of my business. Unless it's something criminal."

"I can't go with you on that one, Kenya. I don't need to know the exact number or every woman's name, but I need to know if it's some astronomical shit. Isn't that as good a barometer as any of a man's view of women?"

"Yeah," Kenya acceded. "That's right up there with his relationship with his mother." She ran some water into a pot and set it on the stove.

"Who knows?" Tonya offered. "Maybe he's tired of tricking and looking to settle down."

"Tonya, do you honestly believe that?"

"No. But it's possible, isn't it? It's better than saying my friend is willingly walking into the lion's den—"

"Which is what you really believe," Kenya said.

". . . wearing a pork chop necklace."

"Hey, don't make me sound like some babe in the woods. Maybe I'm just looking to have some fun," Kenya insisted.

"Yeah, right." Tonya scoffed. "The way you were making goo-goo eyes at him yesterday at the mart? I don't know who was more scandalous, you or Racquel."

"See, now, you're just being plain mean."

They both laughed.

"Guard your heart," Tonya said.

"Will do, skipper."

"Kenya, I'm serious. Remember the creed."

"I know, I know. 'Guard your heart, 'cause most brothas are heartless.' "

"They steal sistahs' hearts so they can have one."

July 15, 1994

"Be still, my beating heart," Amir said as he looked through the peephole. "Who is this beautiful sistah at my door?"

"The same one who buzzed you less than two minutes ago, unless there was another one in the interim."

Amir opened the door to his apartment. Kenya walked in.

"Hi," she said, smiling at him.

"Wow." Amir's eyes widened. "Look, Kenya, I don't mean to stare, but you look good."

"You think? This old thing?" Kenya gave him a comical model's spin, pouty look and attitude included.

Amir laughed. "All right, Roshumba," he said as he closed the door. When he turned back around, he mused, "You know, *that's* who you look like. I've been trying to think who you reminded me of."

"Amir, please. Roshumba is drop-dead beautiful."

He looked directly at her. "Your point?"

Kenya rolled her eyes to the ceiling as if to say, I'm not even trying to buy it—but flattery will get you everywhere.

"So, this is it."

"Yep," Amir said. "Welcome to my humble abode."

"May I look around?"

"Make yourself at home, Roshumba."

Though she knew it was a ploy to get in her panties, Kenya decided to give him something to look forward to—if he did in fact come correct.

So as she started her walk around the living room, she put in a little more strut than usual, making the hem of her rayon dress sway against her runner-sculpted calves. She stopped at a picture over the futon. "Nice painting."

Amir joined her. "It's a Paul Goodnight print. He's an artist from Boston. Hopefully, one day I'll be at the point where I can buy originals."

As she stepped around the coffee table to continue her stroll, she noticed a huge photography book titled *Women of Africa* set in the middle of it.

His place was neat and clean, which was a good sign. There was no dust on the bookshelves. Shelves that were actually occupied with books, though most looked like the kind you had in college courses and decided to keep.

"Well-read, are we?" she asked teasingly.

"Somewhat. Though most are just for show," he admitted.

She laughed. She noticed a pleasant aroma emanating from the kitchen.

"What are you cooking?"

"Baked chicken, spinach, homemade macaroni and cheese, rolls, and for dessert, drum roll please . . ."

Kenya drummed her hands against her thighs.

". . . peach cobbler!"

"Peach cobbler?" she asked excitedly. "Homemade?"

Amir looked at her and scoffed. "But of course."

"How did you know that that is my favorite?"

Amir shrugged. "It was an educated guess. I figured you like any and all things peach. Peach roses, peach dresses, peach cobbler." He looked at her and gave her a wicked grin. "You're a peach, is what you are."

Kenya grabbed her dress and curtsied, which made Amir laugh. She then looked over in the direction of the bedroom.

"Do you mind?" she asked Amir.

"Be my guest," he replied. Amir fixated on her ass as she walked into the room. Go ahead and get familiar, he thought. Believe me, your sweet self will be doing gymnastics in there soon enough. While she toured the bedroom, he walked into the kitchen to check on the spinach.

Kenya looked around the room. It wasn't what she expected. Then again, what did she expect? Handcuffs on a brass headboard, a red light and a—she looked up—mirror on the ceiling?

He had a king-size bed with a bright maroon, blue and yellow comforter. He had four pillows, two with blue pillowcases and two with maroon. The huge wooden headboard had shelves and cubbyholes that contained watches, bracelets, necklaces, and loose change. Hanging over the wall of the headboard was a paddle with Greek letters on it. Aha! Kenya thought, a paddle. I knew he was a freak.

In the corner was a high-back chair underneath a lamp. Kenya chuckled. This was his pensive reading area, no doubt. He had an immense chest of drawers, as well as a dresser that came up to Kenya's chest. On it sat at least a dozen different bottles of cologne.

On the wall were bright, cheery prints of African men and women doing all kinds of activities. There were three men playing the drums. A group of women dancing. Mothers nursing their young. Women carrying urns on their head. Children running, trailing long pieces of colorful string behind them.

Kenya looked closely at the pictures. Each one was primarily comprised of the same three colors in his comforter. She was impressed. That took some doing.

She thought about checking out his walk-in closet, but knew that went beyond being nosy and crossed the line into snooping. She sat down on the bed—and nearly capsized.

She hadn't realized it was a water bed.

As she regained her bearings, Amir walked in.

"So what do you think?"

"It's nice, though I was nearly lost at sea on this bed." She nodded in the direction of his dresser. "I couldn't help noticing all the colognes you have."

Amir picked up a bottle of Obsession and moved it to the front. "A brotha likes to smell good, and a brotha likes variety."

"For whom? Maybe the *variety* of sisters who gave him the cologne?" Kenya teased. She got up and joined him at the dresser.

"Why did you assume women bought them for me?"

"Oh, so you bought twelve different colognes? 'Vanity, thy name is Amir.' C'mon, now, what would you have me believe next?" Kenya asked. "You gonna sell me the deed to the Walt Whitman Bridge?"

"Why couldn't I have bought them myself?" he asked, his face full of innocence.

"I don't know." She titled her chin mockingly. "Why didn't you?"

Damn, she looked good standing there, with her hands on her hips and lips all glossy and pursed. Amir couldn't resist.

He leaned over and planted one. She flinched momentarily, but accepted it willingly.

She tasted too sweet. Amir was sure the rest of her tasted just as good. Like peach syrup, he bet.

"So?" she asked.

"So?" he answered, temporarily mesmerized by the movement of her lips.

"Were the colognes bought for you or not?"

"Yes, they were."

"Let me guess. By your grandmother, right?"

Amir moved from her lips to her eyes. "No."

They stood quiet for a moment. Kenya spoke first.

"That's a lot of cologne." She looked at the dresser again. "A lot of *different* cologne." Tonya's words of caution were echoing in her head.

Amir shrugged his shoulders. "Maybe." He picked up a bottle of Obsession. "Though, if you notice, most of the bottles are almost empty."

"That just means you must use a lot of cologne."

Amir fixed a gaze on her. "Or maybe since I'm looking to downsize to a specific one, there's no need to replace the others."

Kenya turned away. "Maybe." She then noticed a huge picture frame set to face the wall next to the nightstand. "What's that?"

It's about time, Amir thought. That's what I sent you in here for, not for an inquisition about my cologne.

"I don't know—how did that get there?"

Kenya rolled her eyes, went over, and turned over the frame. Inside it was a poster of Jon Seda and Lauren Velez in an embrace. He was looking reverentially at her, while she was looking away with a sly Mona Lisa–like smile. Emblazoned across the bottom in big red letters were the words *I Like It Like That*.

Kenya was taken aback, so Amir spoke first.

"I got the idea that you really enjoyed that movie. Was I wrong?"

"No, I did," Kenya said, reading the credits along the bottom of the poster. "In fact, I loved that movie."

"Good," Amir said. "I went back to the theater this week and bought the poster from them and had it framed. It's for you, Kenya. I figure it will always be a memento from our first date together."

Now, that was too damn sweet. Kenya carefully put the picture back against the wall, walked over to Amir and gave him a warm hug. "Thank you."

"You're welcome." They separated.

"So, you hungry?" he asked.

Kenya nodded.

"Let's go eat."

Yeah, let's go eat, she thought. Or at least get out of this bedroom before I do something I regret.

Amir raised his eyebrows when Kenya reached for another slice of peach cobbler.

"What?" she asked. She sucked some excess syrup off her thumb.

"Nothing," Amir said, and quickly concentrated on his plate. Kenya smiled.

"Hey, I told you, I'm real. I'm not the kind to eat like a bird just to impress a man. If you want that kind of pretension, then you'd better call the sistah from down the street."

Amir looked startled. "What sister from down the street?"

"I don't know, Amir. It's just a saying. You never heard that?"

"Oh," he said, relieved. "Yeah, I heard it before." He looked at her plate. "No, no, eat as much as you like. I want you to be comfortable."

Damn, Kenya thought. The way he reacted, he must really be messing with some chick from down the street.

"Besides," she said, "this food is delicious. Not to partake of it would be violating my most sacred rule after the Ten Commandments. *Thou shall never front on thy stomach.*"

Amir put his fork down and thought that one over.

"Man, that's beautiful," he said. "That should be the eleventh commandment."

They both laughed. Kenya looked at him thoughtfully. "Do you go to church?"

"Not every week like I did when I was a child and forced to," he replied. "Is that important to you?"

"I think it's important that a man is spiritual." She had noticed that he had blessed the table before he started to eat earlier.

"Agreed." He took a sip of soda. "It's foolish not to think that there are forces at work larger than us. God is obviously one of them."

"One of them? What else is there?"

"Well, there's love."

"Oh, really?" Kenya asked dryly.

"Definitely. I believe in the power of love."

"You and Luther Vandross both."

"Oh, you don't respect it?" Amir asked.

"Don't get me wrong, Amir. I respect the power of love—"

"Well, all right, Stephanie Mills!"

Kenya smirked. "May I continue?"

"By all means."

"It's just that I think the word is thrown around so often that it has become trivialized. It has lost much of its weight. People should say it only if they are sure that they mean it, not as a means to an end."

Like getting some pussy, Kenya thought, but did not say. Instead, she watched Amir chew and swallow a bite of pie. She wondered how many women Amir had "loved" on that water bed.

"For instance," she continued, "I would *love* to know who cooked this food for you."

Amir laughed. "What do you mean? I cooked it."

"Amir, on the way back from Great Adventure you asked me, could you cook for me. Correct?"

"Yep."

"You and I got back from Great Adventure at four o'clock. That was the time when you dropped me off at my place."

Amir smiled. He was enjoying this.

"So in the span of less than three hours you would have me believe you went to the store, bought all this food, brought it home, and just whipped this up—baked chicken, homemade macaroni and cheese, peach cobbler and biscuits from scratch, mind you—showered, got dressed again, then cleaned up your apartment and the kitchen? Is that what you're telling me?"

"Yes, Inspector, that's what I'm telling you."

"Impossible," she scoffed.

"Kenya, didn't anybody ever tell you that nothing's impossible for a black man?"

"Yeah, but it was always lying-ass black men that were telling me it."

Amir leaned back in his chair. "All right, I'll admit it. The biscuits are courtesy of the Colonel. I just glazed them with honey."

"Aha! You've been exposed, fraud."

"But the rest *is* homemade. Your premise is false about me having to go to the store to buy the ingredients. I already had everything in the house before we left."

"Oh, really? And you just assumed I would want to come here and break bread with you?"

Amir flashed a wicked grin. Once again Kenya had to make a conscious effort to close her legs under the table.

"I was hopeful," he said.

More like confident, Kenya thought. And he had every right to be. She really liked him, and she was sure he could tell. Could probably smell her attraction the same way his brother dogs smelled fear.

He chuckled.

"What?" Kenya asked.

"I was just thinking that we have some long dates. All-day affairs."

"Yeah, I was thinking the same thing." She studied his face. "Are you complaining? Maybe you're tired of me?"

Amir took the napkin off his lap and placed it on the table. He got up and came around. He placed one palm on the table, the other on the back of her chair, and leaned toward her.

Kenya's mouth fell open instinctively. As his tongue probed her mouth, she tilted her head back slightly and shifted her body. She wanted to make him pursue her. This chase excited both of them.

"Mmm, Kenya . . . mmm, Kenya," he whispered softly as he hungrily reached for her.

No, mmm, Amir, she thought. She was dangerously close to violating her pledge to make any man she liked wait at least six months for sex. About to miss her mark by about five months and three weeks.

The hunter became the hunted as Amir began to pull back.

Oh, don't go now. Kenya strained her neck to keep up with him, but he finally stood up straight.

It had felt the same as the kiss they'd shared in the bedroom earlier. So uncontrived, so unforced. Like it was his inherent right to kiss her whenever he felt so inclined. And Kenya had to admit, she felt he did.

She looked up at Amir. She thought she saw a hint of indecision on his face, like he was deciding whether to carry it further or not.

Amir went back to his chair and sat down. Kenya couldn't decide if she was disappointed or relieved.

"Believe me, I'm not sure if I can even comprehend being tired of you," he said.

She smiled. Damn, she hoped his good-looking ass was coming correct.

"Besides, if you had said no, the food wouldn't have gone to waste," Amir continued.

"No?"

"Nope. I just would've called my chubby brother over here to eat it. He would've had a field day."

That night in Kenya's bed it was just the two of them, her and Amir. In their usual positions. He was occupying his increasingly more frequent spot in her thoughts, while she was lying on top of her covers playing with her nipples and squeezing her thighs together.

The ring of the phone snapped Kenya out of her horniness. She sighed with irritation. Then again, maybe it was Amir calling to wish her a good night. Hearing his voice could only enhance her self-gratification.

"Yes?" she cooed.

"Kenya?"

Damn. Racquel. Kenya released her breast.

"Yeah, it's me. What's up?"

"I'm just calling to let you know I won't be in church tomorrow, so don't you and Tonya bother picking me up. I'm spending the night down here."

"Where are you?" Kenya heard music playing.

"Baltimore. I'm visiting some friends."

"Okay."

"So what you do all day?" Racquel asked. "Did you see that man again?

"Who, Amir?"

"Yes, Amir."

"Yeah." Not that it's any of your business, Kenya thought.

"I was just thinking that I was premature to call him a dog. He's probably a decent guy."

Kenya wasn't sure if Racquel had spoken to Tonya and was trying to be funny, or was being sincere. Nah. Even if Tonya hadn't told Racquel about Amir's past, Kenya seriously doubted she was being sincere.

"I'll tell him that he has your endorsement."

"Maybe I'm just prejudiced against fraternity guys," Racquel said.

Kenya thought about the paddle in Amir's bedroom. She propped herself on her elbows. "How did you know he was in a frat, Racquel?"

She hesitated before answering. "I saw the brand on his arm when I met him."

"Oh." Kenya relaxed again.

"He's an Omega—went to Lincoln, right?"

"Yeah. Why are you so interested in Amir?"

"Hey, if he's gonna be a part of my friend's life, I figure I'd better get used to him."

That was such bullshit, on so many levels, that Kenya didn't bother commenting on it.

"All right. Well, I'm getting ready to go to bed."

"All right. I'll talk to you later."

"Good night." Kenya hung up the phone. "Gonna be a part of my friend's life." Please. First of all, she and Racquel were hardly best buds. Second, though she certainly wasn't opposed to the notion of Amir maybe one day being a part of her life, she had just met the man. Racquel was acting like it was already a given.

Hell, Kenya thought, it may never get past him just being a part of my fantasies.

August 6, 1994

Amir and Kenya were driving back across the Ben Franklin Bridge. They had just come from attending service at Kenya's church.

"What's up with your friend?" Amir asked.

"Who, Tonya?"

"No, the other one."

"Oh, Racquel."

Amir shifted in his seat as if the very sound of her name made him uncomfortable. "Yeah. Are you and her close?"

"We hang out and stuff, but not really. I met Racquel through Tonya. With the exception of Tonya, most of my close friends still live in North Jersey." Kenya looked at him suspiciously. Please don't tell me that you are yet another man that wants to sleep with Racquel. "Why do you ask?"

"To be honest, Kenya, I don't like her. I just get a bad vibe from her."

"Yeah?"

"Yeah. And I don't think she likes me, either."

You're only partially right on that count, Kenya thought. From what she could tell, Racquel didn't like Amir because he didn't bow and scrape in her presence like every other man did. Leer at her and tell her how fine she was. In fact, Amir had ignored her, which really burned Racquel. Which is probably why she had barely seen Racquel since Amir had been in the picture.

"So? Do you care?"

Amir glanced at her. "Only if it's gonna stop me from getting to know you better."

Kenya suppressed a smile. "It won't. Like I said, we aren't that tight."

"Good."

"So how did you enjoy the service?" she asked, ready to change the subject.

"It was good. I like your pastor. He's well-spoken, and he passed my most important test when it comes to judging a reverend."

"What's that?"

"He doesn't drive a better car than me."

Kenya looked at him. "How do you know what he drives?"

"I noticed an Accord in the pastor's parking spot. That's the first thing I look for when attending a new church. Believe me, if it was a Benz or BMW sitting there, I would have turned right around and gone home."

Kenya started laughing. "You're silly."

"How do you mean?"

"They haven't taken a vow of poverty, Amir. Why can't they drive what they want?"

"C'mon, Kenya, think about it. 'I'm a man of God, but dammit, I wheel the phattest car in the congregation'? Hey, why stop there? Why not have him live in a mansion as well? And matching mink coats for him and the missus. So what if many of his congregrants are struggling financially? But, hey, they just better keep those tithes coming. And don't even get me started on those ministers that wear a bunch of jewelry. Rings on every finger. Not only is that disgraceful, it's downright *country*."

Kenya looked out of her window. She had her mouth buried in her hand trying to smother her giggling.

Amir slowed down going through the tollbooth. He didn't have to stop since they were going back to the Jersey side. He then noticed Kenya's attempt to hide her laughter.

"Oh, you laughing? I could tell you some horror stories." His voice turned grave. "There was this one case in a church in

Lawndale a few years back, where a couple of old ladies in the choir kept coming up a little short in their tithes. Well, one day the minister called them in his office to discuss the matter."

Amir paused as he turned on to 295. Kenya turned to face him.

"The details are a little sketchy, but apparently the old women's reason for not keeping up with their tithes was unacceptable to the pastor. And, since he spoke for God, unacceptable to the Big Man upstairs."

Kenya figured she knew where this was heading. She had heard horror stories of pastors defrauding elderly women.

"So anyway he takes these two sisters and puts them in his car—a 525 BMW, mind you—and he takes them for a drive. Do you know where he took them?"

"To the bank?" Kenya guessed. "To empty their life savings?"

"They should've been so lucky," Amir scoffed. "He took them to a seedy, high-crime area of Philadelphia. One that did a good amount of prostitution business. He pulled up to a curb and told them to get out of the car and go stand on the corner. They hesitated, so he picked up a big Bible and said, 'Don't make me put the word of God upside y'all's heads.' When they got out, he told them, 'I'm gonna be back in three hours. You old biddies better have my money! The new seven series Beemers are coming out!' "

Kenya doubled over.

"I don't see what's so funny about it, Kenya," he said. "It's sad."

"It would . . . be if . . . it was true," she said in between giggles.

"Oh, it is. It is," Amir insisted solemnly. "Except I left out one last thing. Before he pulled off, he told them, 'And hitch up y'all's choir robes when the cars ride by. Y'all got a lot of competition out here. Work it, ladies, *work it*!'"

Amir turned into a cul-de-sac and pulled up to the curb in front of the third house in.

"So here we are," he said. "This is where it all began for me."

Kenya looked at his parents' house. It had a brick front and green siding. Three steps led up to the front door. The porch was enclosed by a small black iron fence.

"Are you sure you want to do this?" he asked.

"Are *you* sure you want me to?" she responded.

Amir smiled. "Come on."

"Mom, this is Kenya. Kenya, my mother."

"Hello, Mrs. Moore."

"Hi, Kenya. It's a pleasure to finally meet you. As much as Mir-Mir has talked about you, I feel I already know you."

Kenya glanced over at Amir, who looked like he was about to drop dead on the spot from embarrassment.

"I hope he's been positive," Kenya said.

"Positive? That's an understatement," Mrs. Moore countered. "More like glowing."

"Where's Dad and Myles?" Amir asked. He was more than a little anxious to change the subject.

"Your father is in the backyard fighting a losing battle with the grill. Myles is out somewhere with Katrina," Mrs. Moore answered, still studying this girl that had her son's nose so open.

"Is that idiot still chasing after that girl?" Amir sneered.

"Would you kindly refrain from calling my child out of his name?" Mrs. Moore said. She turned back to Kenya. "He's always picking on his brother."

"Like he doesn't deserve it. Admit it, Mom. He's the white sheep of the family."

Mrs. Moore ignored him. "Kenya, have a seat. Would you like anything to drink?"

"No, thank you." Kenya sat down at the kitchen table. Mrs. Moore also took a seat, while Amir walked over to the window above the sink to look out onto the backyard.

A cute little girl of about seven walked into the kitchen.

"Aunt Eva, I'm thirsty."

"Hey, little girl!" Amir exclaimed.

Jasmine ran over to hug her cousin, wrapping her arms tightly around Amir's waist.

"How's my baby girl?"

"Fine."

"What are you doing?"

"Me and Chantel are playing with Myles's PlayStation." Jasmine then looked up at Amir. "What did you bring me?"

Mrs. Moore looked at Kenya and shook her head wistfully. Her look had "these kids today" written all over it.

"Sweetheart, I didn't even know you were gonna be over here today," Amir said, bending over to plant a kiss on the top of her head.

"That's okay. You can get me next time," Jasmine assured him.

"Jasmine, there are some juice boxes in the refrigerator," Mrs. Moore said. "Get one for your company, too."

Jasmine turned around and for the first time caught sight of Kenya. She looked back at Amir, then over at Kenya again and smiled. She then walked over to the refrigerator, took out two juices and closed the door. Leaning against it, Jasmine looked Kenya up and down before deciding to speak.

"Hi, my name is Jasmine."

"Hello, Jasmine. I'm Kenya. It's a pleasure to meet you."

Jasmine sidled over to the table and sat down. She put the straw from the juice box, popped it into the hole, and started to sip, eyeing Kenya the whole time. Mrs. Moore looked at her in amazement.

"I like that dress you have on, Kenya," she said. "DKNY, right?"

Mrs. Moore's mouth fell open, truly mystified. Amir buried his face in his hands.

Kenya was startled as well. "Thank you. No, it's a Liz Claiborne."

"Well, it looks cute on you," Jasmine said.

Mrs. Moore had had enough. "Jasmine, if you don't get your fast little ass out of my kitchen, I'm gonna—"

Jasmine didn't wait to hear the rest of it. She was a blur leaving the kitchen.

"Grown thing!" Mrs. Moore said, disbelieving. "My sister better watch her like a hawk." She turned her attention back to

Kenya. "Well, anyway, I like you already, Kenya, for convincing my wayward son to go to church. Did it catch on fire when he went through the door?"

Amir sighed. Kenya, on the other hand, laughed heartily.

"Actually, Mrs. Moore, he was a big hit. During the call for visitors, he acquitted himself quite nicely."

Mrs. Moore looked at her son proudly. "My boys were raised in the church, you know. In fact, this one here was the star soloist of the young adult choir."

"Really?" Kenya grinned at Amir, who looked like he wanted to open up a portal and crawl into another dimension.

"Yep. Next time he goes to church with you, have the preacher call him up to sing 'Until I Found the Lord' for you."

"I *love* that song," Kenya said. "I'll talk to the reverend."

"Oh, you will?" Amir asked. He looked at his mother and then back at Kenya. "Y'all must not want me to go to church anymore."

Both ladies laughed.

Mrs. Moore faced Kenya again. "So, Kenya, where are you from?"

"Randolph."

"Really? How did you come to move down here?"

"Well, when I graduated from Farleigh Dickinson I was offered a good job in my field in Cherry Hill. So I took it and moved in with my aunt in Willingboro until I found a place on my own."

"So you do have some family down here. That's good."

A most pleasing aroma was tickling Kenya's nostrils. "Mrs. Moore, what is that wonderful smell?" she asked.

She smiled. "Mir-Mir told me how much you liked that peach cobbler I made. So I'm baking another one for today."

"I sure did. It was delicious." So Mrs. Moore had made the cobbler. Kenya looked at Amir. The fraud was avoiding eye contact as he opened the refrigerator.

"I think Dad is ready for the meat now," Amir said. "I'm gonna take it out to him." He picked up the long platter of chicken and ribs.

"All right," Mrs. Moore said. "Take him that big fork out of the drawer."

Amir walked past them, still managing to avoid Kenya's look of derision. She waited until he got to the doorway before she spoke.

"Hurry back . . . *Mir-Mir*." Kenya mocked, winking at Mrs. Moore.

Amir seized up abruptly, like he had just been poked in the ass with one of those big forks he was carrying. He refused to turn around. Instead, he adjusted his neck, regained his composure, and headed through the laundry room and out the back door.

The two ladies laughed mightily once he was out of earshot.

"Good-bye, Mrs. Moore. Thank you for the meal."

"You're welcome, Kenya." She hugged her warmly. They separated but still held each other by the forearms. "Come back anytime. I mean that."

"Thank you. I appreciate that." Kenya smiled at her. "Bye." She stepped out onto the porch, where Amir and his father were talking.

"Thank you again, Mr. Moore," Kenya said.

"You're welcome, darlin'."

"All right, Pop," Amir said, "we're gonna head on out. I'll see you at the shop tomorrow."

"Okay. See ya later." He walked back inside.

Kenya and Amir were halfway to the car when Mrs. Moore called out from the door.

"Mir-Mir, I need to see you before you go. It'll only take a second."

"All right."

Mrs. Moore closed the glass outer door and disappeared from their view.

Amir sighed. Kenya puckered her lips and started speaking in baby talk. "Are you my good boy? Are you my good boy? Then go see what your mommy wants, Mir-Mir."

Amir laughed. "Hey, now. Watch that 'Mir-Mir' stuff. She's

the only one who calls me that, and I've been trying to break her out of the habit for years." He handed Kenya the keys to the Jeep and headed back to the house.

"Okay," she agreed. "But are you still my good boy?"

Amir looked over his shoulder. "Oh, I'll *be* your good boy, Kenya. As long as you'll be my good girl." He flashed her a lethal smile.

Kenya turned to hide her blush and headed for the Jeep.

Amir found his mother in the kitchen. She was putting the rest of the peach cobbler in a Tupperware dish.

"What's up, Mom?"

Mrs. Moore looked behind him to make sure he was alone.

"Son, I really like that girl," she said. "Now I see what you've been so excited about for the last couple of weeks."

"Oh, by the way I appreciate you telling her that," Amir said dryly. "What are you trying to do, ruin my reputation?" He kissed her on the cheek. "See you later." He headed out.

Mrs. Moore put her hands on her hips. "Since you're worried about staying true to your reputation, then I guess I'll never see her again, huh?"

Amir stopped in the doorway and faced her. "Oh, you will definitely see her again. Trust me. You may not have raised a perfect son, but you didn't raise a fool, either."

When Amir got into the Jeep, he handed Kenya the dish.

"All right!" she said, looking through the clear lid. "I was hoping that's what she called you in for. I didn't want to be greedy and ask."

Amir leaned over, cradled her face, and gave her a long kiss on the cheek.

"Are we—"

Amir cut her off by kissing her again, on the lips this time. He finally pulled back and started the engine.

"Thanks for meeting my parents," he said, taking her left hand in his right.

"You're welcome." Kenya looked at him. "Are we through for the day?"

"Not unless you have something to do," he said, wheeling his way around the cul-de-sac. "Personally, I'm committed to keeping our tradition of all-day dates alive."

"So, you're not done with me yet?" Kenya asked softly.

Amir heard the seduction in her voice. "Not by a long shot, Kenya. Not by a long shot."

Kenya felt downright frilly as she made her way up the sidewalk to Amir's apartment. She looked like she was about to take Center Court at Wimbledon. She had on her brand-new Reeboks, cotton ankle socks, lavender polo shirt, and her too-cute gleaming white tennis skirt, which was swishing in the air as she walked. She glanced at her pink Swatch, so chosen because it matched her shirt. Eight o'clock. Good, right on time.

Earlier, after they had left his parents' house, she and Amir had decided to go home to change out of their church clothes, then meet later. They were staying in tonight, it was agreed, and in addition to watching a movie or listening to some music, Kenya was looking forward to doing some protracted snuggling. As she knocked on the door, she heard music playing.

The door opened slowly and Kenya said, "Tennis, anyone?"

Amir was wearing black from head to toe. Only the bottom half of his wide-collar rayon shirt was buttoned. The top was flung open to reveal his bare chest.

She scanned down his body. He was wearing slacks with no belt and soft leather shoes. He looked like he had gotten dressed haphazardly, almost as an afterthought, which was a remarkable feat considering how good he looked.

You win, Amir, she thought. Game, set, and match.

"I thought we were staying in tonight," she said.

"We are, come in."

Amir took hold of her hand and led her into the apartment, closing the door behind her. The place was dark except for the lamp next to the couch. He kissed the back of her wrist as they sat down on the futon. He smelled as good as he looked. Kenya recognized the scent. She had bought him a bottle of Drakkar yesterday when they were at the mall.

She felt silly. Damn silly. Who told her it was gonna be cute to wear a tennis skirt? In the evening, no less.

Nothing she could do about it now. She noticed the song that was playing, the Luther Vandross and Martha Wash duet "If This World Were Mine."

"I love this song," she said.

"I know you do." Amir walked over to the entertainment cabinet and picked up a cassette case. He brought it back and handed it to her. "I made you a tape."

Kenya squealed when she began reading the list of songs he had written down. It was loaded with her all-time favorite songs, from classics to contemporary. From Marvin Gaye and Smokey to Tony Terry and Babyface.

While Kenya was looking over the tape, Amir laid her feet across his lap and began taking off her sneakers. She looked at him and marveled:

"How did you know that I like these particular songs?"

"We've spent a lot of time together since we've met, Kenya. I listen to you. Mostly to your off-key singing in the Jeep."

She acted like she was gonna kick him. "I'll have you know, I've been told I have a good voice."

"It's okay, but damn, baby, do you have to make everything sound like gospel?"

They shared a laugh.

Next off were her socks. Amir began massaging her feet. Pressing his thumb along her sole and giving tender, individual attention to each toe.

"Roll over, baby."

Kenya dutifully did as she was told. Like a good girl.

Amir leaned over and started kissing her ankles and heels. When the sensation caused by his adept tongue hit her, she closed her eyes. When he started sucking on her heel, Kenya let out a deep sigh of appreciation. Her insides were already turning liquid, and Amir had yet to touch anything but her feet. This was definitely a man who knew how to give pleasure.

Amir began working his way up her legs, managing to be firm yet tender. As he kneaded her calves, Kenya buried her face in an end pillow. Her arms dangled over the edge of the futon, and she dropped the cassette case on the floor.

Next came the back of her knees, which Amir seemed to already know was a sensual zone on Kenya's body. He kissed it softly, first barely brushing his lips along the skin, then darting his tongue along the same spot. Kenya purred contently.

When he started sliding his massive hands up her thighs, she was thankful that she had worn a short skirt. She parted her legs to make his navigation easier. That's right, Amir. Let your fingers do the walking—it's your show. A couple of more inches, just beneath the curtain of her skirt, and it was gonna be showtime.

Amir abruptly stopped his exploration, moved her legs, and stood up. "Get up, baby. I wanna dance with you."

Kenya rolled over onto her back. Amir gently took her hands in his and helped her up.

No words were spoken as they danced. Amir fixed his eyes on Kenya, taking mental snapshots of every luscious contour of her face, the gentle slope of her cheek, the tempting curl of her lips.

Their slow drag to "Secret Garden" turned into a dry hump. Kenya's arms were wrapped tightly around his neck, while Amir guided her hips with his hands. It was like she and Amir had done this before. Their bodies were perfectly synchronized, each anticipating the other's movements.

When Barry White's part of the song came on and Amir started singing along, Kenya was through. She climbed him, wrapping her legs around his waist, so that his bulge now rubbed against her essence. When she began rhythmically rotating her hips, it was Amir's turn to moan appreciatively.

The song faded out, and in the pause before the next song played, Amir took Kenya by the hips and set her down on the floor.

"Let's go to the bedroom." He kissed both her eyelids.

At first Kenya wondered why he didn't just carry her into the bedroom, but then she realized not only did he want it to be of her own volition, he wanted her to *want* it.

And she did.

As she stared at the deep groove that separated Amir's pecs, the same one she had been longing to run her tongue along since the first time she had met him, the seductive bass line of "Don't Be Afraid" pumped through the speakers.

Kenya remembered her promise to make any man wait six months before she slept with him. She was about to break that promise by about five months. She knew it was too soon, but she didn't care.

Kenya took his hand and led him to the bedroom door, which was shut for some reason. She turned the knob and opened it. Then gasped.

Scattered all over the carpet, bed, nightstand, chair and dressers were peach rose petals. They were everywhere—there had to be dozens of them. Flickering candles were spread throughout the room. Kenya recognized the candleholders as the ones that Sister Delores sold. And the scent they were giving off: Opium.

The bedding had been changed as well, to jet-black. She could tell by the pillowcases that the sheets under the comforter were now satin. The contrast between the black and the peach rose petals was striking.

So, he just *knew* he was gonna get some tonight. Kenya turned and looked at Amir.

He knew what she was thinking. "I was hopeful," he said.

Confident is more like it, Kenya thought.

Amir again took her hand and led her to the foot of the bed. He gave her a quick kiss before he gently slid her shirt off her head and tossed it onto the chair. Amir kissed her once more, again teasing Kenya by pulling away before she wanted him to.

He slid the straps of her bra down her shoulders and unfastened it. It fell to the floor. Amir followed suit as he knelt down in front of Kenya, like a servant genuflecting before his queen.

Amir's hands slid up Kenya's legs. He put his thumbs in the waistband of her panties and slid them down her legs and off her feet, then unzipped her skirt and let it fall to the floor.

He held her hips as he softly kissed her stomach. Amir slowly worked his way down to the groove in between her thighs. The one he had been longing to run his tongue along since the first time he met her.

When Kenya felt Amir's lips first touch her wetness, she gripped his shoulders and let out a deep breath. Amir took his time, exploring and savoring every luscious bit of her femininity. He moved a hand inward, delicately spreading her folds to reveal more of her pussy for his knowledgeable tongue to explore. Amir intended to be thorough. No part of her would escape him tonight.

Amir looked up at her, disbelieving how sweet she tasted. Kenya stared back at him and stroked his head tenderly.

When he probed deeper, she crumpled on top of his shoulders. As she quivered, Amir steadied her, holding her tightly as he slowly worked his way up her body. He traced her navel and flicked his tongue along her nipples before finally standing up.

Kenya fell back onto the bed, tugging at Amir's shirt, trying to pull him on top of her. He gently released her.

While she lay on the bed, Amir began to undress. He unbuttoned the rest of his shirt and twisted out of it. The shadows of the candlelight were doing a delightful dance with Amir's athletic body, alternately hiding and exposing each twitching muscle.

Amir kept his eyes riveted on Kenya as he unbuttoned his pants. They slid down, revealing the bulge that had been swelling against Kenya earlier.

She spread her legs wider.

When Amir first entered her, they both gasped. The feel was so perfect, it momentarily startled them. As if fate had long ago created their bodies to complement each other. They were attuned to each other, in delicious harmony. It was as if every caress shared between them was predestined, every gyration foretold. Every nuzzle expected, and every touch necessary.

Later, as they lay in a silent embrace, Amir and Kenya had the same thought, one both overwhelming and empowering. Whatever happened to them for the rest of their lives, they both knew they were now irreversibly changed. Each lover in their pasts had been a way station on their journey to reach the refuge of each other's arms. They had found their home.

Long after her final orgasm had subsided, Kenya lay in bed with her eyes closed, but she wasn't sleeping. She was praying. She sincerely hoped that this man whom she had just given herself to, whom she was already so crazy about, turned out to have substance. That he wasn't now finished with her. She knew she had no business sleeping with someone this fast, but she hardly regretted it. In fact, she was looking forward to the morning and another go-round before they both left for work.

She rolled over and looked at Amir. He was soundly sleeping, dead to the world.

You're worn-out, ain't you, Mir-Mir? Sorry about that, kid, but you asked for it. I had to put that good stuff on you.

Kenya got off the water bed, causing as little motion as possible. She walked across the room, the soles of her feet finding flowers with every step.

She sat down in a chair, carefully taking off a rose petal that was on her shoulder and smelling it. Kenya crossed her legs. It's a bit late for that, she thought, and uncrossed them. She looked over at Amir and wondered how many women he had done this with before. Had most of them held out longer than she did or succumbed even quicker? Most likely she was just another notch in his belt, no more or less special than any of his other conquests. Hell, what did she think? That her pussy was laced with sugar?

So what she wasn't gonna do was hound him when he lost interest in her, which was probably inevitable. She wouldn't give him the satisfaction of feeling like he had dropped her, even if she sensed that there was something special in this man that belonged to her and only her.

But that was only how she felt.

How many women, she asked herself, have felt the same way about a man only to be disappointed? How many women are having the same thoughts running through their heads as I am right now? Wondering if the man they just slept with is or isn't about shit, but scared to find out the answer.

Kenya leaned back in the chair. Regardless of what happened from here on in, it had been a wonderful night. She looked around, soaking in the room. The glow of the streetlamp peeking through the cracks of the venetian blind was her only source of light.

Her eyes stopped on the dresser. There were the rose petals, the candleholders and a bottle of Drakkar. Yet something about it looked different. Kenya walked over for a closer inspection.

She then realized what it was. She looked in the wastebasket by the dresser. Underneath the condom wrappers were all the other bottles of cologne. She turned back toward Amir's sleeping form and smiled.

Maybe, just maybe, she would be the sister that beat the odds.

Kenya crawled back into her man's bed and hugged him tightly around his waist.

May 5, 1995

Nine months had passed when Kenya's phone rang. She grabbed the reciever off the kitchen wall. "Hello?"

"Hey, girl, what's happening?" Racquel asked.

"Hey, yourself, stranger. This is a surprise," Kenya said, walking into the living room. "I was starting to think you moved out of the country."

Racquel laughed. "No, I'm still here."

"Tonya and I barely see you in church anymore," Kenya said.

"I've been visiting other churches over the past couple of months, going with different friends."

"Why?" Kenya asked. "Because the single men in our church aren't up to snuff?"

"You know!" Racquel said, making them both laugh. "Besides, I figure since you have what's-his-name going to church with you now, and Tonya has Brandon, I'd just be in the way."

Kenya decided to ignore her last remark, feeling it was too silly to be worthy of a response.

"But I do miss our girls' nights out," Racquel continued. "In fact, are you doing anything tonight? I wanna go catch a flick."

"Well, Amir is coming over . . ."

Racquel sucked her teeth.

"What's all that for?" Kenya asked.

"I don't know what you see in that guy."

The same thing you do, Kenya wanted to say. "You barely know him, Racquel. Why do you dislike him so much?"

"I just think it's a bad match, that's all."

Kenya sat down in a chair, taking the receiver off her shoulder, into her hand. "How do you mean?"

"You know what I mean, girl," Racquel insisted.

"If I did, I wouldn't be asking."

"C'mon, Kenya, I—I just mean he isn't your type."

Kenya stood up. "And what type am I? Huh?"

"Dag, girl. What are you getting angry for? I didn't mean anything by it."

Yeah, right, bitch. "Well, if you can't answer that, then tell me what 'type' of man I deserve, Racquel."

"You taking shit the wrong way, Kenya."

"Is there another way to take it? My 'friend' telling me that I'm not glamorous enough to be with some man."

"Don't go putting words in my mouth, Kenya."

"I need to be more like you, right? I guess if I had hair—real or not—down to my ass, Amir would be my type. I guess if I was getting my nails filed once a week, he'd be my type. I guess if I wore ten ounces of foundation on my face and spent every waking hour worrying about my appearance, he'd be my type. I guess if I wore clothes that showed off everything God gave me, he'd be my type. I guess if I my skin was high yella, he'd be my type. Right?"

"Are you finished?" Racquel asked.

"Almost." Kenya walked back into the kitchen. "I'm still waiting for you to just come out and say it. That you don't think I'm pretty enough to be with Amir."

After a pause, Racquel answered.

"It sounds like you're doing a good job saying that all by yourself."

Kenya slammed the reciever onto its base.

*　　　*　　　*

"It was nice seeing you again," Hope said as she put back on her sunglasses.

"The pleasure was mine," Amir replied as he tied the cape around the next customer's neck. "I apologize for not remembering you." He studied her face again. "You say you went to Cheyney, huh?"

"Yep, but I spent a lot of time at Lincoln, going to parties and stuff. I remember meeting you a couple of times," Hope said.

Amir didn't remember meeting her, but then again, his college experience had been a whirlwind of fucking dozens of women who were as fine as this one. It was hard enough keeping all their names and faces straight. He looked down at Hope's nephew, Yasin, looking quite dapper with his fresh haircut.

"You take care, little playa. Take it easy on those girls in kindergarten."

Yasin nodded, but was more interested in the lollipop that Amir had given him.

His aunt, meanwhile, was lingering. "So," Hope said, "maybe I'll see you around."

Amir gave her a polite smile. "Okay. Looking forward to it."

There was an awkward pause. She still wasn't leaving.

"I'll be in the area for a while. You know, for the summer. Then I go back to complete my master's at Towson State in the fall."

Amir sized her up. This girl was begging for some attention. And as fine as she was, she probably wasn't used to begging too often.

"Then, I can expect to see you and Yasin in here again," Amir said.

"Oh, most definitely." She rubbed her nephew's head playfully. She grabbed his hand and headed for the door.

A hush came over the shop as everybody stopped what they were doing to watch her leave.

Hope looked over her shoulder to toss Amir one last sly grin. "Bye."

"See you later, Hope. Take care."

As soon as the door was closed behind her, the place erupted. High fives were exchanged. Feet were stamped on the floor. Praise was given to the Lord for creating the black woman and, most specifically, the black woman's body. Two of the customers fell to their knees. Another one, Kendell, ran to the window to watch her walk all the way to her car.

"We're not worthy! We're not worthy!" David and Jamal said from their knees.

"That is, without a doubt, the finest sistah I have *ever* seen in my life," Brian Boyd said. He looked at Amir. "Nigga, if you don't want her, I'll take her . . . I'll take her!"

"Very Lisa from *Saved by the Bell*-ish," Jamal said.

"No, I think she looks more Chili from TLC-ish," David said.

"Nah, baby girl is too thick for that," Brian said.

The men put their heads together, trying to come up with an appropriate description.

"Maxine, from En Vogue-ish?" Kendell offered.

Hmm, they pondered that one for a moment.

"Close, but it doesn't quite do her justice," Brian decided.

The three of them looked at each other wide-eyed. They had stumbled upon it.

"Janet Jackson from *Poetic Justice*-ish!"

A hush fell over them. Just the mere mention deserved a moment's reverence. Kendell broke the silence.

"Whatever she is-ish, she's coming back-ish!"

They all scrambled back to their seats.

Hope came back into the shop and made a beeline straight for Amir. "I forgot to give you a tip."

"That's not nec—"

Undaunted, Hope slipped a couple of bills into Amir's uniform pocket.

"Thank you," he said.

"You're welcome." She turned and hurried to the door. "I gotta go. I left Yasin in the car. Bye."

"Bye."

She left again.

"Yo. I didn't notice that belly ring before," David said.

"I don't know how you missed it," Myles said, speaking up for the first time. "She hardly has any clothes on."

"I'll betcha she's a *freak*," Brian said.

"Most definitely, most definitely," Kendell concurred, nodding his head rapidly.

"What kind of woman wears an outfit like that into a place where she knows there won't be anybody but men?" Myles asked. "With her ass hanging out—what does that say about her character?"

The fellas emitted a collective groan.

"All it says is that it's hot outside, Myles," Jamal said.

"Yeah. Somebody feed Myles a burger, so he'll shut up," Brian said. "Besides, Amir ain't looking for a long-term relationship. Ain't that right, playa?"

That's true, Amir thought as he turned the customer in his chair. That's what I have Kenya for. Kenya.

"Nah, fellas," Amir said. "I'm happy with my girl. I'm not looking."

The boys weren't going for that, and they let Amir know it.

"*You didn't have to look for it. The pussy found you.*"

"*You ain't married, nigga!*"

"*It's perfect, Amir. You heard her. She's only up from Towson visiting for the summer. It'd just be a summer fling.*"

"*This is a sad day!*"

"*Don't do this to me, Amir. You know my dick lives vicariously through you!*"

Myles came to his defense. "Kenya's a quality lady." He looked over at Amir, waiting until he had his eye before he spoke again. "He'd be a fool to risk losing her."

The boys turned their venom on Myles.

"Myles, shut up. Please!" Jamal begged.

"What world do you live in, Myles? Men do not say no to women like that," Brian said. "It simply isn't done. It's against the laws of nature."

"Especially Amir. Dammit, it's his duty to knock that booty," Kendell added.

"You know. He would be a fool if he *didn't* ride that honey train from here to Kalamazoo."

"Besides," Brian said, "he's *not* married. If he can't have a little side booty now, then what are we saying? Think about it. He has the rest of his life to be faithful to one woman after he's imprisoned—I mean, married."

That got a laugh.

Myles walked to the register to make change for the customer whose hair he had just cut, then turned to the men sitting in the row of chairs pestering his brother. David got into the barber's chair to wait for Myles to cut his hair.

"So, let me see if I got this straight. Since 'Mir isn't married, it would be okay to step out on his lady," Myles said. "Though he's happy with her, happier than I've ever seen him before."

Amir didn't look at his brother. He knew he was saying this for his benefit.

Brian looked around at each of the customers for their tacit approval, then back at Myles. He was to be their spokesperson.

"That's exactly what we're saying," Brian said. He held his hands out like he was balancing melons. "On one hand, there is pussy. On the other, there is love." He spread his arms farther apart. "And one has absolutely *nothing* to do with the other."

There was silence in the room, except for the buzzing of Amir's clippers. Everyone was digesting Brian's last statement. Reconciling it with their own beliefs. Myles was the first one to speak.

"You guys are right." He went over to David and tied the cape around him. "Therefore, I think Kenya should be free to look for some stray dick as well."

A gasp rose from the men. They all looked at him horrified, even Amir.

"This cat is scandalous!" Jamal said, pointing at Myles like he was the Antichrist.

"Myles, you are one bitch-ass nigga! Why aren't you next door doing the females' hair, anyway?" Brian asked.

"Nigga, fuck you!" Myles answered, glaring at him.

"Hey! Hey! What's going on out there?" Mr. Moore yelled from the back office. He appeared at the door's entrance.

"Huh?" He looked at Brian and Myles and sighed. They were forever going at it.

"Sorry, Mr. Moore," Brian said.

"Sorry, Pop," Myles added.

"Y'all know I don't allow that in here."

While everyone's attention was on his father, Amir slid his fingers into his pocket and unwrapped the folded bills in his pocket, feeling for and finding the slip of paper he knew they enclosed.

June 17, 1995

What the hell are you doing? Amir asked himself. He was driving along Route 63, on the way to a planned tryst with Hope in the Super 8 motel in Burlington. This morning when he called Hope, she had suggested it and Amir was more than amenable to the idea.

Kenya was at some convention for her job in Atlantic City and wouldn't be back until tomorrow evening.

Unwilling and unable to slow down, he drove by the motel, missing the entrance. He didn't see Hope's car but knew she was there. Parked in the back like Amir had asked her.

Amir turned onto the jug handle so he could circle back. He stopped at a light and accidentally caught sight of his image in the rearview mirror.

What's wrong with you?

You've done this a thousand times with a thousand different women. Amir Moore does *not* leave a piece of pussy unturned. Especially one as fine as Hope. Uhn-uhn, he just doesn't. Go do what you do best, playboy.

The light turned green. Amir turned west down Route 63. He spied the motel again, over the concrete divider in the middle of the road. He turned off onto another jug handle, so he could head east again to the motel. Once again he caught the red light.

What *is* wrong with you?

You know full well that those other thousand times *were* different. And while you may have been cheating on whatever girl was calling herself your lady at the time, you have never had a woman the caliber of Kenya to call your own. You have never had a woman move your heart—and yes, son, believe it or not, you do have a heart—the way Kenya has. It's just buried under a bunch of used condoms, motel receipts, and forgettable encounters with forgettable partners. And lies. A whole lot of them. You see, they are what you needed to make everything else flourish. Sprinkled on top of your dung heap of emptiness. Like maggots. Lies to numerous women, who were probably lying to their men at home when they were out fucking you. But most of all, kid, you've been lying to yourself.

Because now that you've had a taste of something better, you know this shit just ain't enough anymore.

That's right, Amir. You're in love. Deal with it.

Amir was halfway up the steps to the second-floor room when he hesitated. Maybe he should just get back in the Jeep and call Hope from a pay phone to say he couldn't make it. Nah, he was here now. Besides, he wanted to reimburse her for the money for the hotel room and to tell her he wouldn't be seeing her anymore.

When he got to the door, he heard TLC's "Creep" playing. How appropriate, he thought. He knocked on the door.

Amir heard rustling in the room and Hope say, "I'm coming."

Not tonight, you ain't, Amir thought. Though rest assured, fine as you are, if you had caught me before Kenya, I would have had your ass speaking in tongues.

She finally opened the door.

Damn, Amir thought when he saw how her body was popping out of her teddy. Maybe I can start my skank-free diet tomorrow.

"Hi," she said, letting him in. "I was beginning to worry."

"I'm here." He closed the door behind him.

"I see." Hope wrapped her arms around him, burying her head in his chest.

"We need to talk," Amir said, gently removing her arms.

"We can do that, too, later." Hope turned around and grabbed his hands. She let him cup her breasts, which had spilled out of her teddy while she grinded her ass against him. "We don't *have* to talk, do we?"

Damn, she isn't wasting any time. And this feels too good, Amir thought. Asking me not to fuck this skank is like asking a starving man not to eat filet mignon because it's too fattening. Amir ran his hands down to Hope's hips. This here is top-shelf booty. How can I be expected to say no to this?

Amir answered his own question: because you are what you eat. He pushed her hips away and walked over to the chair at the desk and sat down, uncomfortably. His discomfort caused by his already erect penis.

Hope was startled that Amir had pushed her away. She then caught sight of the huge bulge in his pants and laughed.

"I told you, you didn't want to talk." She tried to sit on his lap.

Amir blocked her gently but firmly. "He's dictated my actions long enough. Sit down on the bed, please."

Instead, Hope walked over to the refrigerator. "I think you need a drink. Is rum and Coke okay?"

"I don't need a drink. Sit down."

Hope reluctantly sat down on the edge of the bed, purposely leaving her legs open to give Amir a sneak preview.

"Look, Hope, I hate to disappoint you—"

"Oh, I seriously doubt that you'll disappoint," she said, staring at Amir's groin.

". . . but, I can't do this. I'm sorry for wasting your time."

Amir stood up and reached for his wallet, wanting to get the hell out of there before he changed his mind. Hope sensed his weakness.

"You know, Amir, maybe I'm not enough for you."

You sure ain't, Amir thought. Not when a man has had a steady dose of a lady like Kenya. But Amir wasn't gonna tell her that.

"Naw, Hope, it's not that at all. I would be lucky to call you mine. It's just that I'm already involved. I told you that from the giddy-up."

"You misunderstand." She got up and walked over to him, slipping out of her negligee completely.

Amir's mouth started to water.

"Maybe I'm not enough for you because you need to *double* your pleasure." Hope started playing with her nipple.

Amir was about two seconds from fucking the shit out of this girl. But one second was all it took to walk away. He laid the money on the desk.

"While those are some nice titties you got there, I still—"

"That's not what she meant."

Amir whirled in the direction of the voice. He wasn't sure what hit the ground first. His wallet or his chin.

Racquel walked out of the bathroom, also in possession of a teddy just as scandalous as Hope's. They both looked like they had made their selection from the "Fuck My Triflin' Ass" section of the Victoria's Secrets catalog.

She stood next to Hope and wrapped an arm around her waist, smiling coyly.

Amir knew what that smile meant. It meant two things. One, it was about to get real freaky up in here. And second, you *will* fuck me, buddy.

Amir glared at Racquel. Did this bitch really think she was gonna buffalo him into giving up his dick? Did she really think he would fuck Kenya's friend?

But first he turned his attention on Hope.

"Fuck you."

"No, but I believe that's what you came up here to do, right?" she replied nastily.

Racquel didn't want it to turn ugly. She really wanted to sleep with Amir.

"Hey, we're three grown people here," she said. "I say we make it a memorable night."

"And you." Amir turned on her. "Do you really think I'd fuck Kenya's friend?"

Racquel shrugged. "Why wouldn't you? Because you have so

much regard for her? Hope here tells me your dick tastes like honey—"

"Mmmm, straight from the hive," Hope interrupted, licking her lips.

"I just want to find out for myself."

Amir threw his hands up. "Go to hell. Both of y'all."

"Spare me the outrage, Amir. If you have so much regard for Kenya. If y'all's shit is so tight and strong, then what the fuck have you been doing sneaking around with Hope for, huh?"

Amir had no answer. He reached down and picked up his wallet.

"You and I are cut from the same cloth, Amir," Racquel continued. "We like sex and we're damn good at it. We have a lot to choose from, because many, many people want to fuck us. Maybe one day we'll reach the point where we only need one person, but we ain't there yet. I think you should just recognize it. You can't be faithful. Therefore, you're no good for Kenya, anyway."

"Oh, so you're looking out for your friend's well-being?" Amir asked, disbelieving. "Is that why you're trying to fuck her man? Is that why you enlisted this trollop to go after him? You skank ho-bitches!"

"Like . . . honey," Hope again said, baring her teeth.

Racquel shrugged her shoulders and looked at the carpet before lifting her head to meet Amir's scowl.

"You're only gonna hurt her anyway. The only question is where, when, and with who."

Amir stormed to the door, throwing another "ho-bitches" at them for good measure.

"Wait!" Racquel said.

"Aww, let him go," Hope said, walking toward the phone. "I wanna call this fine West Indian nigga I know, anyway. I know his freaky ass will be down."

"Wait, Amir!" Racquel shouted.

Amir had flung open the door and was halfway down the steps before he stopped. He turned around and looked up at her.

Racquel realized she was half naked and ducked back inside, poking her head out.

"Listen, there's no need to tell Kenya about this."

Amir looked at her. He knew what she meant. They both were guilty. She was proposing an alliance of silence, because both were complicit in their misdeeds.

"Racquel, me and you are *not* the same." Amir turned and left.

July 8, 1995 1:01 P.M.

Kenya pulled away from the red light. She was on the way to the gym to work out some aggression. Some aerobics, maybe a little ab work. Then maybe she'd go into Philly and treat herself to a movie and dinner. She refused to be one of those women who fell apart over a man, or one that was terrorized by the thought of being alone.

To hell with that. She had seen too many women just in her family alone stumble down that path. Settling for sorry-ass men just so they could say they had somebody. That's one thing she always promised herself she wouldn't do. Settle. If a man wasn't willing to do what was necessary to be her man, then she didn't need him.

She wasn't gonna be one of *those* women. Who see all the faults in everybody else's men while turning a blind eye to their own. Thinking that everybody else's man ain't nothing, but that the two-hundred-pound pile of dog shit sleeping next to them is a prince. Because they have feelings for him, and because they "can see the good in him." That they're the exception, *they* know what they're doing. But those other bitches that put up with their makeshift versions of manhood? Well, they're just plain dumb.

No, you'd be a dummy, too, Kenya thought. And if she couldn't see the handwriting on the wall with Amir, she'd be one of those fools as well. Hell, she wasn't trying to want anybody that didn't want to be wanted.

As Kenya was stretching her hamstrings on a mat, she noticed a couple of muscled-up brothers coming out of the hammer-strength room. One of them did a double take when he saw her. Later, while he was waiting for his partner to finish his set on the leg press, he checked Kenya out, realized she had caught him doing so, and then quickly acted like he had been focusing on something behind her.

Kenya reversed legs, bringing the heel of her Reebok up to her crotch and leaning her body over to grab the toe of her other sneaker. She could kiss her knee easily. Her flexibility was an aspect that Amir had loved.

Careful using that man's name and love in the same sentence, she scolded herself.

She came back up right in time to see both of the men ogling her through the mirror. Men are so stupid. What? They think using a mirror makes them invisible? She brought both heels to her body anyway, and applied slight pressure to the insides of her knees. Stick around, boys. I'm about to get on the abductor and then the treadmill. You can see me work up a sweat, if you'd like.

Besides, there was almost something perversely endearing in their clumsiness, their openness, even if it was due to incompetence. Rest assured, a creep like Amir never tipped his hand to a woman until it benefited him to do so.

Wearing these tights without a long T-shirt was a form of rebellion anyway. In fact, she was wearing a shirt that didn't quite reach the tip of her navel. Amir would've had a heart attack if she was out in public wearing this when they were a couple.

Careful again, girl. That man has no heart.

July 8, 1995, 2:02 P.M.

"Hi, Mom," Amir said as he laid his keys on the table. He leaned over and gave her a peck on the cheek. He sat down in the chair next to her. She was reading an article in *Essence*.

"Hi, baby. You feeling okay?"

"Yeah. I just didn't feel like going in today. Why, did Dad say something?"

Mrs. Moore flipped her wrist. "He grumbled a little bit, but so what? He's gonna have to get used to not relying on you so much anyway. Soon you'll be opening up your own shop."

"Yeah." Amir thought about how supportive Kenya had been when he had first told her of his plans. She had a way that made him feel like he could conquer the world. It sickened him to think of her making another man feel so empowered.

"What about you?" he asked his mother.

"My first appointment isn't until four." She turned the page. "So, have you spoken to Kenya?"

"No."

"Why not?"

"It's not for lack of trying on my part, Mom. If I call, she hangs up. If I come over, she doesn't let me in. I've even taken to accidentally bumping into her at places where I know she goes."

"And how does that go?"

"Let's just say that I didn't know one woman had so many vicious, icy glares. One of her looks could put the entire continent of Africa into a deep freeze."

Mr. Moore shrugged her shoulders. "What do you expect? She trusted you, and you hurt her. Kenya's a quality woman with high standards for herself. And as such, she has neither the time nor the stomach for your nonsense."

"But dag, Mom, she acts like I—I mean, I didn't really do anything with that woman."

Mrs. Moore closed the magazine and concentrated on her son. "Boy, do you think all women are stupid, or is it just me and Kenya?"

Amir sighed.

"You don't think I know what you do?" she asked with rising agitation. "You think I'm comfortable knowing I raised a son who has turned whoremongering into an art form?"

Amir pushed himself from the table and stood up. He didn't need to hear this today.

"Sit down!"

Amir sat back down out of respect for his mother. He concentrated on a picture of two ducks kissing on the wall rather than look at her.

"Whether or not you slept with that woman isn't important. The fact that you gave yourself the option to is. In Kenya's eyes, you're guilty just by association. You already had a lady in your life. You should have made that clear to that fast little thang you were running around with—from the jump."

Her voice softened, slightly.

"Little boys think they're supposed to have everything that catches their eye. Part of being a man is realizing that you sometimes have to say no to things you want. Things that are pretty to your eye. You have to weigh the consequences of your actions and make the right decision *beforehand*. Anybody can be sorry later. Even children are sorry later, when they're caught. Son, women want a man who'll do the right thing, even when he isn't being watched. Even if he knows he can get away with something. Why? Because a woman needs to be able to believe in her man."

Amir slumped in his seat, as his mother continued.

"I'm not sure if men are capable of loving like women do. Whether y'all have the capability to or not. Whether or not you do isn't important as long as you understand how we do. Because if you do, you will understand how a woman's heart is ripped up by betrayal."

Mrs. Moore rested her chin in her hand and looked down at the table.

"Sometimes I wonder if men understood—I mean, truly understood—the impact it has on us, would they still do it. You see, it's not just the thought of a woman knowing your man intimately, of sharing his body with another woman, that kills us. That's what bothers y'all when your women cheat. But what hurts us is that this man who occupies your thoughts nonstop, who you devote yourself to so tenderly and faithfully, doesn't hold you in *nearly* the same high regard."

Mrs. Moore looked over at Amir. She saw a pain in his eyes that she had never seen before. She got up, stood behind his chair, and draped her arms on his shoulders around his neck.

"I know you're hurting, baby," she said. She rubbed her hand through his curly hair.

"I guess you think I deserve it, huh?"

"That's irrelevant to me. I'm your mother first. All I see is my child suffering, and I would do anything to make it go away."

Amir looked up at her. "What should I do, Mom?"

"I think you have to lay yourself bare. You gotta be real, so don't go over there 'please, baby, pleasing' because she's too smart to fall for that. She'll see through it. And don't go wasting your money on flowers, teddy bears, or anything else you think is cute or mushy. It's not the time for that, either."

Now she tells me, Amir thought. He wished she had told him five hundred dollars ago.

"What you have in your advantage, and what works against Kenya right now, is that she loves you. She doesn't want to talk to you or see you because she wants to put you in a place where she can deal with you." Mrs. Moore patted her chest. "A certain place women have for men that we *used* to love, that once we relegate you to it, hell or high water won't be able to get you out."

Damn, that sounded like a place Amir didn't want to go to. "So, you mean she's trying to forget me."

"Of course. And it's a lot easier to accomplish when that person isn't around to constantly remind you how much you miss them. Which is why those looks you get from her are so evil." She pinched him on his cheek.

Amir grimaced.

"Love building is a process that takes time. Nor do you fall out of love with a person overnight. It takes time to accept that a person is *not* essential to your happiness. I personally think a woman has to go through five stages to get over a man: from love to hate to disgust to acceptance and finally to apathy to truly get over him. The further you let Kenya get away from love, the harder time you're gonna have getting her back. Right now I would think Kenya is squarely in hate mode."

While Amir mulled that over, Mrs. Moore picked up a mug off the table and went to the sink to rinse it out.

Amir turned around to look at her. "Mom, when did you get so wise?"

"Hey, I read *Essence*. I'm in the know." She dried her hands on a towel while she looked through the window into the backyard. She turned around abruptly. "So what are you saying, anyway? That you always thought I was clueless?"

"Well . . ."

She threw the towel at him. "Boy, don't make me smack you."

He smiled, forgetting his woes for a second or two. "I'm just saying that Dad doesn't seem to be the kind to have done all this wooing and pursuing."

Mrs. Moore put her hands on her hips. "Do you think your father is the only man I've ever known? I was once a young woman, too."

"What?" Amir didn't like where this was heading.

"Where do you think you get your good looks from? Why, before I met your father, I had all the boys—"

"Hey!" Amir said, rising out of his seat with his palms facing her. "That's more information than I need to know!"

They shared a chuckle. Slowly Kenya returned to Amir's thoughts. His mother intuitively knew it, by reading her son's face.

"Lay myself bare, huh?"

"Do you love Kenya?"

"You know I do."

"Then, go to her. But don't go over there half stepping and bs'ing. Tell her how you really feel and be honest with her and yourself. That's all you can do."

"And if she won't talk to me?"

"Then keep trying until she will. I'm sorry, but that gigantic ego of yours is gonna take a few hits. This ain't one of those simple little hussies you're so used to dealing with. Her heart won't be recaptured so easily. Understand?"

Amir nodded. He walked over and gave her a kiss. "I'll stop by there tonight," he said.

"Waiting for the cover of darkness, huh?" she teased.

"No, it's just that I doubt that she's home. She usually goes into Philadelphia on Saturdays." He picked his keys up off the table. "I'm gonna head on out."

Mrs. Moore walked with him through the foyer to the front door.

"One last thing, Amir. I need you to do me a favor."

"Sure."

Mrs. Moore's countenance was pensive as she picked a piece of lint off Amir's shirt. She wanted to choose her next words carefully, and took her time before looking up into her son's eyes.

"Besides telling Kenya what she means to you, I want you to really listen to her. Pay attention to what she's saying. And if she's asking you to do something you don't think you can do, or to be something you don't think you can be, then I want you to leave her alone. Don't be so selfish that you only think of what you want. Think about what's best for her as well. And if you're not it, then leave her alone."

Amir was perplexed. Not as to what she was saying, but his mind was having difficulty grasping the enormity of her words.

"That's right," she continued, knowing he had understood her. "Don't go over there with the mind-set that you'll just say whatever you think is necessary to get back in her life. Even if you can weaken her. Don't be a snake who uses lies and half-truths to worm your way to her core. You don't want that to be the foundation of your relationship. It's weak, it'll eventually rot, and you'll both be miserable, anyway. So go to her as a man, and love her like a man. Meaning, put what's best for her foremost. If you truly love her, you'll do just that. Love her first. Love *you* second."

Amir stared at her, numb.

"I know it's a lot to deal with. It upsets your applecart to think of someone else's benefit, especially if it's to your loss first. But I know my son has a good heart somewhere underneath all that selfishness, ego, and womanizing," she said as she poked him in his chest. "Let Kenya see it when you talk to her, and you might gain more than just your lady back. You just might find your manhood as well."

Amir stood there for a moment to digest his mother's words. He then nodded and walked out of the house.

July 8, 1995 2:32 P.M.

While Kenya idled at a red light, she fiddled with the scan button on her radio. When the light turned green, she stopped so she could concentrate on the road.

It had stopped on an easy listening station, and the song "Friends and Lovers" was playing. Oh, hell, no. No syrupy ballad shit today. She hit the scan button again. Heeyyy. Now we're getting somewhere. Kenya's head started nodding to the infectious beat. The black woman's anthem, or at least one of them, was playing. Mary J. Blige was telling everybody that all she wanted was to be happy. I hear you, girl. That's what I'm talking about.

Kenya was on her way to the Gallery to treat herself to a new outfit, and to pick up that new Brownstone CD. Their songs "If You Love Me" and "Grapevyne" had blown her away the first time she heard them. Now she would have to add Mary to her shopping list.

Kenya turned onto Market Street. She wasn't going to bother trying to find a meter, knowing it would be an exercise in futility on a Saturday afternoon. She would just have to pay to park in a garage.

This day was rapidly turning out to be an expensive one. New outfit, two CDs, parking, and she still hadn't eaten yet. But, hell, she was a frugal person by nature. She could treat herself occasionally. She looked in the rearview mirror at the twisted plaits in her head. A couple of months back she had decided to chop off her hair and go natural. It had been a good decision. Besides saving the beaucoup bucks she used to spend on her hair, she had liked Amir's reaction to it. She hadn't consulted him before she did it and was a little nervous about his reaction. But he had loved it. Said it focused more attention to her high cheekbones and pretty lashes. She loved it, too. Mainly because Amir cut and shaped her hair every week. Or, at least, he had.

Stop thinking about that man. Kenya pulled into a garage, took the ticket, and slowly wound her S coupe up the spiral incline. On the fifth level, she spotted an empty spot and parked.

As she made her way to the elevator, she felt a hunger pang. Maybe on the way back she would stop by Donato's for a bite to eat. Their vegetable lasagna was slamming.

Nah, that was her and Amir's spot, Kenya decided as the elevator doors opened. One of the workers there was sure to ask her about his whereabouts. Everybody in the restaurant knew him. All the waitresses loved him, partly because of his looks and personality but mainly because he was such a good tipper. She had never seen such a Big Willie in her life. Kenya chuckled. A Big Willie barber.

He had majored in business at Lincoln and had told Kenya of his plans to open his own shop in Camden. He had painstakingly planned every detail. That was one thing about him, Kenya thought. He didn't do anything half-assed. Except maybe his relationships with women.

Kenya stepped out onto the street and looked around. She then started the three-block walk to the Gallery. She put her grit on, fixing a scowl on her face. She was in the city, after all, and didn't want to look like an easy mark. Besides, Amir might just happen to "coincidentally" be at the Gallery today as well, and she wanted to be prepared in case he was. *That* nigga. She furrowed her brow even more.

July 8, 1995, 6:10 P.M.

Stupid, stupid, stupid. Amir pounded the steering wheel with his fist at the memory of Hope first entering the barbershop. He should have thrown that phone number in the trash. What had he been thinking? For once he should've listened to his brother.

That's when his slide had begun. Right there. Whenever

Kenya was unavailable to him, he became available to Hope. If Kenya went up to visit her family, he'd be with Hope. Kenya's job took her away, he'd be with Hope. It was all pretty fucking stupid.

Amir looked up through the windshield. He was parked in the gravel lot at Rancocas Park near the biking trail. Next to a sign that read, PLEASE DON'T FEED THE BIRDS. From his vantage point he could see a gaggle of geese walking in a regimented line, making their way down toward the small pond.

Amir studied the geese. He felt a kinship to them. He shouldn't be fed, either. Except his ruination wasn't junk food, but rather junk pussy.

He thought of Kenya's reaction after she heard of his betrayal. Amir closed his eyes tightly, trying to block out the look on her face, but it was embedded in his mind. Her voice was even harder to forget; it had been so filled with hurt. She had kept asking him over and over, "What did I do to you, Amir? What did I do wrong?"

Amir rubbed the bridge of his nose. That he could cause a person who wanted to do nothing but love him that kind of grief was fucking pathetic. That conversation was, without a doubt, the low point of his life. And believe me, he thought, with all the shit I have done, that's saying something.

Kenya slipped the Brownstone CD into her player. The sound of "Grapevyne" flooded her apartment. She noticed the red light on her answering machine was blinking.

She turned down the music so she could play the messages. The first one was from Tonya, asking her if she wanted to come over and watch a movie with her and Brandon. Thanks but no thanks, thought Kenya. She knew Tonya was just trying to be helpful, but the last thing Kenya needed to see was Brandon trying to keep his smug "I tried to warn your dumb ass about that nigga" expression off his face.

The next message came on. When Kenya heard the voice, she sat down and listened to it attentively until the end.

Sorry, Mrs. Moore, no can do. Kenya went over and turned

Brownstone back up. I know you mean well, but while you may
be a very sweet lady, you just happen to have a piece of shit for
a son.

July 8, 1995 8:20 P.M.

Amir hesitated before pressing the buzzer to Kenya's inter-
com. He knew there was a good chance that she wouldn't let
him up, and he wanted to say as much as possible before she
hung up. He thought of different scenarios in his head, figuring
which approach he should try. Maybe he should go with,
"*Please, it's vital I speak to you!*-(click)." Or, "*You can hate me
forever, just let me talk to you now*-(click)" Or maybe even,
"*Kenya, if you have one drop of the milk of human kindness in
your breast, you'll*-(click)"

None of these were palatable, he decided. He pressed the
buzzer.

"Hello?"

"Kenya, it's me. Can I—"

Amir was surprised to hear the door to the building unlock.
Damn, that wasn't hard at all. It was as if she expected him.
Maybe she wanted to see him as badly as he wanted to see
her.

Amir strode through the lobby and pressed the button for the
elevator. Too impatient to wait, he opened the door to the stairs
and bounded up to the third floor, where Kenya's apartment
was.

As he opened the third-floor stairwell door, he spotted
Kenya's door. The second one in on the right. It was cracked
open. Amir took a deep breath and walked to the door, grabbing the knob to go in.

He bumped against the heavy metal door.

"Kenya, can you take the chain off, please?"

"No. I don't want you in my house," Kenya said from the
kitchen.

"C'mon, sweetheart."

"Look, Amir, if you wanna talk, then I suggest you talk." Kenya made her way over to the door. She was still out of Amir's line of sight. "Your mother called me to ask me to listen to you. But I don't have to look at you."

"My mom called?"

"And it's only as a courtesy to her that you got this far. So what do you have to tell me?"

"This is silly," Amir said. "I might as well be on the phone."

"Then go call." Kenya shut the door.

"Wait, wait!"

Kenya opened the door again. This time looking into the hallway. She and Amir's eyes met for the first time.

"I'd rather stay out here," he said quietly. "This is the closest I've been to you in weeks."

Kenya quickly turned away. "Suit yourself," she said nonchalantly.

She walked back into the kitchen. Once there, she leaned against the counter and tried to gather herself. It had been a mistake to look at him.

"What are you cooking?" he asked.

She turned off the stove. "Chicken." She removed the breasts from the oven.

"It smells good."

"I would toss you the bones to gnaw on, but they're fillets. Is this what you wanted to talk to me about?" she asked, irritated.

"No." Amir slowly slid down the wall to the floor. Being so close to her and not being able to touch her was torture. He took a deep breath.

"Kenya, I miss you so much."

"Yeah?" Kenya looked in the cabinet for a side dish for her chicken.

"Yes. And I want my lady back."

"Oh? Where did Hope go?"

"She isn't my lady." Amir peered into the apartment through the sliver of opening. The only part of the apartment that was visible to him was a portion of the living room. "I need you, Kenya."

She slammed a can of creamed corn onto the counter. "Fuck what you need, Amir! Fuck what you want, and fuck what you miss! You know, it's always about you, isn't it? Let me tell you something. I have to look out for what I need and what I want, because it has become painfully clear to me that I can't trust people in my life to do so for me."

The young couple from across the hall came out of their apartment. They were on their way out. Amir knew them, Dave and Rebecca. He had played ball with Dave a couple of times at the basketball courts near the building. Amir could tell by the looks on their faces that they had heard Kenya's shouting.

"Hi," Rebecca said.

"Hi."

No words had to be exchanged between Dave and Amir. He could tell by Amir's face and his posture that he was having serious problems with his lady. Dave gave him a keep-your-head-up nod and put his hand in the small of Rebecca's back, guiding her toward the elevator.

Amir watched them as they waited to get on. Rebecca was looking over at him suspiciously. Like she wanted to be able to give the police a good description, if need be. When the elevator arrived, as she and Dave got on, he looked over at Amir and mouthed, "Good luck."

Amir turned back to the door. He heard Kenya taking a plate out of the cabinet.

"Kenya, I'm a selfish person. I know that. And part of being a selfish person is that I don't want to share anything—"

"That's not true. You don't mind *sharing* your dick."

Amir fell back against the wall, resting his elbows on his knees.

"Right? Tell me, Amir, am I right?" she asked.

His silence was pissing her off.

"What? I thought you came up here to talk. So talk. Tell me, Amir. What exactly did y'all do?"

Amir could tell from her voice she was right behind the door. "C'mon, Kenya."

"Where we going? I wanna know. Is her tongue more nimble than mine? Did her pussy taste sweeter than mine? Did she make you come harder than me?"

"No . . . no . . . no." Amir dropped his head between his knees, shaking it repeatedly.

"Then, what did you need her for?"

I don't know! Kenya, I don't know!" Amir shouted back. When he looked up, he saw that Kenya was looking down at him. "Babe, I don't know."

"What did you do with that girl?" Kenya asked again.

Amir realized she wasn't looking at him out of a desire to see him, but to determine if he was lying.

"I never had intercourse with her, Kenya. A couple of blow jobs is all."

She slammed the door in his face and buried her face in her hands. She hated the thought of another woman taking her man into her mouth. She opened the door again.

"Thanks for those cute little stuffed animals you've been sending me. You touched a lot of people. Folks think I'm Santa Claus, the way I give those things away."

Amir looked up at her.

"And thanks for all the flowers you've been sending me. The girls at my job loved them."

"You gave those away, too?"

"Of course," she scoffed.

Amir looked back down, then up at her again. "Even the peach roses, Kenya?"

She saw the hurt in his eyes, and convinced herself she liked it. "Even the peach roses, Amir."

She closed the door again.

9:27 P.M.

Kenya put her dinner plate into the dishwasher. She walked over to the door and opened it again. Amir was still in the same spot.

"You still here?"

"I ain't going nowhere," Amir answered.

"Do you mean out of my hallway, or in life in general?" She shut the door again.

10:02 P.M.

Amir knocked on the door. Kenya opened it.

"I have to go the bathroom."

"What are you telling me for?" Kenya asked.

"Can I use yours?"

"Doesn't your kind usually just lift a leg?" She shut the door again.

10:22 P.M.

Amir finally realized that Kenya had no intention of letting him go the bathroom.

"Kenya?"

"Yes," she sang sweetly.

"If I run down the street, will you let me back in the building?"

"Hmm, I don't know. Let's find out!"

10:37 P.M.

Amir got off the elevator, back on Kenya's floor. He saw that her door was cracked. As he approached, he heard music playing.

"Thanks for letting me back up." Amir settled back down on the floor, unwrapping his burger. He then recognized the song that was playing. "If This World Were Mine."

"Is that song for me?" he asked.

The song abruptly stopped. He heard some rustling and then

a couple of seconds later the sound of Bob Marley's "Waiting In Vain" cascaded down upon him, right before the door closed again.

11:03 P.M.

Amir knocked on the door. Kenya opened it.

"I don't feel well."

Kenya looked down at the remains of Amir's burger and fries.

"I guess not. You know you can't eat that garbage." She looked at his pitiful expression. "Hold on."

Kenya went to the cabinet and made Amir a glass of Alka-Seltzer and brought it back to the door. Amir stood up and grabbed it. "Thank you."

"Give me that stuff, so I can throw it away."

Amir picked up the food, put it in its bag, and handed it to Kenya.

"I don't know what made you think you could eat this junk," she said, irritated.

"I was hungry," Amir said in between gulps.

"Even so, you can't eat just anything." She looked at his face. "I would've fed you, Amir."

She saw the look of hope on his face that last remark had elicited.

"Don't get me wrong. The same way I would feed any other stray dog."

Amir finished his drink. "Kenya, you can make all the canine references you want. I deserve them. But will you please not close the door anymore?"

As he handed the glass back to her, their fingers touched.

Kenya thought it over for a second, then sat down next to the door. Amir sat back down in the hallway.

They sat in silence. After a couple of minutes passed, Amir finally spoke.

"Kenya, listen. I wasn't being truthful with you before. I do know why I messed around on you."

Kenya closed her eyes, and set the glass and the bag in between her legs. She girded herself for the worst. Amir continued.

"Earlier this evening I was in Rancocas Park. I wasn't doing much of anything, just parked along the side, thinking. Well, I noticed these geese, right? They looked like little soldiers on their way to the front line. Their leader was marching them down to the water, and the rest of them were following him blindly, seemingly oblivious to where he was leading them. If he had walked into the mouth of an alligator, I think the rest would have followed. It was learned behavior: following the leader. Not one of them looked ahead or around the line, to see where they were going. Just at the back of the goose ahead of them."

Kenya opened her eyes.

"Well, I saw myself in that line, but I most definitely wasn't the leader. I was a follower. You see, all my life I've been led to believe that men take pussy when it is offered to them. A man can't be expected to turn down some pussy thrown in his face. It is a rite of manhood, to sample as many women as you can. The finer the woman, the better. The more women you do, the better. Because if you fuck enough of them, you are held in a higher regard by other men. In a sense, I guess you're the lead goose.

"In reality, with men there is no lead goose, because instead of walking in a line we really just walk in one big circle. Chasing tail. I catch the most, so I've been voted the lead goose."

"I thought you said you were a follower," Kenya said quietly.

"I am. I'm a leader and a follower. Niggas admire me, but for what? 'Cause I'm better able to bullshit and use women? The way I see it, even the leader is doomed because he's *following* a faulty belief system. Hell, he sees the alligator's mouth open, but is too foolish and brainwashed to avoid it. For some guys, the alligator is death, killed by a scorned woman or a jealous boyfriend. Or by AIDS. Or it can be unwanted pregnancies, spending your life supporting kids you never wanted and will never see. Or jail, for any of a number of stupid things you can do chasing the wrong tail. My alligator is regret. Because I know

I've lost the love and respect of the only woman I have ever loved."

He took a breath before he continued.

"Kenya, you're the first person in my life that has made me question and redefine what manhood is. Manhood for me would be to hold you in my arms for the rest of my life. I'm in love with you." Amir reached for her.

Kenya avoided his touch by getting up to take the glass and bag into the kitchen. She wiped her eyes before she walked back and sat down beside the door.

"Amir, why did you tell me?"

"What do you mean?"

"I mean, you might have been able to get away with it. I doubt if that bitch Racquel would have ever told me." Kenya looked at him.

"I couldn't have her walking around thinking she had something on you. Smiling in your face while knowing—"

"That my man ain't shit," Kenya finished for him.

Amir shrugged his shoulders defeatedly.

Kenya emitted a soft chuckle. "You missed it. I damn near strangled the life out of that bitch."

"Yeah? I was wondering."

"I caught her coming out of Bible study, in the parking lot. I put the foot to her. People were like 'Sister Kenya! Sister Kenya!' They finally pulled me off her. After I told them what she did, the rest of them were in agreement that she had needed her ass kicked. You should have seen it. Fake nails and tracks were flying everywhere."

They both chuckled. Kenya quickly stopped.

"Regardless of whether you were entrapped or not, you should've known better." Kenya said.

"I know, I know." Amir exhaled and shifted his weight.

"Amir, understand something. What hurts the most is the betrayal. You didn't just bump into this girl and have a onetime fling. You plotted on me. You planned rendezvous. While I was spending damn near every moment of my life thinking about you, how badly I love you, you were scheming on me. That you could look me in the face after being with her . . . that scares me to death. It leaves me cold. Don't you understand that?"

Amir stared at his sneakers. "What can I tell you? I'm an accomplished liar, Kenya. I've been lying to women since I was fifteen years old. This is probably the first totally honest conversation I've had with a woman other than my mother in my entire life. I'm not proud of that."

There was a hush between them. The silence was broken by Kenya's whimpering.

Amir again reached for her. This time he succeeded in grabbing her hand. She squeezed back tightly. She turned to face him.

"Amir, listen to me. I love you to death, you know that, so I'm not gonna even try to deny it. However, it's over between us. I refuse to be your fool."

"Please don't say that to me." Amir let her hand go and rubbed his eyes.

"What do you want from me? Surely you can't expect me to believe it won't happen again. Can you?"

"Kenya, if you want an absolute oen-hundred-percent guarantee that I would never cheat on you again, I can't give you that. Life offers no such guarantees, and anybody that says it does is lying. And as badly as I want to kiss your lips and hold you in my arms, if saying that is what it's gonna take to do so, then I can't do it. What I can tell you is that I have a one-hundred-percent belief that I can make you happy."

"Until the next time you break my heart," Kenya said softly.

"You're gonna have to have faith in me. What I do know is that if I have an ounce of sense, I won't do *anything* to risk losing you again."

She shook her head emphatically. "You're too big a gamble for me, Amir."

"If you love me as you say you do, Kenya, it's a gamble you're just gonna have to take. You can't afford *not* to."

Kenya stared at the floor.

"I wouldn't ask you to bet on me if I didn't think I could make you happy, Kenya. I'm being real with you. I know that I don't deserve you. But as I was saying before, I'm a selfish person. I know that if I don't make you my wife, I'll regret it for the rest of my days."

Kenya closed her eyes at the mention of "wife." She and Amir had never discussed marriage.

"Happy anniversary, Kenya."

"Huh?"

"It's after midnight, July 9. We met one year ago today."

Kenya thought about it for a second and let out a dry chuckle. "Oh, yeah. Happy anniversary," she said quietly.

"Remember our first date? We saw that movie," he said.

Kenya looked over at the picture on her wall. The framed poster of *I Like It Like That*.

"That was an appropriate movie for us to see," Kenya said, "Nino was as roguish as you, the way he ran around on Lisette."

"And Lisette gave him another chance, flaws and all, because she loved him. And knew he loved her."

"That's not how I remember it," Kenya said. "All she did was leave the door open to the *possibility* of them getting back together."

"That's all I want from you, Kenya. To leave the door open."

Kenya stood up and stretched. "I'm going to bed, Amir."

"Good night."

She looked down at him. "You're going home now. Right?"

"That depends. Are you back in my life?"

Kenya shook her head.

"Then even if I wanted to go, I don't think I could. Not when everything dear to me is here and still up in the air."

"Suit yourself. Good night." Kenya decided he wasn't really foolish enough to sleep in a hallway. She closed the door and locked it.

"I love you, Kenya."

I love you, too, Amir, she thought. She ran her fingertips over the door. But you aren't getting back into my bed, pants, or life. At least not for a while you ain't. She turned out the lights and went into the bedroom.

2:13 A.M.

Amir was sitting on the top step in the stairwell. The door was propped open by his leaning against it. He was fighting sleep when he heard a sound that jolted him awake.

Someone on the floor was unlocking a door and taking the chain off. Then again, it could have been someone locking the door and putting the chain on, he couldn't be sure.

But he was hopeful.

Amir got up to go see if Kenya had left the door open.

Money Can't Buy Me Love

E. Lynn Harris

I didn't mean to fall in love. It just happened.

It was the first Valentine's Day in the new century, and like many V-Days in the last century, I was prepared to spend it alone. I know love don't love black women and black gay men, especially like in romance novels or the movies. I'm the latter. So when my best friend, Keith aka Thunder, called me and asked me to help out with a party he was catering, I said yes immediately because at least it meant I wouldn't spend the evening drinking champagne alone.

Thunder, whose mother still calls him by his full name, Keith Dwayne Carey, is the owner of a successful catering firm called Diva Delicacies. He is a tall, slender, tea-colored man with an angular and gentle face. He has remarkable brown eyes, with the long lashes of a female and long braids that could rival pop star Brandy. Thunder fashioned himself as a gay B. Smith and on some occasions Martha Stewart, whose show he watched or taped daily. He only did small intimate parties for members of the Ghetto Fabulous set, white literary types and a few corporations like *Essence* and *Later Today*. The Valentine's affair was for a few members of the GGF, (Gay Ghetto Fabu) up in the Sugar Hill area of Harlem. Keith needed a waiter, because one of his employees decided he shouldn't have to be a server, especially when he was sleeping with the owner on occasion. It didn't matter that he was married and had another girlfriend, besides Keith on the side.

After spending a couple of hours serving a five-course meal, and envying the well-dressed couples drinking imported champagne from tall crystal flutes, I was promising myself that, no matter how much I loved Keith, this was the last time I was going to serve anything but great sex. Not that I'd had the opportunity to do that in recent memory. Which is really where this story begins.

After the event I stopped at Keith's Upper West Side brownstone for a drink and some conversation. We were sitting on stools in his large industrial-sized kitchen. I was feeling warm by my second glass of red wine, when Thunder said, "You seemed kinda uptight tonight. When's the last time you had some dick?" Tact wasn't one of Thunder's assets. When I couldn't remember after two long sips of my wine, I knew I was due.

"That long, huh?" Keith quizzed

"How can I meet anyone? Where is there a time when I'm not teaching or helping out my best friend?"

"When it comes to sex, you need to make time. Besides, I know you got to run across some fine men up on that campus."

"You know my policy about dating students," I said.

"Yeah, but that's your policy, not the school's. They knew you were gay when they hired you."

"I just wouldn't feel right. What if I get with some guy and then have to give him a grade other than an A. I'll have to use my savings to defend myself in a lawsuit," I said as I poured myself a third glass of wine.

When I turned to fill Keith's empty glass, he smiled slightly to himself and then began giggling.

"What's so funny?" I asked.

"I was just thinking maybe I could do a little summthin'—summthin' to help you release some of that tension," Thunder smiled.

"Now, baby, you know I love you but we agreed not to roll like that," I said. I had one rule I always lived by and that was never, under any circumstances, sleep with friends. No matter how horny I was.

"Child, please. Now, you know me better than that."

"Then, how are you going to help me relieve my so-called tension?"

"Maybe you deserve a little bonus for saving my butt tonight. Those grand girls we just finished serving gave me a really nice tip."

"Yeah, but how is that gonna help me with my sex life?"

Keith pulled out a cigarette, lit it, inhaled, and waved the match like it was a magic wand, then said, "Let me worry about that. I need to make a phone call."

After Keith left, I leaned on the large butcher-block island, where Keith usually prepared some of his legendary dishes like stuffed catfish and Slap Yo Mama chicken wings. I was moving toward the sink to wash my hands when Keith walked back in the kitchen with a smile spread across his face. When he handed me a twenty dollar bill, I asked, "What's this for?"

"You need to be home in an hour. I got a little Valentine present waiting for you."

"What or should I say who?"

"I'm not at liberty to speak on it. But trust me . . . you would want to take a taxi, even if that means catching a gypsy cab, Mr. Grand Diva."

"Diva? I'm no diva. Can't I just take the subway?"

"Whatever. Just be at home in an hour. Take a shower and spruce yourself up."

"Should I do this?"

"Don't just do it for yourself. Do it for all of us who love you. Get all that tension out of your face," Keith said as he gave me a kiss on the cheek.

I put on my jacket and walked out into a cool Harlem night. I looked at my watch and realized it was almost eleven o'clock. I walked a couple of blocks east toward Lennox Avenue with the intention of catching the subway, when a small miracle happened. Waiting for the light to change, I looked to my left and saw an empty yellow taxi. I noticed the out-of-service light wasn't illuminated. I made eye contact with the driver, and he nodded for me to get in. And he wasn't black.

"Where to?" he asked with a heavy accent that had a Russian lilt.

"Down in the village, 95 Christopher Street. It's west of Bleeker."

"Which way do you want me to go?"

This was too good to be true, I thought as I instructed the driver to go down the West Side Highway.

My name is James Whitmore Thorton, but my friends call me Jimmy. In another life, right outside of St. Louis, Missouri, I was known as Dr. James Thorton III. I come from a family of physicians, all educated at Meharry Medical School in Nashville, Tennessee. My grandfather was the first African-American chief of staff at the St. Louis Medical Center. My father had a thriving family practice located on Kingshighway and Natural Bridge. There was a time in St. Louis when if you were colored (that's the term they used then) chances were you were delivered into the world by my father or grandfather.

After my father retired, I took over his practice. He and my mom moved to Florida, where they lived until they both died within six months of each other. A year later I sold the practice and moved to New York with the notion I too had retired from medicine.

It wasn't a decision I came to easily. I had many sleepless nights. It just seemed like the right thing to do after several of my father's patients and some of my own left when the *St. Louis Afro-American* published the fact that I was the first African-American president of GDOA (Gay Doctors of America). I thought it was a good thing at the time I was elected. I had done something that wasn't tied to my father or my grandfather. Even though in fairness to them, it would have been a difficult position for them to achieve, since they were both happily heterosexual. And I never would have run for the post or done the interview if either of them were still alive. Yet while wallowing in my sadness over the rejection of my community, I started to think about my life in the first grade. I loved my teacher, Mr. Wilson. He was the kindness man I had ever met. I knew then I wanted to be a teacher. That was my dream. It was only when my parents started sending me to science camps as a teenager that I realized I was expected to go in the family business. It was their very demanding dream.

*   *   *

About fifteen minutes later I was walking through my lobby and into the elevator to my ninth-floor one-bedroom apartment. I took off my white shirt and black tux pants, which smelled like smoke, and threw them into the hall closet. I went into the bathroom and started the shower, waiting a few minutes for it to get hot, and then to the small kitchen. I poured myself a glass of cranberry juice and put in my newly purchased Macy Gray CD.

After my shower, I put on my navy blue rayon pajama bottoms with drawstrings and my white cotton robe. I sprayed on some of my cheap, but sweet-smelling unisex cologne I purchased at the Gap every month. The scent was called Heaven.

I was on my way to the kitchen for my final glass of wine for the evening when the apartment phone buzzed.

"Yes," I said anxiously.

"Mr. Thorton, this is Julio. You have a guest."

"Who?" I could hear Julio ask, "What did you say your name was?" I heard a deep voice say, "Trevor Smith. Tell him Thunder sent me."

"Mr. Thorton, the gentleman's name is Mr. Smith. He said Thunder sent him."

"Send him up," I said. When I hung up the phone, I raced into the bedroom and quickly flossed my teeth. I was rinsing my mouth with mouthwash when I heard a knock at the door.

I put a touch of lip balm on my lips and exhaled a deep breath and suddenly wished I hadn't stopped my thrice weekly workout with a trainer. Thunder had even treated me too; when he realized he couldn't *have* the handsome young man, he begged me to complete his three-month contract. I suddenly realized that having Jeffrey press his hand against my stomach as I tried to do sit-ups was the last time I had felt the touch of a man. That was six months ago.

I opened the door, and my knees seemed to buckle. Standing before me was a handsome man with a huge smile and some corner-store pink roses. His skin was the color of French vanilla ice cream mixed with caramel. Yellow boys were my weakness.

"Hi, I'm Trevor. I'm your present from your best friend Thunder," he said with boyish charm. For a few seconds I was silent, and didn't speak until he pushed the roses toward me and said, "These are for you."

"Thank you," I mumbled.

"Are you going to invite me in?" Trevor asked.

"Oh, I'm sorry. Come in."

Trevor walked in with a confident, masculine-trade aura, as he surveyed the small foyer, right off the living and dining area. "Nice place you got here."

"It's all right," I said. I was feeling a mixture of nervousness and excitement. I couldn't remember the last time a man had brought me flowers or even been in my apartment when he wasn't delivering food or packages. I was wondering what he meant by describing himself as my present. My birthday was a couple months away. I asked him if I could hang up the short wine-colored jacket he was wearing.

"Sure," he said as he removed the jacket. "What time is it?" he asked.

I hung his jacket in the closet and then glanced in the kitchen at my microwave digital clock.

"It's twelve-thirty," I said.

He looked at his watch and said, "I just wanted to make sure I had the right time."

"Would you like something to drink?"

"No, that's okay. I'm not a big drinker."

I walked back into the kitchen and poured myself a half glass of wine. When I walked back into the living area, Trevor was still standing. His jeans were black and tight, and he was wearing a sky blue V-neck sweater.

"Have a seat," I offered.

"Don't you want to see your present?" he asked.

I looked over at the dining room table, where I had placed the roses, and thought I should put them in some water. I assumed he was talking about the roses, so I gazed at the flowers and then back at Trevor. I noticed his steady hazel-brown eyes that were glittering with mischief. His closely cropped hair had so many waves that I was feeling seasick.

"Are you talking about the roses?" I asked. There was that word *present* again.

"I'm not talking about the roses," he said as he began to sway slowly to the sounds of Macy Gray. He moved like a backup dancer, accent on the hips and dips. Without a hint of shyness, he kicked off his loafers, then removed his jeans and sweater seductively. A few seconds later he was totally nude. He had a smooth body and a beautifully defined chest, a butt that looked like water-filled balloons and a splendid erection, which curved slightly to the left. He had several ropelike tattoos on his arms and a butterfly on his ass. I'm not a fan of body art, but tonight it looked just fine. Trevor's body was flawless, his face so handsome, that the total package seemed blinding and I felt almost afraid to look.

"Are you going to join me, or would you like for me to do the honors?" he asked as his eyes and body danced flirtatiously.

I didn't know what to say. It was like my body was taking sides against me. My brain was telling me that I didn't even know this handsome stranger, who could have all kinds of diseases. At least I knew he wasn't carrying a weapon, if you didn't count the banana-sized penis, he was obviously proud of. I tried telling myself that maybe this was the dream man I had been waiting for, and sleeping with him minutes after our first meeting might not be wise. But the lower part of my body was making it's desire known.

The message was loud and clear: *Don't think about it . . . let's git it on.*

Trevor moved toward me and rested his arms around my waist. His hands were firm, and I could feel his penis press against me. I was hard too, and only a drawstring was keeping us apart. He smelled like Dove soap and citrus. I removed his hands, moved back and looked at his eyes and said, "Let's talk. I want to know more about you." Once again, my mind was directing my body.

Trevor game me a sly smile and asked, "What do you want to know?"

"Are you from New York?"

"I've lived here for over ten years. What about yourself?" The tone of his voice had changed slightly from a sexy street sound to one of an Ivy League college student.

"I'm from the Midwest. St. Louis. Have you ever been there?"

"No, can't say I have," Trevor said.

"Why don't we have a seat?" I said as I pointed toward my small sofa.

Trevor took a seat, and before I sat down I still didn't know if I should offer him a drink or a room. I felt more than a little awkward, especially because I was certain this was the first time that I had entertained a naked man on my sofa. I tried to concentrate on his eyes rather than staring at his still-hard manhood. My mind whirled with possibilities. Was this beautiful man a hustler or just being nice to a man in need? Was he some kind of sex addict who just loved sex? There was only one way to find out. Ask the question.

"What do you mean when you say you're my present?"

"Oh, it's just my way of saying I hope that when we finish, you'll consider me a gift in more ways than one."

"So you're not a hustler?" If the answer was yes, then I was prepared to drop a condom on his manhood and ride without feelings or emotions. I knew I couldn't turn a hustler into a husband.

"No, I'm not a hustler. I'm just friendly and horny," Trevor said in an assured voice.

"Are you sure you don't want something to drink? I have water. I mean I have a filter on my sink if you're worried about the water," I offered.

"Naw, I'll pass. Let's talk so we can get down to business."

"How do you know Thunder?"

"I didn't come here to talk about Thunder," he said as he gripped my knee.

"What do you do for a living?" I asked as I removed his hand.

"You mean during the day?"

"Yeah," I said, wondering what the question meant.

"I'm sorta between jobs," Trevor said. "What do you do?"

"I'm a teacher."

"What do you teach?"

"Chemistry."

"I don't really get into the sciences. Do you teach high school or college?"

"College. I teach at Fordham University."

"Aw, Fordham, near Columbus Circle. I took some classes there," Trevor said as he seductively rubbed his chest and licked his lips like there was something sweet covering them.

"What kind of classes?"

"Writing."

"Are you a writer?"

"You can say that," Trevor said as he stared at me with a laser gaze. He licked his lips again and then gently touched the side of my face and said, "Has anyone told you how nice lookin' you are?" I never considered myself attractive. I'm a C-plus on a good day. I'm Tootsie Roll brown with short coarse hair. I do have near perfect teeth from years of braces. I'm about five foot nine inches and weigh about 177 pounds. I got my father's broad nose and my mother's full lips and booty. My sister got our father's high African-like butt and my mother's high yellow coloring.

I felt my face grow warm from Trevor's touch. I knew I was blushing. Instead of answering Trevor's question, I jumped up from the sofa and said, "I know you must be cold. Let me get a robe or a towel."

"You don't have to do that, but if my body makes you nervous, then I'll cover up. This evening is all about you."

I went into my bathroom and pulled out a thick green-and-white beach towel. I was still uncertain as to what I was going to do or should do. Have sex with Trevor, or try and get to know him and pray he'd call me the next day. I started to call Thunder and get some information, but I thought it would be rude to leave Trevor alone. I walked back into the living room and dropped the towel in Trevor's lap, covering up the beautiful view I had enjoyed. I went into the kitchen and got a glass of cranberry juice. I decided I didn't want anything that might cloud my judgment.

I was greeted by Trevor's beautiful smile when I walked back into the living area. "What's that smile about?" I asked.

"Just glad to see you," Trevor said.

I sat down on the sofa and asked Trevor where he attended school.

"You mean college or high school?"

"College?"

"I started out at the University of North Carolina on a soccer scholarship. I finished up at Hunter College on the East Side."

"What did you major in?"

"English and creative writing."

"So what are you doing now? Working on the great American novel?" I asked as I giggled nervously.

"That is my day job. But right at this minute I'm trying to seduce this very good-looking man sitting in front of me. Are you a top or a bottom?"

I hated that question. I felt it limited your possibilities in bed, so I gave my standard answer. "That depends who's on the other side of the bed."

"I feel you. So are we finished talking?" Trevor asked as he picked up his silver watch from the table and stared at it intently for a few seconds. I didn't remember his taking it off during his quick striptease.

"Tell me about your novel."

"I'm not here to talk about my work. I tell you what, though; maybe I'll let you read it one day."

"That would be nice."

"Am I still making you nervous?"

"I'm not nervous."

"Are you sure?"

"Yeah, I'm sure. But just understand that I would like to know more about you before we hit the sheets," I said.

"That's nice. I can't remember the last time someone wanted to know anything about me other than my dick size. Which, in case you're interested, is a solid eight and a half. Thick," Trevor said seductively.

"Good to know," I said, wondering why I didn't just pounce on Trevor. But I wanted to see him again. I can't count how many one-night stands I've had without my permission. I wanted to read his novel and talk about the books we'd read. The movies he loved and what he did for fun. I had a urge to kiss, but feared he might be one of those "I don't kiss" boys. He had been free with his hands, but I knew a lot of men Thunder dated didn't like to kiss. My friend didn't share his men freely. However, anytime he ran across someone who aspired for more than his next forty ounce, then he'd send them me, which wasn't that often. Thunder could discern a wine drinker from a beer guzzler in a heartbeat.

Over the next couple of hours I became mesmerized by Trevor and his knowledge on a wide range of subjects from art to music. When he spoke it was with a passion I found rare in young African-American men. My thoughts of his being a hustler went out the window. Trevor couldn't be a play-for-pay man. Not that I had ever considered paying for sex.

"So tell me more about yourself," Trevor said.

"What do you want to know?"

"Do your parents know you're gay?"

"They did. They're dead," I said, suddenly remembering my very loving, but snobbish parents. They did know I was gay, but we never talked about it. I had known I was gay since I realized Mickey was a mouse. Age nine. I was never interested in little girls with the exception of the power they held over little boys. There were times when I thought I was the only African-American man who accepted my sexuality and didn't try to change it by sleeping with women or pretending to be one.

"I'm sorry to hear that," Trevor said, breaking me out of my trance.

"How tall are you?" I asked, trying hard not to be placed under some type of magic spell. I felt like I was about to embark on a journey where I was looking forward to each and every step.

"I'm six foot three inches and 212 pounds. Solid," he said as he slapped both his hands on his iron-flat stomach. The sound brought chills to my arms.

"Do you mind telling me your age?" I asked.

"Twenty-nine."

"Oh, that's a great age."

"Every year seems to be a little better," Trevor said with a glint of sadness in his eyes.

"What's the last book you read?" I asked.

"Fiction or nonfiction?"

"Both."

"*Jazz* by Toni Morrison and Michael Dyson's book about Martin Luther King."

Morrison and Dyson, I thought. I was impressed. Reading had never been a requirement for Thunder's men.

"I also love Cornell West and Bell Hooks. What about you? What's the last book you read?"

"I don't get a chance to read a lot when school is in session. But the last novel I read was *White Boy Shuffle* by Paul Beatty."

"Never heard of it."

"It was good. Maybe I'll get you a copy," I said as I reached for my juice and took a sip.

"Great. I love gifts," Trevor said as he picked up his watch again. This was not a good sign. I was certain somebody must be waiting at home for this beautiful man.

"What time to do you have to be there?" I asked. It was my smart, roundabout way of asking what time he had to leave. I hoped this guy was married. Thunder knew better. He knew I didn't do married or confused. Which meant bye-bye bisexuals. That was just asking for heartbreak.

"It's getting close. Time just went so fast. I guess that's what happens when you meet someone who's nice to talk to," Trevor said as he stood up. The towel fell to the floor, and his penis still hung beautifully. It was soft now, a little reduction in size, but still larger than an average *husband*-sized dick.

"You have to leave now?"

"Yeah, I think I better. But if you're interested in seeing me again, your friend knows how to reach me."

"Can I get your number?"

"Why don't we wait and see how you feel tomorrow." I already knew how I would feel tomorrow, and the married question popped into my head again as I quickly wrote down my number on a piece of paper.

Trevor walked toward the dining area and picked up his jeans, which were hanging across one of my dining room chairs. As he put them on, he looked at me and said, "If you want to see me again, then you're gonna have to let me know. I'm thinking I might not be your type."

"What do you think my type is?" I asked a I moved toward Trevor. I wanted to smell him one more time before he put his shirt on.

"I'm still trying to figure that out. But I like your style and willpower. I don't know a lot of men or women who can resist my charms when they are so apparent," he said in his cocky tone, which I was lovin'.

"That's fair. I don't mind if I have to do a little work," I said as I watched Trevor tuck his T-shirt into his unzipped jeans.

As Trevor zipped up his jeans, he suddenly patted his backside as if he was checking for his wallet and said, "I can say this was one of the most unusual dates I've ever had. But it was cool and I think you're kinda cool." Then he move close to me and gave me a gentle kiss on my cheek, and I slipped my number in the back pocket of his jeans.

"Till next time," he said as he opened the door. I didn't say anything as the door closed. I was too busy praying that the *next time* meant tomorrow.

About ten minutes after Trevor left, I was still thinking about my family and decided to call my sister, Carmen. I wanted to share my big night with her. She loved hearing from me when I had good news. I dialed her number, but got her answering machine after one ring. This meant she was probably on the phone or not taking calls. Maybe she had gotten lucky too.

"Hey, baby girl. This is your big brother. Didn't want anything. Just thinking about you," I said and hung up the phone.

My family was close-knit, but we weren't like a black *Leave It to Beaver* gang where we would sit around the dinner table and discuss our personal lives. It was more like a don't-ask, don't-tell family. We didn't talk about the fact that I had never had a girlfriend or that my room was covered with pictures of the Jackson Five and Smokey Robinson. I swear I was in love with Tito during the week, and Jackie on the weekends. We certainly didn't talk about the ugly incident that happened at my family's annual Christmas party one year. A party that of all of St. Louis's black elite (a couple hundred in number) waited with baited breath to see if my mother had them on the list.

I was home from my first semester in undergrad at the University of Missouri at Columbia, when one of my parent's guests, Mrs. Lillian Deauville, had a little too much to drink and announced to a stunned crowd that I was having an affair with her husband, Dr. Donald Deauville, one of my father's closest friends. Neither my mother nor I ever cared that much for the hard-drinking Lillian.

I didn't admit it or deny it, but I know my silence and the look on my face and the good doctor's spoke volumes. We also didn't talk about how my parents practically forced Carmen to marry a guy she didn't love because they knew she was their only source for grandchildren. Carmen married Malcolm Kennedy from Columbus, Georgia, after her freshman year at Fisk University in Nashville. Ten months later, my pride-and-joy nephew Darius was born. When I sold the practice, I split the proceeds with Carmen. She used the money to get a divorce, and bought herself a nice house in a gated community near downtown Atlanta. Like me, she was now in search of her soul mate. Tonight I was wondering which one of us was on the brink of that dream.

I woke up the next morning thinking about Trevor. Why would someone as attractive as Trevor want to date someone like me? I was thinking I had been a fool for passing up the opportunity to sleep with one of the most beautiful men I had ever seen. Still, I was hopeful when I dialed Thunder's number to get more detailed information on the mystery man. The phone rang about five times before the answering machine picked up. I hung up because I had too many questions to leave on a machine.

At age thirty-eight, I have been in love only once, since I couldn't count Jackie, Tito, or Smokey. My sexless affair lasted only a couple of months. His name was Jude, and I met him on a Sunday afternoon in Washington, D.C., at a bar called Tracks. When I lived in St. Louis, I would always take a two-week vacation to the East Coat. I would spend a week in New York, a day in Philly and then head to D.C. just in time for Memorial Day weekend, when Black Gay Pride is celebrated with parties and self-love. A lot of friends from medical school lived there, and every night each of them would give a dinner party in my honor. Each day was more festive than the one before. During the weekend the city swells with beautiful, well-toned black men for a four-day fest of parties, sex, drinking, more sex and very little sleep.

Going to Tracks was a Sunday-evening ritual for me. I would start the morning at Metropolitan Baptist Church and have brunch at the Capitol Hill Hyatt. Then it was on to the gym to make sure I was at least looking presentable when I entered Tracks, where looks were everything and a tight body was all. I never really went to Tracks in hopes of finding "true love," but I was happy to settle for a four-day fling and to be able to dance with black men to black music.

So there I was wondering if I had made the right choice in wearing an all-white linen ensemble and open-toe sandals. My friends and I were drinking beer and cruising men, when this tall, beautiful man walked by. He was wearing tight white tennis shorts and a white muscle T-shirt. He looked at me. I looked at him, and then his eyes darted in the direction of one of my friends, Royce, who said hello and invited the stranger to join our small group. While he and Royce were talking, he kept smiling my way. A few minutes later, Royce introduced us, and when he shook my hand, my knees actually buckled. He was golden brown, the color of cashew peanuts, with sandy-brown

hair and eyes to match. He told me he was a professional tennis
player ranked in the top three hundred in the world, which
meant he had to work as a waiter to supplement his income. I
couldn't believe Jude spent the entire evening talking to me, despite the fact that almost every man that walked past us tried to
capture his attention. I was both surprised and pleased when
Jude offered to take me to lunch and to the Frederick Douglass
house the following Monday.

It was the best Monday of my life. I stayed an extra week in
D.C. after I met Jude, and spent every day with him. We cooked
lobster dinners, rode bikes near Washington National Airport
and drank wine until we fell asleep. We smiled broadly every
time our eyes met, which was almost every second of the day.
When my vacation funds ran out, he invited me to his tiny one-
bedroom apartment in Dupont Circle. The three nights I spent
with him, I was as giddy as a high school cheerleader performing in her first pep rally. I had never met anyone whose every
word I hung on, still wanting to know more. The only thing
missing was the passionate lovemaking I longed for. The first
night we met, I asked Jude if he was interested in me. He said
yes with a sweet and simple kiss. But kissing was as far as it
went. I thought maybe he was just being nice and trying not to
hurt my feelings, or was hoping that he felt as I did and knew
we had the rest of our life to make love.

When I got back to St. Louis, Jude called every day for about
a month. I made an unannounced weekend trip to D.C., and he
seemed pleased, but didn't offer his bed. When I returned back
home this time, the calls stopped, and when I managed to reach
him, Jude seemed distant. Some days I would call at least five
times, page him and even leave messages at the restaurant where
he sometimes waited tables. I know in some states they call my
actions stalking. But I became worried that something was
wrong or even worse, that Jude had lost interest in me.

When I finally did reach him, his conversation was short,
telling me he would call me right back. I would spend the
night literally staring at the phone, trying to will it to ring. It
didn't. Then I did something really stupid. I got on a plane to

Washington, D.C., rented a car and drove to Jude's apartment. I rang his buzzer and didn't get an answer. While returning to my car, I saw Jude approaching his apartment, with a short dark-skinned brother. They were both wearing tennis whites, and had several rackets hanging from their shoulders. I turned around so they wouldn't see me and returned to the car to debate what I should do next. An hour later I was ringing his buzzer again. This time he answered. I could tell he was shocked, because he repeated my name twice to make sure he had heard me correctly. When he came down to the door, I could tell from his face he was neither happy nor excited to see me.

"What are you doing here?" he demanded.

"I was worried about you," I stuttered.

"I told you I would call," he said.

"But you didn't. Can I come in?" I asked.

"I don't think that's such a good idea. I have company."

I was heartbroken, but still I couldn't just leave. "Do you want me to wait until later?"

"I don't think so. Look, I have to go. Maybe you should just tear my number up," Jude said as he closed the door in my face.

I cried most of the way home, with my face pressed against the window of the plane, gazing at the clouds, like they were going to provide an answer.

I didn't hear or see Jude until almost a year later. It was Memorial Day weekend, and I bumped into him as I was about to enter the Florida Avenue Grill, near Howard University. Jude looked startled, and so did I. But I was even more shocked, because Jude didn't look like Jude. He was skin and bones, and his handsome face was missing his deep dimples. He looked at me and smiled, then grabbed my hands tightly and said in a whisper, "It's good seeing you."

"You too," I mumbled and then Jude was gone.

Two weeks later, I got a call from a friend of his telling me Jude had passed away. I didn't have to ask how or why, but I did have a question. "How long did he know?" I asked. There was silence on the line, and then his friend Joseph said, "He found out over a year ago. Right after he met you. I know I shouldn't be telling you this, but I think you should know."

"What?" I asked anxiously.

"Jude really loved you."

I was silent and tears began to roll down my cheeks.

"Jimmy, are you still there?"

"Yes," I said. "How do you know he loved me?"

"Because he told me. He was ready to spend the rest of his life with you. That's why he got tested. Unfortunately, when he got the results, he knew he didn't have much time. A year wasn't enough. And when he couldn't have you forever, he shut you out of his life. But even then, he talked about you all the time and the wonderful time you guys had."

"Thank you for telling me. It really means a lot to me," I said as I hung up the phone, cherishing the knowledge that I had loved, and was loved for the first time in my adult life.

After about six calls, I finally talked with Thunder. It was about 11:30 P.M., and I was getting ready for bed when I decided to give him another call. I was a little bit worried, because he usually always called me back, especially when I had called more than twice. I had even tried his cell phone twice.

This time he picked up after about three rings, but his voice was a mere whisper.

"Did you get my messages?" I asked.

"Yeah, baby. I'm sorry. It's been a day from hell. Is everything all right?"

"I'm fine. Why are you whispering?"

"My trade is fast asleep, and, honey, I want to keep him that way. I'm so tired I can't even just lay here and take the dick. I had three events today, and of course two people didn't show up. I'm going to start only hiring Mexicans. They seemed to be the only ones who want to work," Thunder said. "These black children will read you in a minute because they know they can walk right down the street and get another job for a day or two."

"Thank you for last night," I said.

"Did you have a good time?"

"I had a grand time."

"Good."

"Can I get his number? I want to see him again."

"He didn't give you his number?"

"No, he told me you'd know how to get in contact with him."

"He did?"

"Yeah. How long have you known him?"

"Huh?"

"How long have you known him," I repeated. "Where did you meet him?"

"Darling, can we talk about this later? I'm so tired," Thunder said. His voice suddenly sounded evasive.

"Sure. But when? I've been thinking about Trevor all day."

"Trevor?"

"Yeah, Trevor. The friend you sent."

"Oh yeah, I'm sorry, Jimmy. I'm so tired. Why don't we meet at Stella's on Friday night? There is something I need to tell you about *my* friend Trevor," Thunder said.

"What? Is it something bad?"

"No, it's nothing. Can we talk on Friday?"

"Sure. Call me and let me know what time."

"I will. I just have a small party Friday evening, and it's near Stella's. Maybe, I'll even hire a car service so we can do some barhopping. We haven't done that in a while."

"Okay. Sounds like fun," I said as I hung up the phone, wondering what Thunder was going to tell me about Trevor.

Friday came painfully slow. I prayed Trevor would call, but he didn't. Every time my phone rang at home or my office, I picked up after the first ring. I even answered the phone during my conferences with students, something I never did. I kept telling myself that maybe he or his wife had washed the jeans with my number still wedged in his pockets.

I took the subway to the Forty-second Street station and walked the twelve blocks to Stella's. It was a cool, moonless February evening, and Eighth Avenue was busy with theatergoers leaving restaurants and heading for an eight o'clock curtain. I stopped at a restaurant called JR's and had a cheeseburger and some lentil soup, drinking only cranberry juice, since I realized the night was still young. Maybe Thunder had planned another surprise for me and was going to show up at the club with Trevor on his arm. Now that would be the way to end to the workweek and start the weekend.

I paid my check and strolled the last two blocks to meet Thunder. Stella's was one of our favorite watering holes. Both Thunder and I were at that awkward age for black gay men. Too old for the youthful Village crowd, and not ready for the gay old-folks home. Stella's was an interesting mix of young and old, black and white, professional and blue-collar. The only thing I didn't really care about it was the number of hustlers who frequented the place. There were times when I thought I'd gotten lucky with some good-looking man, only to be informed of the cost of their services on the way out. Thunder never seemed to mind and got a kick out of requesting a price list of services. I can't tell you how many times after a few drinks, Thunder would shout out, "Anybody running any blow-job specials?" Most times somebody was.

I walked into the bar a little after nine o'clock, and the first person I saw was Thunder sitting on a bar stool with a cigarette in one hand and a drink in the other. When I saw he was alone, my heart sank a bit.

"Jimmy, over here," he shouted when he spotted me. Stella's was alive for an early Friday night. The lights were turned down low, and the television, hovering over the pool table, played without volume. Several black and Hispanic guys, in tight jeans, hovered over the juke box, flipping through the selections, while a Mariah Carey song played. The crowd would triple around midnight when the shake dancers started performing in a lounge area located downstairs. The men, mostly older white men sitting around the bar, were dressed in suits or the latest trailer-park fashions.

I went over and gave Thunder a kiss on the cheek and sat on the bar stool next to him.

"How are you doing, baby?" Thunder asked.

"Glad it's Friday," I said as I looked for the bartender.

"Sounds like you need a drink," Thunder said.

"I do. How was your event this evening?"

"Oh, it was easy. It was sandwiches, a little fruit salad and chips for a bank not too far from here."

The bartender came over and asked what he could get for us, and Thunder mouthed, "Let me have another rum and Coke."

"And what about you?" The bartender asked me.

"A white wine."

"You want zinfandel or chablis?"

You don't have any chardonnay?"

"No."

"Then, just give me a Beck's," I said.

"So tell me about your Valentine's evening. It musta been something with you calling me every hour on the hour."

"I'm sorry. I really liked him. I don't understand why, but I've been thinking about him ever since he walked out of my door."

"This sounds good. He must have really put it to you. Isn't that body and dick something to behold?" Thunder asked as he took the last swig of his drink.

"You've had sex with him?" I asked.

"Now, you know Mother ain't gonna send you nothing she hasn't tested."

I don't know why I was surprised that Thunder and Trevor had had sex. Trevor didn't strike me as Thunder's type.

"So when did you start going after the light, bright, damn-near-white smart guys?" I asked.

"What are talking about?" Thunder asked with his eyebrows raised slightly as he sipped his drink.

"Well, he's a writer."

"A writer?" Thunder repeated as he almost spit out his drink. "Jamal can barely write his name."

"Who is Jamal?" I asked. "The guy you sent is named Trevor."

"I sent Jamal. This tall, fine blue-black niggah with a big dick and slammin' body."

Now I was puzzled. Where did Trevor come from? I thought.

"The guy who showed up at my apartment was a guy named Trevor. He was big, but he was a yellow boy. Maybe your friend Jamal sent him."

"Maybe. So how was the sex?"

"We didn't have sex."

"What! You didn't have sex?" Thunder asked as he nervously stirred the ice cubes in his now empty glass.

"Naw."

"Then, why did I have to pay for three hours?" Thunder asked.

"Pay who?" I asked.

The bartender arrived with two fresh drinks, and Thunder tossed me a wait-a-minute-before-we-talk look. When the bartender moved to the other side of the bar, I repeated my question.

"Pay who?"

"Your date, honey. I told them to send Jamal, but if you liked this guy, then I ain't mad. Did you think that he was there for free? Ain't nothing in life for free," he said as he pulled the straw from his drink and laid it next to his package of cigarettes. My body was getting warm with anger. Had I heard Thunder correctly? Had he paid Trevor to spend time with me? I knew I was about fifteen pounds overweight, and my wire-rimmed glasses made me look like the absentminded professor. But was I so beat down that I couldn't attract a nice-looking man with my personality and intellect?

"You're telling me Trevor is a hustler?" I asked. My voice boomed with anger. I didn't know if I was more shocked or disappointed. Maybe I wanted to believe Trevor was nice to me because he was interested in starting a relationship with me. All of my romantic fantasies from the week were crashing down around me.

"Don't talk so loud," Thunder whispered under his breath. "People can hear you."

"How could you?"

"How could I what?"

"You know I don't play that shit! I never pay for sex," I protested.

"Trust me, honey. Everybody pays for sex. You might not lay out a couple of hundred dollars for each hour, but you pay. And I don't know this Trevor guy. Maybe he's not an escort or a hustler."

"What's the difference?"

"There is a difference. If I sent you some of those guys I used to meet when Forty-second Street was really Forty-second Street and not Disneyland East," Thunder laughed.

"How could you do that to me? He could have been an ax murderer or something. I let this man into my house. You could have at least told me," I said.

"That's why I asked them to send Jamal. He's fine. He can fuck. And you don't have to hide your jewelry. Besides, what difference does it make? Dick is dick, and I can't believe you didn't get some."

"Now I'm thankful I didn't."

"Why?"

"Just think of all the diseases he could be carrying."

"Oh no, Jamal and, I guess, this Trevor guy are from a service that guarantees all their men are tested for sexually transmitted diseases. It's a top-notch escort service. I mean they have to be at two hundred an hour."

"What's the name of the service?"

"See, I knew you couldn't stay mad at me long. I don't know the name right off the top of my head, but when I get home I can give you the information. Have you ever seen how many agencies there are in the weekly party rags. This dude must be something special. I might need to check him out for myself."

"I'm not going to see him again, but I do think I'm going to let him know I don't appreciate him trying to make a fool out of me."

"Now, how did he do that? Just because he didn't tell you he was on a time clock doesn't make him a bad person. He probably thought you knew. And let's face it, child, everybody ain't making money off the stock market. Things are still tough for brothas," Thunder said.

"But you should have told me."

"First of all I didn't know if I could find somebody that might fit your tastes. You know how you can be picky. No white guys, no guys from West Indies, no this and no that. A lot of these escort services don't have the kind of guys you like. I'm pleased with myself that I got so close."

"You know you're not being fair. I just prefer black men. If Mr. Right came along and he was white, I would deal."

"Now, you know that's not the truth, you only like black men with a leaning toward the yellow ones," Thunder said.

"So you don't know the name of the agency?"

"Are you going to call them?"

"I might. What's the name?"

"I'm not sure. It could be *www.bigdicks.com* or something like that," Thunder laughed.

"Don't play with me. You're not off the hook yet," I said.

"Don't worry. I'm sure I got the number near my nightstand. I'll call you when I get home and leave the number on the machine. Tell them I told you to call, and you might get a discount, since they didn't send you the man I requested," Thunder said as he finished his drink. I could tell he had eyed something interesting at the pool table. A tall Hispanic guy with tight jeans, tight shirt and tattoos. Just what Thunder liked.

"So how long do you want to stay here?" I asked as I looked across the crowded bar. The whole scene suddenly seemed sad to me.

"Don't tell me you're ready to go."

"I'm kinda tired," I said. The truth was I was anxious to get home and see if I could get in contact with Trevor.

"Then, head on home, darlin'. Your sister sees somebody I need to know. I'll call you when I get home," he said as he gave me a kiss on the cheeks and headed toward the pool table.

I finished my beer and headed home not really sure what I was going to do next.

I didn't get the number of Trevor's service until late Sunday. Thunder had fallen in lust for about twenty-four hours and didn't call until Sunday afternoon. I was at the office looking over some papers, and even though I was anxious to talk to Trevor, I didn't feel right about soliciting for sex on a Sunday. So I waited until Monday evening.

I dialed the number, and after a few rings a white guy answered the phone with a cheerful "Can I help you?"

At first I didn't know what to say, so I stuttered a bit when I asked, "Is this Mandingo R Us?"

"Yes, it is. How did you hear about us?"

"Huh?"

"How did you hear about our services?"

"From a friend," I said.

"Does this friend have a name?" he asked curtly.

"Yes. Thunder."

"Okay, how can I help you?"

"I was calling about one of your escorts."

"Do you have a name?"

"Trevor, I think."

"Yes, he's one of our *top* guys. When do you want to see him?"

"As soon as possible," I said nervously.

"Give me your name and number. He hasn't checked in yet, and I have to see if he's available. If he's not available, Jamal is. Are you interested in seeing him?"

"No," I said quickly.

"Okay. I was just asking. I know that's who Thunder requested, but he wasn't working that night. Give me your number."

As I gave him my name and number, I suddenly thought I could be giving my information to someone from the F.B.I. I then asked how long it would be before I heard from Trevor. I started to get an uneasy feeling, the kind I got doing something I knew I shouldn't be.

At such times, I would get the strangest feeling that my parents were looking down on me and shaking their heads in disgust. I viewed my parents as my personal angels and very tough judges. Much like they had been when they were alive. I was glad that I knew they loved me no matter what I did.

"Give me about fifteen minutes," he said as he hung up.

For the next ten minutes I wandered around my apartment excited at the prospect of seeing Trevor and chastising myself for what I was doing. Paying a man, make that a black man, for his company. I tried to tell myself that I wasn't paying for sex, but maybe helping the gay gods to deliver my soul mate. I told myself that Trevor not only had the novel he was writing, but his own story as well. Maybe he was working as an escort to pay for his mother's transplant surgery or better yet donating a kidney to his little brother. No matter why he was doing it, I knew there had to be some noble reason behind his actions. There better be.

When the phone rang, my heart raced, and I picked it up after the first ring.

"Hello."

"Is this Jim?"

"Jimmy," I corrected. Why did white boys always want to shorten your name and make it sound more like them? I thought.

"Okay, Jimmy. Well, I got some bad news for you. I couldn't get in contact with Trevor. It's still early, and he might call in. Could I interest you in some of our other guys? You sure you don't want to give Jamal a look-see? Besides Jamal and Trevor, we have some wonderful-looking, and I mean well-endowed, African-American and Hispanic men. Can I tell you about them?"

"No, I'm only interested in Trevor. Will you call me back if you hear from him?"

"Sure. Do you know our rates?"

"No. How much is he?" I asked. I could feel my skin crawl when I inquired about Trevor's fees.

"It's $250 for the first hour, and $200 for every hour afterward. Since this is the first time you're using our services, we ask that you pay up front. We take Visa, MasterCard and good old American cash. No checks, personal or traveler's, and no American Express. And don't worry. It shows up as a catering charge on your credit cards," he said.

"Okay. You can call me up until eleven."

"Okay. Do you have a computer?"

I thought that was an odd question, but I said yes.

"Then while you're waiting to hear from Trevor, why don't you check out our Web site at *www.mandigoplus.com*? You might see something else you like."

Not hardly I thought. Besides, I only had one line, and if I was tying it up on the computer, I might miss the call. "Thanks. I'll do that," I said as I hung up.

It was Tuesday and I was looking forward to a relaxing evening watching two of my favorite shows, *Who Wants to Be a Millionaire?* and *Will and Grace*. I got off the subway and stopped at the teller machine to get my pocket money for the week. A steady rain fell carelessly from the sky, and I was without an umbrella. Despite being soaking wet and a little bit chilly, I stopped at a neighborhood deli and purchased a cup of mushroom-barley soup and a tuna on rye. A white teenage girl, with multiple piercing on her ears and nose, and hair the color of orange-pink baby aspirin, stood by the door of the store. She was selling rain hats. "I'll give you a good deal on a hat," she said. I smiled at her and said, "No, thanks," since I was only a block away from home.

I entered my apartment, put my food on the kitchen counter, and began taking my wet clothes off in the living room. I went into my bathroom and got out a towel and began to dry my body like I had just stepped from the shower. I pulled on a pair of plaid boxers and was heading to the kitchen for my food, when the phone rang.

"Hello."

"Is this Jimmy?"

"Who's calling?"

"I'm looking for Jimmy."

I don't know why but instead of trying to find out more information on the caller I said, "This is Jimmy."

"I thought your voice sounded familiar. This is Lee from the agency. You called yesterday about one of our escorts, Trevor. Right?"

"Yes, I did."

"Well, I have good news. He just checked in about an hour ago, and he's available this evening."

"He is?" I asked. I felt a knot of excitement tightening my stomach.

"He sure is. What time would you like to see him?"

"What time can I?"

"You name the time. He doesn't have any bookings right now. How about nine o'clock?"

"Nine o'clock works for me," I said. *Will and Grace* would be just as funny on my video recorder, I thought.

"Great. Where am I sending him?"

I gave him my address and last name. I was then given a few rules and regulations for the evening.

"Now, Trevor will need to call me once he arrives and when he leaves. Since this is your first time he will ask if you are involved with law enforcement of any kind. If you respond no, then he will ask for payment for the first hour. Do not offer him anything to drink or exchange any personal information. Do you have any questions for me?"

I was thinking this was worse than a custom's inspection at the Mexican border, and I wondered if Trevor was worth the hassle. The layers of guilt about paying a white man for the company of a black man returned, and I started to shout *fuck off,* but instead I said, "I think you've explained yourself perfectly clear."

I looked at the clock on my microwave and realized I had a little over an hour to get ready for my date.

I opened the door, and there stood Trevor with a sexy and easy smile covering his face. His eyes glittered with mischief, and his hands were placed over his crotch like they were the top of a gift box.

"Come in," I said coldly. I was excited to see him, but I was upset as well.

"How ya doing?" he asked.

"I'm cool. Let me take your jacket."

Trevor took off a yellow, rain-soaked jacket and handed it to me. A navy blue baseball hat he wore was also wet. A tight buttercup yellow sweater accented his chest and nipples. His face was clean-shaven, and his teeth were white like miniature marshmallows.

I put his jacket in the closet, then turned to him with my arms folded over my chest and sighed. "Well."

"Is everything all right?" Trevor asked.

"Oh yeah, everything is just fine."

"Then, what was that sigh about?"

"I'm just waiting," I said.

"Waiting on what? Would you like for me to get undressed right here?"

"That can come later. I'm waiting on you to ask me *the* question and for the money," I said sarcastically.

"No need for the questions. I know you're cool, and we can deal with the money later. I'm just really glad to see you," Trevor said as he walked up close to me and tried to put his hands around my waist. I pushed him back and shouted, "Why didn't you tell me you were being paid?"

"I thought you knew," Trevor said as he stepped back and put his hands up as if to hold me back.

"How was I supposed to know? I've never paid for sex."

"Then, why tonight?"

I wanted to tell him because I wanted to see him, but instead I asked, "Why did you give me that cute answer when I asked you if you were a hustler?"

"I'm not a hustler. I am an escort," he said boldly, as though he was proud.

I was going to ask him what I had asked Thunder, but instead I asked him why he hadn't called me.

"I didn't think you wanted me to call."

"What are you talking about? I gave you my number."

"I thought you were just being nice."

"What?"

"A lot of clients give me their number, but when I call, they act like they don't remember me or how I got their number," Trevor said. His voice was suddenly urgent and low.

"I don't know how your *other* clients are, but I enjoyed talking to you. That's why I gave you my number. I wanted to see you again, but I didn't know that it was going to cost me."

"I'm sorry I wasn't totally honest. Sometimes people want to role-play. They don't want to hear the truth."

"I always want the truth," I said forcefully.

"Understood. Is that what you want to do tonight? Talk."

"I don't know what I want," I said as I turned away and raised my hand in disgust. "I did want to tell you how much you hurt my feelings."

"But I didn't know I was hurting your feelings. I could say I was just doing my job, but I really enjoyed you."

"Well, I don't have a lot of money, and I know you don't have a lot of time. Don't you have to call your pimp?" My anger was back.

"He's not a pimp, and don't worry about that. I can handle him."

"So is he your lover?"

"Look, Jimmy, let's not talk about the business. But he's not my lover."

"So let's see, I have about thirty minutes," I said as I looked at my watch. "Take off your clothes. I might as well see what I'm paying for," I ordered.

Trevor removed his sweater, kicked off his loafers and dropped his pants. Again, my knees went weak at the sight of his beautifully defined and smooth body.

"Is this what you want?" Trevor asked.

At that moment I didn't know what I wanted, but I felt like a jackass for treating Trevor like he was a slave or a piece of cattle.

"Put your clothes back on."

"You don't want to touch me? You don't want to make love?"

"It's not making love when the one of the parties is paying. How long have you been doing this?"

"Is that important?"

"Why are you doing this? You're attractive. You're smart.

Are you really writing a novel, and why doesn't your agent help you?"

"You ask a lot of questions," Trevor said as he zipped up his pants and tucked his sweater into his slacks. "Let's sit down," he said as he took my hand and moved me toward my sofa. I just followed him, as if I were under some spell. Suddenly Trevor seemed as mysterious as the moon and as untouchable as the sun. We sat down on the sofa, and something just came over me. I grabbed Trevor and hugged him tightly. After a few minutes, he pulled back and looked me in the eyes, then asked, "Don't you know that I enjoyed every minute I spent with you? I just couldn't be hurt again."

"Hurt? How was I going to hurt you? I just enjoyed the time we spent talking."

"I could tell, but I couldn't take that risk. For all I know you could have been working as some double agent with the agency. I could be fired for calling a client."

"Does the job mean that much to you?"

"It's all I have until I sell my novel," Trevor said.

"But I could help you find a job. What happens if your agent doesn't sell your novel?"

"I have faith in my work. It will sell," Trevor said confidently.

"Maybe I can ask if there are any openings at Fordham. Maybe I can see if I can find you some freelance writing assignment."

"You would do that for me?"

"If you wanted me to," I said. I knew I wasn't thinking straight. What if Trevor couldn't even write. I would run out of fingers and toes if I tried to count the number of gay men I had met who were writing a masterpiece novel. I would be the laughingstock of the faculty, but I wanted to get Trevor out of this horrible and sad profession. I knew then I wasn't going to pay him for sex. I was going to pay him for his time, but not his body, and this was going to be the last time, no matter how excited I was to be in his presence.

"I can't believe you'd help me out," Trevor said.

"Why?"

"You don't know how many promises men make when they've had a little to drink or after they've gotten their nut. I've become hardened over the years and don't believe anything until it happens."

"So you do this every night?"

"No, I don't do this every night. There are not a lot of calls for black guys. I barely make enough to pay my rent and put a little food on my table. Forty percent of what I get from you goes to the agency."

"Forty percent! That's robbery," I said.

"Well, I'm not going to be walking the streets. At least with the agency I feel a little safer going into a stranger's home."

"Have you ever run across any crazies?"

"What do you mean?"

"I mean have you ever felt threatened?"

"Not really."

"Are you having safe sex?"

"Jimmy, come on. I know you don't know me that well, but I'm not crazy. If a person doesn't have a uniform, then they can't play on my team," Trevor said.

"So everything we talked about was true?"

"What do you mean?"

"What we talked about. Your novel. The books and music you liked?"

"Yes, that was all true."

"Good, because I don't put up with liars."

Trevor lowered his head, and then looked at me and said, "Well, everything wasn't true. Trevor isn't my real name."

"It's not?"

"No, escorts are instructed to never use their real name."

"Which is?"

"Jimmy, I'm sorry. I'm here on an assignment. I can't tell you," he said.

I leaped from the sofa and screamed, "This is bullshit! This is crazy. Here I am making a fool out of myself in front of somebody who won't even tell me his name. Let me get your money, and you get your ass out of here."

I went into my bedroom and got two hundred fifty dollars from my wallet, which I had hidden under my underwear. I went into the living room and dropped the money on the coffee table and said, "I think your time is up. Thanks for coming."

Trevor got up from the sofa, then walked over and tried to pull me toward him. I pulled back and picked up the money, and this time I placed it in his hands, then said, "This is the last time I will pay you for anything, Trevor. Please leave."

"Are you sure you want me to leave?"

"Yes."

Trevor, or whatever his name was, looked at me with child-like eyes. Then he took his finger to his lip and kissed it and gently placed the finger on my lips. He sauntered over to the closet and pulled out his jacket and hat, before walking out of my apartment and hopefully out of my life.

About an hour later and two glasses of zinfandel, I was getting ready to call my sister for a niggas-ain't-shit phone session when the buzzer from my doorman sounded. I wasn't expecting anyone, but I picked up the phone despite my better judgment. I was hoping it might be Thunder so I could have my ain't-shit session face-to-face.

"Mr. Thorton," The doorman said. "There is a Mr. Cummings down here for you."

"Mr. Cummings? I don't know a Mr. Cummings. What's his first name?"

A few seconds later he came back on the phone and said, "His name is Kenoy."

Kenoy Cummings, I thought. I didn't know a Kenoy anyone. So I told my doorman to tell him he had the wrong number.

I refilled my wineglass and was dialing my sister's number when I heard the call-waiting beep. I ignored it, as I listened to my sister's phone ring and then her voice on her answering machine. When I heard the beep, I said, "Hey, sweetheart. Didn't want anything. Just thinking about you and the little ones. Give me a call when you get a chance. It's nothing. I promise. I love you. Call me. Soon."

When I hung up the phone, I started to call Thunder but the phone rang.

"Hello."

"Hi," a somewhat familiar voice said.

"Who is this?" I asked.

"Can you meet me downstairs?"

"Trevor? Is this you?"

"Yeah. Can you meet me downstairs?"

"For what?"

"I'll explain when you come down."

"Where are you right now?"

"A couple of steps from your door."

"What is this about? I gave you the right amount, didn't I?"

"Jimmy! Listen to me. This isn't about money. Meet me downstairs."

"Let me think about it," I said.

"Please come down or let me come back up," Trevor pleaded.

I was a little bit fearful, but I wanted to know why he had come back, so I put on some jeans and a sweatshirt and headed downstairs. I decided against inviting him up, in case he had something sinister planned. At least in the lobby of my building, I had my doorman as a witness or protection. I hoped Trevor wasn't going to cause a scene, even though I was sure my gay-friendly building had seen a little bit of everything.

When I got downstairs, there was Trevor, now wearing a fire engine–red jacket and holding a bundle of wilted pink roses in his hands.

"These are for you," he said as he handed the roses to me.

"What are these for?" I asked as every muscle in my body seemed to lock into place.

"I want to start over," he said.

"Trevor, I don't . . ."

Before I could finish, he put his finger on my lips to silence me and said, "My name is Kenoy Cummings. And that's the truth." He voice was soft and halting, like the spring rain falling out-side.

There was an uncomfortable pause, and then I looked into his eyes and felt a very strange sensation, a knot of excitement tightening in my stomach. Kenoy gave me a boyish smile, and then I said, "Let's go back up to my apartment."

The next evening as I was turning the key to my apartment, I heard the phone ringing. It sounded urgent and I hoped it was Kenoy. I pushed open the door and dropped my briefcase and mail on the floor as I grabbed the phone.

"Hello," I said, totally out of breath.

"What's going on, big brother?" my sister Carmen asked in her perky voice.

"How are you doing, sweetheart? How are the rugrats?"

"I'm fine. They're fine. How are you doing?"

"I'm great. Been singing all day," I said.

"You singing? Where? In the shower?"

"You know . . . it's more like humming. All day I've been humming 'Singing in the Rain' and 'You Make Me Feel Brand-New' by the Stylistics," I said.

"It must be love," Carmen said.

"Why does it have to be love? I'm just happy to be alive," I said.

"I could tell something was going on from your message. Who is he?"

"Who said it was a he?"

"Child, plezze. You're talking to your sister."

"Well, he's wonderful," I said. I was thinking about the night before when Kenoy returned to my apartment. We had a glass of wine and then talked about an hour before retiring to my bedroom, where we slept. No sex, just holding each other tightly, looking in each other's eyes until we fell asleep.

"What's his name?" Carmen asked.

"Trevor . . . uh, I mean, Kenoy," I said.

"Which one is it, honey? I love the name Kenoy," Carmen said.

"I don't know why I'm tripping. His name is Kenoy Cummings," I said.

"What does he do?"

"He's a writer," I said, touting only one of Kenoy's professions.

"Where did you meet him?"

I paused for a second. I started to say Thunder had introduced us, but instead I answered, "I met him at the gym."

"You're back at the gym! That's great. You know we have to look out for ourselves. Mama and Daddy taught us that," Carmen said.

"Are you working out?"

"Jimmy, you forget. I'm still looking for a husband. I'm running five miles a day . . . five times a week. And if that stops working, then I'm going under the knife. So you look out for good doctors up there. I won't dare to do it down here," Carmen said.

"I wish I had the time or the inclination to run five miles a day," I said.

"You can," Carmen said.

When I was getting ready to answer her, I heard my call-waiting beep.

"Hold on, darling." I hit the release button and said, "Hello."

"How was your day?" Kenoy's voice sounded both sweet and sexy.

"It just got better," I said.

"What are you doing?"

"Talking to my sister."

"Do you want me to call you back?"

"No, hold on." I clicked the release button again and said, "Carmen, it's him. Let me call you back."

"Don't worry about it, darling. Call me when you can."

"Give my babies a big kiss," I said.

"I will," Carmen said.

I clicked back over and said, "Are you still there?"

"Where am I going?" Kenoy said.

"How was your day?"

"Like you said . . . it just got better. You should be a writer," Kenoy said.

"You couldn't stand the competition," I teased.

"I don't know. I had a great day of writing today."

"When am I going to read this great work?"

"Soon."

"Is that a promise?"

"It's a promise I can't wait to share with you," Kenoy said.

"So am I going to see you this evening?"

"Maybe . . . maybe not."

"What does that mean?"

"Well, you know I want to see you. But I got something better."

"What?"

"Can you meet me?"

"Yeah. Where?"

"At the docks. How long will it take?"

"About thirty minutes," I said as I looked at my watch. It was almost nine o'clock.

Thirty minutes later, as I approached the docks along the West Side Highway, I saw Kenoy leaning against a concrete embankment with a neon-green windbreaker and tan jeans. When he saw me, he moved quickly toward me, and within seconds he was hugging me tightly. I absorbed his scent and enjoyed the strength of his arms and the gentle way his hug felt.

"So what's this about?" I asked.

"What?"

"Meeting down here. I was hoping we could spend the night in bed. Talking of course," I said.

"That's why I asked you to meet me down here," Kenoy said as he reached for my hands. The docks was one of the few places, besides the Village, where gay men could hold hands and kiss without being stared at. I had walked down to the docks hundreds of Sunday afternoons and envied couples being affectionate in public. Something I never dreamed of when I was growing up in St. Louis.

"So you don't want to lie in my bed again," I teased.

"No, that's not it. Last night was wonderful. I just want us to take it slow."

The expression on my face must have changed because Kenoy said, "Now, don't look like that. What I'm saying is I want us to get to know each other. I want us to take long walks, and long baths, and I want us to share our deepest thoughts and dreams."

"That sounds nice. So where do we start?" I asked.

"We start here. Let's walk. If you want to talk, then we'll talk. But if we just want to enjoy the sounds of the night, then we can do that as well."

I gazed at Kenoy and smiled as I took his hand and we started walking. In silence. Every now and then I would look at him and then at the twinkling stars, protecting a low moon.

About ten minutes later, Kenoy held my hand firmly and stopped walking. I looked at him, and he asked, "Did you dream as a child?"

"Of course, I dreamed. I dreamed all the time."

"What did you dreamed of?"

"Would it sound corny if I said I dreamed of nights like this? Walking hand in hand with a handsome man."

"It doesn't sound corny if that's the truth," Kenoy smiled.

"What did you dream of?"

Kenoy was silent for a moment and said, "I was to afraid to dream."

"Why?"

"It's a long story."

"I got time."

"And you would listen, wouldn't you?" Kenoy said as he gently rubbed my face.

"I would listen."

"Then, one day very soon I will share my fears, but right now let's just enjoy tonight."

I gazed at him and smiled. I looked at the sky and smiled. And then we both began walking and holding hands. Again.

Two days later, I was on the phone catching up with Thunder. I told him about my moon-lit stroll with Kenoy, and how I thought he was a really special young man. There must have been something in my tone of voice because Thunder asked me if I was falling in love.

"No," I protested. "You know I know better than that."

"Are you sure?"

"Of course, I'm sure. Thunder, I know better. I just enjoy talking with him and spending time with him," I said.

"He's not charging you for that, is he?"

"No," I shouted.

"I'm just asking. I want you to be careful 'cause if anybody knows how a dick can make a girl crazy, then it's me," Thunder said.

"I've seen the dick and it's nice, but we still haven't had sex yet," I said proudly.

"What are you trying to do? Reform him?" Thunder asked as his giggles bubbled out like champagne.

"No, we're taking it slow."

"Now, Jimmy, listen to me. I know you are still some little country boy from the South, and . . ."

I interrupted Thunder and said, "I'm from St. Louis. That's considered the Midwest." I was trying to avoid the lecture I knew was coming.

"Midwest, Northwest or whatever. But I'm a hardened New York diva, and I know how to handle men like your boy. You have to treat them like trade. Don't ever let them think you need them, and if you're smart, you should change them as often as you change your underwear."

"What about that man who's been staying with you for almost a month?" I asked. Thunder had been keeping company with some guy named Delvin, who had spent some time in jail at Lorton, right outside of D.C. Thunder told me he was trying to help him get on his feet and was hoping he would introduce him to some of his prison friends, before he tired of Thunder or vice versa. It used to bother me that Thunder only pursued men with whom he had no chance of having a long-term relationship, but I had come to realize it was his way of protecting himself. I couldn't blame him for that.

"Are you talking about Delvin?"

"Yeah."

"Well, thanks to God and Greyhound, he's back in D.C., but

I did meet one fine friend of his when I went to Riker's Island with him."

"You're lecturing me, and you're still pullin' for prison trade."

"But I know better. I'm not falling in love with nobody. I worry you don't know the difference between chicken shit and chicken salad. Most men fall into the chicken-shit category," Thunder said.

"When am I going to see you? We should go out for a drink tomorrow," I suggested.

"I wish I could, but I'm booked solid the next couple of days. I have an event at *Essence,* and I'm doing a big party for the Terrie Williams agency. But I will call you this weekend."

"Okay. But don't abandon me now. I know what you're saying about Kenoy might be right, but I'm gonna need you to be there to keep reminding me. He is one of the most beautiful men I've ever seen."

"Remember, beauty is only skin-deep, and with you a teacher, I know your pocketbook can't go that deep. And if he ain't charging you now, I bet you he's keeping a ledger," Thunder said as he giggled dismissively.

"I hear you," I said.

"Make sure you do," Thunder said as we both said good-bye.

I started to call Kenoy, but my body and sleep had other plans for me.

Days came and went and came again, and before I knew it, Kenoy and I had fallen in a rhythm of some sort of couplehood. And though we had spent many nights in each other's arms, we still hadn't made love, nor had we defined our relationship. I told myself I had to be sure about my feelings before I took the next step, like quizzing him on our status. There was a fear and a hope that Kenoy was going to be so spectacular in bed, that it might be hard to leave or look the other way when he did work for the escort agency. We talked a lot about his past, but not a lot about Kenoy's present. Whenever it seemed we were going in that direction, Kenoy would turn the tables, asking about my prior profession.

"So you don't think you'll ever practice medicine again? I mean that sounds like a total waste," he said.

"I never say never. But right now I love my life the way it is. I love teaching. And my skills are just being transferred to students who will have a passion about medicine. I lost my passion during the day-to-day grind of trying to be perfect," I told Kenoy.

We never talked about the escort business, even though I tried to keep track of his movements without being a nag or giving him the feeling that I didn't trust him. In the back of my mind, I worried where Kenoy might be, when I couldn't reach him, or when he left my apartment early to write.

On the evenings we spent together, it usually meant cooking dinner and watching movies. In the course of a week, Kenoy and I had watched *The Nutty Professor* three times, *Tick* twice and *Living Out Loud* four times. We both agreed the Holly Hunter and Queen Latifah movie was our new favorite all-time movie. Some evenings we would watch television programs like *Biography,* and sometimes we would just lie side by side as I read my schoolbooks and Kenoy reworked his manuscript. I was dying to read his novel, but figured he would let me read it when he was ready. I was still praying that he could really write.

I was so happy and proud when Kenoy invited me to meet him and his agent at a reading by Frank McCourt at the Ninety-second Street YMCA. It was even better when his agent canceled at the last minute, and we got to spend the evening, after the reading, alone.

Kenoy was also reintroducing me to my youth, and it felt wonderful. We began to work out together, and I soon lost about seven pounds. One evening we did something I hadn't done in years. We roller bladed from my apartment down to Battery Park City. I felt like a teenager as the spring wind caressed my face. It didn't matter that I fell at least three times, especially when Kenoy would rush over to rescue me every time.

One evening Kenoy finally invited me to his tiny basement apartment in the Williamsburg area of Brooklyn. I took the L train and walked the few blocks to his place, not knowing what to expect. What I discovered was a small studio, cluttered with books, music and cooking utensils. Kenoy made a splendid pot of spaghetti and meatballs, balanced with a caesar salad. For dessert, he surprised me with two of my favorite delicacies: coconut cake from the Magnolia Bakery topped with Ben & Jerry's Chucky Monkey ice cream. "The way you've been working out, I think you deserve this," he said with a big smile as he served me. I felt like a prince.

On evenings like those, I had to keep telling myself I couldn't fall in love with Kenoy, no matter how young or happy I felt. Yet there were so many things to love. I loved the fact that he appeared so versatile. He was not afraid to show his soft side, and still carried himself in a masculine manner that made my knees weak. So many times in gay relationships, roles were established often and early, and if you tried to go another road, trouble arose.

Almost three weeks had passed since I'd talked with anyone but Kenoy, my students and colleagues. Thunder was not amused. I had left him several messages telling him I was doing fine, and he had left me messages, but we hadn't spoken since he tried to convince me not to take Kenoy seriously.

I arrived home one evening, expecting to spend it with Kenoy. I was going through my mail as I pushed the PLAY button on my answering machine. As I shifted through the bills and credit card offers, the automated voice on my machine informed me that I had two messages. The next voice I heard was Kenoy's. "*What's up, sexy. I hope you had a great day. Look, I don't know if we can hook up this evening. Something came up, and I've got to meet with . . .*" Then I heard a beep. I was expecting to hear the message continued, but instead I heard Thunder's voice.

"*Bitch, are you all right? Are you still alive? I think I need to call 9-1-1, but I don't know the number. So when you get in, call me, but if you're dead or something, I'll just call information and get the number to 9-1-1. I miss you and I love you.*"

Thunder's message caused me to break out into a joyous laughter. *He is so crazy,* I was thinking while I dialed his number and hoped I got to actually speak with him, instead of his answering machine. My prayers were answered.

"Hello."

"What's up Diva Deluxe?" I said.

"Child, it's so good to hear your voice. I guess you ain't dead. I was worried about you. I thought maybe that man had kidnapped you and was forcing you to have sex with him and his friends. Oh no, that's my fantasy," he joked.

"What are you doing this evening?"

"What I do every evening. Working. I got a big party for some rich white folks on the East Side. This ain't no meatball and paper napkins event either. I'm serving lobster rolls for starters and grilled ribs with a my own special dipping sauce," Thunder said.

"That sounds wonderful. What's happening on the man front?" I realized getting Thunder to talk about men would give me some free time to pat myself on the back for not worrying about where Kenoy was spending his evening.

"Oh, it's kinda slow right now, which is okay since I've been so busy. My prison pipeline kinda dried up. But once I get some free time, I'm going down to *The Today Show* and throwing a brick through the window. Maybe that can get me a little vacation at Riker's Island. At least there I know I'll will have a captive audience."

"You're some kind of fool. I really wish I could see you this evening. Kenoy is busy, and it sure would be cool to catch up on your little life."

"You can see me," Thunder said.

"But what about your event?"

"I'm still gonna do my event. I was just thinking how nice it would be to see you all dressed up in a tuxedo, smiling and being gracious," Thunder said. I knew where this was going. Thunder needed a waiter.

"Who just called in sick?" I teased.

"Does it matter? Honey, that's why I should stick to my policy and not hire black folks, especially girls with kids. There must not be a single baby-sitter within miles of Harlem."

"What's the address and what time do you want me to be there?" I asked.

"109 East Seventy-second Street. Meet me at eight o'clock. I promise to cook a special meal just for you and me after we finish. Why don't you bring an overnight bag and spend the night? We could have our own little slumber party and catch up."

"That sounds fun. Let me call Kenoy and leave him a message, and I'll be on my way."

"Oh, we're checking in now . . . huh. I know you've got some stories to tell, honey. We might have to stay up all night," Thunder said.

"Let me go. I can't wait to see you."

I think everyone at some point in their life should have to serve food to a stranger. It would make the world a much humbler place. I showed up at the tony East Side town house, where I rang the doorbell like I was an invited guest.

"May I help you?" an elderly black man with his nose pointed toward the stars asked me.

"I'm here to see Thunder . . . I mean Keith," I said as I shook the slender garment bag with my change of clothes.

"Thunder? Do you mean the caterer?"

"Yes, that's him."

"Are you a server?"

"Yes, I guess I am."

"Then, young man, you need to enter through the service entrance on the side," he said as he pointed to a small alleyway on the side of the building. I gave him one of those *HNIC (head nigger-in-charge acknowledgment)* and went to the side entrance. I rang the doorbell, and a handsome Hispanic man open the door.

"I'm looking for Thunder," I said.

"Come on in," he said.

I walked into the massive kitchen and saw Thunder directing a group of handsome and well-built young men. Some were wearing tight black pants and white shirts, while others were wearing hospital white where you could tell what type of underwear they were wearing or not wearing. When Thunder saw me, he came over to give me a big hug and whispered, "I owe you one for this."

"What else is new?" I teased.

"Did you have any problem finding the place?"

"No, but I almost went home when old boy *Benson* tried to give me shade for showing up at the front door," I said.

"I'm sorry. I should have told you. You didn't read him, did you?"

"No, but not because I didn't think about it. He sorta reminded me of my great-uncle, and I know he comes from another era. I don't know why, but I forgot a lot of people do domestic jobs their entire lives," I said.

"But don't tell them they ain't running things," Thunder said.

"What can I do to help out?"

"Get your shirt on and start putting those lobster rolls on that silver platter," Thunder said as he pointed to a butcher-block island in the middle of the kitchen. "I'm doing a French service tonight."

"What's that?" I asked. Sometimes Thunder forgot I didn't read *Martha Stewart* or *B. Smith Style* on a regular basis.

"Just follow my lead. It just means everything is on a platter tonight."

"Yes, sir, boss. Where do I change?"

"There is a small bathroom over there," Thunder said as he pointed to a lighted hallway.

"I'll be with you in a few shakes," I said as I grabbed my drag for the evening.

Once inside the small bathroom, with its beautiful cobalt-blue tile and white border, I was thinking about my mother for some strange reason. Maybe it was the way the butler had treated me when I came to the wrong door. My mother wouldn't have handled that situation too well. She was light-skinned, went to college to meet a doctor and lifetime Links member to the end. Hattie Ryan Thorton wore those adjectives and organizations like badges of courage. She used to brag to my sister and me on how she set her sights on Daddy when she found out he was a first-year med student, who was also the son of a doctor. Maybe I didn't overreact to the butler because as a child, I had seen my own parents treat other African Americans less than kindly. It wasn't that they were mean. It was more like, *Don't expect any breaks here because we've worked hard to get here, and if this is the best you can do, then don't blame me for holding my head a little high.*

I also was thinking about Thunder and how much I appreciated his friendship, one I might have missed if I had held on to my mother's high standards. I had met Thunder when I first moved to New York. A close friend of my mother's as well as being my godmother, Mabel Taylor Watkins, had given an upscale dinner party in my honor when I moved to New York. It was on the Upper East Side, about thirteen blocks from this place, and Thunder catered the affair. When I became a little bored with Mabel and her friends' lively gossip, I went into the kitchen and asked Thunder where I could get a little more wine. I don't know how my tone was, but Thunder read me immediately by saying, "It's in the icebox, Mr. Thing, or is it Miss Thing? Sister is off the clock, packing up and heading home."

When I looked at him with a puzzled look, he informed me he already knew my story, and when I asked how, since I was wearing my best black suit, Thunder said, "Who do you think those old biddies were talking about before you got here? Tell me about your daddy's friend whose heart you broke." We have been friends ever since.

I left the bathroom, now dressed in my waiter's monkey suit. I must admit my tux wasn't as tight-fitting as the two other servers Thunder had hired, but that didn't bother me. I hoped it wouldn't bother his clients. The first person I saw when I walked out of the hallway was Thunder.

"You look good, child. Romance is wearing well on you."

"Thanks. Where is my platter? And what's the mood for the room?"

"Rich old white girls with a few of us sprinkled in for good measure," Thunder joked.

"Real girls?"

"No, honey. Girls like us."

"So this is a gay gig?"

"You got that right," Thunder said as he handed me a platter of beautifully golden-brown lobster rolls.

About ten minutes later my tray was empty, so I returned to the kitchen for more food. Thunder was busy supervising his staff, but he stopped to ask me how it was going.

"They love the food. One of your sisters is out there trying to be grand, but overall they seem like a nice bunch of chaps," I said in a mock British/Boston accent.

"Do I need to go out there and slap her?" Thunder asked.

"Naw, that won't be necessary. I can still give *it* to the best of them."

I returned to the elegantly appointed living room right off the library with my tray in hand. The room was swimming in festive light with some type of classical music playing in the background, while several middle-aged white men gathered around the bar with drinks in hand. I could hear the clicking of ice cubes and voices floating in the air like summer lightning bugs.

"Would you like a lobster roll, sir?" I asked one portly gentleman standing alone.

"Indeed I would," he said with a smile. I handed him a linen napkin, and he lifted a roll from my tray, then dipped it into the plum sauce and into his mouth in one fell swoop.

"These are heavenly," he said as he quickly grabbed another.

"I'll tell the chef how much you enjoyed them," I said as I eyed a tall and slim black man entering the room. Our eyes met, but he quickly looked the other way. He spotted someone he recognized, and in a high-pitched voice he said, "Darling." I wanted to shout at the top of my lungs *bitch*. But I knew the drill. He was probably one of those *I want to be the only monkey at the zoo* types. That's what Daddy used to say when he attended affairs and was snubbed by the only other blacks in attendance. It drove my father crazy when the person in question was light-skinned. I smiled to myself when I thought about

Kenoy's skin color and my mother's and realized my father and
I did have some things in common.

I walked back into the kitchen and announced I was out of
lobster rolls.

"There are some more over there," Thunder said as he
pointed to a large tin pan on the counter. "Serve them a few
more, and then it's on to the rib tips."

I loaded my tray with the rolls and reminded Thunder of his
promise to make me dinner.

"I already got you covered, doll," he said.

"Do you mind if I bring someone?"

"No, I don't mind. Who you gonna bring? Your PNB (poten-
tial new boyfriend)?"

"No, I'm going to bring my PNH. My probably new husband." I smiled. I was thinking about Kenoy and how hungry I
was for food and to be lying in his arms.

I walked back into the room and noticed the crowd had
grown in size. There were a few more men of color, one who
smiled warmly and one with his back to me, standing next to a
very tall and thin white man holding court with several of the
guests. His voice was large and filled the room. I moved closer
to the group and I heard him say, "This young man is going to
make me a lot of money." Then I heard him break out into
laugher as he patted the young man on the back. I slid next to
two men talking with each other and suddenly was in front of
the tall man and his court.

"Would you like a . . ." I stopped in midsentence when I realized the man standing next to the tall and loud man was Kenoy.
I felt my knees buckle. I was shocked, and it took everything I had
to hold on to my tray. Kenoy had a drink in his hand and the look
of someone who had been caught in a bank robbery.

"Jimmy," he said. But before he could finish his sentence, I
was back in the kitchen. My face was warm, and my heart was
beating so fast I felt as though it were going to burst out of my
body, rendering me heartless.

"Thunder, I'm sorry, but I can't go back out there," I said as
I placed the tray on the counter.

"What's the matter? Did someone say something nasty to you? Tell me 'cause I don't take no shit from these uppity mutherfuckers just because I'm cooking for them. They can't treat the doll and her friends like we don't count. Just tell me who it was."

"Nobody did anything. I just can't go back out there. Kenoy's out there with some tall white man bragging on how much money he's making for him. It must be his pimp. What kind of sick party do you have me working at?" I asked angrily.

"Wait a minute! Don't get your panties in a bunch. Let me see what you're talking about," Thunder said as he walked out of the kitchen into the living area. I went into the bathroom. I felt embarrassed and sick to my stomach. Kenoy had lied to me to be with his fucking pimp, I thought. Even though he had never said he had left the escort business, it was the impression he gave me. I felt like the biggest fool in New York for thinking I could change a whore.

I walked out of the bathroom to find Thunder standing near the door. He looked at me with a sad expression and said, "Well, honey. You were right. He is fine."

"Did you speak to him?"

"No. He was standing there looking down in his drink. He whispered something to the tall man, and they left right away."

"Good, but I feel sick. I'm sorry but I've got to go home."

"That's fine, honey. I understand," Thunder said as he gave me a gentle hug.

I was doing everything within my powers to keep my tears in the corner of my eyes and not allow them to escape to my burning face.

I'm getting used to being lonely. I have no dreams about a love life with a happy ending. That's what I keep telling myself each time love's empty promise disappoints me. During my cab ride home, I suddenly hated New York and it's residents. I wanted to live in a place where the world didn't move so fast. New York had too many people waiting to hurt you.

When I got to my apartment I poured myself a strong glass of brandy and took a bath. I didn't check my answering machine or quiz my doorman if someone had come by and didn't leave a name. I put on my light-blue-striped pajama's because they made me feel like a little boy. A time when I felt safe and never lonely. I slipped into a deep nest of white cotton sheets and king-sized pillows and prepared to drift into an uneasy sleep when the phone from my doorman buzzed.

I hoped it was Kenoy. I prayed it was Thunder. I made up my mind to ignore the sound and then changed it when the buzzer sounded again.

"Hello."

"Mr. Thorton, there is a Mr. Cummings here to see you."

"Send him up," I said without hesitation. I looked at the clock, which was blinking 2:06 A.M.

I poured myself another sip of brandy, drank it quickly and then rushed to the bathroom to rinse my mouth with Listerine. Just as I was spitting the mint-flavored liquid into the sink, I heard a knock at the door.

"Be forceful and strong," I said to myself as I gazed into the bathroom mirror. I moved through my bedroom to the living room and opened the door.

"Why didn't you let me explain, Jimmy? Why did you look at me like I had done something wrong? Like I was the last person on this earth that you wanted to see."

"Come in," I said as I turned my back and headed toward the kitchen. I needed another drink. I was pouring my drink when Kenoy walked into the kitchen.

"What did you think I was doing? Did you think Paul was some client?"

"Oh no, I didn't think that. I heard him. He's your pimp. The man you're making a lot of money for with your wonderful body," I said. I was feeling the effect of the brandy and my emotions.

"Paul was not my pimp or a client. He's my agent," Kenoy said.

"Agent, pimp. They are one and the same," I said as I swirled my glass around in a circular motion.

"He's my literary agent. That party was for some gay group of publishers and editors. Paul thought it would be good for me to meet some of them in person before he sends out my manuscript next week," Kenoy said.

"Then, why did you tell me you had a meeting? Why didn't you just say you were going to a party!" I shouted.

"Because I didn't know. Paul just told me to dress up. That he wanted to discuss our strategy. He didn't say anything about a party."

"I don't believe you."

"Then, how can we have anything? You've got to trust me," Kenoy pleaded.

"I can't," I said. The liquor was causing tears to form. I looked at Kenoy's sad eyes, and I wanted to hug him, kiss him and tell him everything would be find. But I couldn't.

"So you're saying you can never trust me? I thought you were different. Why should I think that?" Kenoy said in disgust. He walked out of the kitchen and toward the sofa.

"Kenoy," I said with volume and force.

He turned around and gazed at me with a puzzled look on his face.

"You have to leave. You have to leave now," I said.

"Why? Can't we talk about this?"

"No. You have to leave now," I repeated.

"Why?" Kenoy repeated.

"Because if you stay here another minute, another second, then I'm going to fall in love, and I can't do that," I said sadly.

Kenoy was silent, and then he said, "Naw, you wouldn't want to do that. Fall in love with a whore. But how could you fall in love with me when you don't even know me? Who I am. Where I've been and why. You know, selling my book has shown me that where I've been and how I became the man I am is important. Maybe it's time I share some of those dreams, or why I was once afraid to dream with you."

"How are you going to do that?" I asked.

"I want you to read my book. Take your time. And after you read it and still feel you can't be a part of my life, then just burn it. But if you change your mind and think I might be worthy of your love . . . well all you have to do is call," Kenoy said, and he walked out the door.

The next evening when I got home, the doorman presented me with a brown-wrapped package. There was a small piece of paper on top of the manuscript. It was a note from Kenoy.

> *Jimmy,*
>   *Maybe, just maybe after reading this you will understand my life and why I do some of the things I do. If you're willing to give us another chance, give me a call. I hope your time reading will be well spent and that you will be totally honest with your assessment.*
>   *Fondly,*
>   *Kenoy E. Cummings*

I gazed at the cover sheet, which read, *Mother's Day . . . a novel by Kenoy E. Cummings*. I thumbed through the manuscript and realized it was 356 typewritten pages.

I went into my kitchen and pulled out a small plastic bottle of carrot juice, then went to the living room and dropped into the comfort of my sofa. I placed the cover sheet on the coffee table and began to read.

> *I love my mother. And when she could, my mother loved me. Fiercely.*

Five hours later, I was crying a river of tears. I wiped my eyes dry and then picked up my phone to call Kenoy. But after dialing about four numbers, I hung up. I had to pull myself together before I spoke to him.

Kenoy's novel, *Mother's Day,* was a heartbreaking story of a young man's love for his drug-addicted mother, and his trials and tribulations through an ill-equipped foster-care system. Not only did I fall in love with the main character, Austin, but his extremely flawed mother, Viola.

Kenoy's writing dealt with issues of race and self-loathing within the African-American community and the battle to save the life of not only the mother, but the son as well, when he became the victim of an abusive foster father. I couldn't remember reading anything more riveting since I had read *I Know Why the Caged Bird Sings* and *The Color Purple*. Both of those books provided me a cleansing cry. Kenoy's was my third.

After my cry, I picked up the phone, and this time completed the call. Kenoy answered after a few rings.

"Hello."

"Kenoy, this is Jimmy. Can we get together tomorrow evening?"

"Sure. Did you read my book?"

"Yes, I did. It was wonderful."

"You really liked it?"

"I love it," I said.

"You mean it?"

"I mean it."

"Where do you want to meet?" Kenoy asked.

"It doesn't matter."

"What about Café Rafaella?"

"Where is that?"

"It's on Seventh Avenue, just north of Christopher Street," Kenoy said.

"That's fine. I'll see you at seven tomorrow."

"Cool. I can't wait."

"Good night, Kenoy."

The day moved slower than snails, and I was looking forward to the evening. I didn't know what I was going to say to Kenoy or even allow him back in my life. All I knew was that I had to see him at least one more time.

When I arrived at the restaurant, Kenoy was already there. He was looking handsome in a black silk shirt and tan pants. When I approached the table, he stood up and smiled and gave me a kiss on the cheek and whispered, "It's so good to see you."

"You too," I said as I sat down. The restaurant was beautiful with antique chairs and sofas. It had the feel of an Italian grandmother's ice cream parlor, with round wooden tables.

"The food and desserts here are amazing," Kenoy said.

"I'm really not that hungry," I said as my eyes roamed the room and noticed several tables filled with Eurotrash gay boys.

"Can I order for you?"

"Sure, but make sure I get a glass of wine."

The waiter came over, and Kenoy ordered a couple of focaccia sandwiches and glasses of pinot grigio wine. When the waiter left, I looked at Kenoy and asked, "So was *Mother's Day* a true story?"

Kenoy was silent for a moment before his eyes began to gleam with tears. When he lowered his head, the tears began to run down his cheeks. I started to reach over the table to dry his face with my palms, but I decided to wait until he spoke. A few minutes passed, and finally Kenoy said, "Most of it is true. Of course, I changed a lot of the names and places. But a lot of what Austin went through actually happened to me."

"What about the Rice Krispies treats?" I was curious about a particularly moving section of the book, where Austin and Viola spent a week in their new apartment. Viola had made a pan of Rice Krispey treats, but when Austin, then nine, asked for a glass of cold milk, there was no milk in the refrigerator. Viola went to the store to purchase the milk and didn't return until a week later. Austin had eaten the treats like they were war rations, but had saved one and kept it wrapped in aluminum foil. When he was sent to a foster home, he took it with him, protecting it like it was a block of gold.

"Yeah, that actually happened. As a matter of fact, I still have it," Kenoy said as the waiter placed glasses of wine in front of us.

"You do?"

"Yeah, but I haven't looked at it in a long time. Just knowing it's there gives me a sense of solace."

"Is Viola dead?"

"If you mean my mother, whose real name was Alma, she died about three years ago of AIDS-related complications," Kenoy said sadly.

"Is this why you were working for an escort service? To get your mother in rehab?"

"Yes, that's how I got started in a way. I was also working two jobs as well. Every time I got Alma into a clinic she was fine. The problems occurred when she got out, and I couldn't keep an eye on her every minute of the day. I mean she tried, but it was tough on her to stay clean. I don't think I realized how hard it was. All I knew was that I wanted a mother," Kenoy said.

"What about your father?"

"Never met him," Kenoy said sternly.

"Do you know who he is?"

"No. Alma told me it was some Italian guy she had a brief affair with. The funny thing was he tried to get her off the streets and drugs as well. When he realized he couldn't change her, he left. Leaving me behind. But I wouldn't give up any of the time I spent with my mother to spend one second with someone who left me and my mother." His voice was punctuated by brief pauses, as if he wasn't sure how much he should say, or share with me.

"You don't do drugs, do you?" I knew that often children of addicts usually followed their parent's path.

"I've never taken a drug in my life."

"That's good," I said as I gently patted the top of his hand.

"Do you think some of the sex stuff was too graphic?"

I recalled a passage in the book where Austin was seduced by an older boy in a group home. Some would call it "molested." I started to tell him how I thought it was quite sexy, especially the way he had written it, but instead I told him I thought it was important to the story.

In many ways I felt the hours I spent reading *Mother's Day* were like watching a videotape of Kenoy's painful life. I felt guilt at ever questioning the middle-class life I had been blessed with and ever passing judgment on Kenoy's life of selling his body for sex. I wanted to know why he still did escort work, when his reasons for starting were over. I was trying to figure out a delicate way of asking him, but instead I blurted out, "If you're not working for your mother anymore, why do you keep doing the escort thing?"

"I've asked myself that more than you know, and I don't have an answer. Maybe I'm an addict in some other ways. Maybe I do it to protect myself."

"Protect yourself from what?" I asked as the waiter placed our food on the table. It was a few seconds before Kenoy spoke again.

"Don't you know?"

I shook my head and said softly, "No."

"To keep myself from ever falling in love," Kenoy said. His voice sounded bruised, and his eyes drifted away from me, like he was searching for something or someone in the busy restaurant.

I wanted to asked Kenoy if his work had succeeded in keeping him from love, but he looked so sad and serious. I picked at my sandwich, and Kenoy did the same for about ten minutes. Then he looked at me and asked, "So are you going to give us another chance?"

Just as I was getting ready to respond, a thin white boy with dirty blond hair, jeans with holes at the knees and a tan T-shirt walked over to our table, folded his arms and said, "I've been wondering when I was going to run into you."

Kenoy looked up and said, "Excuse me?"

"Now, don't tell me you don't remember me. As much money as I spent on you."

"Look, I'm with someone," Kenoy said as he positioned his eyes in my direction. I suddenly felt warm with embarrassment and pulled the napkin from my lap and dashed to the restroom without even excusing myself. I didn't have to use the restroom, but I had to remove myself from the situation.

Once inside the restroom, I cupped my hands under cold water and splashed it on my face. I looked in the mirror and asked myself in silence how I could enter a relationship with Kenoy, despite my strong feelings for him. Even though I didn't think that I was better than him because of my family background and what he did for a living, I knew big problems could be around every corner. Misunderstandings and questions about every man Kenoy would come across. How could I fall in love with a man I could never trust?

I went back to the table. Kenoy stood up, came over toward me and said, "I'm sorry about that. It won't happen again."

I didn't sit down, but I asked him, "How can you be certain?"

"Most of my clients aren't like him."

When Kenoy said the word *client,* I wanted to scream. They weren't clients like a law firm or an accounting agency. These were people who at a moment's notice could demand that my boyfriend leave our bed and come to theirs. I couldn't live like that. I wouldn't.

"Kenoy, this is not going to work. I loved your book, and I think it will help a lot of people. But it won't help us," I said.

"Can we try? I've never felt the way I feel about you."

"I can't. I have to go. Please give me some time to sort this out, but I don't think I'm going to change my mind," I said, then dashed out of the restaurant with Kenoy standing stunned.

April seemed endless. Each day echoed the last. I went to work, came home, ate, drank, crawled into my bed, and made love to my pillows. Even though it was spring, the weather was unseasonably cold and wet. The only people I spoke with were Thunder, my sister, and my doorman for food deliveries. I had stopped going to the gym for fear of running into Kenoy. I had gained my weight back, and the pounds had returned with a few friends. I was in a self-inflicted *I love my man* depression.

I was looking forward to the semester ending. I was toying with the thought of seeking a teaching position in Atlanta, or a research position at the CDC, so I could be close to my sister and her children. I also thought about returning to St. Louis and applying for something at Washington University. I suddenly longed for a town where the local beauty pageant was a really big event.

I was finally willing to admit that New York had won and it was time to return to a simpler life. Whenever I listened to music, which was usually old Aretha Franklin or Patti LaBelle,

I sometimes found myself playing Jay Z's *It's A Hard Knock Life,* where he sampled lyrics from the Broadway musical *Annie.* I was thinking that little bitch Annie had no clue as to what a hard-knock life was.

I had not spoken with Kenoy but I still thought of him constantly. I missed talking with him and feeling his body against mine. I missed his smile and the sexy gleam in his eyes. Every time I thought of calling him or going to the gym at his usual time, I would force my memory to recall the dinner party and the skinny white boy confronting Kenoy with his arms folded in a huff. Those memories alone kept me from dialing his number.

I did hear his voice almost every day. Kenoy had left me several messages on my answering machine. Even though I never returned his calls, I listened to the messages over and over. Sometimes I reread portions of *Mother's Day.* It was my way of enjoying a small glimpse into his life since I walked out of the restaurant over a month before.

Today I was missing him, so I listened to the tapes again.

"Hey, Jimmie. This is Kenoy. Are you there? Please pick up the phone. Call me. I miss you."

"Hey, Jimmie. I thought I'd give you a little time. Hey, I got some great news today. Call me. I miss you."

"Jimmie. I hope you're all right. I hope you're getting my messages. You know a couple of days ago I told you I had some good news? Well since I haven't heard from you I guess I'm going to have to leave it on your answering machine. It's about my book. My agent has gotten a lot of interest from publishers. In a couple of days they are going to do something called an auction. Do you know what that is? Oh, shit, I think my time is going to run out. I will—"

"It's me again. I knew the tape was going to run out. So I was telling you about the auction. It's where publishers bid on the right to publish my book. Right now there are four publishers interested. Keep your fingers crossed. And if you're praying, please ask God to bless me. Call me. I miss you."

"Jimmie, it's me. I'm nervous. The auction has been going on all day. Two publishers have dropped out. But it looks like I

might be in for a windfall. I miss you. Please, please call me. Call me. I miss you."

"Hey, it's me. I sold my book. Viking is going to publish it. I met my editor and she's a nice lady. She loves the book. It got down to Random House and Viking. They offered me a little over three hundred thousand dollars. Can you believe that? I never thought I'd ever make that much money my whole life. God must have heard your prayers. Thank you. Call me. I miss you."

"Hey, I've sold my movie rights. Warner Bros. bought them. Fox 2000 tried to get in on the action, but Warner came ready to play. Angela Basset is pegged to play my mom. She will be great. May get her that Oscar she deserves. They are talking about Carl Franklin directing . . . you know, he did One False Move *with Cynda Williams and Michael Beach. I love that film. Who do you think should play me? There aren't a lot of young actors out there of mixed race. I miss you. . . . Call me."*

I wanted to call Kenoy and congratulate him. I wanted to hear him say that not only was he getting a lot of money for his book, but that he was out of the escort business forever. But I never heard that message. It had been over a week since Kenoy had last called. I wanted to call him. I missed him still.

When I looked around, it was the middle of May. The weather had suddenly gone from cold and wet to hot and sun-drenched within a couple of days. I still hadn't heard from Kenoy, but I had received a package from him that I hadn't opened. I planned to, but not yet. I spent nights staring at the package and wondered what was in the tiny box the size of a checkbook.

I was in the last week of finals and I had forgotten that my birthday was a few days away. Carmen called and asked what I was planning for my last birthday in my thirties, and I told her I wasn't planning anything.

"Then come and spend some time with me and the kids. We'll cook you a great meal, and I'll even bake you a cake."

"I don't know. I'm kind of depressed," I said.

"That's okay. Be depressed. What did Mom always say?"

"What?"

"Love happens more than once."

I missed my sister, so I decided to visit her and see how the city of Atlanta felt to me. I arranged my flight for early Saturday morning. Each day of the week, I placed an item of clothing in my suitcase in anticipation of my trip. It was Wednesday and I placed a pair of new warm-ups in my brown leather bag. I was ready to start running again, because I knew the first thing out of Carmen's mouth was going to be, "You're not getting fat on me, are you?"

I was getting ready to have dinner when the phone rang. I hoped it was Kenoy, so I turned the volume up on the machine.

"Diva! Are you there? Pick up the phone. I need you," Thunder said.

I picked up the phone and said, "I know you're not calling me about passing out food."

Thunder laughed and said, "Not quite. But I do need your help. I'm doing an event tomorrow for The Ladies Who Lunch Bunch up here in Harlem. I need some help assembling some gift bags."

"Ladies who lunch? Is that a new group?"

"I don't know. But it's the Old Harlem divas. You know, Sugar Hill girls. I got some fierce bags for them. Even a little aqua box from Tiffany's. Please help me. After we finish, I can take you out to dinner to celebrate your birthday. How does that sound?"

"That sounds good. I'm through packing for today."

"When are you leaving for Atlanta?"

"Saturday."

"You are coming back, right?"

"Yeah, I'm coming back. What would you do without me?"

"Oh, you know me. I'd miss you, but I'd survive. I'm just happy you're not going to let a man drive you from the greatest city in the world. Has he called?"

"Not recently," I said sadly.

"From that sound in your voice, I guess you still miss him. Right?"

"Yes, I miss him. But I hope we're not going to spend the evening talking about Kenoy," I said.

"No, but like I've told you before, you can't sleep with love or pride. I still think if you feel so strongly about him you should call him," Thunder advised.

I ignored his last statement and asked, "What time do you want me to be there?"

"Give me about an hour and a half. Wear something nice. Pull one of your good dresses out of the closet," Thunder laughed.

"Why?"

" 'Cause we are going someplace fancy. This is your last year before people will start calling you middle-aged. We're going to kick our heels up before arthritis kicks in."

"Okay. I'll see you around nine."

"Be on time, and don't bring that sad look you've been wearing since . . . well, you know."

"I'll do my best," I said as I hung up the phone. I walked to my closet to see what nice pants and shirt I could still fit in.

I located a pair of black linen pants that I prayed wouldn't make my ass look bigger than it was and a long-sleeved black silk shirt. While slowly sipping brandy, I took a long bath with bath beads I had purchased from the Body Shop. I was looking forward to seeing Thunder, and I was going to use this evening to reignite my social life.

About thirty minutes later I walked a block from my apartment and hailed a taxi. Minutes later, cruising up Eighth Avenue, the taxi was crossing the Disneyfied Forty-second Street, and I started to think about what I loved about New York and how I would miss it. I looked to my right and smiled at the bright lights of the Broadway theaters and realized it had been months since I had seen a Broadway show. When I first moved to New York I went to a show at least once a week. I made sure I didn't have classes on Wednesday afternoons because I would often attend a price-reduced matinee.

As we approached Columbus Circle and Fordham I wondered if I was making a difference by teaching. Could I do more in research or by returning to practicing medicine? And then my thoughts returned to Kenoy. What was I accomplishing by blocking him from my life? Was I making a moral judgment? Or was I simply running from love? So what if he had sold his body for money? I had done things in my life that I wasn't proud of. I remembered a time when I was in med school and this dufus named Alex Moore had this terrible crush on me. I wasn't the least bit interested in him because he was wrong for so many reasons. First, he talked like a white boy; I think he was from Fort Worth, Texas, or someplace like that. Alex, like me, was a member of a little society of closeted gay med students at McHarry. I always avoided being one-on-one with Alex because he always made his attraction obvious. During our last week of school, after we had completed finals, our little unofficial group had a potluck dinner at Lloyd Rice's house. Lloyd, a built, light-skinned beauty, made my dick increase in size just with his mere presence. Of course, he wasn't interested in me. Yet on this night I was determined to show him what he was missing. Lloyd wasn't buying it. When I told him I wanted to git with him, he looked at me and said, "We're probably interested in the same things. Let's just be friends." Even in the gay world those words are the kiss of death.

Well, Alex was waiting around just like a spider, and since I didn't have a car, I needed a ride home. Waiting on a cab outside of Nashville could take months. Alex had a car and offered me a ride home. I was drunk, horny, and feeling sorry for myself. I accepted the ride. Long story short, Alex and I ended up in bed, and the sex was average, as I had imagined it would be. He was in love and wanted to spend the night. I looked at him and said, "You don't have to go home, but you've got to leave here." He looked sad. I didn't care. I needed a ride home. He had a car. Wasn't I using sex to get what I needed? Sometimes in life, you have to use what you have, to get what you want or need.

*   *   *

The taxi pulled up in front of Thunder's brownstone and I was looking forward to an evening of drinking and eating with a friend. I gave the driver a twenty dollar bill and told him to keep the change. It was a five dollar tip but I was feeling generous and wanted to reward him for not having a physical reaction when I told him to take me up to Harlem. He gave me a huge smile and said, "Thank you, sir. Thank you very much."

As I was walking up the step, I noticed that Thunder's house was lit up like a Christmas tree. I saw someone look out the side window and then quickly close the curtain. Thunder didn't tell me he had company and I prayed a silent prayer that he wasn't trying to set me up again. I rang the doorbell and there was about a minute wait. *Where* is Thunder? I thought. He knew I was usually on time. Then I noticed that the well-lit house suddenly went dark. Then the door opened and there stood Thunder, with a glass of champagne in his hand and a party hat on his head.

"What is wrong with you?" I asked as I stepped into his foyer.

Then I heard a word I had never heard directed toward me. A huge crowd of people shouted, "Surprise!"

About fifteen familiar faces all focused on me. I was in semi-shock and for a few seconds I had their undivided attention, like I was the star of a Broadway show taking my final bow.

"Close your mouth, honey. I guess you're surprised," Thunder said as he put his arms around me and moved from the foyer. We walked into the living area, where a waiter handed me a glass of champagne, and then Thunder led the crowd in a rendition of "Happy Birthday." I just kept looking at Thunder, shaking my head in mock disappointment. But I was beginning to feel extremely happy. This was not the first birthday party given in my honor, just the first surprise one. When I was growing up my sister and I had lots of birthday parties, but this was the first one I had to celebrate an odd-year birthday. My parents would give us a party every other year. For me it was even-numbered years and Carmen had parties on odd numbers. On my odd-numbered birthday, I was expected to perform community service and donate my birthday money to charity.

After the second chorus of "Happy Birthday," I hugged Thunder's neck and whispered, "You got me this time."

"I ain't finished yet," he replied. "The night has just begun and I got even more surprises up my sleeves."

Several of the well-dressed men started making their way toward me to give me a kiss on the cheek and wish me happy birthday. The first was a short, brown-skinned man named Ivan, who was an amateur bodybuilder. He had bad skin, and word on the street was that his dick was shorter than a minute because of all the steroids he took.

"Ivan, how you doing, man? I haven't seen you in a long time. How have you been?"

"I been good," Ivan said. "Were you really surprised?"

"You couldn't tell from my face?" We both chuckled. Then I asked, "Are you still competing?"

"Yeah, I got a contest in New Jersey next week, so I can't stay long. Got to be in the gym first thing."

"Well, you look good."

"Thanks. So do you. I'm going to move out of the way so the rest of your friends can get their hugs," Ivan said.

"Thanks, Ivan," I said as I leaned over and gave him another hug.

For the next fifteen minutes, I stood in the archway of Thunder's huge living room greeting guests like I was the king or queen of England. A lot of the people I didn't really consider friends, just associates I saw at the bars or at some of the black circuit events, like D.C. on Memorial Day, Atlanta on Labor Day, and Los Angles during Fourth of July. When I didn't remember their names, I would just say, "Oh, it's good to see you, baby," or "Boy, you still look good."

As the line came to an end, Thunder came and whisked me upstairs, where several guests were drinking wine in his den while soft music played in the background. Waiters carried platters of food from room to room of Thunder's three-story brownstone.

"So are you having fun?" Thunder asked.

"I'm having a ball. How did you pull this off? You can hold water better than you can keep a secret," I teased.

"Oh, it's not hard when your best friend is in a constant state of doom and gloom. I hope tonight changes that for good."

"I can't tell you how much better I'm beginning to feel," I said.

Thunder and I left the den area and went into his large Victorian-style bedroom, where a thin light-skinned with a large afro was sitting on the bed, watching a basketball game.

"This is my new baby's daddy, Samuel Tucker," Thunder said as he swayed over toward his bed.

"Hi, Samuel," I said. "Nice meeting you."

"Are you the birthday boy?" he asked.

"Yeah, I'm afraid so," I said as I moved toward the love seat directly across from the king-size canopy bed.

"Then we ought to celebrate," Samuel said as he reached under the bed and pulled out the top of a shoe box covered with weed and rolling papers. "You do indulge, don't you?"

"Sometimes. But I think I'll pass," I said as I finished the last of my champagne.

"You want some more to drink, honey?" Thunder asked.

"Sure."

"Where are those damn waiters? I told them to make sure your glass was never empty. I hope I don't have to *read* somebody on your birthday."

"Don't worry about it. I'll go downstairs and get some. Do you need anything?"

"Naw, baby. I got everything I need right here," Thunder said as he wrapped his arms around Samuel.

I walked down the stairs, exchanging smiles and kisses on the cheek with several guests who had arrived late. Thunder told me he had invited about thirty-five people and it seemed that all of them showed up with a few guests in tow.

I moved into the kitchen, where a handsome waiter greeted me with a full bottle of champagne and said, "There you are. I've been looking for you."

"Thank you," I said as he filled my thin flute to the top.

I walked back into the living area, where guests were now dancing to house music. I wasn't feeling house music, so I went back upstairs to the den, where the music was producing a mellow mood, the kind of mood the surprise and the champagne were putting me in.

A few hours later, I was feeling no pain. As guests began to leave, Thunder announced from the top of the stairs, "It's been fun. But you girls have drunk all my liquor and eaten all my food. It's time to press on. You don't have to go home. But you got to leave here."

I was getting ready to leave as well before there would be no chance of getting a taxi out of Harlem, when Thunder whispered to me, "Go up to the white room, darling. I got one more surprise for you."

I gave him a puzzled look, and he just waved his limp hand in the air like he was scooting me up the stairs.

"Are you coming up?" I asked.

"Don't worry about me. I got to make sure I get these girls out of my house."

I walked slowly up the three flights of stairs toward Thunder's white room. It was a large open space, with deep, plush white carpet, white sofas, and white scented candles. Thunder used this room to meditate and drink champagne with guests one-on-one. It was the only room in his house where he insisted you remove your shoes before entering. When I reached the third floor, I could hear soft music playing, which sounded like Vanessa L. Williams singing, and I noticed a pair of black boots sitting by the door.

I walked into the room with my shoes still on. The space had a golden glow from the lit candles. I could see the shadow of a man sitting in the windowsill. As I moved to the center of the room, I got the second shock of the night. It was Kenoy.

"Happy Birthday, Jimmie," he said with a huge smile. He was dripping with sex appeal in black leather pants that were as tight as skin and a cranberry silk shirt with the top two buttons open.

"Kenoy. What are you doing here?" I asked.

"I was invited. I heard you might need a ride home," he said.

I stood still for a moment, unable to believe Kenoy was only a few feet from me. Our eyes were locked in a gaze like we were sending each other secret messages, and I suddenly decided I had been acting like a spoiled child for too long. I wanted to touch Kenoy. I wanted to kiss him and spend the night in his arms. I moved toward him and my arms began to tremble as I reached up and put them around Kenoy's neck. He kissed me gently on the mouth and then his tongue slipped through my parted lips. I felt a strange and comforting calmness, as if my body had been dipped in ice-cold water, making my body feel numb.

After we finished a minute-long passionate kiss, Kenoy mumbled, "I've miss you so much."

"I've missed you, too."

"Are you ready to go home?"

"Sure, but do you want to take the subway? We'll never catch a cab at this time of morning," I said as I looked at my watch, which showed it was a little past 4 A.M.

"We don't have to take the subway, and I will get you home safely," Kenoy said.

"How did Thunder get in touch with you?" I asked. I was praying he wouldn't say through the agency.

"He got my address from the guest book from the party and he sent me a really nice note. I was touched."

"Is that why you stopped calling?"

"Yes, I didn't want to give away the secret, and knowing that I would see you made it much easier to resist calling or showing up on your doorstep," Kenoy said as he took my hand in his. I smiled as I was savored the idea of spending days and weeks with Kenoy.

"So are you ready to go?" I asked.

"Ready when you are," he smiled.

We walked out of the white room and Kenoy put his boots on. I heard Thunder's voice and a few seconds later he was standing there with a big smile on his face. Then he looked down at my feet and said, "Now I know you didn't go in the white room with your shoes on, Miss Thing. I know you're gettin' old but you haven't lost *all* your senses."

"I'm sorry. I got carried away."

"I'll forgive you this time, but don't make it a habit. So how is this for the finale?"

"Wonderful," I said as I kissed Thunder on the cheek.

He whispered, "Now don't be a fool twice. I've talked to this man and he's the real deal."

"Thank you," I said as I grabbed Kenoy's hand and started toward the steps, before Kenoy pulled back and said, "Wait a minute." He turned and gave Thunder a big hug and planted a kiss on his forehead. Then he grabbed my hand and we raced down the stairs like we were little boys racing for a spot on the last swing.

When we got outside, Kenoy pulled me against him and kissed me while standing on the last step of Thunder's place. It was a tonsil-touching kiss. I had never kissed a man on the streets of Harlem.

"How are we getting home?" I asked.

"Your chariot awaits," Kenoy said as he grabbed my hand again and we walked about half a block. We came upon a silver-blue convertible BMW and Kenoy pulled out a set of keys and pointed toward the car. I heard an alarmlike sound and the lights of the beautiful car came on.

"Is this yours?"

"Yes, sir. Do you like it?"

"It's beautiful. When did you get this?"

"Yesterday. I want you to be the first one to sit in it besides me," Kenoy smiled.

"You're going to make me cry," I said as Kenoy opened the door for me and I slid into the front seat and inhaled the new-car smell I loved as a kid. Every year either my father or mother would get a new car and I would wallow in the backseat, trying to cover my body with the scent of the car.

"I know it's kinda cool, but would you like to ride with the top down?"

"Let's do it," I said.

Kenoy and I enjoyed the chill of the early morning and the stars dancing in the blue sky along motionless clouds as we sped

down the West Side Highway. When we reached my neighborhood I noticed that the early-morning light made my block look
gray. Kenoy put the top up on his car and we walked into my
apartment building holding hands like teenage lovers.

Once inside my apartment I kissed Kenoy passionately, full
on his mouth, and he responded with equal passion. He then
pulled back and gently touched my face, our eyes meeting in a
penetrating gaze. I felt wonderful at the sensation of being
touched.

"I have something I need to say," Kenoy said in a low and serious voice.

"What?"

"I want you to know that from this moment on every word
from my mouth will be the truth. In the short time since you've
come into my life, so much has changed. So many dreams have
come true. I am out of the escort business for good and I'm
ready to devote my life to my writing career and you . . ." Kenoy
said and then paused. I was looking at him with loving eyes, still
silent.

"If . . . if you let me," he finished. "Will you let me love you?"

My heart was racing and I was absolutely lost in the moment,
not having a clue what to do next, what to do when everything
you've ever dreamed of happens. This wonderful man was asking me if he could love me.

Finally I broke my silence and asked, "Are you sure?"

"Sure about what?"

"Sure about loving me? Sure about leaving the escort business?"

"More certain than I've been about anything in my life."

I was stirred by so many emotions and questions as I stood
close to Kenoy. Could he forget a childhood of pain and love me
without complications? Could I trust him? Could I love him
completely? Again my body was pulling me in different directions, like the first night I had met Kenoy. But this time I listened
to the part that told me to give love a chance, to throw caution
right out the window and love this handsome man asking me to
do just that.

I pulled Kenoy close to me and began kissing him and slowly unbuttoning his shirt. Moments later we were still kissing passionately and undressing each other. The smell of Kenoy's body aroused me, sweat and cologne combining for a sexy and sweet aroma. I pulled back to admire his stomach, a rippling wave of muscles. I opened the top of his leather pants and Kenoy took over, unzipping his pants, kicking off his boots, and ripping his pants off in a matter of seconds. He was standing before me in some black nylon see-through underwear, with the head of his dick sticking out above the waistband. I clumsily removed my pants and took Kenoy's hand and we raced to my bedroom.

We dived onto my bed still holding hands and I allowed myself to enjoy a wonderful, all-enveloping feeling of love and lust. Kenoy and I kissed slowly and sweetly as we removed our underwear and tossed them to the floor. He then whispered to me sweetly, "Can I make love to you?" I took a deep breath and said, "Yes." Kenoy's eyes widened and he kissed my lips and then my neck and ears. His tongue moved toward my nipples and he sucked them softly like they were fresh strawberries. Kenoy's dick hardened against the muscle of my legs and my own sex stiffened.

I was feeling a mixture of excitement and fear, wanting the sensation of Kenoy inside me, but dreading the possible pain. I knew I wanted to love him with my whole body.

I moved Kenoy onto his back, then reached into my nightstand and pulled out a condom and some lubricant. I tore the condom wrapper open with my teeth and slowly placed it on Kenoy's brick-hard dick, and then covered it with the cool slipperiness of the lubricant. Then I straddled Kenoy, securing a comfortable spot on his lap. "Am I too heavy?" I asked.

"You feel great," Kenoy said as he moved up to kiss me. He then entered me slowly, taking his time for a long, long fifteen minutes, then gradually building to a moaning and pumping crescendo. The feeling of Kenoy inside me left me breathless and I began to ride him like he was a rocking horse. The sensation became almost too much and I thought I was going to collapse on Kenoy's chest. He was moaning and breathing deeply. I leaned over him and heard his voice softly in my ear saying, "Ride that dick, boy. Take this dick. Is this your dick, baby?"

It had been a while since I'd had passionate sex with a man, and very rarely with someone who talked, but I had to answer Kenoy. "It's my dick, baby. It's my dick."

"Come on then, boy, ride that dick," Kenoy said as he pumped faster and breathed harder. I could hear exhaustion weighing heavy in his voice and the sensations in my body were feeling multiplied over and over.

It was as though our bodies were colliding and slowly preparing to break the surface of the ocean, when Kenoy started to scream, "I'm getting ready to come . . . Oh, shit, I'm coming!" I started to ride Kenoy's dick faster and then, within seconds after feeling the condom fill with semen, I released a powerful climax onto Kenoy's chest without even the slightest touch of my own sex. That was the first time that had happened in thirty-nine years.

Kenoy's sleepy moan startled me. For a minute I just lay on my side with my left arm supporting my head and gazed at the handsome man sleeping on the left side of my bed. A few moments later Kenoy's eyes opened, and he smiled at me as he rubbed his entire face with his large hand. He pulled me close to him and kissed me softly. It didn't matter that we both had the dreaded morning breath.

"Good morning," I said.

"Good morning to you, sir. How did you sleep?"

"I slept wonderfully," I said.

Kenoy sat up with his back against the headboard and pulled me even closer, and I lay against his chest in silence. After about ten minutes I looked up at him and asked, "Are you hungry?"

"I'm starved. But let me take you to breakfast."

"No, let me cook for you. I don't have a class until this afternoon. Besides, if we have breakfast here, I get to see you naked," I joked.

"For you I'd walk into any restaurant in the city butt-ass naked," Kenoy joked back.

"I'd have to beat the boys off you."

"No, you wouldn't. They'd know I was with you."

I gave Kenoy a peck on the cheek and went into the bathroom to wash my face and brush my teeth. I started to take a shower, but I decided it would be better to do that with Kenoy. I put on my pajama bottoms and went into the kitchen and pulled four eggs, some turkey sausage, cheese and milk out of the fridge. I broke off pieces of cheddar cheese and mixed them with the eggs and milk. I located half an onion and cut chips to add to my breakfast mixture. I placed the sausage on my George Foreman grill and popped two slices of bread in the toaster. I could hear the water running in the bathroom and imagined Kenoy was washing his face. *Toothbrush,* I suddenly thought. I hoped I had a spare. I went to my small towel closet and looked in a white plastic bag where I kept extra toiletries. I spotted a new black toothbrush and a blue disposable razor. I walked into the bathroom, where Kenoy was bent over the washbowl splashing water on his face.

"I thought you might need these," I said as I handed him the razor and toothbrush.

"Thank you," Kenoy said as he smiled like he had a secret.

"Breakfast will be ready by the time you finish."

"It smells good."

"I hope you'll like it," I said as I moved out of my small bathroom.

I had taken only a couple of steps when I head Kenoy's sexy voice say, "Come back here."

I turned and he pulled me toward him and gave me a sweet kiss and asked, "You're not going to spoil me, are you?"

"Only if you deserve it."

Kenoy and I enjoyed breakfast in a peaceful silence. Every now and then I would look over at him, and Kenoy would return my glance with enormous tenderness. I felt like I could float to Fordham.

Kenoy smiled and opened his mouth to say something, but instead he just shook his head.

"What are you thinking?" I asked. I couldn't believe I had uttered a question I myself hated hearing.

"I'm thinking about you, and how wonderful last night was," Kenoy said.

"Right answer," I smiled.

"So what are we going to do tonight?"

"What do you want to do?"

"Spend it with you."

I suddenly remembered my planned trip to Atlanta and said, "Aw, shit."

"What's the matter? Do you have plans?"

"Not tonight. I was just thinking about Saturday. I leave for Atlanta for a week. Now all of a sudden I don't want to leave."

"Then don't," Kenoy said.

"I promised my sister."

"I understand that. I remember how close you told me you guys are."

"But the week will go fast," I said, trying to convince myself.

"Let me take you."

"Take me where?"

"To Atlanta."

"What are you saying?"

"Why don't you let me drive you? I don't have to stay with you and your sister. We can take our time. Stop in Washington, D.C., and Charlotte. Stay in wonderful hotels and have breakfast in bed. What do you think?"

"It sounds wonderful. Let me think about it."

"What's there to think about? We get to spend time together. We can talk about our dreams. Our future. We can stop when we want to, and make love. I need to give you a taste of the other things I have to offer. It will be wonderful. I don't want to spend another day without you," Kenoy said.

"You're right. There is nothing to think about. Let's do it."

"I'll be off the hook. When you're busy with your family, I can start the outline on my next book."

"What is it going to be about?"

"I think it's going to be a love story."

"That sounds nice," I said as I smiled and gently rubbed the top of Kenoy's hands.

The two of us were silent for a while, and then Kenoy said, "You haven't said anything about the package I sent you. Were you surprised?"

I thought about the package in my sock drawer, which I had never opened. For a brief second I started to bluff—no, lie . . . and then I thought of Kenoy's words about truthfulness the night before, so I said, "I never opened it."

"Do you still have it?"

"Yes."

"Where is it?"

"In my drawer."

"Will you open it for me?"

"Right now?"

"Please."

I pushed back my chair and went into the bedroom and pulled the package from the drawer. I quickly tore open the package, and just when I was getting ready to examine the contents I noticed Kenoy standing in the doorway. I glanced up and gave him a nervous smile. When I lifted the top off the box I saw three crisp one hundred dollar bills with a small note card on top. I looked at the card and read, *Jimmy, With you it was never about money. I learned long ago that money can't buy love. Especially real love . . . true love . . . Kenoy.*

Feeling my eyes brim with tears, I looked at Kenoy and asked, "What's this for?" I held the money between my fingers.

"It's the money you gave me to spend time with you. I returned Thunder's money as well. You've taught me that no amount of money is worth the risk of losing a chance at love."

I felt numb. I thought about the first time I saw Kenoy, and when I found out what he did for living. Then I thought about how I had felt the night before, and I stood up and pulled him close to me. I buried my head in the groove of his shoulder and cried as he gently stroked the back of my neck. I realized no amount of money could ever make me feel the way I was feeling at this moment. I wanted to feel this way forever. I think I can. I think I will.

I'm Still Waiting

COLIN CHANNER

(for my radiant daughter Addis,
and my curious son Makonnen)

chapter one

Like a manatee, the big Mercedes dove into the traffic and pulled itself ahead with ease despite its bulk and weight. It was summer—humid and hot, and the sky above Manhattan was the color of a tropic sea.

Sitting in the back of the car, slouched against a door, her twirly Afro banded with a length of purple cloth, Patience Olayinka felt her stomach crunching as the eight-cylinder engine pulled her down the FDR.

It was a little after two; the meeting was at three, and as she felt the car begin to slow, and heard the driver suck his teeth, she knew she would be late.

Her eyes were closed behind a pair of silver shades with undulating edges; and she tried to clear her mind by guessing where she was. On the left she knew there was a park—she did not know the name—a grassy park with leafy trees and baseball fields; and on the other side there was a clump of housing projects brown and squat.

What an irony, she thought, that roads, whose very idea is to bring us closer, can often work to keep us from the things we love.

And as she thought of this, she began to hear a song, a sad song about a little boy who wants to cross a highway just to fly his kite. Then she remembered that the FDR was spanned by many walkways, and that some years ago, late one night, after a performance at the Roxy, she had juiced a man on one of them—a man who was no longer in her life—her ankles crossed behind his back, her body arcing back and down across the rail, the humming of the traffic whirring through her spine.

She wanted to forget her past. She switched her mind again and thought of where she was. She was somewhere south of Houston Street, she knew; and in her head she saw the oily river through the trees.

There would be boats in the river, she thought. Pleasure boats and freighters. And as she thought about the boats, she saw the esplanade between the river and the park. And she saw Latino men with glowing skin like polished pine standing with their knees between the iron railing, catching fish with simple poles the way they would have done at home.

And as she thought of Puerto Rico, where she'd gone to live eight years ago when rumors had begun to plague her, she said inside her head: "I have lived too many lives."

By the time she was sixteen, she had been around the world. Her father, who was Nigerian, was an international banker, and her mother who was Irish, was an anthropologist; but most of her travels were on her own.

In the early 1990s, Olay, as she used to call herself, was the princess of the realm of teeny pop—a wormy-waisted piece of chesty jailbait whose songs of unrequited love and boys who moved away had galvanized her compact discs in platinum.

Now, at twenty-four, so much had changed. She hadn't had a label for the last three years, and had been signed and dropped before that many times. But she was holding fast to her belief that she had learned enough from life to make an album of intelligence and grace, a work as deep and penetrating as a novel.

As she thought of this the car began to move again. Eyes still closed, she reached into her bag, which was large and sailor-striped with polished bamboo handles, and rummaged elbow-deep for a lighter and a spliff, feeling, then discarding a tin of mints, a vodka flask, a jar of body cream from Kiehl's, a diaphragm, a Coptic cross, a journal and a candle.

She lit the spliff and pulled it hard and felt the heat suffuse her like a drop of ink in water. Then she heard her manager's voice, measured but insistent: "Get there late. Smell of weed. This is what we need right now."

"I thought we weren't speaking," she replied.

Her voice was soft and furry, the vowels elongated like a stretching cat.

"Well, I'm speaking to you now."

"I'd prefer if you didn't."

"I will do what I have to do to rightly do my job."

She had hired him a month ago, which to her meant that she owed him nothing; and she hooked her glasses down her nose to say this with her eyes, the movement agitating her bracelet, a knotted length of plaited silver threaded through with common stones.

"Patience," he continued. Like her he was a Londoner, but he was twice her age and white, with an oblong face that turned to mush along a quickly tapered jaw. "Do you follow what I am saying? Things are rough out here. Yes, you are my boss, but you have to let me do my job." She didn't reply. "If you think that I am not doing it, then you should tell me. Tell me right now. I know my way around this place. The driver can let me out if you don't think that I have something to say. He can pull over. I can get around. I am not a stranger to this place. If you don't want to listen, Patience, then go to the meeting alone."

She watched him, the black of his suit, the brown of his center-parted hair, the blue of his eyes, the white of his shirt against his orange tie. Since they were sitting down their eyes were level—for he was short—and she promised herself to bully him later, when they were standing. Then his head would be the height of her nipples.

As the car began to rise with the grading road, she removed her glasses and held them in her lap. Higher up now she could see the gray of the river below her, then the blue Manhattan Bridge above. The river was moving swiftly; and a subway train was rushing on from Brooklyn; and she could see the flashing sparks along the rails and sunlight glinting on the silver cars, which were striped with shadow from the cables of the old suspension bridge.

She felt his hand on hers, and she did not pull away.

"I believe in you," he said, a little tightly. "That's why I took this job. I just need you to work with me." Of the spliff he added softly: "Just put it out. You can smoke all you want when we leave."

She handed him the spliff as they flashed beneath the shadow of the bridge, and raising her hips to pull her body in a bow, she reached inside the pocket of her yellow cargo pants.

"This is our problem," she declared, holding up a DAT. "Not weed. These tunes are full of shit. I know it. You know it, and depending on the traffic on the Brooklyn Bridge, Don will know it soon as well. These are not my songs. This is not my idea of music." She shot up, closed her eyes, took a breath, then flopped down again, shifting her weight as if she had sat on a stone, continuing to speak in a strident voice. "This isn't music, Peter. This is the shit you hear on radio every day. It's like crack—a very basic formula that anyone can make in their house. Fuck, it doesn't really matter anymore. I'm already done."

"I cannot say I agree with you," said Peter. "You're not ruined. Radio is exactly what you need right now. The sound of black music is changing. And we have to give the people what they want. If radio doesn't play it, then you haven't got a chance." He plucked the tape away from her. "This is the sound of today. Use it to get where you want to be tomorrow. That's the thing you should be looking at. Tomorrow. You are already where you are."

"So you think it's great?" she asked. "Be honest."

"It's the only way I know to be."

When he turned his gaze outside the window, she sucked her teeth and told him: "You're completely full of shit."

chapter two

Across the river, in a nineteenth-century factory with rows of arching windows on a cobbled street in Dumbo, Donald Kurtz was staring at this image in a tinted pane and mouthing to himself, "I can't believe this shit I'm hearing."

Dressed as usual in pajamas and knee-length cowboy boots he leaned up off his horseshoe desk and paced around his office, his heels thud-clunking on the varnished floors, his shadow pitched against the grain of the high brick walls, one hand on the telephone, the other briskly pointing the remote toward the eighteen-unit video wall suspended from the ceiling.

"Listen," he said, raising the volume on MSNBC. "I don't need this shit from you . . . well . . . if that's the case, then fuck you too . . . money is money . . . no, no, no, no, that's not the problem . . . the problem is you're wasting my money . . . listen to the pronoun . . . *my* . . . and you don't seem to be respecting that." He paused to pay attention to the value of a stock. "This is the music business . . . not the music game or the music charity . . . the music *business* . . . as a matter of fact, I've got business to do . . . so I gotta go." He grabbed a fist of matted hair, blond with darker roots. "I love you, man . . . don't gimme that shit . . . you know I love you. How could I not love you when you schooled me in this shit? But bullshit is bullshit . . . and you're making me feel as if you're trying to punk me out? Anyway, that is how I feel right now. So tell Saran Rap that he can fuck himself . . . yeah . . . with a motherfucking nuclear missile . . . yeah, yeah, tell him to suck my dick, then, if that ain't

big enough . . . yeah, yeah, blah, blah, bling, bling, Sony's got a
contract with his name on it . . . contract my ass . . . yeah, the
way he's playing himself, the only thing he's about to contract is
that VD."

He passed between the maple-finished conference table and
his paper-laden desk and stepped up on the platform where his
telescope was set up on a tripod.

A train was moving fast across the bridge; and he peered
across the river, searching through the windows of the multi-
storied buildings just behind the FDR to see if he could spot
some naked flesh.

Back at his desk he dialed his assistant, who sat outside the
double doors.

"Have Patience and her baby-sitter called?"

Off the telephone now, his voice had lost its edge, and he
sounded like himself: a graduate of Dartmouth with a chemistry
degree.

"Of course they haven't come yet." Her voice was Trinida-
dian. Her cadence was a song. "They are usually late."

"Call them please and let me know what's going on?"

"Okay . . . I have some calls for you."

"Okay . . ."

"Wyclef, Timbaland, Dr. Dre . . ."

"Oh, you are so fucking evil." He reached out for her picture,
which was framed in cherry wood. "Has anyone ever asked you
why a honey like you is hooked up with a short fat Jew like
me?"

"All the time."

"And how do you explain it?"

"I told them that I dropped a little oil in your dinner."

He smiled and briefly looked like thirty-one again. Weight
and sleepless nights had aged him fifteen years; and as he marveled at her beauty, he thanked her in his heart for all that she
had done to help him build his label when he'd lost his job in
A&R at Virgin. So much had changed since then. Now they
lived together, with a baby on the way; and his dad, who owned
a fleet of cabs, was pulling all his money from the label. There

would be more changes soon. For better or for worse? As he pondered this, Diane began to speak again: "Peter just arrived."

"Patience isn't well," said Peter as he sat down at the conference table.

Donald said: "I've always known that."

"She's not *feeling* well," said Peter.

"Whatever."

"I don't know what you mean by that."

"Of course you do. You're around her every day." On a plastic tray between them were some water and some glasses and a bowl of melting ice. Donald helped himself and then continued. "In the NBA, Patience would be the kind of player they call 'uncoachable.' You know that kind of player . . . a nigga with mad game who just can't pull his shit together. Mary can't sing like Patience. Toni can't sing like Patience. If you wanna talk about people in her league, you've gotta talk Whitney or Mariah—and that is if you're talking about this generation right here. But this business ain't about who can sing and who can't sing. It's all about two things: who you're willing to fuck and who you're willing to listen to." He was about to rest on this, but Peter seemed unmoved, so he continued.

"And forget this shit about fucking your way to the top. The farthest you can fuck your way is to the middle. To get to the top you have to listen. But Patience doesn't seem to know that."

"I would disagree," said Peter. "She knows she needs to listen. The thing is that she knows she should be listening to her soul."

"Oh, that's a loada shit. An artist has to listen to the radio and ask herself, 'Why is that song being played over mine?' An artist has to listen to the producer who will get her that sound that's getting radio play. An artist has to listen to the songwriter that will give her the kind of lyrics people wanna hear. An artist has to listen to the publicist to know what people wanna hear her say in interviews. Now, once upon a time, twenty million albums ago, Patience Olayinka used to listen. Then she stopped. Now she doesn't have a career."

"It's a little bit more complex than that."

"No, it's not. She began to take her fans for granted." He leaned across the table now to emphasize. "There were millions of little girls around the world who used to use her songs to help them through their growing pains." As Peter glanced around the room, Donald asked, "Do you know what a song is . . . not to us . . . to the people who buy records?" He did not wait on a reply. "A song is a part of the sound track to the film they think their life is. The people out there are not living in reality. They are living in a movie world, a TV world, and they want their lives to have its own personal sound track. See, the more fake their life is, the more they believe it's real. And Patience betrayed a lot of people when she came out with her so-called grown-up music. The kids were like, 'What the fuck?' And adults were like, 'Little girl, please.' And that's how Patience fucked herself."

"Anyway," said Peter as he found himself compelled by Donald's logic. "We have some other things to talk about."

"The tape."

"The tape."

At a smaller rack beside the video wall, Donald placed the tape in a machine, and as he moved toward the table, he stopped to listen to the opening of the lost-my-lover ballad. The strings were soft. The kick drum thugged it out.

"Is this pretty much the way it sounds?"

Peter couldn't read his face. Twenty minutes later when they'd sampled all the tracks, Don was sitting with his elbows on his knees.

"I want you to be honest, Peter. Do you think this shit is any good?"

Peter crossed his arms and said, "It all depends on what you mean."

"Good for me is an album that'll earn me back the hundred grand I gave her. Better is an album that will make some noise and earn a little cash so I can begin to build a catalog with value. Best is an album with lots of singles that radio will like and that people will buy—in other words the kinda album that will make me say, 'Patience is wack but I'ma keep her around.'

That's the kinda album that I gotta have right now. Anything else don't make no sense."

Peter walked around the room, his hands in the pockets of his buttoned-up suit.

"It's a better album than anything you've put out so far," said Peter. "On principle, you'd have to drop everybody else as well. Don't forget that people know who Patience is. Her first and second albums sold eleven million copies. As a businessman, I'm sure you know that it's unwise to bet against those kinds of numbers."

"Who knows?" Donald said, standing up and leaning on the table. "She might have something left. But basically, Peter, I simply can't afford to take the risk."

"Oh," said Peter, "it has come to this."

"Don't get sentimental, Peter. You've been around this business too long for that. Artists have hits. They don't have careers. Careers are for guys like me and you."

"Tell you what," Peter said as Donald shook his hand and began to move toward the door. "Give us another month or two, and I'm sure we'll work it out. We're not far off, I don't think."

"I don't know, man."

"Look, we take a day or two to process this whole conversation. We go back to the studio, and we do the tracks the way you think is best."

Donald shook his hand again and said: "I can't do this anymore."

"You can if you want to," blurted Peter. He recovered quickly, though, changed his tone and said: "Let's make something happen, man. Let's make history. We could make history if we make this album work. We just need a little time."

"I can't do this anymore."

They were standing at the door now. Donald had his hand above the knob.

"We can if we decide we want to," Peter said.

"I can't, man. I just can't. Patience doesn't give a shit. She isn't even here."

"She's ill."

"Whatever."

"Look—"

"I can't. You win some, Peter, and you lose some. That goes for money and that goes for friends."

"What are you saying, then?"

"I am saying what I said. I know what I am up against. I know the things that I've got to do."

chapter three

The building was located on a narrow street that elbowed near the entrance of a park. The street was gently graded, and the buildings were old, most of them in brick, nineteenth-century structures with elaborate facades.

Peter headed down the street and made his way inside the little park, picking up a footpath that slanted at an angle to the boardwalk, which was painted powder blue. Following the boardwalk, the river on his right, to his left a lawn of sunning people, he began to trot a bit and jog.

Beyond the railing was a bulwark of granite rocks; and as Peter thought of what he was about to say, his mind was flooded by the sound of lapping water. Ahead of him he could see the huge foundations of the Brooklyn Bridge, the gray stones in titanic columns; and beyond the bridge he could see the thick agglomeration of steel and glass on Wall Street; and he noted to himself how the buildings cut each other off from total view as if in competition, the rows and rows of windows rising higher, soaring like the market.

At the end of the boardwalk, he passed through another gate, crossed a narrow street that ended at the water and moved along the cobbled esplanade that spread out from the buttress of the span, into whose shadow he passed, emerging into light again, his shoes crunch-crunching on the stones.

Rounding the bridge with the esplanade, he came upon a pair of iron gates that opened on the driveway of the River Café, whose driveway, lined with brick, made a crescent through the shadow of a tree around whose roots were planted many flowers.

The driveway put him out on Old Fulton Street, which was broad and fairly busy. Restaurants were clustered there; and from the ridge of Brooklyn Heights, narrow streets cascaded, bringing pedestrians and trickling streams of traffic.

At the end of Old Fulton was an old lighthouse made of wood, and beyond the lighthouse was a jetty as wide and deep as a Broadway stage; and there, parked at an angle, the driver leaning on the trunk, reading a magazine with his face toward the city, was the car.

When the driver turned around, Peter signaled him to take a walk.

The heat and the tension and the tempo of the journey had opened Peter's pores, and he could feel the wetness of his shirt against his freckled back.

Bending with his palms against his knees, he brought his face against the lightly tinted window. Patience was lying on her side along the khaki-colored seat, apparently asleep, her sandals off, her face against her palm, a loosened finger from her fist inside her mouth.

Peter tapped the window. Patience did not stir. He called her name. She did not answer. He called her again. She did not move.

He opened the door and the light and sound aroused her, but she quickly closed her eyes on seeing him and tried to will herself to sleep again. Peter held the door, watching her, and she began to feel unnerved by his presence, but this feeling soon gave way to a feeling of embarrassment, a sense that she had done something for which she ought to be ashamed. And as she thought of this, she admitted that she had; yet she vowed to not admit it.

"So how did it go?" she asked as she lit a cigarette. She sucked it deeply, and her cheekbones pointed through her skin. She looked at him, looked askance, then looked down at her feet and saw the white of her nails against the beige of her skin and the black of the mat.

"It could have been worse."

His head was hanging low to see into the car. One arm was on the roof, the other on the frame of the open door.

She began to fidget now, and her bracelet clanked and clamored.

"We have some things to finalize," he said, glad that she had looked away and did not see him swallow.

"What does that mean?"

"That we wait to hear from him about some things and then we're off . . . cooking with gas."

The cigarette between her thumb and pointing forefinger, she tilted her head and smoked it for a while, the smoke coming out in ribbons and puffs, her lips held in a circle like a crater. Things were bubbling inside, he knew. Soon they might explode, which concerned him even more when he saw the empty vodka bottle peeping from beneath the driver's seat.

She turned to him and smiled and motioned him to sit beside her, the bracelet clanking now, and he felt a sadness coming on, and he asked himself if he should tell her the truth as he knew it, or tell her the truth as it could turn out to be. This had always been the hardest part of management—when to lie and when to not; for truth can liberate as much as it can kill.

Halfway in, one foot still outside the door, he asked himself again if he could chance it, searching for a clue in her face. Her forehead was high, smooth and round as a river stone, with a ridge of bone to shade the sockets of her eyes, which were deeply set with copper irises. Her cheekbones, which were angled out, were sharp and roughly hewn, showing through like reefs in shallow water.

"So what's the word?"

"The word," he said, "is good."

"Okay, I'll put it to you another way. To be or not to be?"

And as he saw her with the cigarette and the bottle at her feet, he realized that he had to say: "To be."

She held his hand and kissed it, and he rubbed her spit into his skin and held her face, wondering as she cried, if he had made the right decision.

*   *   *

Returning to Manhattan, they had lunch in a restaurant across the street from their hotel, a white cast-iron building with windows framed by columns on a narrow street in Soho.

The restaurant was large—two floors and a basement—with octagonal tiles and, in the mezzanine, a barrel-vaulted ceiling.

At a well-proportioned table with an orchid in a pewter vase, Patience had a beet and apple salad with a sherry vinaigrette, and Peter ordered mutton, which he found a little salty and he asked the waiter for the sole, which was served with hearts of palm and roasted carrots.

It was a little after five, early for the dinner crowd, and the service, though efficient, was unhurried. It had begun to rain, softly at first, but the water was beginning to come hard now, clattering like a beaded curtain. Outside, people had begun to scurry past the cafés and boutiques that lined the street.

"So when do we go back to London, then?"

"In about a week."

"And what is there to do between now and then?"

"For you," said Peter, "very little. For me, quite a bit."

"Did I tell you thanks?" she said, tilting her head to rest upon her angled palm, a smile subtly pleating the corners of her eyes.

"You didn't have to," he replied. "Some things don't have to be said."

"But others ought to be. Thanks for saving my bum."

She raised her glass. He raised his too, and he felt his stomach twitching as he thought of what would happen if he couldn't make the deal. Would she fire him and hire someone else? Would she go to pieces? Would it ultimately help her by teaching her to listen? Yes, she didn't like to listen. But so much was her talent that whoever could contain her would be rich.

"So tell me?" she asked brightly, as he considered all of this. "I want to buy a present for you. What do you want? I don't care. Whatever it is."

"You're joking of course."

She had always managed money well. So life without a label had not ruined her.

"I can't take anything from you," said Peter. "I was only doing my job. I'm just happy that you're happy. Didn't I tell you it would all work out?"

"You did."

"Yes, I did."

She kissed her palm and placed it on his face.

"So," he said, acknowledging the gesture with a nod and a smile. "What are you doing tonight?"

When he said this Patience felt something fall inside her, something indefinable, a drop of something potent shading her mood into darkness.

It was the memory of the night before. It had happened to her too often, she who had lived so many lives—drunk on cosmopolitans, and buzzed with a line of coke, she had gone home from a bar with a man she didn't know. And as the drop of doubt began to tint her recollection now, she wondered if she'd fucked him. She closed her eyes and tried to see the moment but could not. Could not see the man. Could not see the house. Could not see the details of the night That is why she and Peter had been late that morning. Peter had to wait for her return.

"Tonight I'm going to stay at home and sleep," she said.

"I didn't mean to kill your mood."

"It's not you. It's me. Don't worry."

"Worrying is a part of my job, I'm afraid."

"Okay, you're off duty now. I have to go to the toilet."

As Peter watched her take the stairs, he dialed Donald.

"Diane, this is Peter. May I speak to Donald?" He was leaning forward with his elbows on the yellow tablecloth, his face toward the window, watching the stairs in the reflection. "Don . . . hi, this is Peter. How are we looking? Look, we need some time and money for the remix. I know the budget is tight." He ran his fingers through his hair as he listened. "You are absolutely right. You have spent a lot already, but . . ."

He gathered his hair in his fist now, and began to shift his weight; and the waiters held their breath as he tugged the petals off the orchids. "You are absolutely right. You have spent a lot already, but there is no way I can tell her that. That would make her lose her mind. Can I tell you something? I've already told her that everything is fine. Don't make me out to be a liar, man."

With his hand he called the waiter for another glass of wine, pausing to listen, his hand suspended near the apex of a wave. "No, I cannot do that." He stopped abruptly and began to listen again, his shoulders, which had been raised, falling slowly now. "Okay, okay . . . okay. But all I'm asking for is"—he calculated on his finger—"okay, but could I have six weeks?" He began to smile now, cautiously. "Well, there is a little left . . . but there is no way that we can . . . right . . . right . . . you're absolutely right . . . no . . . I agree with you. Okay, that is all we have. We'll just have to do our best, I guess. Okay, then. Good news. Didn't I tell you we could make history if we tried? All the best to you. No . . . you're the best. Bye."

And as the waiter filled his glass, he said, "I'm fucked."

When Patience came back, she and Peter tried their best to speak, but their need to be alone separated them; and they sat together though apart, gazing through the window at the hissing rain.

The man—whoever he was—had not called her, and the darkness of the day and the presence of the rain intensified her sense of loss and longing. Now that she was gloomy, she felt the need to write a song, and she began to hunger for the neck of her guitar, a custom-made Ovation that was lying in her bed now, its headstock on her pillow. From somewhere deep inside herself she felt and heard a crack, and she closed her eyes again and heard the jar that held her darkest feelings break and spring a leak. But if she began to cry she knew that Peter would inquire and she did not want to lie, so she turned her face away.

As she looked around the restaurant, she noticed at a table, sitting by himself, a man who caught her interest. At first she could not explain it; then she stopped trying, telling herself it was because she liked the way he ate. He ate in small portions and chewed his food slowly, and maneuvered his utensils with quick but subtle movements of his wrists.

As she focused more and more on him, she lost her sense of

space, and as she reached out for her glass again, her finger caught the edge and tipped it over.

The man looked in her direction when the goblet hit the floor, then quickly turned his gaze toward his meal; then he looked again.

Soon he was picking up the napkin from his lap and moving in her direction. He was tall and slim, with broad shoulders, and carried his height in his waist. His hair was flecked with silver, and his cheeks were hard and flat below his eyes, which were hammocked and awninged by folds of fatty skin.

"Oh, my God," said Peter when he saw him. "Where the hell have you been? What have you been doing?"

"I'm doing okay," the man replied. Like Peter he was dressed in black. His cuff links were a pair of screws. He crossed his arms across his chest.

"Are you living in New York now? Shit, I haven't seen you in a thousand years."

"A little more than that," the man replied. "You're still in the business."

"It's a curse. What can I say? And you?"

"Naw!" He waved, then crossed his arms again, laughing. "I'm doing something different now."

Peter cocked his head.

"And how is that going?"

The man paused to think.

"Good. The check is regular."

"And I am Patience."

The man turned and bowed slightly when Patience interjected and shook her hand with both of his and quickly said politely: "Nice to meet you."

"Oh, forgive my manners," Peter said. "Patience Olayinka, Michael Chin-See."

Patience saw the meaning of his surname in the angle of his eyes . . . the softness of his hair. Her bracelet in a riot, she shook his hand and studied him, reading in the subtle pattern of his stubble the history of his genes. He grew no hair along his cheeks, and his mustache grew more thickly at the corners of his mouth. He was part Chinese, a quarter or a half. And by his accent he was from the Caribbean.

When she let him go, he quickly turned again to Peter.

"I have to go," he said. "Here's my card. Call me."

And he dashed out into the rain without a coat.

"You just shook hands with a genius," Peter said to Patience. "He's the greatest music mind I've ever met. He's worked with all the reggae greats . . . Marley, Tosh, Jimmy Cliff, Burning Spear. You name it. He's even worked with Sting and Peter Gabriel. Shit, he's worked with everybody."

"Doing what?"

"Producer . . . engineer . . . guitarist . . . bassist . . . keyboards. Whatever they needed at the time."

"He's Jamaican?"

"Yes. They are Chinese on his father's side. His grandfather came from Hong Kong in the thirties. His dad was very wealthy. Owned four supermarkets and some duty-free shops. But Michael was an outside child. It's hard for you to tell, but he grew up really rough. The last time I saw him, he had locks past his shoulders."

"How'd you meet him?"

"Working with Peter in the seventies."

"Peter Gabriel?"

"Peter Tosh. Mike was only fourteen then, and he was mixing tracks at Federal and Channel One—famous studios down in Kingston."

"So why've I never heard of him?"

"He left when you were starting out. One day in the early eighties he just walked away from everything. Everyone was shocked. I've never asked him why."

chapter four

The next day over lunch at his office in Tribeca Michael told Peter of his early days in America: of how he had arrived without a visa in 1982 and taken a job as a production assistant at an audio postproduction house until he had saved enough to pay a citizen to marry him; of working as an editor on movies and commercials; of switching sides and working for an agency, producing commercials for TV and radio; of moving from shop to shop until he was offered the position that he knew he deserved—creative director; of how the title felt like tweed against his skin, itchy and hot; of the emptiness he felt inside his soul.

After that, they agreed to meet again, and two days later Peter came to see him at his house in Brooklyn and told him what was going on.

"You have to tell the truth," Michael emphasized, his body rivered by a large white shirt. "Patience needs to know the truth of her situation. That way she can try to change it."

"But how can you speak to me of truth," said Peter. They were drinking lemonade from jelly jars. "You head an advertising agency. You lie for a living. You make a living from people's insecurities. First you tell them they're defective; then you offer them the remedy to fix it."

They were sitting on the roof of Michael's brownstone in purple Adirondack chairs, shaded by a pyramidal canopy, brown with khaki candy stripes, the flaps rolled up and tied against the frame. The sun had begun to set, and they could see the lay of Fort Greene Park: in the nearground the gray stone fence, then the line of trees that threw their shade along the undulating asphalt track that swung around the playground in the corner of the lawn, which was slightly overgrown and generally flat. Beyond the lawn the land began to rise, gently on the left up to the tennis courts, but steeply on the right—swooping to the wooded hillock where a fluted column soared toward the sky, a memorial to war.

The sun had truly ripened now. Soon it would fall, and evening light would dramatize the details of the old brownstones, their windows framed like portraits, their chandeliers like clustered grapes.

"A lot of what you say is true," said Michael. "I struggled with that for the longest time. But who is the real enemy? Commerce, which has always been about the lie, or art that masquerades as truth? When I was involved with music, working with people like Marley and Tosh, I was working with people who were searching for truth—in fact, people who had found the truth and were trying to bring it to the people."

"Music is a business."

"Yes," said Michael, "but so is selling fish. So for the same reason that you shouldn't sell rotten fish, you shouldn't sell rotten music, you shouldn't write rotten books. I don't make bad commercials, Peter. I make very good ones."

"And still you are not happy."

"Not really. No. That is why I just ran out of that restaurant. I just had a feeling that you would see right through my shit. I am sounding a little dramatic now . . . but between me and you, Peter, I've been thinking about leaving my job for a while—to do *what* I don't know—but something that will satisfy my soul. So there I was, deep inside this heavy vibration, just running different scenarios through my mind, and I began to feel somebody really looking at me hard as I was getting this really heavy music vibe. Then I looked up, and I couldn't believe that it was you. That's the kind of thing you call a natural mystic." He took another sip and wiped his mouth against his sleeve. "Seeing you I think is a sign that something has to change. I have to leave this place I'm in, man. I need my exodus. Bob said open your eyes

and look within . . . are you satisfied with the life you're living.
I was there when Marley made that song. At my age Bob was
dead. What have I done with my life?"

A gloomy mood descended, and each man, in his head, began to
tabulate his hurts and disappointments. Below them people were
streaming from the park. On the horizon birds were flying home.

Peter broke the silence. He handed Mike the tape and said:
"Let's go inside. Tell me what you think."

Later as they drove across the Brooklyn Bridge in Michael's
Audi roadster, Peter reiterated: "Tell me what you think."

It was one o'clock in the morning, and the traffic on the
bridge was light. Down below, the FDR was straight and clear.

"She can sing," Michael said, the wind rippling the bright
white shirt. "She can definitely sing. She can sing so well that
she knows the songs aren't right for her, and you can hear her
reaching for herself within the songs. She has a wicked tone. A
soothing tone. You know what her voice is like? You ever been
to the beach at night and heard that sound when the waves
come in and pull back from the shore? That kind of buzzing
sound? That is what she has in her voice. But the instrumenta-
tion isn't bringing that out. If anything, it is cluttering it up.
Who produced it by the way?"

Peter told him, but he didn't know the names. Yet they had a
ring to them that told him they were popular.

Coming off the bridge, Michael held the roadster in a falling
turn. High above the river, but falling fast, he shoved the stick
in third and pressed the gas and felt the silver roadster pounce,
growling as it left the slope, the hot wind coming cool against
his contemplating temples.

"I need your help," said Peter when they arrived at his hotel.
They were sitting in the car, streetlights playing on the hood.

"What kind?"

"Anything you have to offer. As I told you, they're gonna
drop Patience unless we bring them what they want in three
weeks. Ten grand is all we have. She doesn't know what she has
hanging over her head."

Peter shifted on the leather seat and took a draft of humid air. Could he ask for what he wanted? He had thought of asking Michael to book some studio time and roll it into another client's bill. Agencies billed millions. Who would notice? But after hearing Michael's view of truth, he couldn't say this. So he sat there, stalling.

"So," Michael was concluding, "now that we've seen each other again, we shouldn't let it go." He had thrown the car in first, but had not released the clutch. In the stereo was his favorite driving CD, *Sarge,* by Delroy Wilson, an underrated reggae singer with a voice as brittle as a cinnamon stick—island spice with notes of Memphis soul.

"I'll call you next week or so," said Peter.

"Next week," Michael said distractedly. "No . . . next week won't be good." At his temple a vein had begun to worm. "I'm taking all of August off. I haven't had vacation in a while." He began to fidget with the short-throw gear stick now. "And as I said," he continued, looking over Peter's shoulder, "I have to figure out some things."

He had been drawn into himself by the angelic opening harmonies of "I'm Still Waiting," a melancholic reggae ballad with a spare arrangement—drum, bass, and two guitars.

Delroy Wilson had died a pauper from cirrhosis. Marley, who had written and recorded the song in doo-wop back in sixty-five, had died of cancer at thirty-six.

And as Michael thought of this, he began to see a night in Kingston . . . him and Marley sitting in a mango tree . . . gazing on the city lights below . . . 1978 . . . *Babylon By Bus* had just been released . . . and the Wailers were the highest-grossing touring act in the world . . . bigger than the Stones, bigger than the Grateful Dead, bigger than Earth Wind & Fire.

That night in the mango tree, Michael was remembering now, he had spoken to Marley about redoing the song. Marley was wearing a white mesh vest and dungarees. His hair was out, and he laughed and said he liked the way that Delroy had approached it. And Michael told him that he should forget Delroy and approach it like a new song, the way that he'd remade his early sixties hits like "One Love" and "Sun Is Shining," and Marley said his voice had lost its subtlety, that "I'm Still Waiting" was a supple song, that he would need some help with it. He would only chance it as a duet, he said. But since he'd broken up with Peter and Bunny, he didn't like to sing with other people. No, he wouldn't do the song again. But he would like to hear it, though. He would like to hear a woman sing the song.

And as Michael sat there in the car, thinking of Bob and Delroy and Jamaica and the life he used to have, sadness overcame him like a film of perspiration, sticky and damp, and he began to think of the woman to whom he had been married then, the woman he still loved today.

Open your eyes and look within. Are you satisfied with the life you're living?

He was not satisfied. And as he thought of this woman, he felt a muscle twitching in his thigh, and he told himself that some kinds of loss are like an amputation, that you will feel that loss for years to come, although you cannot have that thing again. How long had it been since he had seen her? A little over twenty years.

As he thought of this, he thought of Bob again, of how Bob had told him to be careful with this woman, for she lusted too much for the things of this world.

As he remembered this he became sadder now, and he began to think of Bob again, of what he had said about the song, that the song was really a woman's song, and he began to think about Patience, and he began to feel sad for her . . . sad that she did not know the truth of her situation, and he began to see her in the way that he had always seen Delroy, who had had his first hit at twelve, and Marley who had had his first hit at eighteen; and as he thought of Bob and Delroy, he began to think about himself . . . saw himself at six in tattered clothes with ringworms in his scalp, hustling around the studios at the age of eight, running errands for money, dusting off the console, tuning up the drums . . . earning tips to buy a little lunch at school.

"Peter," he said, redirecting his gaze, "gimme a chance to work with her."

Peter laughed, as was his way when he was nervous, showing for a flash the bone beneath his mushy jaw.

"Let me do the remix, Peter. As it is, I have the time."

"I can't afford you."

"Is not a money thing," he said, shaking Peter's hand. "As Marley always said: 'If money fi come it wi come.'"

Later, the telephone awoke Michael from his sleep. His room was on the second floor toward the front: chevron-patterned parquet floors, pocket doors with paneled glass, two club chairs, a ceiling fan, a wooden bed on rounded pegs dressed in lemon-yellow sheets, a box guitar in a rack beside the window.

On the walls were photos from his previous life—touring with the Wailers, playing guitar with Jimmy Cliff, having lunch in Barbados with Roberta Flack and Nina Simone, college graduation, smoking weed with Jacob Miller, and on the night-stand, a picture of a high school girl with Afro puffs, a diamond face and eyes with dreamy lids. The inscription was simple: *For Michael from Mia, con amor.*

"Peter told me," said the voice on the telephone. "I don't know what to say."

In yellow boxers he sat on the ledge of the big bay window, ankles crossed, the action flexing muscles in his thighs.

"I understand," he replied, noting that Patience had not introduced herself.

Her voice was soft but crisp around the edge.

"This whole thing is pathetic," she went on. "The way that Peter lied to me. The way they run this business. I can understand why you just wanted to get out . . . just wanted to run away from the whole thing. Sometimes I feel the same way. Why do you want to get involved with this business again, though?"

He glanced at the picture on the nightstand.

"Because I think you can sing."

"So I'm a charity case?"

"And if I said yes you would hang up the phone, and if I said no you would get quite feisty, so I might as well not say a thing."

She sucked her teeth. "And what can you really do for my career?" she asked.

He had not thought this far.

"I don't make promises—"

"That you can't keep."

He glanced at the picture again.

"Promises period."

"That's refreshing."

He felt an itch along his side.

"It was just an idea, you know. You don't have to do this."

"I know, okay."

He began to think that he had been hasty, that he had not thought it through. And to be caught this way embarrassed him.

"Let me know tomorrow what you want to do," he told her, opening the way for her to call it off.

"And after tomorrow?"

"I'll be on vacation."

"Where?"

He raised the picture to his face, remembered something and turned it down.

"Jamaica."

"I think the whole thing is a waste of money and time," she said.

As he often did when he was getting annoyed, he reached for his guitar and began to strum it absentmindedly. The phone between his ear and shoulder, his fingers spidered up and down the strings.

"Is that you?" she asked in a friendly way.

"This is the number you dialed."

"Playing, I mean."

"Oh, yeah."

He had begun to play a flamenco now, the notes in a flutter like a ruffled skirt.

"Hold that," she said excitedly. Through the phone he heard the twanging as she tuned up her guitar.

Then she said, "I'm back." And without invitation she began to play along with him. At first she shadowed his notes; then she ran ahead to lead him; soon their voices had been silenced and there was just the sound of concentrated breathing as they focused harder and each began to see an image of the other's pliant fingers climbing up the other's spine.

An hour later, when they were done, she said: "Take the job. It is yours. But you shouldn't go alone, though. You should let me come with you. I like it that you make me work. That you make me stretch. That you make my skin perspire. You are a groove master, baby. How did you learn to groove like that?" She began to laugh and flirt more boldly now. "I like your licks, man . . . the way you stroke your strings like that. You want the gig, Mike? Take it. Crack it. Whip me up some twelve-inch singles."

Michael passed his palm over his head, felt the smoothness and the sweat, and saw himself being caught up once again in a web of his own making. The details were new; the pattern was old. He should end it now, he thought as he raised the photograph again. He felt as if he saw the girl in the photograph shake her head.

"That won't really be necessary," he told her. "I will send you a DAT with the remixed tracks, and you can tell me what you think."

"I have never been to Jamaica."

"It's not sinking. You have time."

"I really want to come."

"That is your cross to bear."

"And you? Do you have a cross as well?"

"Baby, my crosses are legion."

"So, you are legionnaire? A soldier?"

"Patience, it is late. I have to go."

"Michael, I will let you know when I am coming."

chapter five

When he arrived in Jamaica after twenty years, Michael's first impression was that things had hardly changed. The hills were green, or even greener, the flowers still blared with the force of trumpets.

People dressed differently, though—in a distinctly American way—and they drove newer cars—Japanese sedans and hatches; and houses had been sown in what had once been open fields and rolling hills and pasture.

Many of the houses were large, most of them in white; and as he flew along the coast in a turboprop to Port Antonio, he saw the large hotels that had been built along the coast from Montego Bay to Ocho Rios. Flying below the clouds, he could see the rivers coursing through the forests to the sea, and little villages and hamlets holding fast to steeply sloping land, and where the land was flat, he could see the fields of cane arranged in squares of green that ranged in shade from speckled lime to olive.

The plane was half empty by the time it came in to land. The runway was short. The reception hall was low and small: a single room, a counter and a Coke machine.

Waiting there to meet him was Azania. Slim but strongly built, she had bushy brows that drew attention to her closely shaven head. Her skin was smooth and dark and she wore a denim dress despite the heat.

"So what do you do at Magic Mountain?" he asked as they began to drive. The windows were open and the roof had been popped, and the cabin of the SUV was filled with noise and heat and light. She was driving with speed and daring, one arm on the steering wheel, the other on the shifter; wrangling with the bucking lane that rose and fell and twisted.

With her eyes still on the road, she said: "I am the engineer." They had just passed through a little town. The sea was on their left. On the right was bush and farmland. "I told one o' my friends I'd be working with you," she continued, "and he was like: 'Wha? Wicked. The great Chin-See? Dem man deh wicked, star. And ray-ray-ray.' Nuff excitement, man. Chuss me. Nuff excitement you create."

He looked at her. She looked at him. Her lips were dark and smooth and shine. She giggled, and he saw the stud of silver in the center of her tongue.

When they had passed through Port Antonio, the sleepy parish capital, a maze of narrow, cluttered streets with nineteenth-century buildings, they turned into the hills and he heard the engine mount the challenge of the sloping country lane that had partly crumbled through to gravel. A gully on their left, the mountain always on their right, they took a turn that led along a ridge, and after passing through a little settlement of wooden huts, they saw a rambling house.

It was an old white house in a grove of trees with a shingled roof and porches hung with ferns. The shutters were black, and the banisters green.

Separated from the house by grass and mango trees, the studio was a concrete box with a flat, slab roof, surrounded by a metal fence.

Inside, at the mixing board, which looked out through a window on the skylit studio floor, Michael took a seat and addressed his young assistant: "I have a reputation as a perfectionist," he said. "In many ways that is true."

"So I hear," she replied, shifting her weight on the dark gray carpet. "I heard you made Bob Marley take the vocals on 'Redemption Song' thirty-five times. Is true that?"

"What I am trying to say is that I need the best from you right now. I don't know anything about you. You came with the studio. So tell me who you are."

Her face began to crumple, but she recovered quickly and told him who she was. She was originally from Negril, but she had grown up in Montego Bay, and had studied drums in Kingston at the school of music. She did a three-year stint on the hotel circuit, then studied engineering at a polytech in Canada. She had been back in Jamaica nearly three years now. She was twenty-eight, divorced, had a child, and had been the resident engineer at Magic Mountain for the last three years. In that time she had worked on projects for U2, Duran Duran, Angelique Kidjo and Phil Collins. She lived in Port Antonio, but she often stayed inside the cottage by the pool, which she explained, was outside, behind the studio. You couldn't really see it from the road.

She sat, smiling nervously, unsure of how to read his face; and as she crossed her legs, he saw her thigh—powerful and brown like a river in flood.

And he felt something shake inside him. Shake then fall. And as it fell he heard the stirring of a sleeping lion, and he was overcome by a sense of disappointment. It was not just that he had lusted, nor that she was young, nor that she was his assistant. The disappointment came from the admission that the wetness in his mouth had not come from knowledge, nor hunger, but from instinct, greed and habit.

"We cannot start today," he aid, standing up and moving quickly to the door. "There are a couple of things I have to work out." And slipping into dialect now, he said, "Sleep a-tear me down."

Her chin rose appraisingly, she swiveled on the chair and said: "Well, your room is ready in the house. I won't bother to go home tonight. If you need anything in the laters, let me know."

In the morning they had breakfast on the second-floor verandah, which was hung with ferns and overlooked a stand of trees. The sun had barely risen, and the air was cool and smelled of ripened mangos. Miss Lydia, the cook, brought them boiled bananas, fried breadfruit, snapper in a thyme and butter sauce, and buttered bread with coffee sweet with condensed milk and sugar. Azania wore her pajamas, and Michael, who had swum and meditated, wore a light green shirt and shorts and sandals. He had a stack of studio manuals at hand, and Azania had a memo that outlined her job.

"You not a morning person?"

"Not really."

"Well, you not a night person either, clearly. I came to your door last night to ask you something, and you acted like you were sleeping."

"I was in the studio."

"Oh," she said. "From what I heard about you, I thought you were rooksing a girl. I hear you used to be a senior cocksman in your time. So what?" She cocked her head. "You get too old to fuck off all the girls now? Fuck too much. You dick get cloyed."

In America he would have chided her; but here in Jamaica, where innuendo is intuitive, and a certain right to roguery is the inheritance of men, he felt obliged to laugh it off, although this was not his way—laughter or any kind of bold expression.

He was an introspective man who had learned to hold his joys and hurts inside. He had learned to do this early. When he was eight years old, and living with his mother in a squatter camp beside the Kingston dump, an older boy had told him that the man that he'd begun to call his father was heading to his mother's job "to sink a machete in that blasted whoring gyal."

Barefoot, in tattered briefs and a vest that caught him at the knee, Michael grabbed some stones, and ran off down the dusty lane, leaping over pools of stagnant water, sending chickens fluttering over barricades of rusty sheets of zinc.

By the time he reached the factory, she was dead; and he was taken to a family he did not know.

It was the family of his father, a wealthy Chinese merchant who lived in one of the houses on the hill that turned to sparkling gems of light at night.

On the night of his arrival, his father took him out on the

tiled verandah and, without touching him or looking at his face, said while pointing to a clump of darkness: "That is where you live. That is where you come from. If you cry, I going send you back to that. Inside, is your brother and sister-dem. If you call them 'brother' and 'sister' or tell anybody is your brother and sister, I going send you right back to that. I hear you working as an errand boy at Studio One. I hear you getting on well, but I don't want you to concentrate on that. I going send you to school. If is education you want, I going give you that. But if you don't take learning, if it turn out that you like to tief and skull school and create botheration, I going send you right back to that. You have a naygah modder. But I going grow you up the Chiney way. You see, we Chiney, we build our strength off three things: business, education and family. If you show that yuh doan believe in these things, I going send you right back to that, to the dump, right back where I tried to take you modder from, right back down there where you doan see nutten but darkness. Right back to that. I see like you want to be a studio engineer. That is not the Chiney way. You see any Chiney singer or engineer? We know where the money is. The money is in the label, the studio-dem. Is not to sing. Is to be a producer. Is to own the songs and own the master tapes. Ask Leslie Kong. Ask Joe-Joe Hoo Kim. Ask Herman Chin Loy. We Chiney know where the money is in this music."

Michael ran away from home at twelve, after his father beat him yet again for playing with his siblings, and was taken in by a Venezuelan pianist named Junior Pareles who owned a flower shop and visited the homes of the well-to-do to teach their daughters classical music.

When Junior returned to Caracas in 1969, Michael kept the house and raised himself, working after school in studios to pay the rent; and although he had run away from his father, he did not turn away from his teachings. He finished high school, and went on to get a first degree in business. By then his father had passed away, and although he was the firstborn child, he was left no inheritance but the genetic evidence on his face and a deeply rooted sense that if he showed his deepest feelings he

would end up right back down there where yuh doan see nutten
but darkness.

One day, as she transferred tracks from two-inch tape to
Macintosh, Azania said to Michael: "A message came that Patience is coming here next Wednesday. That means we have nine
days to do eight songs, according to your schedule of eighteen-
hour days."

Michael didn't answer. Focusing on something else, he
slapped his finger on his lips and pointed to the speakers on the
wall.

He had heard inside his head the chords that he would use to
subtilize the song, and he was thinking to himself that if he had
a month he would have Patience take the song again. But if she
was coming on Wednesday . . .

What if by then he and Azania had done everything on schedule? Yes, she should retake that song. But there were other songs
that he would have her take again as well.

All the love songs. All the love songs on the album needed
major work. And he began to think about the album with the
passion of the mother of a bride, and felt within himself a gathering passion as thought became idea, idea became opinion and
opinion turned itself into the rule of law.

Patience must redo the songs. And why hadn't they allowed
her to play guitar? She should play guitar on some of these.
That is what they needed. Some rass guitar. Softer instrumenta-
tion and some acoustic guitar for a more intimate feel. It would
be a shame to let this album go this way. More than a shame. A
waste. For her own good. She has to do this. I have to talk to
her. I can't have her go off and ruin her life.

chapter six

In the mornings Michael would rise with the sun and meditate out on the verandah among the hanging ferns and potted plants, a pillow beneath his haunches; then, he would swim in the pool for an hour, his legs and arms tadpoling in the cool blue water, which was flecked with yellow leaves from the overhanging trees that had been planted as a colonnade around the water's edge.

In the water, he felt weightless, and his mind was free to float, and he would feel his muscles pulsing with the cadence of the great pop singers. Sometimes it was Marvin Gaye and Fela Kuti. Sometimes it was Sting and Shirley Bassey. Sometimes Chaka Khan . . . Bob Marley . . . Sly Stone . . . Stevie Wonder . . . Dennis Brown . . . Gregory Isaacs . . . Elis Regina.

In the mornings, as he swam, their songs would swirl inside his head, and he would close his eyes and bring his thoughts to bear on them, squeezing out the essence of the songs . . . the chords, the horns, the runs, the fills, but most of all the groove, the intercourse between the drum and bass.

In Michael's mind the bass was woman; the drum was man. The bass led. The drum followed. The bass line dipped and rolled, then settled. The drum struck deep and hard.

This was the problem with the album, he came to understand one morning as he dried off with a towel—as in hip-hop, the baby-mother music of the rhythms on the tracks—the man and the woman, the drum and the bass, were either in conflict or estranged; so there was no significant intercourse, or interplay, or flirting, or heat, and therefore no sense of seduction.

Lovers rarely shout. They mostly sigh and moan and whisper. On this album, though, even on the softest songs, the drums were raging, yelling, cursing, shouting—harassing and assailing the bass.

"We should work on the dance tunes first," he said when all the transfers had been done. "They are the easiest to do. If you find a groove, you're all right. Plus, this is the kind of stuff that labels like as singles. For the first three tracks let's go back to what Sly and Robbie did for Grace Jones on tunes like 'Pull Up to the Bumper.' We need some bass lines with hips . . . bass lines that can birth a song. But to make it work, the drums have to really stick it, though . . . just boof-baff, boof-baff . . . just sink it deep into the middle . . . just hold it steady and stick it right. After that we can fill it out with tambourines and shakers . . . soften it up."

That week, they started work at ten A.M. and went to bed past midnight, waking up at five again to meditate and swim.

Using ProTools on the Macintosh, they stripped away the tracks, leaving just the vocals, Michael giving directions as he watched a virtual version of the studio on the wide computer screen, Azania controlling the edits through a remote control as wide and deep as a shoe box.

In the world of advertising, where thirty-second TV spots can cost a half a million dollars, Michael took technology for granted. But, engaged with music now, something so intimately coiled around his spine, technology was alienating him, making him ill at ease, like making love with rubber gloves.

Sometimes as he supervised Azania he would close his eyes and bring to mind the days when making music was a tactile thing, like pottery or weaving . . . sometimes when the reels of tape began to spin you would look at all the dials and get the sense of sitting in a cockpit, the music blowing in your face, drawing water from your eyes, and you would feel your soul arise in flight. It was too easy now, he thought. Too distanced. Then, a song was edited by splicing tape with razors; now you clicked the mouse to cobble several takes to make a song.

Still, he acknowledged, technology was saving time; for what would have taken a month in those days was taking them a week.

This became his comfort as he thought of better days—this and the maturation of his friendship with Azania.

As they worked together, building up the rhythm tracks, him on keyboard bass, she on a drum machine . . . him playing the woman and she playing the man, the sexual attraction, confounded by the shifting roles, lost its sense of purpose and began to drift away.

When he looked at her legs now, he saw only form. There was no longer a consideration of function, of agility or endurance. And he began to surrender his guard to the point where he would joke with her and repeat for her amusement all the Chinese words he knew, most of which were curses. Azania liked to listen; and when he had an able charge, Michael liked to teach, and he taught her about the history of Jamaican music, about the other Wailers—Vision Walker, Junior Braithwaite and Beverly Kelso—who left before the group was famous; about the antics of producer Lee Perry, who used to bury master tapes in his yard; about the genius of King Tubby, who invented dub . . . Peter Tosh believed in UFOs . . . Marley only checked for light-skinned girls . . . Bunny Wailer told producer Leslie Kong that Selassie would strike him, and the man fell down and died.

On the day of Patience's arrival, Michael awoke when it was barely light, and lay there on his back in the four-poster bed, his palms between the pillow and his neck, staring at the slowly turning fan. It had rained last night, and the breeze was cool, and as he stood up on the sisal mat a draft of air came through the door, biting on his nipples. As he walked across the wooden floors toward the bamboo chair beside the double-doored armoire, he felt an easing of the weight between his legs.

With the light his cock had risen.

On other mornings he would have returned to bed and licked his palm and slowly shined his veined magnificence, which was thick and long with a head whose hood of skin correctly indicated that it was initiated in the martial art of fucking, an art in which speed and strength and stamina were admired, but not as much as agility and finesse.

This morning, though, he gathered his trunks from the chair and opened up the paneled door, his shadow playing on the frosted panes.

The awning was raised, and over the trees he could see in the nearground, traces of the road below the embankment. Beyond the road he could see the tumble of the land into a steady slope of trees and grass and bushes, then the land leveling off into pasture marked by wooden posts and wire—the lemon-colored grass, the blobs of sleeping cows, then the blackness of the road that curled along the coast; then there was the sodium whiteness of the sand against the mentholated sea.

He began to think of how much he missed this place, these hills, this sun, this life. And as he thought of this, he told himself that this was not this place, that the countryside had never been his place. His place was Kingston. And as he thought of this he began to feel a need to travel to the capital, but he was afraid, because twenty years ago he had left things there untidily. This now was his exile.

As he thought of this he began to think about the girl in the photograph beside his bed, and he began to think about his life in music and saw a strip of faces pulled across the aperture of the sun, and he began to see his life as in a film and admitted that his life had been a tragedy, for he had caused an awful thing to happen. He closed his eyes and felt the heat against his body as the sun began to crane, heard the twitter of the birds, smelled the freshness of the earth, and felt his finger burning for the ring he used to wear, and he lamented, for himself, for the girl in the picture, for the marriage that had grown out of this soil into a tree, only to be felled by his axing indiscretions. Oh, delinquent husband, this is your fate—returning as a stranger to your paradise.

Through his room he made his way along the curling stairs, his feet padding softly on the runner and passed through the parlor with its wood and wicker furniture and let himself outside; there, he followed a rising path into the shade of leafy trees and stopped abruptly as he made the crest . . . for sitting by the pool, in a yellow dress that buttoned down the front, her golden hair in plaits, her legs stirring the water, was Patience Olayinka, whom he had believed would be arriving in the afternoon.

She did not see him, for she was lost in her own considerations. And he quickly turned around and jogged toward the house.

The songs had been completed; but there were three of them, he thought, that needed some guitar for ornamental flourish. He had planned to sketch the lines today. But now she was here. The studio needed cleaning. Azania had spent the night at home. Call her now. She has to come. Where is Peter? What's the time? How come no one told me of the change in plans?

Dressed now, in a white camp shirt and light gray pants and lace-up shoes with squared-off toes, he came downstairs to speak with her and found instead a note:

dear michael,
i am sorry for dropping in like this, but i just couldn't contain my anxiety. the truth of the matter is that i have been here in jamaica for the last five days. call it what you will—madness whatever—but i just feel that i need to be close to my work in a physical way. i am sorry for making you feel out of sorts in new york. sometimes i can tease too much. sometimes i do things and say things without thinking of what these things and words will do to others. my apologies again to you. i have been listening to your work a lot. not that i am checking up on you or anything. not that i don't trust you or anything. i just like to know. doesn't everyone? the mix on kaya is brilliant. the stuff with grace jones is pure class. i am there with you, man. i am there with you on everything. say no more. i'm there. peter is in new york. he should be getting here in two days or so. as far as he is concerned i am on vacation. which i am. this is such a beautiful country. such a beautiful place. it makes me write in a tremendous way. i have written so

many songs since i've been here. i am eager to hear
what you have to say about them. maybe, and i don't
think this is really possible, but i would like to try some
of them, one perhaps, or two, on this album. i hate the
songs that were written for me. i am staying at the
dragon bay hotel. do come for lunch or dinner today.
we can listen to the tracks on the morrow. that was the
original schedule. have a nice day. don't work too hard.
i can be difficult at times. but please—and i don't often
beg—work with me. something tells me that you are
good for me. going for a swim. wish that you could
come. patience. always. patience.

After reading the letter, Michael felt something growing deep inside, something that was making him sit, that was weakening him, that was drawing on his energy—something with a focused will to grow and grow—a cancer or a child?

Squatting on his haunches, his back against the wall, his bottom on his heels, he read the letter again, the pressure of the growing thing inside him pulsing now, commanding his attention. What is this? he asked himself. This thing that I am feeling? Sometimes emptiness is good, he told himself. Because things that grow inside you change your life.

He arrived at her hotel in the early afternoon, and read *The Observer* as he waited. Unable to concentrate enough to move beyond the headlines, which were big and thick and black, he clasped his hand behind his back and paced the terra cotta tiles.

The central building called to mind a rustic inn in southern Spain. He gazed out through the arches at the central plaza, which was wet with sunlight down below. Surrounded by a parapet, the plaza opened on a flight of concrete steps that clattered down the terraced hill through frothy palms and ferns and bushes in the flame of efflorescence. Through the swaying foliage he could see the whitewashed villas, the stucco walls, the balconies, the roofs of rippling tiles whose glimmering scales of reddish brown overlapped like schools of fish.

"Are you always this quiet?" Patience asked him as they walked along a snaking concrete path that led them past the villas that were closest to the sea.

They had made their way together, down the steps, she ahead of him, pausing on the landings to look out on the bursting waves. Now the sea was on their left, across a lawn of new-mown grass that ended at a buttressed wall.

Ahead, the grass began to grade down to the level of the water and opened out to sand.

The sand was umbrellaed by a giant tree with tiny leaves and nobbly, golden flowers. And behind the tree there was a beach bar with a roof of thatch beside an open-sided restaurant, thatched as well, paired like cow and calf.

At the bar, she took a lemonade; he took a sparkling water; and they sat there for a while, unsure of what to say. Around them young Italians carried on flamboyant conversations. In the shadow of the giant tree some German men were playing volley-ball. At the water's edge, where children played, a lobster-colored man was clawing at a pretty Cuban girl who laughed him off and dove into the surf.

"Are you always this quiet?" Patience asked again.

"I am," he said. "I like to listen more than talk."

"They say I don't like to listen," she replied. "But I do. I don't want to talk today. I just want to listen to you. That is why I am here, Michael. Talk to me. Tell me things. Make me listen to you."

She wore a tangerine and olive dress that caught her at the knee. Days of sun had warmed her skin. Salt had further bleached her hair. Around her neck she wore a string of cowry shells. Around her wrist was her bracelet made of stones.

"We've finished six songs," he said. "We did the fast ones first. They are the easiest to do, as you know. You also took those vocals better."

"Tell me something I don't know."

She swallowed when she said this and turned away to gaze out at the sea. He saw the tendons surface through her skin, cabling from her collar up along her neck. And as he watched her, the roundness of her forehead, the way her jawline angled sharply just below her ear, the sharpness of her cheeks, he realized that he'd never really seen her when he had met her in New York, that he had come to know her through her voice, which was beautiful—as beautiful as her face.

"I didn't mean to sound sarcastic," she told him when she turned around. "You just make me really nervous."

"How?"

"You challenge me."

"I don't know what you mean."

"I can't fool you. And that is good and bad. It is good because I need someone who won't take my shit, you know, someone who can make me listen. If I don't respect you, then I don't listen to you. That's just how I am."

He began to smile now as he thought of what this meant—that maybe she'd indulge him and rerecord the vocals on the ballads.

And he began to speak with animation now, gesturing with his arms and laughing loudly, sharing anecdotes about the music life. And she began to know him in a different way.

After talking for a while, she asked him if he liked to dive, and they went out in a motorized canoe. She wore a modest suit with an open back, and he wore a pair of rented rubber pants. In the boat she found herself admiring the smoothness of his skin. Like a manila envelope he was golden brown, his chest delineated like a folded flap, his abs in a block like a scrawled address. Watching him she felt the urge to stamp him with her lips.

Below in the water, silver light above, creamy sand below, white tanks on their backs, their flippers navy blue, they sloped across the easy current, and glided to a stand of waving pink and orange coral; there they paused to hover, legs and arms in languid circles, watching as a manta ray, black and speckled gray, floated past their faces, trailing in its wake a school of iridescent fish.

They stayed below the water for a half an hour, slipping through caves and twisting underneath a sunken wreck, surging on a wave of bold adventure—dolphin and sea lion.

Back inside the boat they found themselves continuing in the silence of the water. A mile away from shore, the boat began to cut against the chop of the waves, and as the prow began to heave and fall, she leaned against his side and felt the heat returning to his skin. Ahead of them, the whiteness of villas called to mind a flock of sheep. And she remained within the safety of his slender arm, frightened as a lamb.

When they landed they proceeded to the dive shop to return the tanks, and, paired as they had been beneath the water, their clothes across their shoulders, they followed the electric current that was pulsing through their blood, up along the steps, she ahead of him, toward her villa.

Ascending through the foliage, they felt a sense of possibility, a sense of newness, as if the lives that they had led before were loofahed off and scrubbed away with salt and left along the ocean floor, there to be nibbled by fish and spread by radiating currents.

Inside her villa reigned a hush of elemental silence—the silence of a breeze among the rafters, the silence of a lizard sleeping on a rattan chair, the silence of a vase of orange birds of paradise, the silence of a slit papaya, the silence of humidity, the silence of reflections of a room on rounded glass, the silence of coffee, the silence of rum, the silence of a panty on a polished marble floor.

He waited in the living room. She went away, returning from her chambers with white towels. Then she left, leaving him to go downstairs to bathe.

As she took her time to shower, the water coming hard and hot, misting up the mirror, pebbling on the curtain, she imagined that her suds were spurting through his showerhead, burning his eyes, foaming up his face. She lathered with an almond-scented soap, arching her back to hoist her nipples to the water, bending forward so her hands could slide across her back, raising the triangles of her shoulder blades. Her knees turned out, her buttocks tight to hold her, she dipped and closed her eyes as her fingers soaped her delicates; and she began to smile as she thought of how her pussy called to mind his eyes—fatty folds of flesh around a slit.

Downstairs, in the smaller bath, Michael held a different kind of image in his head. In this image, Patience was singing, her slender body shrouded in a muslin dress, her hair cut short like his, flowers at her feet, sitting on a slatted chair, singing "I'm Still Waiting" as she strummed a box guitar. To her right there was a chorus, behind her was a band. The audience was a pond of flaring lighters. In his head he heard her oceanic timbre percolating through the grit of Delroy Wilson's baritone and Marley's salt-encrusted rasp. The water was warm. And the cardamom soap had melted to a slippery grease, which he was slowly rubbing on his body, his fingers sliding through the grooves that ran between his muscles.

They met again in the living room, and sat adjacently in padded rattan chairs across a coffee table. The curtains had been opened and they could hear the buzzing of the sea and the fluttering of the leaves in the breadfruit tree whose leaves were larger than a human hand.

She was wearing white. A dress with buttons down the front. Her shoes were off. Her hair had been unbound, and she smelled of almond soap and ginger oil.

There were papers on the table. He looked at her. She looked at him. He accepted her permission. And as he read the scribbled lyrics, she reached for her guitar. She stroked it softly and watched him mouth the lyrics, his lips of dusky rose, his hair like new-mown grass. The gray ones caught the light like flecks of broken glass.

The things you say make the green in the hills
Flame up and dance, make my skin catch a fire
It's the way you say it, that gives me the thrills
You've got a word for each season, sweet words take me
  higher

Play me like a song
Play me soft and slow
Breathe it nice and long
When you say come, I'll come
Let the music flow

Tonight I don't need the fancy stuff, the frills
Just a wood fire burning like my heart's desire
Sweet me with your music, show me your skills
A word for this season, sweet words take me higher

Play me like a song,
Play me soft and slow
Breathe me nice and long
When you say come, I'll come
Let the music flow

Not calling it love
That woul d be too easy
This is a groove
Full up with mystery
This old, old romancing
So long mellowing
Before time I knew you
Before time I knew you

Could play me like a song
Play me soft and slow
Breathe me nice and long
When you say come, I'll come
Let the music flow

He looked up from the paper and listened as she played. When she was finished she gave him the guitar, and he watched her mouth the lyrics as he plucked, her nostrils flaring as she caught her breath. He played the song in a different way, slowed it down, double-chopped instead of strummed the chords, defined the downward stroke.

Leaning forward now, her elbows on her slowly gapping knees, she watched his fingers fan, then slide, then stop then grip along the neck, whose tone of ambered pine was close to their complexion. She saw in his fingers the desire of her legs. She wanted him to make them fan and slide and grip like that.

He finished the song with a locomotive run. His face was tense. His lips were clamped against his teeth. His eyes were focused far away, his fingers pumping piston hard, and she realized that he had traveled to a place she didn't know, somewhere in a tunnel inside himself, a place of great emotion, and she wanted to burrow there to hold him.

He slumped against the chair when he was done and closed his eyes, and she watched his stomach heaving through his shirt. His knees were apart. His ankles were crossed. And she knelt in front of him and placed her face against his belly and listened to his feelings steaming there.

Soon she felt his hands along her back, gathering her dress, and she felt the need to take it off.

When he opened his eyes she was standing in a pool of rumpled cloth. Holding his gaze she kicked the dress across the room, and, facing him always, never turning away, she retreated through an alcove to her room, her knees held tight, her legs hardly moving, her arms at her side, as if she were being carried by a company of ants.

He watched her from the door. She was lying on the bed; and his looming shadow spilled toward her, splashing on her freshly lathered skin.

He moved toward her nakedness and placed a knee upon the bed, gazing still. She arched her back, and he saw her ribs like twigs beneath her straining skin, which in the clarity of the tropic light revealed its secret moles and scars and folds that would mature to wrinkles.

As she sunk her fingers in her hair and massaged her tender scalp, she rolled from side to side, rubbing her legs against the sun-warmed cotton sheets, and he glimpsed the spot of dampness underneath her.

He lay beside her on the bed, wet his palm against his hand and rubbed her, kissing her soft and slow, but with reserve. He surprised her with his knowledge of her secret hollows . . . the inside of her wrist, the curves between her eyes and nose, the corners of her mouth.

Sometimes as he rubbed her he would stop and hold his hand above her skin, and with the heat of both their bodies in his palm, she would tingle as her hairs began to quail, often, to her surprise, in places where she thought she had been smooth—her cheeks, her ears, the insteps of her feet.

She began to rub her hands across herself to see if she could feel what he was feeling. She slipped her little finger around the curve beneath her breasts, slid her palm along the hollow of her belly, up toward her pubis, where the hairs resembled sprinkled grains of demarara sugar.

He watched her as she touched herself, then took away her hands, crossed her wrists and bound them in a grip above her head and ran his hands along the contours of her side.

Binding her still, he reached between her legs and felt among her slipperiness a tiny thumb of flesh, which he rolled between two fingers as he kissed her with the languor of mature experience.

On the off-white dresser, among the creams and keys and lotions and the plate of mango crescents, the lizard from the rattan chair, awake now from siesta, puffed the fold beneath his neck, watching as the woman looped and writhed as if she were a severed tail.

"Tell me," Patience said as she and Michael lay across the bed, "why didn't you want to be inside me?"

"There is a time for everything," he said.

"It seemed as good a time as any."

"There will be more times."

Disappointed in himself, he felt the urge to leave but thought about how she would take it.

"When?" she asked.

"When the album is completed."

She was on her side, and he was on his back with his hands behind his head. She raised her leg and placed her knee against his stomach, and he felt the smoothness of her inner thigh against his pelvic bone.

"Is this how you plan to control me?" she asked, nuzzling his shoulder.

"You can call it that."

"Is it or isn't it?"

"Can't reveal my secrets."

He said this in a joking way. She was quiet for a while, then said: "Tell me a secret. Something that you have never told anyone."

"I would rather tell a lie."

"Who would know you could be silly?"

"Anyone that knows me." To take the focus off himself, he dared her. He had begun to feel an urge to talk about his feelings, and he didn't want to open up. Not with her. Not at all. Not about him and his previous life. "Tell me something about you," he challenged. "I want to hear about you."

She began to chuckle nervously.

"Go on," he said. "See, it's not so easy."

"I had an abortion when I was twelve years old," she recited after stuttering several times. "Did it myself with a hanger. The man was my gym teacher. My father found out and beat me. I botched it, so I can't have children. Does that matter to you?"

"It does and it doesn't," he said, sliding his arms around her now. "It does in the sense that I am sorry about what happened, but it doesn't change the way I feel about you."

He held her even tighter and rocked her even more.

"How do you feel?" she asked.

He tried to find the words, then settled on "Confused."

He felt her slump against him; then he felt her pull away.

"I have to say I'm disappointed," she sighed.

"What did you want me to say?" he asked. "I didn't mean to ruin a moment."

"I wanted to hear: 'I love you too.' "

She squirmed and he felt her corrugated ribs against his side.

He contemplated what to say. She was hurting now. Soon, in less than two weeks, they would be going their separate ways. Would any of this really count?

"Okay, I love you, then," he said. "See, it doesn't change a thing whether I say it or not."

"Yes, it does," she told him.

"How?"

He was becoming irritated now. Not with her—but with himself for lying, especially so easily about a fundamental thing like love. Now, it seemed, the lie was causing complications. But she needed to hear it so badly. In less than two weeks they would be going their separate ways, he told himself again. So would it really count?

She interrupted his thoughts: "I think the ballads sound the way they do because I wasn't in love when I recorded them. How can a woman sing of love when her head and heart are hurting? When she doesn't believe the song? When she can't become the song?"

Outside, the sky was firing with reds and yellows. Soon it would be dark.

"We should go," he said. "You haven't had a chance to hear the mixes."

"Let's retake the vocals on the ballads," she said. "Is there time?"

"It all depends on you. It all depends on how hard you want to work. If you sing with concentration. If you are willing to take the song again and again until you do it right. If you are willing to listen to me."

"I am your slave."

"You will have to do as I tell you."

"I have done things before you told me. I have stopped smoking. I have stopped drinking. I have stopped everything. Haven't you noticed. Can't you see the change?"

He wanted to remind her that he did not really know her; but this would have made the conversation tedious.

"See how good I've been to you?" she continued, sliding her calf along his shin. She kissed his collarbone. "See . . . now you tell me a secret."

"What is it you want to hear?" he asked. Maybe it would be trivial.

"Okay, why would a man with your ability just walk away from music?"

He closed his eyes and felt her move her head across and down his chest, felt her hair against his belly, then a lightness rise toward her tongue as he experienced the need for release in two places: his body and his soul.

"I was in love with a woman, and I was in love with music," he confessed. "I thought I could serve both when I couldn't, and she left me. After that there was nothing. But that is my burden to bear. That is my cross. That is nothing for you to worry about." He brought his hand across his cheek. Felt the sting of water in his eyes. "When I think about it, it is none of your business," he continued. "Why am I telling you this? It doesn't matter. Forget I said anything to you. It is an irrelevance. She does not count anymore. She lives somewhere in California, I think. That is far away. She doesn't count. That is dead and gone. Ancient Arawak history. We haven't seen each other in twenty years."

"What is her name?" said Patience, lifting up her head to look at him.

He placed his arm across his eyes. He didn't answer. She asked again. He didn't answer. She took him in her mouth.

chapter seven

Sixty miles away in Kingston, three days after Michael failed to come in Patience Olayinka's mouth, Mia Fortuna Gonsalves, a small-breasted woman of medium height with hips like sacks of sugar, gathered her nightgown about herself and ran toward the bathroom as she felt the urge to vomit.

She was not pregnant. She was sure. For she no longer fucked her husband; but something wasn't right, she knew. What, she wasn't sure.

For the last eight days, she had been suffering from what she thought was fever. She was weak. Her memory was a script with missing pages. And her eyes had fallen out of focus.

According to her G.P., she was suffering from anemia. According to her homeopath, her body was absorbing too much zinc. And a chiropractor told her that her problem was a larger one, one of physics and engineering, that a bottom such as hers, thrust in any direction, suddenly, and with force, would certainly misalign her spinal column.

Her husband, who had married her, because, he said, she had a truly regal name—which she had come to suspect had never been a joke—had told her of a woman who could read her. That too had had its genesis as humor, but as she brushed her teeth to take away the taste of bile this morning, she began to take it seriously.

Vain in her youth, confident now, but concerned that she was aging, she raised her lips to examine her gums, which were reddish brown like clay. She ran her tongue against her teeth, which shone like limestone pebbles—pouted, puckered, grinned, then smiled, and traced the grooves around her mouth with nails in need of care. She felt like celebrating. There were no new lines today.

Her face was shaped like a diamond, broadest just below the eyes. Her brows were calligraphic, lush and dark and thick with upward serifs; and her hairline formed a widow's peak that clawed her oval forehead. Slave-girl black with the nose of a mulatress, she had a mouth whose lips were a flared extravagance, and eyes that appeared to be lit by candles, for they were warm in tone around the iris, with lids like velvet drapes.

Mia Fortuna slept in a room of heavy furniture in a modern house on sloping land that overlooked the capital. The house was large, with rows of picture windows in the California style, and a platform roof of poured concrete.

Opening the double doors that led to her verandah, her dreadlocks in a fat chignon, she left the thickness of the carpet for the hardness of the streaked and speckled tiles.

From the verandah, which was cantilevered on a precipice, Kingston was a forest. The trees were tall and the houses microscopic, and the roads resembled bridle paths. But a closer view, she knew, a view from ground level, revealed that Kingston was a city of great drama, closer in personality to Lagos or Johannesburg than it was to Port of Spain—an unruly city of traffic and noise and rutted roads where cops and disenfranchised youth continued an ancestral war; a creative city of art galleries and small theaters and dance companies and more recording studios than clinics or markets or photocopy shops; a city of intuitive entrepreneurs who believed in the principle of profit; a city that defined allegiances in terms of politics, school and blood; a city of jokes; a city of threats; a city emerging from a colonial adolescence with pimples on its face.

Trusting by nature, cautious by training, imperial when it furthered her designs, Mia Fortuna Gonsalves was a Kingston girl, the youngest of five, the daughter of a Panamanian stone mason and a Jamaican dressmaker who, despite their modest means, raised children of high ambition.

Looking on the plains now, panning like a camera, she recalled her path to where she stood, a scholarship to board at
Hampton, another one to Cambridge, returning to apprentice in
prestigious chambers, marriage, divorce, relocation first to England, then to Holland, then finally to San Francisco, marriage
again, then returning, changed forever, no longer striving to be
but just being.

But why did she get married again? And to him? She had been
asking this for the last five years and had never liked the answer.
Her husband was the kind of man she would have normally dismissed as a "money Syrian," or a "backra" . . . a man with no
education who had inherited money from his merchant family,
had little appreciation for the arts, and thought that people were
poor because they were too blasted lazy to find some land and
farm—a clichéd caricature of "the man on the hill."

Now she lived on the hill as well; and so did many of her
once-progressive friends; up where the air was cool, tooting the
horn of the SUV and waving as she passed the man who managed her bank, and the woman who did her mammogram, and
the ambitious hustler who had just transshipped two tons of
coke from Colombia to Miami, risking extradition so that his
children would not have to end up washing windows at the traffic light or renting body cavities to tourists.

Is there anything wrong with that? What is so wrong if people like me can finally own a little of what *they* have always
had? she would often ask herself.

Around her and down the hill were houses set in groves of
trees and flowered gardens, the houses of people who could easily live in America but would not because moving there would
lower their standard of living, people with maids and gardeners
and cooks and drivers, people who imported from America
everything it seemed but air.

This morning more than ever, Mia Fortuna Gonsalves felt
opposed to all that she had become, and as she looked around
her, she began to feel light-headed, and had to concentrate to
draw her breath as the colors in her view began to pulse and
swirl and blaze . . . the tall white columns, the red tennis courts,

the blue swimming pools, the flat green lawns. And she leaned over the railing and vomited again, telling herself that she would see the blasted spiritualist for whatever it was worth.

In a neighborhood of broken bungalows with octagonal bedrooms at the ends of small verandahs, Mia Fortuna, dressed in jeans and a mannish shirt cotched her BMW so that other cars could pass.

Standing in the shade of an Afroed mango tree, she further tugged her hat across her brow. A dog with tits like paper bags began to yelp, drawing attention from the neighbors, who craned their necks and noted to themselves with bored excitement that the wealthy lost their fear when they were troubled in the spirit.

"What dead don't dead," came a raspy voice before Mia Fortuna had time to push the gate. "The past don't pass."

At a door whose frosted panes were patched with cardboard sheets, a woman in a shift appeared. She nodded and scratched her side, then disappeared inside. Mia followed her.

They sat on stools in a tiny room whose purple walls were damp with smells of rum and mold and garlic. The woman put some pebbles in a kerosene pan and jumbled them like dice. Focusing, she tongued the gap between her long eye teeth, the shaking of the pan flip-flopping her wrinkled breasts.

"So what does it mean?" said Mia Fortuna. The woman had shuffled the stones on the wooden table, which was dusted with cornmeal and white flour.

"What dead don't dead."

"I don't know what you mean."

"That thing that die don't die."

"There are many things," Mia challenged. "What things?"

"Something in the blood."

"A sickness."

"Something in the blood that you remember like how I remember the old African language that they use to talk on the plantation in slavery days. I know that language, y'know."

"So I have a blood disease is what you're saying? Like anemia. The doctor said I have anemia. That it is connected to this no-meat thing that I've been on now for a while."

"No. This is something different. This is something you did catch when you small. All doctor do is tell bare lie."

"And you are different?" Mia said impatiently. "So since you know so much, then, since you know so much truth, then tell me the truth about myself."

"Me no gamble people life. Me no take neither bet nor dare. You come 'cause you feeling poorly. That is what you come for. That is what you get."

"You're a fraud. I don't know why I came here," Mia said, shifting around.

"Is who living fake life? Me or you? Is me not sleeping with me husband or is you? Is me never send in my GCT to government or is you? Is my head doctor open or is yours? Is me or is you?"

"Look. I have to go."

Driving past Sabina Park, the famous cricket ground, annoyed with herself for having listened to her husband, Mia called her assistant on the speakerphone to see who had called her. Her hat was off, and she drove without shoes. Her toes were long and thin like fingers.

She heaved, but nothing came up; and she called her sister Zenobia, an officer in the army, and was informed by an adjutant that the colonel was en route to Newcastle to inspect a batch of new recruits.

Mia leaned forward to search the sky for Zenobia's helicopter, then settled in her seat and went to lunch alone, hoping that she wouldn't vomit in her own café.

She arrived at the café in fifteen minutes. One of two adjoining houses that she had acquired and refurbished when she came back to the island, the café was located in a neighborhood of rambling forties bungalows with shingled roofs and crescent drives and bowered porches set with concrete columns. The yards were full of trees that used to serve as parasols for garden parties; and the lawns were smooth enough to play croquet.

Located on the upper plains, walking distance from the diplomatic mansions and the central business district, Café Kofi was white, with espresso-colored awnings and a driveway lined with whitewashed stones and royal palms with trunks of silver-gray.

Inside, the floor was made of cream-and-blue Iberian tiles with walls of milky tangerine. Adjoining the café, connected by a walkway, was the gallery, which was open only by appointment now, because of the recession.

The other houses on the street had also been converted to commercial use: advertising agencies, architects, florists, and directly across the street, a sound and lighting company that also rented instruments.

As she often did when the café was crowded, Mia parked behind the gallery, took the flagstone path and entered through the kitchen. The path was shaded by a columned trellis hung with flowered vines. At the end of the path was a wooden gate that Mia often scaled because the rusty latch was temperamental. But she did not have the strength to lift her legs this morning.

"Good morning," she declared as she sauntered through the kitchen door. "Good morning. Good morning. Morning gone already, but you people are still working on morning time. Is afternoon now. Catch up. Catch up. Chef, what you studying today?"

The short, fat chef looked up and flashed his tongue at Mia, who flashed her tongue and crossed her eyes, then kissed him just below his lazy eye.

"Morning, Mia," said the cooks in chorus.

"Sinners. Let delicious, well-presented food be your repentance," she said with a laugh as she washed her hands and put on an apron herself. An intern from the girl's home appeared confused.

"Peaches, what happen, baby?" Mia asked as she tucked the girl's hair beneath her cap.

"Which one name sauté again, Miss Mia?"

"That is the one where you heat up the pan first," she said in common English to relax the girl, "then put in a tip of oil when the pan get hot, and you put in the food till it brown—"

"And use the spatula and move it fast," the slender girl completed, with a smile of confidence renewed.

"No, that one is stir-fry when you move it. Sauté is the one where you leave it just till it brown."

"Her head tough you see," exclaimed the chef.

"Chef, anybody head tough like yours?" said Mia in retort. "How much time I tell you that you have to make sure to batch up the food for the golden-agers home before you serve the lunch? You want the old lady-dem dead for hungry? God bless the little that government providing. Don't behave that way because is free we giving them. People is people. And make some ginger tea for me. Not feeling so good at all."

In her office, which was hung with art, she sipped the tea and fanned herself. The air-conditioner took its time to cool the room. What was she going to do? she thought. Should she go back to the doctor again? This thing was serious. And when was her husband returning from the country? And did she speak to the kitchen staff in any kind of way? Too many questions. She needed some time for herself . . . away . . . perhaps Paris or Barcelona.

As she reached for the telephone to call her travel agent, there was a knock at the door. She had her feet up on her desk.

"Come," she said sharply. It was a waiter.

"Mia, sorry to bother you, but a gentleman wants to know if he can use the phone."

"Tell him two minutes. I going to make a call quick-quick. And where is the tea?"

He clapped his head and smiled and left. Soon there was another knock.

"Come," she said, looking up as she dialed. And there, before her, in a bright white shirt was Michael Chin-See, whom she knew by instinct had been the source of her mysterious fever— the man whom she had married in 1974, against her mother's wishes at the age of eighteen a month before she went away to study law at Cambridge . . . the first man she had ever kissed and loved, the man to whom she had surrendered her virginity.

And in a match-lit moment, she saw that first time, and remembered that he too had bled, that he had cut himself . . . that one of her wiry pubes had sliced him . . . that she had helped him pull away the foreskin and had seen the wonder of the crescent line, red against his copper complexion . . . that they had held each other close and cried, crying from the pain, crying from the sight of the proof of their transgression, which was fresh and wet against the sheet that they had bought with their lunch money and spread in all its florality on the broken mattress on the old trunk bed beside the sewing machine in her mother's room, playing man and woman when they were just teenagers—oh, how they had cried, oh, how they had cried when the blots began to drift, as the islands of blood became a continent, binding their tribes—oh, how they had cried.

They had cried because they knew without knowing that the larger meaning of the moment was beyond their years . . . that you don't just bleed into a person and come away unchanged, because things are carried in the blood, antidotes and sicknesses, traits and states of mind, memories of our future pasts . . . for blood is life . . . and when another person's life flows through your veins and goes into your cells and binds up with your plasm, it is hard to purge that life from yours. All things move in cycles. The cycles of the body are the cycles of the earth. Spring always follows the longest winter.

"You make me sick," she said. "I hope you understand that."

Behind the shirt his body was a strip of dull silver. And there were flecks of gray in the hair that in another life she used to wash with rosemary and moisturize with coconut oil to leonine exuberance. But in the way in which he bowed slightly from the waist and clasped his hands at shoulder height, the almost Buddhist sense of calm that he exuded in the most dramatic moments, she recognized him as her yin. He had gained a bit of weight, she noticed. Still, he was as slender as a bamboo stalk.

"Come," she said, "let me smell you. Just come. Don't ask me why."

Smoothing out her shirt, she walked toward him, stretched

around to shut the door and pulled him close; and they held each other with a quiet desperation, as if they were compressing time, as if they were distilling the essentials of their history, the good and the great, hoping that the rest could be collected in a pan and thrown away.

The smallness of the room, the white blinds barring their bodies, they felt like prisoners now. And as she thought of how much she was in need of release, she remembered how he used to squeeze the fattage on her hips; and she reached for his hand and placed it there, indulging herself, because the man with whom she lived now did not remind her of her softness, did not like to press his hands against her thigh and pull his thumbs together just to marvel at the marbling that showed beneath her skin.

Michael's hands were on her now. The touch, the squeeze, the glancing pat, then just the slightest shimmer.

"How you fat so?" Michael murmured as he touched and squeezed again. "Mummy, how you fat so still?"

She pressed her face against his chest and laughed, and he felt her laughter radiating through his bones. Then he began to laugh as well. And they laughed and held each other until Mia thought of something that she wanted to forget.

Laughing still she gave a little shove, and he let her go and backed away, aware of what had happened.

"I didn't know that you were back here," he said. He had placed his hands behind his back. His voice was formal but not distanced.

"I've been back now, five years, going six."

He raised his head appraisingly.

"I presume you're not a lawyer still."

"No." She ran her palms along her temples and scratched her head behind her ear. "I have the gallery next door and the café here. What can I say? Times change. People move on. Different times bring out different things from people."

"The dreads look really good on you."

She shook her head and sucked her teeth.

"Coming from a womanizer, that is not a compliment."

He chuckled in recognition, remembering now the bluntness of her irony.

"*Former,*" he said. "In your own words, different times bring out different things from people."

"Are you here with her?" she asked.

"Who?"

He leaned on one leg and piled his hands atop his head.

"Your new wife."

He shifted to the other leg, slipped his hands inside his pockets and glanced down at his shoes, gathering his thoughts.

"I don't believe in divorce," he said.

"You don't believe in marriage either."

He sucked his teeth but kept the sound inside his head.

"Well, I have been remarried for a while," she volunteered. But as soon as she said this, she began to feel trivial, as if her husband defined her. Not that a husband could never define a wife at times. But this one, her husband, was too small and inelastic in imagination and kindness to contain her.

"So life is good, then?" Michael asked.

He had shifted his weight again and was standing squarely now, and she read the question for what it was—a challenge.

"So if the woman is not your wife," she countered, "then who is she? Your latest concubine?"

"A singer," he replied, assuming that he had been seen. "Patience Olayinka. I'm doing some work with her."

He felt something shift inside him when he said this. It shifted but it did not fall. It must not fall. Not in front of Mia. He held it fast.

"Why did I think you were out of music? I think I heard that once. That you were working in movies or advertising or something like that."

"That's true," he told her; then he explained how he came to be doing the project, about feeling dissatisfied with his life, about the serendipity of meeting Peter again. Her eyes began to warm as he spoke, and he began to get the feeling that she cared about and understood the meaning of this moment in his life.

"So you still use your name?" he asked her. He leaned against her desk and crossed his arms. His feet were planted firmly. His knees were locked and wide apart.

"Which name is that?"

She crossed her arms and leaned her head. Nervous energy rocked her legs.

"Chin-See," he said, feeling playful now.

"You're funny," she replied, biting back a smile.

"You're Gonsalves still."

"Will always be."

"Mia Fortuna Gonsalves."

He turned her name in his mouth, and she could feel his tongue on her, wetting her down.

"What is your husband's name?"

"I do not want to say."

He crossed his arms and cocked his head and put a thumb beneath his chin and told her in a teasing way: "Lemme tell you who he is now. A big-belly Syrian with a bald head who likes to laugh 'Haw-haw-haw' . . . the kinda man that Peter Tosh lampooned in 'Downpressor Man.' So, baby, you really get married to a Downpressor Man? You hooked up with a Crazy Baldhead? Boy, the next time Bob dream me, I have to tell him this one, that Mia is now a dread and her husband is a baldhead."

"You're only behaving this way because you're jealous."

He swallowed quickly but continued: "Tell your husband that somebody says that his wife is looking very, very good and that he must never leave her careless 'cause her real husband will take her away. Lemme rub your hip again, nuh, Mummy."

She raised her arms but her fingers were limp. Did she want to defend herself or was this a request for him to grab her wrists the way he used to do? No, she must not let him touch her.

"Go feel up the little child you have out there," she told him as she backed away. "Go feel up the little child you came here with. I bet she's skinny. Leave big woman alone . . ."

"Lemme feel the fatness, baby."

He held his open palms toward her.

"When it was yours, it was never enough."

"Baby, that's the past."

"The past is right," she said. "The past is right. Your time has passed. Just leave me alone and go."

That evening she arrived at home to see her husband's car. Clay was compacted in the treading.

Inside, she entered from the carport through the kitchen, which opened on a sunken den where Afghan rugs were held in place by Indian chairs and tables draped in prints from Java.

On a chaise inlaid with plates of bronze and topped with saffron cushions, the husband lay in purple briefs engrossed in watching TV.

He looked up when she entered. He had been dozing and seemed a little startled. On an ottoman beside him was his favorite pistol. She waved and rolled her eyes and shook her head. He smiled and settled down. Leaving him behind, she took the stairs in twos and ran along a skylit hall whose walls were lined with Cuban art.

In her bedroom she wriggled from her clothes and rushed into the shower stall to bathe away the memories of the day, but the memories rose around her with the steam. Memories filled her nostrils. Memories stung her eyes. And she began to soap herself with a new consideration—how she would feel to him. He had never been a romantic, had never been the type to bring flowers or send poems . . . had never been the one to arrange the grand parties . . . had never been the one to find the clever gift. That is not the way in which he showed his love. He showed his love through touching. He would hold your face as if it were a hive of sleeping bees. He stroked your side like water shaping earth. His arm around you was a vine. Still, he used to fuck so hard. There was a way in which he fucked you hard but slowly. Like a root he would take his time and burrow down inside you, and wait for you to feel as if he was a part of you; then he would slowly take his time to pull away, and you would feel a rush of air as if you'd lost a tooth, and you would panic, and he would sense it, and he would slip it in again, and he would take it out again and make you want to rise to meet him, so desperate you'd become, so badly you would want to have him fill you;

and he would do this with you for a night, and you'd feel as if he'd rammed you when he'd really fucked you slowly. Sometimes you would really want it hard, but you wouldn't know how to say it. What would he have thought? That you were common? It was hard to say. He didn't like to talk about his feelings. You either knew him or you didn't.

She emerged from her reflection when she heard her husband shuffling in the bedroom, laughing to himself. "Haw-haw-haw." She closed her eyes and placed her face beneath the water. Through the rushing stream she heard some pedal steel guitar.

"Why you taking so much time?" said the husband through the door. "You know when you hear country music the cowboy want to mount the bucking bronco."

"Coming," she said. "Coming. Just wait. I'll be there in a minute."

Freshly bathed, she latched the door and examined herself in the mirror, which was mounted on the linen closet. Blotting herself with a soft white towel, she slapped her hip and watched it jiggle. And for the first time in her forties, she felt good to have some overage.

"You seem disturbed," the husband told her as they lay down in the bed. His belly was a whale above the deep blue sheets. "You're upset about the gun."

"I don't worry about the things I can't change."

"From I hear you, I know it was the gun. This is Jamaica—everybody has to have a gun. People in America have guns. What is so big about a gun. You're going to let a little gun mash up me and you tonight?"

"It is not about you," she said. "And it's not about me. Some things in life—believe it or not—are bigger than me and you."

"I had a meeting with the people down at Treasure Beach today. It went well. I can taste the money already. The south coast is ripe, man. Ripe. The first man to get in there in a serious way going to be a rich rass man. Six hotels. A cruise ship pier. Condos. Jesus Christ."

"So what about the fishermen? You worked that out? What

kinda provisions you making for them as far as making sure the development won't displace them?"

He sat up on his elbows and looked down at her.

"Mia, I don't understand you and this conscience thing, y'know. You think the small man have conscience when him coming to broke into your house? You don't understand how this world run."

"I am not the only person in opposition. The National Conservation Trust is against it as well. Thousands of petitions too."

"You see all that little guy that heads the NCT? You know what I woulda really like to do? I want to keep a big vegetarian party for all those lesbians and faggots and say all I going to do is play Bob Marley and Tracy Chapman. And when him and all his nonprogressive friends come down, I just gas them and kill them. Haw-haw-haw."

"And you think that is funny?"

"Haw-haw-haw. Haw-haw-haw. Haw-haw-haw-*hawwwwwwwww*."

chapter eight

The Dragon Bay Hotel, the beach at night, white tables arranged in rows between the beach bar and the giant tree; black sky, cool breeze, stars that pulse like living things; toward the beach, in front of a bright bonfire, a stage garlanded with fuschia bouganvillea; to the side a buffet table set with chafing trays of curried goat, jerk chicken, escoveitched fish, oxtails, shrimp creole, lobster in a butter sauce, rice and peas, cassava, dumplings, hardough bread. Jamaica Night.

Michael wore a purple shirt. Peter wore a yellow vest. Patience wore a T-shirt with an image of a giant spliff.

"So they didn't have all the things we wanted when you went to Kingston, yesterday," said Peter. "So what are we going to do? Don should have the DAT by now. So we should be hearing from him tomorrow. I think the stuff went great. But recording five ballads in five days is a really risky thing."

"This is the way I see it, Peter," Michael said. "If the label likes the songs, then they will give us a little more time. If we get another two weeks, then—"

"Who's paying for the studio time?"

"If they want the songs, then they will come up with the money. Nothing in this business is cast in stone. If they believe in a product, they will back it. The thing is that we must be ready when the green light comes. That's why I went to Kingston. I need certain things—certain keyboards and certain modules, certain outboard gear, a live drum set for Azania. For what I want to do I need a Hammond . . . I need guitars . . . a bass . . . a lotta things. My thing is that if we are going to do it, then we should do it. The call will come. I know it. I can feel certain things."

"I'm concerned about the time, though, Michael. You were there the whole day yesterday . . . and what?"

And what? Michael thought. And everything. I met my wife again.

"Peter, this is not New York," he said, as his shoulder blades began to shear.

"Which means?"

"Some of the things will be coming tomorrow."

"And you're also going back you said?"

"We need a certain module," Patience interjected. "The first place didn't have it, and time ran out on us, so we have to go and get it somewhere else. We also need guitars."

"So why not let Azania go?"

Patience emphasized: "Because I like the drive."

Peter's mushy face began to stiffen now.

"If it doesn't work, we're all in shit," he told them. "But fuck it all. Let's eat."

They were joined by Azania, who brought along her toddler T'zo, a pleasant boy who wanted only bread and butter. The presence of the child eased the mood, and soon they were joking, improvising bawdy lyrics for the music emanating from the speakers, which were set on tripods—calypso from the sixties, Kitchener and Sparrow, and contemporary reggae, Luciano, Frankie Paul and Gregory Isaacs.

As they talked and laughed, Michael felt a hand against his shoulder and turned around to see a friend he had not seen in years.

"Chin-See the Dragon."

"Rumba the Rock."

"Years, me bredda. Years."

Short and bow-legged, brown-skinned and hazel-eyed, his hair aligned in braids, Rumba placed his hands atop his belly, cocked his head and smiled.

Michael shook his hand and said, "Respect, veteran. Respect," and introduced him to the table as a member of his earliest band, the Young Ruffians, which he had started up in high school.

"So you playing with the band?"

"No, man," Rumba chortled. "Leave out the playing thing long time. I have the entertainment contract at a couple of the hotels out here. The band thing dread, y'know. No portion o' music naah play inna Jamaica again. Is not like Ruffian's days."

"Was this a reggae band?" said Patience.

"An everything band," said Rumba. "In those days you had to play everything on a bandstand. And you had to play it good too. From samba to blues to jazz to calypso . . . and everything from Volt and Stax and Motown. And not to mention Philly soul. Yeah, man. In those days you never had reggae musicians—you had musicians who could play reggae. Nowadays you don't even have that."

Michael shook his head.

"What do you play?" said Patience.

Michael interjected: "Bass. If I had him the other day, I wouldn't bother even try."

"Just cool, man," Rumba said. "Just cool. You is a bassie in your own right." To Patience he said, "And you, my dear, you are in music too?"

"Sort of," Patience said. "I'm doing a little thing with Michael."

"So you should sing a little song for us tonight," said Rumba, flexing his brows good-naturedly. He did not recognize her.

Patience looked to Michael for permission.

"You want so sing?" he asked her. "Sing."

"You still love 'I'm Still Waiting'?" Rumba said to Michael. "You used to wear out that song."

"Right," Michael said, introspectively. "You played bass on that with Delroy Wilson."

Soon it was sorted. Rumba would play bass as a favor to Michael, and Azania would play the drums. For Patience, Michael transcribed the chords and lyrics and hummed the melody a half a dozen times. They would use the keyboard player from the band. Michael would play guitar. Harmony, like water, would find its own level.

When they took the stage, however—the hotel band was on their break—Michael realized that he was nervous. Since 1978, when he had toured as the Wailer's engineer and was called upon to play guitar in Paris when Junior Marvin badly sprained two fingers, he had not played live onstage. He was also feeling melancholic after seeing Mia yesterday. And as he stood there on Azania's right, the sea to his back, the tables in front, the beach bar to his left, he asked himself: How the fuck did I squander such love?

Was he in love with her still? Could it not be the idea of love? The idea of an idea?

Maybe he was feeling melancholic because he was unhappy with his life or because he was having second thoughts about the way he had remixed the songs. Maybe he should have done something more conventional? More radical? Fuck, if he had only seen Rumba earlier, he could have brought him in to listen before he sent the DAT away. And Mia . . . and Mia . . . what was she doing now? How was she feeling?

He thought of her with her husband—whoever he might be— and felt the urge to spit. How could she do that? How could she ever be with a man like that? He just *knew* the kind of man that she had married. They used to laugh at men like that. They used to call down fire on men like that. And now she was married to a man like that. Maybe at this moment kissing a man like that. Being caressed by a man like that. Listening to music with a man like that. And what kind of music would a man like that listen to? Not this kind of music. Those kind of men hated reggae music, used to fight it down, used to complain when it was played on radio, used to say things like "serve them right" when the police would stop you on the street and beat you up for having locks.

How could Mia marry a man like that? Those kind of men were the ones who left the country when Manley came to power and said that education must be free, that women must get equal pay, that hotels couldn't ban Jamaicans from the beaches in their own country, that America must respect our right to talk to anyone including Cuba.

How could Mia marry a man like that? How did they meet? What was the attraction? And as he thought about Mia, he began to get angry as he remembered how beneath her leftist stance she had always been a striver . . . that she had always found it hard to accept the fact that she was a girl from the flat, although she'd gone to boarding school with people on the hill . . . how she would cringe when he spoke patois in public places . . . how she used to get excited for American food . . . how she used to remind him how to dress when he would go to visit her at Cambridge . . . as if he were a fucking common boy. And who was she? She didn't come from anything either. So her parents were married, and she was born in a concrete house.

And how did the womanizing really start? She didn't take an interest in his work. He would play and she wouldn't come. She would make his friends feel weird when they came to the house. As a rasta, he didn't drink. Yet he would let her lawyer friends sip their Johnny Walker Black on the terrace. But if one o' his bredrens should roll a spliff, it was worries.

Tchicky. Tchicky. He began to scratch a riff now. Azania took this as a cue, and began to roll, and Michael was caught up in the cycle of the song, the revolution of the song, and he felt himself becoming transformed by the mood of dread.

The pick in his hand was a match, and the kick drum was a bomb, and locked in with Azania—tchicky-boom-tchicky, tchicky-boom-tchicky—he began to feel the phantom weight of locks against his shoulders, began to feel his knees dropped down in a guerilla crouch, the Telecaster copy on his shoulder like a rifle. Rumba's rumbling bass notes rolling, then stopping, exuding awe and danger, became an armored car. And at the edge of the stage, legs spread wide, feet turned out, Patience was skanking with her arms outstretched, fists like palmed grenades, head cocking back in the pauses, then firing again, jerking to the high hat like someone sprayed with bullets, high stepping now as the shock of the rhythm took her over, doubling now as the lead in the rhythm took her down, then leaping up again, undeniable as a drumroll detonated her fists, and flung her to the stage to utter words of great lamentation, feminizing the lyrics, curled up on her side, brutalized by love, all this while Michael and Rumba doo-wopped sweetly:

I said my feet, won't keep me up anymore
With every little beat my heart beats, boy
It's at your door,
I just wanna love you.
And I'm never, never gonna hurt you, boy
So why don't you come on to me now, boy
Can't you see, I'm under your spell
But, I've got to, got to ask why, boy
Oh, why, boy
And oh, my gosh, the rain is falling
And I just can't stop bawling

I'm still waiting.
And I'm still waiting, still waiting for you, baby,
I'm still waiting.
I'm still waiting.
I'm still waiting.

There was no turning back now, Michael thought, as Patience wrung the meaning from the song. They would have to record this one as well. They would have to go to Kingston in the coming days. So what if they ran into Mia? He had made his choices and so had she. But as he looked at Patience, he could not prevent himself from comparing. She didn't have the fattage. Just muscle and flesh. No jiggle. Yes, she was younger. Yes, she was slimmer, but she was attractive in the way of a new guitar. She had not matured yet, the sound of her soul was too bright, too thin; she had yet to mellow, to age and ripen like wood.

chapter nine

Later that night, upstairs in his lamp-lit room, Michael poured himself a glass of water. He took a sip. He tried to swallow, but it wouldn't go down; and he leaned against the wall and held it there, squishing it through his teeth.

The water began to thicken with his spit, and he began to move his jaw slackly, his tongue against his palate, reaching through the sludge.

Loosening his shirt he moved toward the bathroom. In the base of his neck a vertebra was feeling like the nut that held his shearing shoulder blades. In the mirror his torso was a copper line that halved his cotton shirt. And as he watched without watching, saw without seeing, a man who looked like him—oblong face . . . high, flat cheeks . . . eyes like cowrie shells—placed his palms atop his head and dribbled down his chin and neck.

The water was warm from being in his mouth—the temperature of piss. And he was embarrassed in his own reflection.

He touched his fingers to the glass. The tips were raw from playing. Both hands on the mirror, he tried to hide himself. But the man was still observing him through cracks between his fingers, brows underscoring scribbled lines of worry.

He let his hands fall and felt the sting against his thigh, and took his time to peel away the shirt, which he heaped between the hamper and the toilet.

Back inside the bedroom, he lay down on the floor, his arms outstretched, his ankles crossed, vexed and disappointed.

As brilliantly as she had sung, Patience had failed him in a fundamental way. After the performance, he had felt a single tear roll into the hollow where his collarbones met. More would have fallen. But he had tilted his head, and they were channeled through the grooves along his forehead to his temples, which glowed with sweat and arcing strands of silver hair.

To call them tears of joy would have been simple. But simple would have been correct, for these were simple tears, tears as pure as dew condensed from mountain air, tears sprung from the most elemental form of happiness—experiencing God's greatness through the greatness of his creatures.

In the presence of such greatness there is nothing else to do . . . laugh perhaps . . . but laughter is inappropriate in church, and greatness sanctifies the most ungodly place: the stadium, the theater, the club, the screen, the ring where Ali won the title for the final time.

Michael had heard it for himself—Patience Olayinka, in one take, of a new song, without rehearsal, in reggae, a genre to which she was unaccustomed, had not just sung, but had *performed* the song as if she had composed it.

After the performance Michael had felt rising up inside him a sense of possibility, a sense of firm assurance that Patience, on ability alone, in his informed opinion, was one of the greatest pop singers he had ever seen or heard—and that the rerecording of the ballads would be his proof.

Her impeccabilities astonished—timing, feeling, pitch, texture, tone, agility and breath control; but more importantly she had an understanding of rhythm and tempo. Like a stripper with a pair of perfect breasts, she used these gifts to tease the song until the song became her slave. This was the secret of the great pop singers like Sting and Marvin Gaye: they could seduce a song and make it yield up secrets that it held from everyone including its composer.

But as he lay down on the floor, the happiness at Dragon Bay seemed so far away. Because after the performance Patience had done something unforgivable. In the presence of Peter and Azania, she had leaned across the table, kissed her palm and rubbed her hand against his face and said with authoritative nonchalance: "I'm going to bed. Do you want me to wait up for you?"

She recovered in an instant, and laughed and made a joke about the heat. And Peter and Azania laughed as well. And the question was so unexpected and the mood had been so light that the question was soaked up by the humid air like all the other jokes that they had told that night.

No, he had not been exposed. But the slip had served to warn him. Patience Olayinka was a brilliant singer. But she was young and unpredictable, and most importantly, in love, and to the point where she was losing her discretion.

Discretion. That was something that he had always admired in Mia. And as he lay there on the floor, unbuckling his pants now, weaseling as he slipped them down his thighs, he thought about the day they met.

He had not thought about their meeting for a very long time. There had been a time when he used to think about it often. He could not remember when or why he had stopped. But there had also been a time, he was remembering now, when he had tried to see and feel the moment again, but he had felt like a man trying to wade into a frozen lake. But this night, though, the memory parted like memories do when they are ready to be forded; and as he lay there on the floor, naked on his back, one leg drawn up, round heel pressed into sweating thigh, he rode a stream of consciousness toward a sea of recollections . . . Kingston . . . 1970 . . . Brazil had won the World Cup with Jarzinho and Pele . . . Cross Roads . . . in the median the clock from colonial times . . . the Woolworth's . . . all the buildings low and made of concrete, the patterned tiles on the sidewalk . . . up the road the market with the iron fence . . . below, the busy bus terminal . . . the buses silver-gray with streaks of green . . . the smell of diesel fumes . . . the bus stop like a grandstand . . . covered in zinc with metal columns . . . people chucked together on the bleachers . . . beside the bus stop the little wooden record shack cotched up on some stones . . . through the open shutter the owner dealing forty-fives . . . the box on the sidewalk . . . speakers blown and baffled . . . a mad-man dancing in the middle of the road . . . the buses swerving around him . . . his penis roping through his holey-holey jeans . . . his hair greenish gray and flat like cow manure . . . everything right but the rhythm . . . and people laughing . . . and people whispering . . . and people arguing . . . people dark and sweaty like beer bottles . . . soul boys Afroed like the Jackson 5, baldheads wearing Tony Cs—short but full in front like actor Tony Curtis—then there were the dreads, the rastamen, who were rare and awe-inspiring, with their matted hair and clotted beards like Old Testament prophets, selling brooms or peanuts and calling out to all who wouldn't turn away: "Peace and love. Peace and love. Rastafari means peace and love."

The stream had brought Michael fully in the memory now, and everything was clear. He was standing at the corner of the market, looking south along Slipe Road. The bus stop and the record shack were on his right. Across the median to his left, he saw the post office set at an angle a little way back from the road, the line of stores. And straight ahead, above the fuming buses, was the Carib, one of the largest cinemas in the Americas, ornamented, white and grand, its broad steps trampled by the polished shoes of two thousand children, most of whom had come from rural areas on a Saturday morning for a special viewing of *To Sir With Love*.

Like the other boys, he was dressed in khaki shirt and pants. But being mannish, he kept his school insignia in his pocket as he moved toward the crowd.

He was fourteen, tall, with a head of boisterous hair, and walked with an affected dip. It was the middle of summer; but with so many students in attendance, the principals believed that uniforms would "better assist in preventing infiltration by reprobates and hooligans."

Although he was late, there were no friends waiting to meet him. At school he was a loner. His peers seemed immature; but there was a more important reason. Mr. Pareles, who had adopted him, had gone home to Caracas, and now he lived on his own. If the teachers found out, he would be returned to his father or sent to a home for wayward boys, both of which for him would be like prison for he led a life with few restrictions.

Most of his friends were in their twenties, most of them leading singers and musicians. And they would allow him to smoke and drink. Because he was tall, light in color, and part Chinese, women often thought that he was wealthy or connected. And whenever he was lonely he would gather up the women who had fallen bruised and dusty from the shoulders of the stars— simple women, common girls . . . barmaids and go-go dancers . . . women with names like Pinkie, Norma, Jean and Dimples . . . women who would ask him for a bus fare and patty every time they made him come.

He was passing by the record shack when he saw Mia Fortuna that day. She had crossed Slipe Road and was standing on the median in the shadow of the clock in the blue tunic and white blouse of Hampton, an elite girls' school on the apex of a hill in St. Elizabeth. Her hair was center-parted with two fat plaits whose tips were held together by a navy blue barrette between her shoulder blades.

At first he was taken by the fact that a girl of her complexion went to Hampton. She must be rich, he thought. Maybe her father was a lawyer.

Her arms were folded across her chest; and the tone of her skin was so even that her color seemed enameled. The box outside the record shack was thumping with the hottest forty-five, Bob Andy and Marcia Griffiths' reggae version of "Young Gifted and Black," and the madman was skanking in the middle of the road, his head down, his elbows out, his legs rotating, riding a unicycle only he could see to the place where all his dreams had been deferred.

In a flash of inspiration Mia began to imitate the dance, cautiously, her movements imperceptible to everyone but Michael, who had begun to watch, jaw gaping as if he had seen a mythic bird. She was rare, he thought . . . rare and different . . . and he began to feel closer to her than to the other people around him because he felt as if he had been given insight into the secret of her other self. Along with this, he was drawn to her because he went to a prestigious school as well, St. George's, which had been founded by Franciscans in the middle 1800s. There, few students were dark. Most were high mulattos, with a strong contingent of Lebanese, Jews and Chinese. Whites in Kingston went primarily to Priory, Campion, Wolmer's or Jamaica College—if they had not been shipped to rural boarding schools like Munro or DeCartret.

Thus intrigued, he tracked her.

Inside the lobby of the Carib, which was hung with chandeliers and noisy with echoes of adolescent excitement, he watched her as she tipped, her arms still folded, looking for her friends. There was a grace to her movements, a pointing of her toes, an imperial carriage in the bearing of her shoulders, something floral in the graceful elongation of her neck.

But how did she speak?

He soon found out. When she saw her friends—all of whom were white or mixed—she sprinted in a mannish way, dodged and wove across the room and leaped onto the curving stairs. Unnoticed he followed, rounding out his shoulders, tucking his hands, trying to hide himself.

In the skirt of the stairs, he cotched and listened. Mia and her friends were true adolescents he discovered—fourth-form girls who slept in bunks and limited their rebellion to mimicking teachers and lending credence to the lie that a secret tunnel linked their school to Munro, whose headmaster was a retired English major.

She had not lived he thought . . . and already she was dead, for she was concerned with trivial things. Hadn't she heard of black power? Still, her voice endeared him and he continued to listen. Her tone was adult, deeper than he had expected, and from her diction it was clear that she was sharper than her peers.

Her friends, he surmised, were the children of old money, of the planter class—rural—for with all their wealth they were quite thrilled to be in the capital, which they referred to as "town." As they talked excitedly about the things that they had seen through the window of the bus, one girl said that she had

heard that town had an amusement park with a zoo and a roller
coaster. Then another confessed that she had never seen a movie
in a theater with a roof because the ones in her parish were
open-air and could only show movies at night—so, although it
was corny, she was glad to see "a stupid movie with Sidney
Batty Hair." And they giggled and snickered, hands over their
mouths, he could tell—at the use of the Jamaican word for
"bottom."

The teachers had begun to organize their students now, and
Michael prepared to go. He saw some boys from his class, boys
with Tony Cs, one of whom was dangling a motorcycle key. He
nodded and they nodded back. And he knelt and tied his shoe,
averting eye contact and any possible conversation.

As he fiddled with his lace, something fell against his head. It
was a rolled-up note on composition paper. To his right, at the
concession stand, he saw a girl much younger than himself.
With a movement of her chin she held his stare and raised it to
the steps above. The note said:.

> Dear Follower:
>   Leading would suit you better. If this is your
> predilection, repair to the concession stand. I will
> follow you.

He obeyed.

"What is your name?" Mia asked him, while holding up her
money so the counter girl would see. It was crowded and noisy,
and they were being jostled on all sides.

"Michael," he whispered. "Michael Chin-See."

He followed the crowed and raised his money as well.

"Mine is Mia Fortuna," she told him.

"Fortuna is your last name?"

"No. That is one name. You don't like your school? You're
not wearing your tie."

"We don't wear one at George's," he said. "We wear
epaulets."

"I am aware of that fact."

She looked at him and cut her eyes.

"So how come you saw me?" he asked, intrigued to know the source of her wiles.

"I like to be addressed by my proper name," she told him, ignoring his question.

"So how come you saw me, Mia Fortuna . . . what's your last name again?"

"I didn't make you aware of it." She looked down at his shoes. They were desert boots by Clarks. "And what are you? A little chukky-boo who wants to be a dread? Why you didn't comb your hair this morning? And you have such nice hair too? I really don't know why you're spoiling it so. You're cute all the same."

"Cute is for boys and puppies," he cautioned in the mannish tone that he had sought and found.

"And you are what?" she ricocheted.

"You don't want to find out," he said coolly, as a dare he knew she would not take.

"That is true," she said a little nervously. Then she switched the subject: "Are you the tallest boy in your class?"

"No."

His voice was confident and breezy. Almost flip.

"The skinniest?"

He was slightly offended at the word, but his tone remained the same: "Maybe."

"But are you the cutest?"

"I am not cute," he warned.

"Take it from me. You are."

Her insistence annoyed him. Most girls in his age-group were obedient. And he began to find her confidence unsettling. Who was she? What was she about? Where did she come from?

"Are you the only black girl at Hampton?" he asked casually.

Her reaction was a shock. She cringed and turned toward him and looked him up and down. A tear escaped her dreamy eyes and rolled along her diamond face.

"Black," she said through trembling lips, "is what you call a maid."

"Sorry," he said softly. He wanted to hold her hand to reassure her. But he couldn't. He didn't know what to do. And felt an urge to wipe his face. Her tears were feeling like his own.

She quickly wiped her face against her sleeve. No one had noticed. But before he had a chance to explain himself, there came a voice from behind them: "Gonsalves."

They turned around. It was a teacher.

"We're assembling now. Come."

They did not get to say good-bye. And as Michael watched her being led away, her hands interlocked on her bustled behind, Mia flipped her middle finger and turned it.

When the film was over he waited on the steps, transfixed like a tree in floodwaters. Around him waves of colored tunics flowed. And as he watched each color streaming into its bus, he felt bad that he had hurt her, but worse, that he had lost the chance to inform her that women who made vulgar signs were known as leggo beasts, and that if she wanted to be considered a decent girl, she should refrain from slack behavior.

It was a little after noon. The sun was a magnifying glass, and they were ants. The sno-cone men were busy squirting Day-Glo-colored syrup on domes of ice that sparked like balls of powered glass. The children from the country looked on furtively, thirsty but afraid to break the line. What if they broke the line and missed their bus? How would they get home?

"You want one?" Michael offered a group of first-formers. "Gimme the money and I'll buy it." And he began to shuttle between the buses and the sno-cone men, four cones to a hand, sometimes tilting back his head to hold one in his mouth, as the cheering students stretched their arms outside the buses.

He was going to the vendor for the fourteenth time when he saw Mia Fortuna in the distance, walking straight-elbowed toward St. Luke's, heading south along Slipe Road; and he gave the children back their money and chased her as the buses steamed with boos.

"Hampton," he said, when he was twenty yards away. In his confusion and excitement he had forgotten her name. "Hampton."

He ran ahead of her and blocked her path. People paused to look, but continued when they realized that the girl was in no danger, whereupon they would have ganged the boy and beat him.

"Listen," he said, "I want to talk to you."

"Can you just eggs off, please." Her tone was flatter now. "Didn't you call me black? What business do you have with me?"

She kept on walking, and he turned and walked beside her.

"But I didn't mean anything," he said. His need to chastise her was waning now. "Black is just a color like white. I didn't mean anything."

"Yes, you did."

She glanced at him and cut her eyes.

"Okay, if I did mean something, what did I mean?" he challenged.

"That you think you better off because you are a Chiney."

He was stunned.

"By the way, you're not taking the bus?" he asked, pointing behind him in the direction of the cinema, the market and the clock.

"Why?"

The road was busy with traffic and the sidewalk was streaming with shoppers. The buildings here were low with overhanging roof lines for shade—hardware stores, patty shops, rum bars and tailoring and wholesale establishments.

"Don't you go to Hampton?" he asked. "Hampton is a country school."

"I *board at* Hampton," she said, sarcasm flexing her twisted brow. "We are on summer holiday."

"Where you live, then?"

"That is of no concern to you."

"Why not?"

"Because there is nothing to know. Black is nothingness."

"I only said that you were—"

"Try your best . . . don't say it again."

Exasperated, he touched her wrist and stopped her and began

to speak in patois to show that he was grounding. "What? You not black? You know, when I saw you I thought you were a conscious daughter, but you not conscious. You still living in colonial times. You never hear 'bout black power? You never read how Tommy Smith show the fist at the Olympics? Look, Brazil just win the World Cup last week and what they call Pele, the greatest footballer in the world? The Black Pearl. So what so bad 'bout black, then? You consciousness not really straight, Hampton. You consciousness not straight. You not listening. To Walter Rodney? You not listening to Stokely Carmichael? You not listening to what Mr. Manley saying? Is socialist time coming y'know, baby. Is black man time coming, y'know, baby. You not listening to reggae music? You not listening to what the rastaman saying?"

"So what?" she said, crossing her arms as she looked him up and down. "You're black too?"

From an adjacent lane a rastaman robed in white, his locks tied up in calico, strode into the sunlight, smelling of ganja, sweat and carbolic soap.

"Nyah," Michael called out as Mia shook her head in mild amusement, "this sister want to know if I am black."

The dread stroked his beard and studied Michael up and down, fire coming to his eyes.

"Which part a you black?" he demanded as he pointed with an open hand. "Which part a you black? When revolution come, all you going dead too. All Chiney. All whitey. All Syrian. All red man. All Babylonian. Dead. One time. Fire bun."

"I think he's kinda mad," Michael said as Mia doubled over and staggered as she laughed.

"No, he's not," she said, straightening up and taking ahold of herself. "You're the mad one."

"And if I am mad, then you are what?" he asked, smiling in defeat.

"I am nothing," she said, wiping her eyes. "I am fine."

Now that he had seen her common side, he liked her even more. She was a girl within his reach.

"How old are you?" he asked her in a courtly way.

They had begun to walk again. Way out in the distance was the sea. In the nearground on their left was the Tropical, a hangout for thieves and petty gangsters, the roughest cinema in the Cross Roads area. The other three were Carib, State and Regal.

"Fourteen," she said. "And you?"

"Fifteen," he replied.

"And I live here in Kingston," she told him, walking with some swing in her hips as she enjoyed the kind of interest usually shown to lighter girls.

"Where?"

She was hesitant. He pressed her.

"Rollington." But she added quickly, "We're going to be moving soon. The area is changing."

"Oh, I like it over there," he said. It was a neighborhood of ordinary people like them . . . bus drivers, cashiers, policemen and entry-level civil servants.

A man on a mule cart filled with coconuts nodded as he clopclopped along his way.

"Easy for you to say," she said. "I would really like to live where you live."

"Which is where?"

"On one of the hills, I suppose."

They were crossing Torrington Bridge, a twenty-meter span across a concrete drainage ditch whose silt-lined floor had sprouted vegetation, twisted trees and prickly shrubs that nourished goats and herds of swine.

"Where do you live?" she asked directly.

"Range," he said, "but I was born in Riverton."

"By the dump?" she exclaimed.

"Yeah," he said more calmly than he felt. "But after a while I went to live with my father up in Cooper's Hills."

"See, I knew you were a little uptown boy—"

"But, I couldn't take the vibes up there, so I kinda ace the spot."

He said this is his mannish way.

"Just you and your mother live together now?"

"My mother died."

"Hush."

She brushed his hair as if she were his sister.

"Is awright," he replied as he willed her to continue. "Don't worry. Is awright."

They had crossed the street and were passing Blissett's now, a store that custom crafted bicycles for racing. Ahead of them was George V Memorial Park, which everyone called the racecourse, a grassy circle about a half a mile across. The national heroes park was there, a velodrome and a boxing gym. On the northern side was Wolmer's Boys, whose oldest buildings was erected in the 1700s; on the eastern side was the ministry of finance, and on the southern side the ministry of education. They approached it from the west.

"So what you doing for the summer?" she asked as they came along the northern quadrant.

"Work," he said proudly.

"In a store?"

"In a studio. A recording studio. Mostly Harry J, Channel One and Federal."

"What do you do?" she asked suspiciously.

"I am a prento . . . an apprentice. I do everything. I mike up the drums. I tune the guitars. I run the board. I buy cigarettes. I play piano and bass. I do everything. I even sing sometimes if they need someone to do some backup. I have my own band, you know. You soon hear of us. The Young Ruffians. You soon hear of us. You know who we going be like? You know The Now Generation . . . Geoffrey Chung, Mikey Chung and Val Douglas?" He held her hand to stop her, but quickly let it go in case an older person saw them. "You see this new beat that coming up now, this reggae music, it going take over the world, you know. Take it from me. This is a boss beat you know."

She crossed her arms and rolled her eyes and chortled.

"Personally I find it butu-ish."

He laughed and shook his head with self-righteous cool.

"Hampton, you can't say that. Only regular people like it now, but watch me, this thing going take over the whole wide world."

"Why?" she asked, churlishly. "How? Nobody in the world even knows about Jamaica much less. All they know about Jamaica is Mobay and banana boat. Chiney boy, you crazy? Is only on jukebox in rum bar you can hear reggae. And if our own JBC and RJR not playing it, how is anybody going to hear it? Boy, you mad. Plus all of our stars sing rocksteady. They not going change. Is only the little hurry-come-up singers singing reggae."

"You don't know what is going on," he said. "You know the Wailers? Well, their new album is not rocksteady. Just pure boss music. The Paragons doing reggae. The Heptones. Ken Boothe. Alton Ellis. Toots and the Maytals. Even Delroy Wilson. Mark me, reggae going take over Jamaica, and then it going take over the world. You ever hear 'bout Count Ossie? Count Ossie and The Mystic Revelations of Rastafari? The Count is a great congo drummer and a rasta elder out in Rock Fort. And I heard the Count announce one day that reggae is the music that come to liberate black people all over the world. Black people time coming up hot, y'know. See, in sixty-two we got independence, the Count said, and that was brown man time. Before that it was colonialism, and that was white man time. The seventies going be black man time, though. Mark me. Mark me. And every time need a music. You better get on board, Hampton. Mind the Black Star Liner leave you."

"Why you like to go one like a big man so?" she said languidly. She was looking at him dreamily, and her tongue had sought the softness of her inner lip.

"Because I am a big man," he declared. "You have to be a big man to spar with musicians, y'know. If you go on like little boy, they will ask you to ace the spot. Plus, when you spar with big man, you learn all the things they don't teach in school."

"Like what?" she challenged.

"Marcus Garvey, Kwame Nkrumah, Angela Davis, Huey Newton, Malcolm X."

"You read *Malcolm X*?" she exclaimed.

"Cover to cover," he confirmed. "Page to page. That and the Macabee Bible."

"But how you read these things and government banned them?" she asked naïvely.

"Stick by me, Hampton, and you will learn plenty things. When you spar with musicians, you learn everything there is to know about everything. Because they travel. And they see things. And they bring it back."

"Is that what you want to be? A musician?" she asked, looking at him appraisingly.

They were on the northern edge of the park. Committed to no direction, they moved with the curving circle.

"Yeah, man. Yeah, man. Definitely. Music is my first love. Nothing can come before that."

"So I guess everybody and everything has to settle for second," she said.

"It all depends, I guess," he told her. "It all depends."

chapter ten

Morning. The curtains were drawn. The room was dim. Through the crack of the barely open door, the world outside was silver. A wind was up, and Michael could hear the sound of it, fluffing up the hanging ferns.

Since the night at Dragon Bay, three days now, he had found it difficult to sleep alone. And to recapture the clarity of the memory of the day that he had met Mia Fortuna Gonsalves, he would lie in the same spot each night after working all day in the studio. Through Peter he had communicated to Patience that he and Azania needed time to work on the ballads without interruption, and that although she would be missed, her presence would have more value when the tracks were closer to completion. Still, Patience had been calling, constantly, or in the words of Miss Lydia, "like she hear telephone going outta style;" and Miss Lydia, who had been instructed to take messages only, despite receiving promises of money and other favors, did not give in, presenting the proof of her commitment in the form of folded messages tucked beneath the door.

The hardness of the floor and the heat of the night had kept Michael from falling deeply into sleep; so when he woke to see a naked woman in the room, he thought that he was dreaming. She moved as if she were a puppet, as if invisible wires were being used to jolt her up and down. Her breasts were large and round. Her hair was very short; and her pubic mound, freshly shorn, revealed a mole above the cleft. She was speaking rapidly, in a language that he could not place, a language whose words had many syllables, and whose tonalities shifted quickly from the nostrils to the throat. She had brought into the room the smell of alcohol and coffee; and her navel was surrounded by a painting of the sun in a walnut-colored tincture that had stained her palms.

On reflexes alone, Michael scrambled to his feet with a speed that cleared his head; and through the lifting daze he realized that the woman was Patience, who had shaved all her body hair except her brows.

"What time is it?" he asked, covering his mouth to hide his breath. "And what is the great excitement?"

Her clothes were strewn across the bed.

"I was so excited I was speaking Yoruba," she said. She leaped and did a back flip and landed on her bottom, but she lost her balance and fell sideways against the bed, and as she raised her leg to hold her poise, he saw a flash of pink between her legs.

"What time is it?" he asked again as he turned away. He was naked too, and the sight of her shaven lips aroused him.

"It is almost noon," she whispered, as she closed her eyes and lay on her back with her legs together and her hands along her side. "But I don't give a fuck about the time." Her stomach muscles tightened, and her lips began to wrinkle as they pursed. And he could see her eyes darting underneath her shuttered lids. "Don called Peter this morning," she said.

"And what?" Michael took a worried step toward her and leaned against the bedpost. "And what?" he asked. "And what?"

Up on her elbows now, Patience looked away across the room, swallowed hard and whispered, "This is what Peter told me. He said that Don said—and I quote: 'This is not what I was thinking, but it's motherfucking better. I'm willing to commit another hundred thousand dollars if you bring those ballads back within a month.' " And she flopped against the bed and laughed and ululated and kicked her thighs.

Michael didn't speak; and for a while he didn't move. And as Patience indulged herself in joy, he put on his pants and went out on the verandah. There, he placed his hands against the railing as his gaze was drawn toward the distant sea.

In his chest he felt as if someone had wrapped his heart in Styrofoam. He could not hear it—even when he closed his eyes and listened. He put a finger on his pulse. It was normal. A month and a hundred grand, he thought. Shouldn't he be excited? What the fuck is going on?

He was not by nature ecstatic. But there had always been a sense of guarding, a sense that his emotions might escape and cause real damage if he didn't watch them closely and beat them down if they did not heed his orders to shut up and sit down.

But if his emotions were like prisoners before, they seemed like mental patients now, sedated and lobotomized, alive but not living.

What was he going to do? He had earned another month, but did he want it?

His original intent had been to take a month to think about his life, to figure out what he was doing and where he was going—and he had not had the chance to do this. Another month would go beyond his leave of absence. If he started on the ballads, he knew, he would not find the will to leave. What would that mean?

His reel, which included six Clios and an Addy, would get him hired anywhere. But another month for someone else? What about *his* month? Another month would be a sacrifice. But a sacrifice for whom? For him? For Patience? For the both of them? The both of them together or the both of them apart? And how would she read his sacrifice? He did not know. She was young and unpredictable, and worst of all, in love.

As he thought of this he heard her singing in the room, a song he did not know. Fuck, he thought, he had the money now, and a little bit of time. If she listened, and worked, and if they could make their time together not so much about themselves but about the opportunity that lay ahead of them, they could make an album that could do the same for both of them—return to them the dignity they knew that they had lost.

As he thought of this he heard her coming, and he closed his eyes and felt her arms around his waist, holding him close, her breasts soft against the middle of his back, her hot cheek against his shoulder blade, her words reverberating through his bones.

"Baby, I don't know how to thank you," she murmured. "I don't know. I don't know." And he felt her body give her weight to him as she began to sob. "I was just this fucked-up, arrogant child who needed straightening out, and you just came along and . . . I just love you, okay. I just love you. Don't leave me, please. I don't know what I would do without you."

He stood with his hands on the railing, his face toward the sea, holding her weight as she heaved. He wanted to tell her that they needed each other for a little while longer, but that they had to go their separate ways.

But he did not tell her this. The truth might make her run. And if she ran too fast too quickly, then the chain that bound their destinies would break. And if it broke they would both be cast adrift. And all would have been lost.

"I need you to hold me," she pleaded. "Come inside and hold me."

On the bed, they lay together, and he held her close against his chest and felt the new smoothness of her hair.

"When did you cut it?" he asked.

She raised her head and looked at him. Her eyes appeared larger now. And she kissed him on his neck and rubbed her head against his belly, softly like a brush and said as she unzipped his fly: "This morning when I got the news. To me it just means that I am starting over."

"It suits you," he told her.

"I don't look like a boy, do I?"

"You're too curvy for that. But come up here where I can rub it."

She put her head on his chest again, and he was relieved.

"And you painted yourself as well?" he asked.

"Tia Maria . . . the coffee liqueur. I was hoping you would lick it off."

He pretended that it was a joke and laughed.

"We should celebrate," she said. "We should do something exciting. Let's get high."

"Let's do something with everyone," he insisted. "And you stopped smoking, remember? You told me that you had stopped smoking. You said you had done it for me."

She shrugged as if this was a petty observation.

"I wanna do something with us alone," she pleaded in a girlish way.

She began to wriggle, and her skin against his body was suddenly too warm, and he began to think of reasons to get out of bed.

"Okay, but let's celebrate another day," he told her. "I have to go to Kingston for the equipment. In fact, I have to get ready right away. Think about the celebration while I'm gone—what you want to do—and then we will do it when I come back."

"I wanna come," she blurted.

"The drive is too much hackling for you. You know. You went with me the other day. Rest today."

"I'm talking about fucking me," she said.

"We shouldn't talk about those things."

"Why?" she challenged.

"Because they fuck things up sometimes."

"You are so unfair."

She rolled out of his arms and stood in the doorway with her palms against the joists, shifting her weight from leg to leg. Beneath her arms he could see the curve of her breasts, and between her legs the shadowed crescent of her bower hanging lower then the arcs that marked the crescents of her ass.

She sucked her teeth and leaned against the joist and crossed her arms, and he saw her now in profile, her head as smooth as someone just emerging out of water, her stomach flat with just the slightest pouch below her navel, her pelvis slightly cocked. She turned toward him, and he acted like he did not see. She turned away, and so as not to look at her, he rolled onto his side; there, he leaned over began to stroke the ridges of the sisal mat.

He heard her suck her teeth; then the floor begin to shudder. And he felt his muscles bracing for a blow.

She did not hit him. Instead, she spread out on the mat, her head toward the door, her toes toward his face, and pulled apart her lower lips and caught a shaft of light inside her delicates. He watched her . . . disgusted but engaged . . . angry but aroused . . . watched her cup her ass and raise her hips and slip her middle finger deep inside herself with grunts and moans of effort, searching for something that eluded her, pulling out the finger now, wiping it in on her belly, haloing the tinctured sun that spun around her navel. She began to rub her fingers on her nipples now, her body in an arc, her poundage balanced on her neck and toes.

"See," she said, "your dick is getting hard."

He had begun to stroke himself.

"Patience, this is not the time."

"When was it? Not last night. Not the night before, nor the night before that. Last night I slept alone when I wanted you so bad. So, so fucking bad. What is so wrong if I want to suck you off, Michael? Is that really such a bad thing? If I just wanna pull the skin back and watch the head swelling like a cobra. Would your cobra bite my face if I kissed it? Would it be jealous that its tongue is not as dangerous as mine. Mike, my tongue is dangerous. I can suck your balls and make you do my bidding. I can lick your ass and bitch you out. Don't fuck with me, Michael." She rubbed herself slowly as she spoke. "I love you, but there is a bitch that lives in me. Understand that." She was trembling fiercely, and he saw her nostrils flare and close like valves. "I can't believe you didn't fuck me," she said as she gritted her teeth. "Son of a bitch, I hate you."

He opened his arms, and she crawled into the bed again. He felt safer now that she had come. If he consoled her, he thought, he could calm her down and make her listen. She could not come to Kingston. She had to stay.

"You know I didn't meant that, don't you?" she whispered as he rocked her. "I could never hate you. I can only love you."

"It doesn't matter," he told her as he rubbed his hand along her side. Now that she had found release, her muscles were relaxed and she was softer to the touch. With perspiration she smelled of salt, and he began to remember the beauty of the time that they had swum together underwater. She wasn't so bad he told himself. Just young.

When he got ready to leave for Kingston, he took her face in his hands and said, "Be good until I come back."

But she insisted that she had to go.

"Baby," he said to her, "let's talk about this when I come back. I have to go now."

"I don't want to be without you," she replied. "Last night was horrible."

"Last night was last night," he told her. "Tonight will be tonight."

"Will we make love tonight?"

"Tonight is its own night," he said as he held her and rubbed her head.

She did not hug him in return.

"What does that mean?"

"Exactly what I said."

"Are you fucking anyone, Michael?"

"No, I'm not."

"Because if you are," she began, backing off to look him up and down completely, "I would be the bitch that brings you down. I wouldn't give a shit what would happen. If they threw me in jail and I never had another record again . . . I wouldn't give a shit. I know myself. I know how ridiculous I can get."

He placed his hands across his lips. "Shhhhhhhhh," he said. "Miss Lydia is downstairs. Have some consideration. Have some manners."

"Is she the one you're fucking?" she screamed.

As he watched with snide bemusement, she clapped her head and laughed.

"Look at me?" she said, holding him close now. "Did I just say all that stupid movie shit? Oh, God, Baby, I just love you, that's all. Is that so bad? Is that so bad that I just want to come with you? That I want to drive with you through your country? Is that really so bad. Does that make me like a bad person? Tell me that it doesn't. I couldn't stand it if it did. I wouldn't be able to stand that at all."

"Just cool," he said as he rubbed her head. Against the hardness of her skull, he could feel his blood pulsing through his finger.

"Don't say that!" she screamed.

She was rigid in his arms; then he felt her go soft. If she cracks her voice, he thought, we're fucked.

"Come," he said, finally. "Come."

"I already did," she said flippantly. "And you promised me I'd come again tonight."

"You are not as funny as you think," he said as he released her. "And you are not as charming either."

"So what is the secret of my success?" she asked through a laugh, as if she had just returned from a safe adventure sparked with hints of fear.

"You have a fantastic voice," he said without a smile. His mouth had barely opened.

"A fantastic pussy too," she said. "But you would never know."

On the road now, in Azania's four-wheel drive, Patience said to Michael: "You didn't tell me that you love me."

They were coming up on Dragon Bay, and he fought the urge to tell her that he'd left something important in her room; when she went to get it, he would drive away.

"If you have to say it all the time, it isn't real," he said.

"Is it real, though?"

"It is as real as you want to make it."

She was sitting very formally, with her seat back straight and her hands neatly folded in her lap. She wore a calico dress with natural linen pockets and espadrilles that added inches to her height.

"I cut my hair to look like you," she said.

He pressed his sandaled foot against the gas and glanced at her. She had taken off the bra; and as her breasts began to shimmer with the roughness of the road, he began to wonder how her nipples felt against the fabric.

"I cut my hair to look like you," she said again.

"It looks good on you, whether you did it for me or not. It is more important for you to do things for yourself, you know. You have to find out what things mean to you, the value of things to you. Then you defend those things and try to hold on to those things, because if you let them go, they are sometimes hard to find again; and sometimes you can find them, but due to circumstances you just can't get them back, and then you spend a lot of time worrying about getting them back—and that kind of fretting can carry you down, can bring you way, way down."

"That song we did the other night, 'I'm Still Waiting,' was all about that. And your friend, the bass player, he was brilliant. How is he by the way?"

"He is in Negril. We spoke one time since that time. He is coming back in a week. So we'll link up then."

"I see."

"You talk about Rumba. But you are the one that really fucked up my head. To sing the song that way without rehearsal, without really knowing the lyrics. That is what really fucked me up."

"What do you mean?"

He should not have said that. He had not meant to say that. But he had. If you couldn't sing then all of this would be so easy, he wanted to say. If you weren't such a fucking fantastical once-in-a-generation kind of singer, I could just walk away from this and say that I had tried—that I had tried to make you the best that you could be but time and money and personal conflicts didn't make it happen. But you are. And that is why I felt nothing this morning, I have begun to realize now. I have become addicted to the idea that you and I can do great things; and now that Don has given us some extra time and money, I realize that I am fiending, that I need a hit to feel alive again. That is what is fucking worrying me. That I am going to Kingston to see Mia, and yet I am bringing you because I would hate for you to leave me when we have so much to do together, me and you. What a fucking tragedy.

But he did not say this. He said: "I'm confused that other producers weren't able to get that out of you."

She kissed his cheek and said: "They just didn't know how to rule me."

chapter eleven

The day was hot. Even for the tropics. The sun was striking hard—cracking up the pavement, hammering the roofs, beating down the shoulders of the folks who had to walk.

It was already one o'clock when they arrived in Kingston; and coming over the mountains from the north, they were bottlenecked in traffic at the roundabout in Constant Spring, whose shopping centers, service mart, and covered produce market catered to the owners of the multilevel houses on the overlooking hills.

The other day when he had first seen Mia, he had come through the parish of St. Thomas, in the east, and had plunged into the city's heart and had not had the time to really take it in.

But now, as they moved beyond the golf course in the clotted traffic stream, he took the time to trace his recollections on the view outside the freezing glass.

Along Constant Spring Road, sometimes he would see the phantom of an older house floating by the entrance of a new apartment building. Sometimes a tree beside a parking lot would tell him that he'd passed a wooded lot where bredren used to go to smoke and catch a little country vibe or play some pickup ball.

As they came down into Half Way Tree, shopping centers penning them for nearly half a mile, he began to think about the way that things had changed.

More people, more buildings, more vehicles, more money. Yet

the roads were still the same, narrow and rough with only basic signs.

The place felt bigger, though, and with its wider range of restaurants and heavy use of mobile phones, Kingston felt layered, firm and self-assured. In this he found a lot to praise.

But there was something quite unsettling. At first he couldn't place it. Then it began to come to him after he had switched the speakers from the tape deck to the radio.

When he had left Jamaica nearly twenty years ago, there were four stations on the air, two of which were government owned and modeled on the BBC.

Now the airwaves were commercial; and there were probably a dozen. And as Michael found himself switching constantly from call-in shows to music shows and as he paid attention to the style and content of the news and advertisements, he understood.

Like a body built on steroids, Kingston had grown too much too fast. In its vain pursuit of touched-up, cabled images of life in North America, the capital was neglecting to develop its mind, and was using cocaine-tempoed beats to satisfy its soul. Turned on by the smell of cash, noisy as it howled for sex, and Rambo in its attitude to violence and guns, Kingston had made the rastaman a prophet.

A music festival was scheduled in Montego Bay that coming week, so the equipment rental houses—which were few and, by the standards of America, petite—had placed their most requested stock on hold. So what had been planned as a simple trip soon became a quest.

In some ways, though, it was easy. So much time had passed that no one recognized him, so no one asked him about his life, about why he had left, or what he had been doing. All the faces that he had known, it seemed, had moved on, replaced by young men in their twenties who did not seem connected to tradition—which disturbed him. In his time to be in music meant committing to a long apprenticeship, an apprenticeship from which you graduated with discipline, technique and a sense of history . . . you knew who played what song on what album, who produced what track. If he had been forgotten, then it meant that many of the other minds behind the music had been forgotten too . . . great producers like Geoffrey Chung . . . Errol Brown . . . Keith Hudson . . . King Tubby . . . Niney the Observer . . . Jack Ruby . . . Lloyd Charmers . . . Errol T . . . Augustus Pablo . . . Lee "Scratch" Perry . . . Striker Lee . . . Harry J . . . and Alvin "GG" Ranglin . . . men whose names were rarely seen in books.

Immediately, however, he was faced with something else. Operating in North American mode, he had called ahead to make appointments at the rental shops, but would arrive to find, in accordance with the languid laws of Kingston, that the boss was not available. Not here. Soon come back. Or in a meeting at the moment. Usually, no one else was authorized to help. So he would wait, and pace, and listen to the workers talking idly among themselves about a dance or a car they'd seen or the state of their immigration papers; and after half an hour he would go outside to Patience—who was not allowed to go inside because her accent would inflate the price—and tell her that they had to go somewhere else; then she would make a pointed but ill-timed remark about how much Jamaica called to mind Nigeria, which would piss him off because the first time that she'd said this he had asked her what "Nigerian" meant, and her reply had been: "Disorganized, dishonest, and disgraceful."

In Molynes, at a rental house in a little shopping center whose other tenants were a security firm, a locksmith and a cobbler, the clerk, a well-spoken teenager with a square jaw and a cleft chin and braided hair in crescent rows, glanced over his shoulder, his blue shirt dark in spots from perspiration, and told him that the amp that had been placed on hold was broken. But as Michael sucked his teeth and glanced outside to see if all was well with Patience, the clerk looked over his shoulder, made sure that he was unobserved and wrote on a piece of paper taken from the Bible in the pocket of his shirt, *The Ark of the Eternal Covenant Congregation of Christ the Redeemer*, followed by a whispered confession: "We don't really have the things. When you call us, we get it from the church. Just tell them Brother Tommy send you."

The church's name was painted in blue letters on a small billboard that was partly shaded by an almond tree. Set back from the road on a grassy rise in Vineyard Town, it used to be a cinema when the neighborhood was middle-class. The surrounding houses—verandahed concrete bungalows with gabled, shingled roofs—had become commercial now, and many of them were tenements.

Inside the church, the seats in the mezzanine had been replaced by benches; but the high-backed thrones in the balcony remained, their scarlet velvet ripped in places. On the walls, which had once been draped in pleated velvet curtains, there were pastel-colored paintings in which a mulatto Christ performed the miracles of the Gospel on the shores of Kingston harbor.

The man who met them at the door and led them through the foyer into the mezzanine and up the stairs along the balcony through a door marked *Staff Only,* was a fat Indo-Jamaican whose white smock and black pants made him look like a dentist. The door opened onto a corridor that led to the luxury boxes, which overlooked the mezzanine from the sides. The seats had been removed here and replaced with folding chairs.

Through another door now, they followed a catwalk, which led behind the stage, and saw up close the canvas screen, yellowed now and cracked and torn in places, then made their way past video cameras and TelePrompTers and other crucial paraphernalia of the modern Gospel ministry, then took a flight of stairs that ended at a door marked *Ministerial Music Market, Inc.*

Michael and Patience had entered the building in a mood of tension; but as they moved together in the semidarkness, unsure of what they would find, a hand reached out for comfort and was at first denied; but as the journey progressed along corridors and stairs, the hand reached out again and was embraced, held, squeezed, and tightly gripped, reaffirming the idea of their braided destiny. At the door, the man in the smock reached into his pocket, smiling over his shoulder as he dipped for the key, whose ring was a yellow plastic cross emblazoned with the church's name.

He called them forward with his head and entered the room, and they felt the chill of air-conditioning before he flicked the light, which sparked a row of fluorescent tubes. The room was the length of a barracks, with racks arranged in rows. At the far end were a pair of iron doors, which, judging from the heavy gear stacked in their vicinity, opened on the loading dock.

Time was going. It was already four in the afternoon. The man in the smock was not the person who handled rentals, and shrugged good-naturedly when he was asked when the rental man would return.

They moved through the racks together, scanning for specific pieces, testing them. Most of them were newish, caught between the crack of cutting edge and vintage. Still they found some gems in good condition: a '63 Fender Stratocaster, a '65 Gibson Les Paul; a '61 Fender Precision and a '59 Hofner viola bass, similar to the one that Paul McCartney played as a Beatle. The keyboards were in poor condition; and the drums were over-priced. But they could not leave the vintage amps, a Fender Twin Reverb and an Ampeg SVT, the favorite choice of Aston Barrett, bassist for the Wailers.

They left there in a different mood—lighthearted, optimistic, and as they drove through New Kingston, the central business district, heading to a church that had been mentioned by the dentist, Patience apologized for her nastiness and asked Michael in a cheery voice if things had always been this way. He explained to her that until the early eighties there was no equipment rental here at all; that bands or their managers used to own all their gear, and if you wanted something extra you either borrowed it or rented from a bredren. There were no rehearsal studios either. You used to rehearse in the back room in one of you bredren's house. And a rehearsal was a big thing, almost like a carnival when the big bands like Skin, Flesh & Bones and the Soul Syndicate were rehearsing. Big crowd outside the gate, and people skanking out on the sidewalk or just talking and idling . . . or kicking some football. Cars couldn't pass. It was like a roadblock. And sometimes you would see a sporty car with rims and all that coming, and you would know it was a musician's car . . . a Cortina Lotus or a Mini Cooper S or a Ford Capri.

In the early seventies a bike was a big thing because it was like a horse, and cowboy shows were a big thing . . . so you wanted to chuck it outlaw style, so you would wear a vest without a shirt, and you would sit right up on the front of the seat with your balls right up against the gas tank, and if you had locks you would let them out to fly in the breeze, and you would have on your construction boots and your straight-leg gun-mouth pants and your welding goggles to hide your face and protect your eyes, and you wouldn't wear a helmet, and you would rev that Honda S90, and you would rev that Yamaha 100, and you would rev that Suzuki 250, and you would double-clutch every gear change, and lay the bike low into every corner; and when you had a stretch of straight road you would dillydally, ride like you were zipping through a mine field—in and out . . . out and in—and sometimes you would throw the bike toward a van to make the people gasp, then pull it out and straighten up and dash between a lorry and donkey cart and come out on the other side and cut back through the traffic stream and lie down in a corner with your shoulder almost on the ground—and while the bike was angled low, you'd double-clutch and pick it up and leave the crowd to cheer and flash their fingers . . .

But . . . whether they came by bike or car, a musician would always cause excitement . . . you would get excited but you wouldn't *act* excited . . . you would kinda look without looking to see who is who, if it was Jimmy Cliff in the car or Big Youth . . . maybe it was one of the newer deejays like Dillinger, who used to ride a Honda CB 200. But no matter who it was, a rehearsal would always be pure excitement. No one asked for autographs or that kind of thing. You were too cool for that. If you showed excitement, they would say you were acting like you just came on the bus from country. But in those days so

many people didn't know how to read and write that after a
while they wouldn't be able to remember which one came from
who. After a while the bigger bands would buy a regular house
and turn it into a base to rehearse and keep the gear and carry
a girl if they didn't want to take her home. If a band was doing
well, or if they were a house band, sometimes they would rehearse at a recording studio if nothing else was going on. Sometimes you would rehearse in a nightclub during the day . . .
especially go-go clubs . . . cause that is where a lot of us used to
get the early gigs. Now you have a few rehearsal studios.

"What about Rumba?" Patience asked, snapping her fingers
and sitting up straight with widened eyes as they left a rental
house in Portmore, a community of prefabricated housing
schemes on land that was reclaimed from water west of
Kingston Harbor. "Rumba has to know someone. He has a
band. He's bound to have equipment."

They were on a narrow strip of land that connected to a
causeway. Ahead of them the double lane rose up steeply to the
bridge. On either side were ragged lines of shacks with sheets of
zinc to keep away the sun, and Michael ignored the question
and told Patience that the ground beneath them used to be a cay
where fishermen had lived for generations, that what she saw on
either side of her where fragments of another life. On the right,
in the distance, around the crescent of the bay, they saw the el-
evated cranes of the west container port. Gulls were wheeling in
the sky. A tug put-putted past an anchored ship. A man dipped
an oar in the oily water, the canoe tossing in the current like a
watermelon cut.

From outside, the vented air brought smells of brine and wet
garbage; and in a flash-lit moment Michael had a memory of the
shack where he was born, began to feel dry dirt between his
toes, and began to see the hills of garbage through the cracks between the boards that a man before his time had fixed with nails
and tape to make an outer wall. Inside, the space was quartered
up by curtains.

Driving around Kingston for the first time in years had

brought back other memories—Fabrics de Younis, where in 1974 Mia had bought a length of tulle to make her wedding dress . . . York Pharmacy where Mia had taken him in 1972 for a milk shake and a burger on his sixteenth birthday . . . Sinclair's Garage where in 1975, the year she entered Cambridge and he went to university at home, they had paid down on a custard-colored Beetle . . . the National Stadium, where in 1978, while on summer holiday, she had watched him play guitar with Marley at the One Love concert . . . Modern Furnishings, where they had bought their first bed from Leo Henry . . . Abdullah C. Marzouca, where they had bought their fridge and stove . . . the house in Mona Heights, where they had rented maid's quarters just before she left for England . . . and the apartment house in Oxford Road, walking distance to New Kingston, where in 1978 they had settled into married life . . . the Carib, where they had met. Now he didn't want to talk anymore, not about music, not about bikes, not about nutten.

"Rumba must know somebody," Patience continued. She punched him with excitement on the shoulder, a glancing blow, and he sucked his teeth and glared.

"He's in Port Antonio," he said in the kind of measured voice one uses with a simpleton. They were on the bridge now, and he felt the engine work to take the grade. His animosity was rising like the road, and he began to search the distant hills, trying to identify the house in which his father used to live. So many houses had been built since then. "We can go there now to Rumba if you want," he mumbled. "And I can come back here tomorrow by myself."

She put her feet up on the dashboard and reclined the seat until it almost touched the cushion of the seat behind.

"Well, take me now," he heard her say. "I wanna go. What a mood for celebration."

With the memory of his former life occupying his thoughts, and with his thoughts still clogged with recollections of the day that he and Mia met, Michael did not answer her. He simply held the wheel and let the vehicle take him where he knew he had to go. To face his future with assurance, he had to have permission from his past; for like an ancestor put to rest without honor, a past denied returns to haunt the soul.

He had to see Mia. He had to see her now. But what if she wasn't there? He began to feel anxious as he thought of this. And he began to drive more quickly now, drawn toward the memory, drawn toward the mystery, drawn toward the woman whose vulva was the shrine where he had shed his ritual blood.

chapter twelve

"Why are we here?" said Patience as they turned into the gravel-lined driveway of Café Kofi. "I want to go home. I told you that. Why are we here?"

"I am hungry," he said, without looking at her. "Hungry and tired and not in the mood to argue. Don't worry. This is not our celebration."

It was a little after seven. The sky was the color of diluted curry. Through the crackling of the tires on the shifting chips of stone, they heard the peck of steel guitar from the tiny speakers nested where the columns met the eaves. Guided by the colonnade of royal palms, Michael parked beneath a guinep tree, wedging up against a BMW and a Rover, and entered the verandah by the walkway, which was lined on either side with white hibiscus.

The verandah was moderately busy. And as they waited for the maître d', Michael noticed to his left a group of women of his own age-group having drinks and tapas at a flowered table, women of substance from the comfort of their laugh and the ease with which they wore their simply cut expensive dresses, sophistication manifesting in the fabric and the colors—cinnabar, moss, mountain mist and parchment. In their presence Patience seemed so thin and insubstantial. But what if she embarrassed him in front of them? Coming here was wrong, he thought. And stupid. But he could not bring himself to leave. So he compromised and asked the maître d' to seat him in a private room.

It would have been a bedroom in its time. The walls were milky tangerine. The window frames were royal blue. The window view was clotted by a hedge of red-and-yellow crotons. Above the hedge there was an orange tree, with dangling fruit like glowing lanterns. The other tables in the room were empty, and believing that the room had been requested for a tryst, the maître d' had told the waiter to take the orders quickly and depart.

In white pants and a navy shirt, the waiter breached the beaded curtain with some bread and bottled water, raising his brows when he thought that Patience was not looking.

They ordered wine. Merlot. A papaya-mango salad for her and chicken with roasted beets for him. The wine had notes of plum and oak and a finish of smooth vanilla, and they drank it chilled as wine was often drunk in the Caribbean.

As they ate without conversing, it occurred to Michael that a brooding kind of silence like the one that fogged the room was a clear articulation of romantic discontent; and Mia Fortuna Gonsalves, who was trusting by nature but cautious by training, would know that he had lied.

"How is your meal?" he asked, nudging her feet, staring across the rim of his glass.

"I am eating it," she said stonily, without raising her head. "It is nourishing me."

"I did not mean to sound that way."

"How did you mean to sound?" she asked, having put aside her glass, her chin resting on the heel of her hand, her fingers loosely wrapped around the handle of the upright fork. The stones in her bracelet clattered. She spoke with the fatalistic languor of a student on the verge of sitting for an exam for which no studies had been done. "You sounded like how you felt . . . like I was annoying you. I mean, how did you mean to sound?"

"It was not about you," he said. "Some of it was and some of it wasn't. Most of it was not, though. Just some. The fact still remains that I am sorry."

"All I ever want to do is please you," she sobbed. "All I

wanted to do was to help you. I know that this isn't easy for you, Michael. I know what it is like to be somebody when you are young and to lose that younger self and then try to find yourself within a newer, older self. I know what you are feeling, and I was just trying to make it easier for you by saying, 'Let's get Rumba,' and you treat me this way."

"It's okay," he whispered, reaching out to stroke her face, naturally now, having already grown disgusted with the flavor of capricious words. "Don't cry. Don't cry."

"What else is there to do?" she sobbed. "What else is there to do?"

"I don't know," he confessed. "I don't know."

"Just hug me," he sobbed. "Just hold me. That is all I need right now."

Her eyes were closed, but she felt the change in air pressure when he moved away from her, and she opened her eyes to see him leaning back, his palms against his temples, wincing.

"That is all I am to you," she blurted out. "A burden."

He recomposed himself and leaned across the table, reaching out for her. She slapped his hands away; and he leaned away again and felt his biceps twitching and he allowed his arms to dangle till they lost the urge to grab her.

"You can't speak to me like that," he said. Like frozen lakes his eyes were hard and showed no sign of life. "I don't care how you feel. Or what you think I've done to you. You cannot speak to me like that. I am a grown man. And this is my home . . . my country. You can't come here and expect to talk to me like that . . . as if I work for you."

One of the women from the verandah, short, with glasses and center-parted hair, passed and paused to nod good evening, and Michael felt the anger surge again as he began to wonder what he would do if Mia should appear. And he thought of the embarrassment, and said no more.

"I have to go the bathroom," Patience said as she wiped her face.

"Okay," he replied, reaching out to thumb some water from her cheek. She held his wrist. He opened his hand against her face and felt her kiss his palm. "Let's talk when you come back, okay? Let's work this out."

"I promise," she sobbed as she rose. "I was only trying to help."

Sympathetic toward Patience but clinging to the possibility of seeing Mia again, his legs trembling from nervousness and anger, Michael thought, God, did I really think of grabbing her? For him this was a new kind of anger. He had never grabbed a woman before, had never even thought of doing it. In arguments with women he had always tried to sort it out, to see their side and try to meet them halfway in a place where they could reason. He was in no condition to see Mia now. Was she even there? Mia! The mere articulation of her name in his mouth was giving him the pleasure of kissing. It would be too much. He should leave his telephone number and go. He wrote a note and gave it to the waiter, with instructions: "Take this to your boss for me and let me know what happens."

> *There are things that I believe we should discuss. If*
> *this is your predilection I would repair to your office to*
> *discuss them.*

He felt silly after sending the note. He had not signed it, hoping to draw her into a moment by the phrasing. Predilection. He gnawed on his knuckle and laughed. In many ways this mix-up was so frigging adolescent.

As he thought of this, the waiter slipped his hand between the beads, parted them enough to show his face and said the line that had been sent with him: "Come."

"Come?" said Michael, pointing at himself.

"Yes, yes. Come."

Michael felt queasy as he walked along the corridor. Previously, when he had not anticipated seeing her, he had not paused to look at the decor. Today, though, to slow the passage of time, to give himself the chance to run if he did not have the fortitude to go in, he began to cut his steps, noticed the patterns of the cream-and-blue Iberian tiles, the copper scones stenciled with Adinkra symbols, which nozzled light against the walls of milky tangerine.

More diners had arrived and conversation tinkled through the beaded doorways. Busy waiters sidled by with trays above their shoulders, trailing smells of coconut and curry. At the end of the corridor was a mirror, and he began to watch himself approach. His guava guayabera was road-worn and wrinkled, even in the dimmest light. He began to feel self-conscious now, and he turned his head to sniff his arm, and blew against his shoulder to check the freshness of his breath. At the mirror he turned right and left the sound of conversation for the clamor of the kitchen, the waiters coming faster now, erupting through the gap between the swinging doors.

He knew the door. He stopped . . . unable to knock. His stomach felt queasy as if he had dined on raw cassava. He would be glad if someone told him that she was not there, or would soon come back or was in a meeting at the moment. This was too much. As he thought of this, he heard a rattling of the knob, and before he could move, the door had opened, and standing there before him was a man he knew by instinct was her husband, a warm-complexioned Lebanese with tufts of hair protruding from the placket of a lemon-yellow polo shirt.

He wore a watch with a metal bracelet, and his hair, which was dark and closely trimmed, was thin on top. And Michael thought, How could Mia marry a man like that?

"How you doing, sah?" the husband said, reaching out for Michael's hand and coaxing him to come inside. "Haw-haw-haw. I got your note, man," he said as he closed the door behind them. "What happen? The food not tasting good? Well, if that's the case, well, dog eat your supper, 'cause I don't know a thing about a damn."

"The food is fine," said Michael, standing in the spot where he and Mia had hugged four days ago when he had come to rent equipment from the place across the street.

"But you said there were things you wanted to talk about," the husband said, returning to sit behind the desk. He spoke with friendly gestures of his hairy arms, which were short and deeply tanned.

"I wanted to ask you about the music," Michael said. Glad to find an alibi, he sounded quite enthused.

"You like it?" the husband asked, reaching out to shake his hand. "This is not the kind of thing my wife likes to play. But I love my Marty Robbins."

How could Mia marry a man like that? The thought of Mia kissing him began to cross his mind, and anger seeped between his shock and disbelief.

"This music makes me ill," he said. He turned and walked away. At the door he said over his shoulder, "That is what I came about. Can you turn if off until I leave?"

"Yes, yes," he heard the husband say with the gleeful resignation of one who thinks his tastes are not peculiar but distinctive. "What you want to hear?"

"Anything," said Michael, "but that."

Back at the table now he ate in silence, his shoulders drawn up to his ears, his emotions hovering in a mist of anger and amusement. How could he have been so stupid to have written a note like that? And what a stupid explanation he had given to the man. And what a silly man he was? And what a silly laugh? Haw-haw-haw.

"Is everything okay?" said Patience, marking her return to self-confidence by displaying the capacity to rise above her own concerns. She had been sitting there when Michael had flung the beads aside and sat ungraciously, his face in his hands, his elbows on the table, sucking his teeth.

"I am okay," he sighed, straightening up and reaching for some water, brushing his palm across his temple as a nervous itch began to stitch its way across his scalp. "Just working out some things."

"The first time I saw you, you were eating," she said, by emphasis turning a simple recollection to a plea. She had begun to console herself by smoothing out the waves in her new-shorn hair, slowly, as if the undulations were the imprint of her brain against her skull. "I think I fell in love with the way you ate."

"People fall in love for all kinds of reasons," he said brightly, exposing the romantic mood that was trying to steal into the conversation.

"Oh, fuck you," she sneered, tugging at her ear. "Just fuck you." She bit her lower lip and balled her fists, her head cocked in an angry pose, one fist pressed against her chin, the other at her slanted temple, her lids drawn low, tracing the pattern of the tiles with her narrowed eyes, trying to distract herself before she focused on her rage and lost her cool and hit him.

Heavy with indecision, Michael's head fell forward, and he sat there breathing heavily, his chin against his heaving chest, tapping his foot against the table. What would he say to her and how would he say it?

Before he could decide, however, he heard the husband's laughter: "Haw-haw-haw," and as he arranged himself and looked toward the door, the smiling husband entered, leading an aproned Mia by the hand.

"This is the gentleman who sent me the note," the husband said, letting go and pointing at Michael, whose shock at seeing Mia made him lean backward until the chair had partly lifted off the floor. He wedged his knees beneath the table, steadied it, felt the backrest touch the window ledge, and, thusly reassured, folded his arms across his chest and met her eyes with a look of stunned elation, which she misread as true contempt. "For hurting your ears, sir, dinner is on the house," the husband continued. "See, Mia, you're right. I have the worst taste in music."

"I didn't mean to cause a fuss, y'know," Michael said as Mia crossed her arms and bit her lip. She was standing to the left, just behind the husband, who had placed his arm possessively on her shoulder. She wore a key-lime dress with a scooped-out neck and buttons down the front. Her hair was pulled away from her diamond face, and in her ears were golden hoops with emerald stones.

"This is Patience," Michael said, pointing with an open hand, which he moved in a great arc, trying to fan away the tension before it was detected by Mia or the husband.

"We were here the other day," said Patience, leaning forward and stretching around the husband, taking Mia's hand. "The place is really nice."

"You make a lovely couple," Mia said, testing as she thought that she had been. "How long?"

Michael felt a metal rod expanding in his chest, and he eased the chair toward the floor and drank some water from his glass, wondering which was better: to warn Patience with his eyes and risk appearing nervous, or to trust that Patience was so angry that she would not want Mia and the husband to associate them?

"Oh, we're not a couple," Patience said fussily, as Michael felt the husband's eyes appraising him.

"Oh, forgive me," Mia said, smiling through her nostrils, which were diamond-shaped like eyes. "You just look like two people in love."

"We just *work* together," Patience emphasized for Michael's sake. "We could kill each other, I think."

Michael glanced at Patience and shook hands with the husband as everyone laughed. With the glance he had seen that Patience intended to continue the argument when company was gone, that what he was witnessing was not surrender, but a temporary truce.

For the moment Patience was committed to being mellow, and Mia didn't seem to think that he and Patience were involved. If Mia sat beside him, perhaps, and if the world were fair, maybe his knee would find her thigh below the table, reconnecting with a place of rest and welcome.

"Have a seat," he said, being careful to address the husband, pulling out a chair on either side. "Tell us all about his place. It is so nice." As Mia and the husband sat, he added: "By the way, you should bottle that laugh."

"Haw-haw-haw," the husband chortled as he slid behind Patience to the chair on Michael's right. Mia rolled her eyes. Michael caught her doing this and subtly shrugged as if to say, "I don't know what to tell you."

Two conversations developed: one between the husband and Michael and the other between Mia and Patience. Following the husband's lead—partly as a way to keep away suspicion, and partly as a way of teasing Mia—Michael indulged the husband in a open conversation about the ways in which he and Mia disagreed, realizing that the husband did not realize who he was, for the introductions had been made with Christian names.

Mia was idealistic, the husband teased, reaching out to pinch her as he winked at Michael. Idealistic to a fault. Rather than hiring all professional staff, she would often hire novices and take the time to bring them up to speed. And every day the kitchen cooked two sets of food: one for the restaurant and one for a government retirement home. She gave away the food for free, although with their connections she could get an easy contract from the government.

As the conversation continued and expanded, Michael brinked a deeper understanding—the husband was attempting to embarrass his wife. He simply knew no other way of bonding. He was his own cliché.

Speaking indirectly to Michael, Patience began to quiz the husband on the ways of men, the way that men can never seem to know if they are coming or going. Men could not be trusted. The minute that women let on that they liked to fuck as much as them, men begin to hold it back, using this as yet another means of power and domination.

The husband revealed, to Mia's chagrin and Michael's great elation, that he didn't have that kind of problem in his house because . . .

And he would have continued, but Mia interjected: "It's getting a little personal now."

Still the conversation continued, albeit in a more general kind of way—the women lamenting the ways of men, the men hawhawing the ways of women—and as Patience and the husband proved repeatedly that as partners they were "special and unique," Michael and Mia were drawn into the warm excitement of performing an act of great deceit, rewarding themselves with languid strokes of knee on thigh each time that Patience or the husband displayed some kind of lapse in etiquette or logic. He would tap her feet. She would wince. Once he even reached beneath the tablecloth and bunched her dress. Another time she rubbed her instep on his calf.

"So," Michael said to the husband after they had ordered more wine, "you love your country and western music?"

"There is no better music in the world, man."

"Yeah, who you like?" said Michael, tapping Mia's foot.

"Haw-haw-haw. Tennessee Ernie Ford. Conway Twitty. Hank Williams. I like the old guys."

"Why do you like it so much?" said Patience.

"I like guns. And if you love guns, you like to watch westerns. And if you love westerns, you love cowboy music. Jamaicans love cowboy shows, y'know, Patience. We are a gun-loving people."

"Stop telling the child foolishness," Mia said impatiently. She took a sip of wine to hide her face.

"Is not foolishness, Mia—is the truth," the slighted husband scolded.

"I love guns as well," said Patience. "They're frightening in a sexy way. And I haven't been called 'girl' in a very long time."

"I beg your pardon," Mia told her, rolling her yes and shaking her head with neither ambiguity nor guilt. "But guns are just unsexy. They are gross."

"They're sexy," Patience insisted. "It's a power thing. I was with a guy one time, and we were in bed doing what we do, and just out of nowhere he just pulled this giant fucking gun and just stuck it to my temple, and it freaked me; but then he started saying all this threatening words, and it just turned me the fuck on." She took another sip of wine. "Then he turned me out."

Mia looked at Michael. They tried to laugh but couldn't find the spirit, and looked at each other, perhaps for too long, trying to come to terms with the change in atmosphere.

"What's the matter?" Patience asked, looking around the room but focusing on Michael. "Did I say the wrong thing again?"

"You said the right thing," the husband said. "Some people like to act as if they want to control everybody's life."

Mia sucked her teeth. Michael looked away. Angry and embarrassed. It was time to leave.

"I love my guns and country music," the husband muttered sourly.

"Can you sing?" said Patience, cheerily.

"Sure."

"Quit while you're ahead," said Mia stonily. "Let it alone."

"Allow the man to sing," said Michael, quietly, patting Mia's shoulder in a way that told her that he was agreeing with the husband just to get the chance to openly touch her.

As a vein began to pulse and writhe at Mia's temple, the husband began to sing. He was a good singer . . . a tenor . . . who chose his notes with care and embroidered favorite lines with little warbles.

"That was great," said Patience as they cheered the husband, who felt vindicated by the pureness of his voice. "How did you meet?"

"Another time," said Mia through a laugh as Michael softly kneed her.

"On the phone," the husband volunteered. "My first wife died leaving some money and property in California, and Mia was the attorney that executed the will."

"So you guys were living in California at the time?" said Patience.

"Right," Mia said. She sipped her wine and pursed her lips unconsciously.

"And you were an attorney?"

"That's correct."

"And over the course of a couple of months, we got to know each other over the phone," the husband interjected. "We had things in common. See, she had lost a spouse as well."

"Oh, is that right?" asked Michael. He pulled his knee away from Mia's thigh and spoke directly to the husband.

"An evil son of a bitch," the husband said. "Put her through a lotta shit."

"Why bring up unpleasant things?" said Mia. She reached across the table and took her husband's hand, clenching her jaw as she felt the glare of Michael's eyes against her cheeks.

"So what did he die of?" Michael asked, turning to the husband now. "I hope you don't think I'm morbid, but this is a fascinating story."

"Well, is not the kind of thing you should discuss over food," the husband said. "But as you have probably figured out, I have more tack than tact."

"Go ahead," said Michael. "You really have me eager now."

"A woman cut off his cocky, and he bled to death. Haw-haw-haw-haw-hawwwwwww."

Michael patted Mia's hand and said, "I'm sorry. That must have been hard for you . . . even though things were over."

"And you know what is even funnier?" the husband said, "She said he didn't have much of a cocky to begin with. Haw-haw-haw-haw-hawwwwwww."

Outside, along the pathway, they walked between the rows of white hibiscus, the petals turned to silver in the scattered light. Behind them the verandah was clotted with shades of skin . . . from caramel to lightest flan. Overhead there was a night of throbbing stars, ahead of them the driveway lined with royal palms and cars jigsawed beneath the trees.

The evening had been spoiled. After the husband had told the story of Mia's husband, Michael had abruptly said that it was time to leave, and Patience had insisted that she wanted to stay . . . had sucked her teeth and leaned against the husband and said in a teasing way, that invited him to side with her, that Michael was old and boring.

So it came to be that they were walking to the parking lot unmatched: Patience and the husband, walking ahead, prolonging the joke, amusing themselves, and Mia sauntering now, cutting back her steps to speak with Michael, who had been deep in thought as they left the verandah.

"So, I didn't know I was dead," he muttered.

Mia crossed her arms and said, "I wanted you to be."

He swallowed hard and asked, "Because?"

"Because if you were, then I knew I could stop loving you."

Ahead of them, the husband was crouching with his fists at his temples, swinging like a bull, his index fingers pointing out like horns, chasing Patience, laughing and mooing as she screamed. Standing now, the husband took off behind her and disappeared from sight along the crescent of the driveway, which was unlit.

"Look at the fucking man I married," Mia sighed. "Just fucking look at him."

When they caught up with Patience and the husband in the parking lot, Patience said to Michael: "I'll meet up with you later."

She was leaning on the side of the SUV, her hands behind her. The headlights of a passing car side-lit her, and he saw that her face was tightly rolled.

"Where are you going?" he asked matter-of-factly. They had to return to the studio, he was thinking. After all, they still had business to do.

Michael looked at the husband, who scratched his head and looked away.

"I'm . . . we're going to a gun range," Patience said, touching her chest, then pointing at the husband.

"For what?"

The husband slowly raised his shirt. And when Michael saw the shadow of the handle of the gun, black against his tapioca belly, his instinct was to treat it like a threat.

"We're just going to squeeze a few," the husband said. "I'm a collector, y'know. Is not Mia alone that likes to collect. She has art and I have guns. I like guns, if you know what I mean."

"I don't know what you mean," Michael told him.

"That is good," the husband said. "You don't want to know what I mean."

Michael looked at Mia. Mia looked away and placed her hands behind her as if she were afraid that they might swing. Tendons were showing through the skin along the neck. Along her jaw a muscle started twitching as she grit and ground her teeth.

Chuckling as he shook his head, the husband drew the gun and held it pointed to the ground. He gripped it by the muzzle and handed it to Michael, who raised his hands and brows and did not take it.

Patience took the gun and bobbed it in her hand to weigh it, her lips pursed in concentration, then passed it to her other hand, the muzzle pointed down. She held it now with all her fingers wrapped around the grip, and as Michael and Mia watched in disbelief, she began to jig around with the gun held low between her legs—excited.

"See," the husband said to Mia when Patience passed the gun to him, "this is how you should be. Gun won't bite you if you behave yourself."

"How long are you going to be?" demanded Michael, staring Patience down. "There are things we have to do. Things we have to talk about before we start to work again."

"Does it matter?" Mia said. "Let them go."

"What time?" Michael insisted. "Port Antonio is two and a half hours away. It's dark. We're going over mountain roads. The mountain roads are narrow. I have the people's equipment to carry back safely. I need to know what time."

"Around tennish," said the husband, crossing his arms.

"Why are you being a pain?" said Mia stonily. "Why are you embarrassing me and embarrassing yourself in front of strangers?"

Michael sucked his teeth and turned his back and walked away. Patience came behind him. When she caught up, he took her by the arm.

"What are you trying to do?" he asked her. Twenty yards away he saw Mia and the husband arguing with whispered words and heated gestures.

"You have been ignoring me all night," Patience blurted. "You've just treated me like shit. I can't do anything right. You don't talk to her the way you talk to me. How am I supposed to feel?"

"She who?"

"Mia or whatever her fucking name is."

"And that is why you're going to a gun range at this hour of the night?"

"I am doing what I feel like doing. And right now I just want to be around someone who is happy, who is up, who is willing to have a little fun. And that means not you."

"You are hopeless," Michael said, releasing her. She stumbled back, then caught herself, paused to seize a new idea, then threw herself against the ground.

"I didn't push you," Michael said. "Don't even try that. I didn't push you."

She stood without his help and brushed her flanks and back. She was so pathetic.

"Don't go," he said softly. "Don't go. Look at what we've come to."

"There is no we," she said. "And that makes me so fucking angry."

"I don't know what to tell you."

"Tell me that you love me."

"Or else what?"

She crossed her arms and looked away, then stared at him with baleful eyes.

"I wouldn't be able to continue to work with you. I would just pack up and go. I don't need to sing to live."

"You would just walk away and waste everybody's time?"

"Yeah," she said, hoisting up her lip toward her nose as she turned to walk away. "Believe me. I would."

At the car, Patience said to the husband, who was standing at a distance and glaring at Mia: "Are we going or staying?"

"Since nobody can tell me what to do—I know I'm going."

"Okay, I'm going with you."

"Patience, what time are you coming back?" said Michael.

"That is not what I need to hear right now," she said coolly. "And you know that."

Mia looked at Michael. Michael looked at Mia, then at the husband, who sucked his teeth and began to walk toward his car. Patience pushed her way past Michael and began to follow him.

"Patience."

She raised her hand and fanned his voice away.

"I fucking hate him," Mia said beneath her breath.

"What's wrong?"

"He said that I disrespected him in front of you."

"He saw?"

"No. Just that whole shit about the cowboy song. He said that I had embarrassed him. He is so small-minded. He wants to play pussy watchman, and he doesn't even know what to watch for."

"Are you sure he doesn't know me?"

She tapped him on the elbow.

"He said that you're a faggot. The words are his, not mine. What can I say? He's clearly clairvoyant. There is something going on between you and Patience, he said. I told him, no, but he said that there had to be . . . said he could read a tension . . . that she wanted you to sleep with her and you didn't want to . . . which means of course you're gay. He's very homophobic. That is why he was testing you. That is why he gave you the gun. To see if you had the heart to take it. In his head you are this gay man siding with his wife against him."

"I see."

They stood there for a while without speaking, listening to the voices from the restaurant, the breeze above them in the treetops . . . heard car doors open and slam, heard an engine start. Then they saw the headlights tunnel straight ahead, the shafts of metal-colored light coring through the darkness.

"What time are you coming back?" Mia asked the husband as he edged the Volvo wagon through the crowded parking lot. The husband neither stopped nor looked. And as Michael watched, helpless, angry and embarrassed, Mia began to jog beside the silver car, her palm against the roof—lowered and disgraced.

"Ten," the husband snapped at her. "Ten . . . ten-thirty."

"So Michael has to wait here all that time?"

Patience leaned across and said to Mia, "We will be on time. Me and Michael have some things we need to talk about tonight."

Michael and Mia began to walk along the driveway, but lost the will. Drained and disoriented, they leaned against a brown sedan; then Michael led her down between a row of cars for privacy. From over the hedge-lined fence, the traffic on the street was coming louder than the voices and the music hovering near the porch.

"This feels strange," said Mia.

"What feels strange?" said Michael.

"After all that just happened, all I can think about is that I am here with you. And it feels illicit. As if I'm cheating on him. I mean, he doesn't know who you are. Inside I took it for a joke. But now it is not the same. Now that I have seen how much trouble and strife can come of this. Jesus Christ . . . all that drama with the gun."

"It feels strange for me as well," he said.

"Why?" she asked. She touched her temple to his shoulder and quickly pulled away.

In the dark he reached for her and missed, and his knuckles brushed her hip, and he felt her fattage shimmer through the cloth. Like him, she pretended not to notice, but it stirred the recollection of the way that they had touched beneath the table, his knuckles like the nutty hardness of his knee.

"It feels strange," he said, "because I'm feeling things for you, and risking things for you and I don't know if I know you anymore. You've changed so much—your hair, your job, your whole attitude."

"For better you think or worse?"

He laid his palm against the car in the space between them, afraid to touch her, afraid to look. If he looked at her, he knew, he would want to kiss her. And if she kissed him back he knew that would be awful. And if she did not kiss him back it would be worse.

"That's not really for me to say," he told her. "People have a right to be whatever they want to be."

"I think it's for the better," she said, angling now so that her back was turned toward his side.

"How has your family taken it? Mr. and Mrs. Bombo?"

"Oh, be nice."

"To them? After everything they did to mash us up? They never liked me from morning, Mia. My mother wasn't married. You weren't marrying into a family—not just a family of means, but into any kinda family at all. I was a musician. I was from Riverton and lived in Range. I didn't have the right address. I didn't have the right profession. I didn't have the right nutten."

They fell into silence again, and he stood there thinking of what he wanted to do, feeling the coolness of the metal on his palm, the thickness of the air against his skin.

"I don't want to talk about my parents," Mia said, eventually. "I want to talk about you."

"What do you want to know?"

"I don't know. Just everything about you."

"It could take all night."

"They might come back and interrupt us," Mia said, turning now. "Let's walk."

They began to drift along the driveway, passed the walkway lined with white hibiscus and sauntered through the gate. On instinct they took the path along the verge, and streamed along the gentle grade toward Trafalgar Road, his bony hands behind his back, her fleshy arms across her breasts.

At the corner now, traffic coursing left and right, they stood beside each other, unsure of what to do, unsure of where to go—feeling quite exposed as they were splashed with looks and noise and lights.

"Where you want to go?" he said.

"Anywhere," she told him.

Approaching was a city bus, a new Mercedes, long and tall and white. Instinctively, he flagged it down. She saw a muscle flex along his arm.

Her pulse boop-booping along her wrist, she touched his hand to say that people of their stature did not take the buses anymore, that even welders and cooks were drivers now because Japan dumped reconditioned older cars on markets like Jamaica.

When she touched him, her finger slipped against his oily perspiration. Yes, he was so well preserved, his muscles still conditioned, his skin still tight along his jaw. In the time they were together, he used to eat of neither meat nor salt, and avoided alcohol, caffeine, and artificial drinks. He used to begin each day with prayers, exercise and meditation, and although he sometimes saw the doctor, he trusted in the medicine of plants and herbs. He used to tell her that this kind of life . . . this kind of livity would keep him young . . . preserve him . . . and she used to laugh. But oh, how he was right.

"How did you go from being a lawyer to running a café?" he asked as they settled into a seat. The bus was almost empty, and the lights inside were bright. They sat in the last seat before the long bench in the back, four rows separating them from the nearest passenger, a woman in a church hat, who sat across from an older man who was sitting with his feet extended in the passage, reading the *Observer*.

"Well, you know the old Jamaican saying: 'Hog ask him mooma how her mouth so long, and mooma say grow come see.' A lot of time has passed, but I have to say it still—a lotta the things you used to say to me began to make sense while I was away from you. I had to go to California to appreciate meditation and natural living, had to see African Americans wearing locks before I felt entitled, had to go to an ashram before I understood the importance of giving up my attachment to material things." She began to puff her cheeks now, blowing out the air in spurts. "I thought a lot about you in the recovery room."

"Recovery? What happened?" He took her arm with both his hands. "What happened."

"I had an aneurysm."

He slumped against the window, holding his breath, then breathing slowly.

"A what?"

He passed his hand along her cheek.

"Yes," she said, placing her hand on his as she remembered what the spiritualist had told her. "That. Yeah. It happened to me. I thought I was going to die. The doctors said there were many factors, but that one of them was stress. So while I was recovering, I did a lot of thinking. And I thought of all the things that were important in my life. And I realized that all the quote-unquote big things didn't really matter. Status and class and titles and money and all that. They couldn't save me."

"I am sorry I wasn't there, baby. If I had known—"

"I know. But I wasn't alone. I was married by then. I have to say he was really good to me. That's really why I care for him."

She had spoken in the present tense. Michael took his hand away, and ran it through his hair. Looking straight ahead, he said: "Well, I guess you didn't need me, then."

"That's not true. I did."

He placed his hand against her cheek again. This time she held it with her hands.

"I am so sorry I wasn't there," he said, slipping his other arm around her and holding her shoulder now. Her shoulders were narrow and steeply sloped and firmer than the rest of her.

"Don't worry about not being there for that, Michael. Things happen. You are here for me now."

Powerful and agile with smooth acceleration, the bus moved quietly through the mansioned avenues of the diplomatic quarter to Old Hope Road, the border of respectability. Through the window on their left, they could see the outline of Beverly Hills bending away—in the dark a ridge of pulsing lights, in the day a thick agglomeration of modern concrete houses from the sixties. To the right, Old Hope Road sloped down to Cross Roads and the Carib cinema, where they had met thirty-one summers ago.

Pulling smoothly, the bus went straight ahead, and Michael felt something rear, then fall inside him when he passed the intersection of Roosevelt Avenue, a broadish street, where, in 1974, twenty-seven years ago, at Harry J's, a recording studio in a converted bungalow, he had assisted during the final mix of Marley's album *Natty Dread*.

Mia was about to study law at Cambridge then, and did not think that Marley or reggae would amount to much, although there was good evidence: Clapton had covered "I Shot the Sheriff" the year before on the album *Ocean Boulevard,* and the Stones had recorded all of *Goat Head Soup* in Kingston at Dynamic Sounds. He had seen Mick Jagger doing the early takes of "Angie."

The next intersection was Mountain View, which was straight and wide, two lanes in each direction with a flowered median poled with metal lights.

Here, on this road that sloped in the direction of the harbor, they felt the engine of the bus appreciate the help, and the wind came rushing through the open windows, thick and wet and warm.

They were parallel to the mountain now, which flickered through the window at the end of cul-de-sacs.

On the right they passed the stadium, and the cemetery for soldiers, some seventies prefab houses with inventive alterations, then farther on, a high school and a college. Soon, at a service station, four lanes of traffic were funneled into two, and as the mountains began a slow retreat, the road began to weave and undulate, and the bus began to slow and the view began to change.

They passed derelict old houses with shingled roofs that looked like mouths with missing teeth. Occasionally, there were dirt lanes lined with sheets of zinc that drained off into darkness; sometimes there were lines of shacks with signs for simple things: ice, coal, animal feed; and sometimes there were rows of concrete shops with bread and cheese and sweets behind a wooden case with panes of glass, a listing scale and a cashier in a cage of wood and chicken wire. Sometimes there was a little church behind a tumbling fence, people milling in the compact dirt that formed the yard. Sometimes a sign would be all it took to change a house into a garage or a bar or a go-go club, a lumberyard or beauty shop. And on the road there were people walking, dressed for the heat, most of them young, in their twenties or their teens, the men in vests and baggy jeans, the women in shorts and miniskirts, the men with freshly shaved hair or sometimes beauty parlor locks, the women be-wigged and be-weaved, everyone part flesh part shadow in the dim streetlights, everyone talking loudly, everyone gesturing with their heads and arms. Sometimes on a verandah, they would see a mother braiding hair, or men slamming dominoes or flipping cards. Sometimes there were children, crossing the road in pulsing clusters or hooked into their mother's arms. Sometimes there would be the sound of sirens in the distance. Sometimes there would be a sound like fired shots. Sometimes there would be the sound of rap or R&B, but most times there was reggae—dance hall music, rough and loud, the lyrics slamming hard like pelted stones.

The area was dangerous. Gangs were at war. To go on would be risky. They had to turn around.

When they stepped off the bus, however, they felt a sense of reconnection with the place. Range, where Michael had been living when he met her years ago, was a half a mile away. So was Rollington, where she had been born and raised. And without discussing their decision, they followed the momentum of the slope, south, pushing deeper into Kingston's darkest heart.

"So advertising doesn't stifle you?" she asked as they crossed the road and moved along the pavement. "Working nine to five? Having a boss like that?"

"Well, a jingle is just a short song. And a mixing board is a mixing board. It really wasn't hard to make the change."

"What I meant to say is that I can't imagine you in any kinda structured job. Well, I shouldn't say I can't. I can now. But I couldn't, if you know what I mean. When I knew you, you were just . . ." She searched for words.

"Wayward and immature," he volunteered.

"Not that. You were never really wayward. And you were in many ways more mature than I was. Well, force ripe." She linked her arm in his as they walked along the verge. "You just had very definite ideas about America and capitalism and consumption. No, you were not wayward or immature—you were idealistic. Principled. Romantic. Not that you are not now. You know what I mean."

"People change," he said, agreeing with her inside.

As they passed a tree where a man was selling cigarettes and crackers from a wooden box, she said in a casual way: "How come you never got married again?"

"I did . . . to get a visa. A purely business thing."

"Yes, yes. But after that?"

"Forget the marriage thing," he joked and raised his hands. "See any rings?"

"You would hardly wear mine."

He reached around and pinched the lip of fat around her waist.

"In those days Jamaican men didn't wear wedding rings. That was such a new thing that you wanted to bring in on me. And also, rasta never wear jewelry, baby. It was a macho thing. A rasta thing."

"Like fucking lots of women."

"I didn't sleep with half the women you thought I was sleeping with, y'know."

"Michael, if you screwed a quarter it would have been a lot. If you screwed one it woulda been too many."

He resisted comment on the subject, then finally said: "But that is water under the bridge, though, isn't it?"

"I guess," she said. "I guess."

"And, you?" he gambled, stopping in front of a shop, acknowledging with a respectful nod a group of men in vests and baggy jeans. "Have you ever slept with anyone except your husband?"

"No," she said softly. "No."

"You're not telling the truth," he bluffed.

Mia contemplated how to tell him what happened: "He was younger," she began, "young and strong and charming. It was pure lust. Nothing else. He would come to the house, and we would have small talk and then"—she looked over her shoulder at the young men standing there and began to walk again—"and then we would just do it. It went on for about two years.

He is not in my life anymore." She reached up and ran her hand along his neck and let it fall along his side, and feeling his body growing tense beneath his shirt, but wanting to be close to him, she hooked her thumb in one of his loops. "I'm sorry . . . I shouldn't have said that. Now you're going to think that—"

"It's water under the bridge," he told her. He felt as if his veins had turned to rods of steel. "These things aren't always simple."

"No. Not at all."

He touched her arm and stopped her and peered into her eyes. "Did you love him?"

She thought of the meditative poet, his curly locks, his limbs thick and muscular, the tattoo in the center of his chest, his skin like roasted cashew nuts, the glee that would invade him when she let him suck her out, his tireless cock, his patient tongue.

Michael sensed what she was thinking; and as she sensed him reading through her, she offered him a further explanation.

"It was nothing like love," she said. Michael felt the hairs along his arms begin to flame as if they had been candlewicks. "Nothing like love. Nothing like love. Love for me is hard. That was just a physical thing."

The road had begun to curve now. As they came around the bend, they heard above the sound of cars and conversation, a rhythm more insistent than the rest.

Turning off the main road, they followed a trail of people down a well-lit street of modest houses, holding hands in silence, working out the meaning of her confession.

As they came upon the crowd, she felt her clitoris lick her in the crevice where it touched her lower lips, and she began to wonder if she felt this way because she had been thinking of the meditative poet.

Beside her, Michael was brooding as he held her hand, and she began to feel guilty for being indiscreet. She did not have to tell him. He would not have been insistent. That was not his way. But she wanted him to know because . . . ? Why did she? Could it be because she wanted him to know that she had learned to fuck without commitment? That he shouldn't feel as if he had to make her any promises?

When she came out of her thoughts, they were already in the club, a small house on a lot that had been paved. The trees had been left for shade and privacy, and the surrounding high fence was lined on top with broken bottles. The trees were strung with pepper lights, strings of red-and-yellow bulbs whose circuitry was processed through the amps to make them pulse to the beat of the music.

At first they were surprised when they entered. Judging from the size of the crowd outside, they had expected to see more people in the yard.

They soon realized, however, that the crowd was in the back, which was accessed by a narrow path of stones placed in mud that smelled of beer and mold. At a gate of beaten metal, they paid another fare, and were admitted to another world. There, on three round stages, each accessorized with shiny metal poles, were topless go-go dancers, their pubic area fringed with tasseled thongs.

As Mia and Michael made their way toward the back, they glanced across and saw a slender woman with a muscled back tipping up, her arms along the pole, her grip above her head, twitching her ass and stopping it a second off the beat, giving the impression that her bottom had the power to conduct a band. On another stage a woman mixed with Indian blood jumped up on the metal shaft and twirled from top to bottom like the stripe along a barber pole. On center stage, a square-faced girl was leaning back, her torso undulating like her backbone was a hose.

"Is okay," said Mia, laughing, as she sensed that Michael wanted to apologize for coming. "It doesn't bother me. You want to stay?"

He nodded. It was a place to sit. They headed for the bar, which was made of wood and roofed in thatch. The counter was covered with rum glasses and beer bottles. And the stools, which were scattered out of line, were largely empty. Off to the sides there were people standing, mainly young men, although there were some women, some of whom had come alone, some to be aroused, and some to learn the finer arts of fucking from these artisans of skill and dedication.

"Drink, Mr. Chin?" the barman asked. "And what for the lady?"

Michael ordered for Mia from memory—a beer with lemonade—and for himself he got a Ting, and he sat with her, his arm against her thigh, watching the show and laughing.

Moving through the crowd were other dancers, tight-waisted and fat-bottomed, who would lean against a man and shake their flesh for tips, pelvis cocked and back leaned forward, horsing up their fat.

"Does that turn you on?" said Mia. "Watching them dance like that?"

Confessing an indiscretion, Mia had discovered, was an aphrodisiac; and as she sat there, watching the women unfold themselves, feeling her own clitoris worming through her blood, trailing her veins with come, Mia Fortuna Gonsalves was hit by a blunt revelation—that to fuck without love was not simply bad behavior, but a wonderfully complicated pleasure, like speeding, shoplifting or spanking disobedient children.

"I wouldn't say they turn me on," said Michael.

"Is that because you don't know how I'll take it?"

"Nothing as sophisticated as that."

"But that is the kind of woman you would go for. You used to always like the little ghetto girls. Which in a sense was good because I can never say you fucked my friends or anyone I knew or knew of."

He took a sip of Ting, rolled it in his mouth and swallowed hard, searching himself to see if he liked this kind of openness with her. He did not like to talk about sex with women, especially her. Unlike men, women felt a sense of entitlement to be directors in bed, to say, do this, do that, hold me here, not so fast. Moreover, women felt a sense of entitlement to pout and be indignant if the man was unable to follow through. Unlike men, women felt a sense of entitlement to openly discussing their satisfaction. They felt as if they had more at stake because

the process of their orgasms was so involved, so finely cali-
brated, that one misstep would ruin it. Yes, the mechanics of
coming was simpler for men, but emotionally they were just as
needy. And how does a man come, then say to a woman when
she asks if it was good, well, yes, but no, that what she really
needed to do was this or that, that she needed to fling it up so,
and dash it back so, and cock it up backways and turn and
watch the fuck over her shoulder like a champion . . . without
making her feel inadequate? Because they would ask you what
you want, then you would tell them what you want, then they
would either want to know why you would ever want that or
why you thought they were the kind of woman who would be
able to do those things. These two you could live with. The
thing that was hard was when she tried to do these things and
failed, when you told her that you wanted her to go on top and
she went up there and thought you wanted her to pose and then
you started to move and she couldn't find the rhythm and your
cock would slip out, or when you told her that you wanted her
to lie down on her belly, and the most that she could do was
brace and take it, or at best move from side to side—but
couldn't really turn it, couldn't make her waist and ass move
like a wrist and a balled-up fist. What do you do then? What do
you do when she just couldn't do it? You would sleep with her
and love her, and sometimes you would wonder what it would
be like if she could do these things? And sometimes you would
close your eyes and picture another woman in the bed and you
would take the fuck from her, but you would kiss your woman's
flesh. And sometimes when you did this your woman would
disappear, and you would kiss the woman in the bed with grat-
itude and your woman would make you dinner for a week because of the way in which you took her both hard and soft that
time. And sometimes you would leave the bed frustrated because your woman would start to complain that she couldn't
keep her legs up that long or that her back was hurting her . . .
and then, sometimes it would happen you would go to that
other home.

   It. Yes, sometimes it would happen.

It. He didn't want to say what it was. Not even to himself. Not even in his own mind. Not in Mia's presence. He had done too much to hurt her in the past.

But Mia was sure that this is what he wanted; and she was sure that she should give it to him. In the time that they had been apart, she had grown and changed. Since she had played with other lovers now, her body knew the patterns of different rhythms. She could tambourine her bottom now, accordion her waist, and when she was in the mood, and the man proved himself deserving, she would offer her rump, depending on his predilection, as djembe, tabla, timbale or snare—and she wanted Michael to know this. But it was already after nine o'clock.

"Let's go," she said.

"Where?" he asked.

"Back to the café, I guess."

"Right," he exhaled. "To that whole other world."

"Are we above that world or below it, you think?" she asked as one of the dancers slipped between them and waved to the bartender. "Is this heaven or hell?"

As Michael contemplated this, they heard the dancer ask: "My yute deh inna de yellow shirt waah me work him. How much fe de room again?"

They overheard the price and watched the woman return to the man and take a palmed note. The dancer took the money to the barman, who gave her a key, which she slipped into her bosom before she went to get the man, whom she led around the side toward the front.

"You like that, don't you?" Mia said.

"I'm thinking about heaven and hell," he said. His elbows were on the counter, and he was holding his face in his hands, sucking on the inside of his upper lip. "Being with you is heaven," he said. "But the sight of you is making me into a devil. Where does that leave us? What does it mean that I want to fork an angel?"

"You want to fork me, Michael?"

"Yeah," he said.

"We don't have the car."

Her new boldness, her fuller body, her new comfort with herself, the music, the girls, all combined to make him more direct. "What happened?" he murmured. "You got soft in your old age? Remember when I used to come to you mother's house . . . right down the road . . . we can go there right now and ask the tamarind tree if you want . . . and you used to come out on the verandah without any panty and turn around and lean against the grill, and I used to cod you through the bars while you mother was sewing inside? We used to watch her shadow through the curtain and laugh. That is why I used to look forward to summer. 'Cause that is the only time I used to really get to see you . . . when you came up from country."

"I'm not convinced you want me," she dared. "You might be saying this because you believe I wouldn't say, 'Yes, yes, come cock me up and fuck me.' Maybe you just want to make me feel good because I said the little ghetto girls used to be your predilection."

"I don't want a girl," he told her, pinching her leg. "I want a big woman. I want a veteran. The other night I was in Port Antonio, and I ran into Rumba—yes, Rumba from Young Ruffians, and we did a song without rehearsal . . . him on bass and me on guitar. And the music was so sweet, see because we just knew the choon. And we could have played a hundred choons that night because that is the way that veteranship works. See, the little young musicians now, they might know one choon or two choons but after that they start asking you to hum the melody or to remind them of the original key. And most times they don't know the choon from the inside, the subtleties of the choon. See, baby, veterans are like that. They don't need no rehearsal. They get better with time. Come, I want to cut a record with you. Old school stylee . . . pull panty one side and lean up on the grill . . ."

"Michael," she said, reading his face and ignoring all signs of love. She was afraid that love would only bring them greater trouble. "I want you to take me the way you used to take those girls. I want to feel the way I shoulda been feeling all those years. I'm ready to let you take me as if you want to use up all of me in one night. There is nothing to be gained by holding back. It took me a while to realize, but I realize it now . . . that at my age if a man tells me that I'm intelligent, he hasn't told me something that I don't already know, that that is nothing to yearn to hear and give a man points for . . . that at my age no man cyaah use me up . . . that I can give you all my substance and make some more in the morning from the fatness on my hips. I know that now. There is no reason to hold back anymore."

"Mia," he said, scraping his lip against his front teeth, trying to decide if her offer was a gift or a challenge. "Don't fuck with me."

She watched his narrow eyes shyly gazing through his lashes, and his face becoming dashed with a cinnamon flush. The thought of unleashing her new self in rebellion against the man whose mind and soul and cock had ruled her for so long was gumming up her lower lips. And she said to him: "Go and buy a condom from a higgler by the gate."

He seemed appalled. Stunned. Shocked. Disappointed. But he went. And she turned to the barman and said in a voice whose articulation made it clear that she was a woman of means out for adventure and not a common gyal: "I need a key."

She waited for him beside the short front steps, which led to the verandah. The verandah was enclosed with grillwork, and the rudely welded bars resembled keloids.

Like the dancer, Mia had placed the key in her bosom; and she stood there, one leg thrust in front of the other in a pose that was intended to discourage conversation from the idle boys in vests and jeans who milled about, smoking cigarettes or talking animatedly about girls and sports and guns and cars as they appraised her, this stranger, wondering who she was. CID? Reporter? Lonely oldster trying to find a man?

The one-chord dancehall music dripping down like Chinese water torture, the dusty concrete yard, the high white fence, on top the strip of jagged bottles glinting, the trees aflame with pulsing lights, bodies in half shadow moving through the haze of smoke, the different kinds of smoke, the blue-gray smoke of cigarettes, the ash-gray smoke of cess, the peanut vendor's smoke enlaced with salt and coal, the cloud of garlic-flavored smoke that hovered near the oil-drum grills, where men in tunics jerked hot chicken.

Mia's senses were on edge. And as she stood there in her key-lime dress, the line of buttons sparkling with the ambient light, she saw her lover floating through the gate and almost ran toward him.

"I have a key," she whispered as she hugged him.

"You mad or what?" he asked her. Yet he felt a muscle flexing in his cock, which squeezed a drop of semen in his blue-and-yellow boxer shorts.

"Of course, I'm mad," she said. "What else could explain what I'm about to do?"

"I have a missing screw as well," he said. As they took the stairs, he passed his hand along her rump. She was damp.

"You've been marinating," he told her.

"Yes. I am so seasoned now. Cook me slowly in your oil."

They passed through the front door and paid another fee, a tip to a man whose face showed acid burns. Through a beaded curtain they passed along an unlit corridor, rubbing hips and shoulders with dancers making special deals before they slipped the key inside the door.

Here, the music was as loud as it was outside, but muffled in tone, and the cream walls, which were stained with leaks and perspiration, held the smell of perfume, piss and smoke.

As they shuffled in the dimness, anxious to reach their destination but being careful not to start an argument by bouncing anyone, they would sometimes lose their footing on the chipped and broken tiles, which tacked their shoes on pads of gum and dried-up pools of Coke and beer.

As they came to the end of the corridor, they left the crowd behind, and saw ahead of them the shadow of a fridge. The sharpness of the odor told them it was old and out of use. Across the way they saw the cardboard box that carried its replacement.

Turning sideways to pass between new box and old fridge, they began to touch and press each other. Protected from view, she leaned against the wall and opened her mouth and closed her eyes before she felt his kiss, which came smoothly, in a stream, warm and soft and tinged with salt.

Behind the fridge, the darkness had the quality of first light—deep but optimistic, all-encompassing but fragile—and in this accidental dawn, the lovers felt obliged to show their newest selves.

With Michael's hand against her hip, squeezing up her fattage, Mia arched her back and spread her legs and drew her stomach flat, then pressed her humping fatness on his cock.

So tightly were they twinned as she dipped and rose while closing and unfolding her legs with concentrated languor, that they could have been mistaken for a butterfly hovering in the elation of release, the box their broken cocoon.

He was screwing so hard against her that she could feel her panties, which were wetly pressed against her cotton dress, being stuffed inside her body by his clothed erection; and it crossed her mind that they could do it there, that she wouldn't have to slip out of her clothes, that she could simply hook her finger in her panty crotch and gash it.

She reached between her legs and tugged the silk aside and felt her fingers sinking in a salty marsh, and undulating still, her head against the wall, her fattage shimmering on her hips. She pulled his fly and rubbed her come along his veined magnificence.

"Am I inside you?" he sighed as a folded softness gloved his cock.

"No, that is my hand," she breathed into his chest.

"I want to be inside you now," he told her as the ragamuffin rose inside him. "Don't let me haffi buss yuh draws waist."

"Jesus Christ," she mumbled. "Look at what we're doing. We're here like animals. Let us go inside the room."

"No, no, no," he cautioned. "Gimme here. If we go in there, I might fuck you too hard."

"If you want it here, you have to fight me," she dared.

She bit him through his shirt and heard him gasp. But as he took her dare and grabbed her wrist and jammed his fingers in her hair, he heard approaching voices. Leaning back, he saw the looming silhouettes.

With the loss of privacy went their performance as antagonists, and they kissed each other softly and went inside the room.

In the musty darkness Michael felt against the wall, his short nails flaking chips of plaster.

When he flicked the switch, the single bulb that dangled from the ceiling by a frayed electric cord exploded like a sodium flare, and they were stunned again into darkness, frozen like an image on a negative.

Still, they had in a moment seen the room: square, to the left a closet with a door depending from a broken hinge, a dull tile floor, cream walls, jalousies with frosted panes, a pair of oilskin curtains. The curtains were hung on plastic tension rods that started half a foot below the highest windowpane; and as their eyes recovered from the shock of quick immersion first in light and then in gloom, they could see each other in the mist of silver radiance that filtered through the speckled glass.

Standing in the center of the fusty room, which smelled of cigarettes and beer and moldy bread and chicken bones, Michael unbuttoned Mia's dress to her waist. Holding his gaze, she slipped her arms out through the straps and reached around her back to tug her bra, which she slung around his neck as he undid his shirt.

A furrow halved his body from his neck down to his pelvis. His chest was demarcated from his stomach by a ruler-guided line. She placed her finger in his navel, then trailed it up along the furrow to his neck, then traced the line beneath his chest, and closed her eyes and said a prayer when she realized that she had prefaced fornication and adultery with a signing of the cross.

She couldn't look now. Couldn't face him now that she was feeling guilt. And as she turned her back, she confessed inside herself that she wanted him to push her up against the wall, and, further, that she wanted him to break her, that she wanted him to make her want him in her life again, that she wanted him to take her in a way that she would have to tell him that she wanted him to steal her from her husband, that she wanted him to take her in a way that would make her feel as if she had the power and the right to ask him once again if he was fucking that little blasted Patience gyal.

And as she stood there thinking this, she felt his hands upon her, his thumbs finding hollows in her shoulder blades, his palms encircling her back.

With his slender fingers he filigreed the stretch marks on her elongated breasts. In a dip behind her ear, she felt a liquid kiss begin to burn. Then there was a kiss along her neck, then another on her shoulder as a hand began to palm and knead her stomach.

Caressing her breasts, kissing her neck, he rubbed his hand across the padded softness of her belly, and gripped the ridge of fat below her navel. She sighed and leaned forward and planted a palm against the wall and reached between her legs and hooked her panty waist and wriggled as she pulled it down. She left it just above her knees, felt it bind and slice her thighs.

Tipping on her toes, as she felt him raise her frock, she said, "Don't make love, just fuck me."

As he bunched the cloth into the saddle of her back, he pressed her to the wall and motioned her to hold her dress above her waist, and she tucked it with her elbows to her sides. He stepped away to look at her, watched the way the light carved out her contours, bringing out her darkness on the oatmeal-colored wall, the fattage on her hips like riding pants, the golden streaks along her rump as if she had been clawed.

As he watched her she began to shuffle back; and she planted her hands against the wall again, her soft breasts hanging down, the dip of her back like a hammock, her bottom hoisted up, cheeks spread apart by a secret muscle, revealing for his scrutiny and admiration the fleshy folds of nappy hair, the glistening silver line that made him want to plunge into her depths.

"Don't make love, just fuck me," she said again, reaching back between her legs and guiding him inside her.

He kissed her back and watched her muscles focus on the touch, and laid his copper face between her shoulder blades, a thumb inside her mouth, a palm against her glimmering hips, which shone with perspiration.

"You cannot tell me what to do," he sighed, his eyes widening as he felt the softness of her bottom slapping wetly on his pelvis, which was figure-eighting tightly up against her. She had learned to fuck with the abandon of a common gyal, but her movements were delivered with finesse.

"Don't love me," she commanded as she bit his salty finger.

He pulled her hair and smacked her ass, leaning off to look down as he rode her, her coat of darkest flesh awash with sweat and ripples.

"Don't love me," she exhorted. "Don't love me."

"That is not for you to say," he whispered. "Loving you or not is my prerogative."

"Do you love me, baby?" she asked.

"Yes, I do."

"If you do, then come inside me," she dared. "Breed me. Fatten me. Steal me from my husband. Make me yours again." She had begun to really open now and felt that she could goad him into fucking her the way that she imagined that he used to fuck those little common gyals, his cock stampeding in their belly.

"Turn around," he whispered. "I want to see you."

She obeyed, and leaned against the moldy wall, raised her diamond face, her mouth already parted for the kiss.

One hand on her cheek, feathering her brows, the other hand squeezing her fattage, Michael, his lids like slit pods, gazed into Mia's hooded eyes.

Nibbling her upper lip, his body, like hers, misted with sweat and silver light, music bleeding through the sound of throttled breathing, footsteps just beyond the door, Michael pierced her once again, dipped into her flesh like a needle in a cushion.

Thusly joined, his narrow torso stitched to hers, her legs folding and releasing once again, they felt inside their bodies some-

thing climbing . . . and they climbed . . . and they climbed and
they did not return to earth until her eighth orgasm, when his
heavy seed inside her brought them down.

When they came out of the room, wet and wrinkled, drawing
stares from strangers for their exuberant feat of stamina—for
which they were obliged to pay another set of fees because the
keys had been assigned for half an hour—they saw that it had
rained. The air felt fresh, the wind was light, and with the smell
of smoke and sweet perfumes rinsed away, they detected in their
pores and hair the nutmeg smell of fornication and from their
delicates adultery's sweet magnolia scent.

They walked toward the main road, holding hands, a line of
blood congealing in a crescent where she'd bitten him through
his shirt, which had been torn.

It was two o'clock in the morning. The buses had stopped at
midnight.

At the corner, they waited for a half an hour, wondering what
to do. In this part of Kingston, at this time of night, death
moved at random, like breeze-blown paper. From behind them
came a crackling sound, and they turned to see two boys coming slowly on a mountain bike, one towing the other on the
frame. If something happened who would see?

The boys rode by and offered a ride, laughing as they imi-
tated Mia's sounds of passion. One was drinking beer. The
other was smoking weed. Doddering, they disappeared
around a bend, leaving Mia and Michael to contemplate the
truth of their condition, to watch every shadow, to lean
toward the sound of every distant car, to hold each other and
wonder. Should they even hold each other? Would that make
them look like prey? Should they break a branch in case they
had to fight. Should they start to walk? Should they just go
back to the club? But could they really do this after causing
so much scandal?

Cak! Cak! Cak! They cringed but did not duck. Someone,
somewhere was firing guns. From behind the hedges came the
yelps and barks of khaki dogs.

Mia and Michael crossed the road and stood beneath an overhanging cotton tree, holding hands, watching, waiting, temples shine with sweat.

Cak! Cak! Cak! More shots. Kadda! Kadda! Kadda! An urgent reply.

"Let's walk," he said.

"To where?" she asked. "The shots sound like they're coming from up the road. How the fuck did we come to this? What the fuck are we doing here?"

"Calm down, baby. Calm down." He paused to rub her back as he slipped his arm around her shoulder. "Just cool. Just cool."

As he said this they heard the sound of engines and they peered around the bend to see the headlights of a car. Easing Mia back against the wall, Michael stepped off the curb and flagged it down and it swerved and picked up speed. He clapped and chased it down. The brake lights flared. It was a cab, a battered Nissan Sentra.

Michael fanned his hand for Mia to come, and he led her to the door. From behind them came a line of army jeeps, with soldiers dressed in battle gear crawling through the night, their rifles gripped, their fingers cocked inside the trigger guard.

"What are we going to do?" said Mia when they settled in the car. She muttered to the driver where to go, and closed her eyes and let the vinyl take her weight, trying to catch the thoughts that swirled inside her head.

She could not live with her husband anymore. This she knew. How could she go back to living with a man with whom she would never be a butterfly? Why shouldn't she break from her cocoon? What did it mean that she had not fucked her husband in almost two years, yet had barebacked a man that she hadn't seen in twenty? What did it mean that she had asked this man to come inside her? What did it mean that she could become pregnant for the first time at forty-five? Would she ever see Michael again?

"What do you want us to do?" Michael asked her as he drew her close.

"What have we done?" she asked him, throwing up her hands. They slapped against her thighs and stung. "What did we just do?"

She shrugged and leaned away from him.

"I cannot speak for you," he said cautiously. "I can only speak for me. But that is not what I want to think about. I want to think about what you are going to do. Your husband . . . he is going to be waiting. He has a gun."

"You don't have to come," she replied, placing her hand to her face to shield it from his gaze. "You can drop me off and go where you have to go. A little fuck doesn't mean I expect you to be my hero."

"Mia, this is not about fucking."

"What is it about, then?"

"It is about love, Mia, and coming back to where you used to be and finding out that's where you are."

"That is deep," the driver interjected. He wore a tam and smelled of liniment and Limacol.

Mia leaned toward the driver's neck: "Can you just mind your business, please!"

"The car is small," the driver reasoned. "Anything you talk I can't help but hear."

What was there to do but laugh? Only in Jamaica, they thought. Only in Jamaica. Only in a country where knowing other people's business was a basic human right.

"Michael, do you love me?" Mia asked him when the laughter settled. "And I don't need you to lie to me or anything."

"You are making it sound like a last request."

"Do you love me, Michael? Seriously?"

He looked at her, reached out for her hand and held it in his lap.

"I love you, Hampton."

"Jesus Christ, don't call me that. Don't call me that and take me there and mash up my fucking life now, man. Don't do that, Chiney boy. Don't do that. I am already heading into a sticky situation. Don't pour sweetness on it now and make it worse."

"Hampton, I am telling you the truth. I love you. We coulda died a while ago while we waited for the cab to come. Look at what we just went through. You really mean to ask me that?"

"If you love me and you're telling me the truth," she said,

"then tell me all the truths. Tell me the truth: is Patience your woman?"

"No."

He shook his head and looked away.

"Something like that?"

She leaned across as if she were trying to look around him into his eyes.

"We never had sex," he began.

"Did you fuck?" she demanded.

"Bredren, shut your mouth," the driver said.

"It's okay," Michael cautioned as Mia leaned toward the driver again. She closed her eyes and hugged him, and he felt her body heave and spread its weight; and as he thought of her crying, he began to cry as well.

"Why are you crying?" she asked.

"The same reason you are crying."

"I am not crying," she chuckled. "I am laughing."

He straightened up and saw that she was telling the truth. And he began to laugh again.

"So you fucked her, Michael," she asked. She wiped her eyes as he composed himself.

"We came very close. And I am telling you this because you told me something about somebody, about a complicated relationship that you had with someone."

She lay down on him again, deflated. Was he going to throw it in her face? She should have shut her mouth.

"What do you want me to say?" she asked.

"That you forgive me," he said weakly. "That you forgive me."

"I have already forgiven you," she whispered with relief. "You have to forgive yourself."

They fell into silence, leaned against each other and listened to the tires, which were hissing on the road.

"Are we really going to the café?" he asked, starting conversation once again.

"I don't know," she replied.

"Your husband has a gun," he said slowly.

"And your girlfriend?"

He sucked his teeth.

"I don't believe you when you said you didn't fuck," she said.

"We did not," he said, pulling her toward him as she leaned away.

"I have put so much on the table for you tonight," she said. "The least you could do . . . the least you could do . . ."

Michael thought about what Mia had at stake compared to him. Mia was gambling her entire life . . . he was betting an old career. He had to tell the truth . . . and he did . . . from the beginning . . . everything from meeting Patience until now. And he confessed that the impulse had taken ahold of him, but that he had fought it, that he had fought and fought but had lost, but had not lost completely. That he had not done the things that Patience had wanted him to do. That they had not fucked. That in his effort to raise himself and walk along the path of truth, he had lost his footing and stumbled. But no, he had not fallen. And he was proud of that, because right now, at this moment, he did not have anything else to be proud of beyond the fact that he had been forgiven and had found the power to forgive himself.

They had come to the point where the road opened into four lanes now, and were riding in the lane beside the median. The hills were to their right, far away but closing in. The stadium was up ahead, on their left, beyond the graveyard for the soldiers; there, the road was veiled in mist.

"What a calamity," said the driver, glancing in the mirror. "I know you don't want me in your business, but I can't see things and don't say mutten. You, Mr. Chin, are a bigger man for telling the empress the truth. Me, personally, couldn't do that. But whether you like or not, your life done now. Her life done too. Is like is a new life have to make now—whether together or apart."

"True words," Michael said. "True words."

"Hold on tight as I go through this fog, y'hear. I don't know what I might buck up on the other side. This life not certain, y'know. This life not certain at all. All you can do is hope and pray."

Michael closed his eyes and felt the car slowing down as it puttered through the fog. Soon he felt Mia's leg across his lap, and her body on his, sobbing, crying this time for sure.

"What a calamity," said the driver. "What a calamity. So your album thing get fuck now, Mr. Chin, 'cause this singer girl sound bilious and bitter."

"True words," Michael muttered. "True words."

"I'm so sorry," said Mia. "I didn't want you to destroy your life."

He stroked her face and placed his palm against her hip and rocked her.

"What are you going to do?" she asked.

"What you want me to do?" he replied.

"Whatever will make you happy," she sighed.

"Give me another chance," he said. "Let's just fuck off with the past and just start all over again."

"You have a life in New York. A career in New York."

"And here I have a woman . . . and possibly a child. Just tell me what you want, and I will be it, Mia."

"I want you to be happy. I just want you to be you, that's all."

"I love you, and you love me. I know you and you know me. I trust you and you will learn to trust me. Let's start out there and work from that."

They opened their eyes. Around them was the fog, pressing them in, not letting them out. Everything white. Nothing visible.

"No one else will be there now," she said. "Only him, only them." She was thinking of the restaurant now.

"We can't go back where we came from, Mia."

"I know," she said. "I know."

"We have to turn around."

"Turn around and go to where? Where is there to go, Michael?"

"I don't know, Mia. I don't know. We can start anywhere, but not right there. Your husband has a gun. Mia, if we have to start from scratch we have to start from scratch. We know what it is to do without, to not have, to suck salt until we can do better. The question is this: are we willing to do it? I know that I am.

Thirty-odd years ago when we just met, I told you that music was the thing that I loved most in this world. Mia, I love music. But music won't suffer without me. Music will live on. And I won't suffer without music. And if I have to suffer, I will suffer because I cannot let you go back to a man like that. As I said to you before, I don't believe in divorce. That man is not your husband, Mia. I don't care what you want to say. Anywhere you sleep tonight, that is where I am sleeping too. If is in a hotel, is in a hotel. If is by the road, is by the road."

"What you want me do, Mr. Chin?" the driver asked, turning around.

"I don't know right now, bredren," Michael said as Mia closed her eyes and snuggled in beside him. "We'll figure it out. Just drive. Don't worry about the money. Just drive. Just drive. Just drive."

about the authors

Colin Channer is the author of the #1 Blackboard bestselling novel *Waiting in Vain*, which was selected as a 1998 Critic's Choice by the *Washington Post Book World*. A naturalized American of Jamaican origin, he teaches fiction writing in London and New York. He is a regular book reviewer for the *Minneapolis Star-Tribune* and the bass player for the reggae band Pipecock Jaxxon. His new novel, *Satisfy My Soul*, will be published in 2001 by One World/Ballantine. His e-mail address is colinchanner@hotmail.com. He lives in Brooklyn, New York.

Eric Jerome Dickey is the author of *The New York Times* bestseller *Liar's Game*, as well as the nationally bestselling novels *Cheaters*, which was chosen as Blackboard's Novel of the Year for 1999, *Milk in My Coffee*, *Friends and Lovers*, and *Sister, Sister*, all of which were #1 Blackboard bestsellers. He is also author of several pieces of short fiction, a memoir, and the screenplay for the film *Cappuccino*. A former computer programmer, middle-school teacher, and stand-up comic, Dickey attended UCLA's creative writing program on a SEED scholarship. Originally from Memphis, Tennessee, and a graduate of the University of Memphis, he currently resides in Los Angeles. His next full-length novel will be published by Dutton in July 2001.

The author of five award-winning, national bestsellers, **E. Lynn Harris** attended the University of Arkansas at Fayetteville, where he earned a degree in journalism. A former computer sales executive with IBM, he wrote and self-published his first novel in 1991. Later published by Anchor Books, *Invisible Life* was nominated for Outstanding Book of the Year by the American Booksellers Association Blackboard list, and inspired a sequel, *Just As I Am* (1994), the winner of Blackboard's Novel of the Year in 1996. Harris is also author of *The New York Times* bestsellers *And This Too Shall Pass* (1996), *If This World Were Mine* (1997), *Abide with Me* (1999), and *Not a Day Goes By* (2000), all published by Doubleday. Twice nominated for the NAACP Image Award and the recipient of the James Baldwin Award for Literary Excellence, Harris has published in *American Visions, Essence,* and the award-winning *Brotherman: The Odyssey of Black Men in America.* He is currently at work on his memoirs, which will be published by Doubleday this spring. A popular college lecturer and avid Arkansas Razorbacks fan, Harris divides his time between Chicago and New York.

Marcus Major's debut novel, *Good Peoples* (2000), was a Blackboard bestseller and a selection of the Barnes and Noble Discover Great New Writers program. Born in Fort Bragg, North Carolina, Major graduated with a degree in literature from Richard Stockton College. A former middle-school teacher, he now writes full-time and resides in South Jersey. Major's next novel, *Four Guys and Trouble,* will be published by Dutton in April 2001. His e-mail address is MarcusMajor@aol.com.